Also by Richard Pitman & Joe McNally

Warned Off
Running Scared

Also by Richard Pitman

Good Horses Make Good Jockeys
Guinness Guide to Steeplechasing
Steeplechasing
Martin Pipe: The Champion Trainer's Story

About the authors

A former champion jockey, **Richard Pitman** rode the winners of over 470 races over the jumps including the Champion Hurdle, Hennessy Gold Cup, Mackeson Gold Cup, and the King George VI Chase twice. He has been a broadcaster for the past nineteen years with the BBC, and writes on racing for the *Sunday Express*. He also owns and breeds horses in his small stud in Oxfordshire. **Joe McNally** has always been employed in the racing/betting game and now works for Satellite Information Services as a Regional Manager. **Hunted** is the second racing novel by Richard Pitman and Joe McNally. Their third, **Running Scared**, is now available in hardcover from Hodder and Stoughton.

Hunted

Richard Pitman and Joe McNally

CORONET BOOKS
Hodder and Stoughton

Copyright © Richard Pitman and Joe McNally 1993

First published in Great Britain in 1993
by Hodder and Stoughton,
a division of Hodder Headline PLC

Coronet edition 1994

The right of Richard Pitman and Joe McNally to be identified as the
Authors of this Work has been asserted by them in accordance with the
Copyright, Designs and Patents Act 1988

10 9 8 7 6 5 4 3 2

All characters in this publication are fictitious and any resemblance to
real persons, living or dead, is purely coincidental

British Library Cataloguing in Publication Data

Pitman, Richard
Hunted
I. Title   II. McNally, Joe
823 [F]

ISBN 0-340-62864-2

Printed and bound in Great Britain by
Cox and Wyman Ltd, Reading, Berks

Photoset by Rowland Phototypesetting Ltd, Bury St Edmunds, Suffolk

Hodder and Stoughton
A Division of Hodder Headline PLC
338 Euston Road, London NW1 3BH

To Mandy, a wife who recognises the
thin line between constructive and destructive criticism
Richard Pitman

For my father, Tommy and his children:
Mary
Joe
Frankie
Joan
Tam
Jim
Kevin
Gerard
Clare
Andy
Martine
Stephen
Christy
Paul
David
Martin
Michelle
Joe McNally

Many thanks from us both to Helen Whitaker
for her editing skills

Prologue

The cold woke me. Shivering. Freezing. Very bad headache. The wind blew hard outside. Every time it gusted
an icy draught cut a line across my spine. I lay on my side.
The draught was there all the time. Worse when it gusted.
My shirt must have been pulled out of my trousers exposing my back. I reached round to pull it down. Nothing
there. No clothes. Naked.

Consciousness returning now making me feel even
colder as I came to my senses. I was lying on cold damp
wood. There was something round my neck, something on
my face. I reached up. A metal chain, thick links. A hood
over my head and sewn into the chain links. I followed them
with my fingers. Two feet from my neck the chain looped
around a big square piece of wood, the leg of a table, a
bench or something. A heavy padlock clasped the links.

I tried to lie on my back but the chain tightened, stopping me. I edged closer to the padlock and tried again.
Made it this time though something crunched below my
left buttock and jagged my flesh. Easing my hips up I felt
for it. It came away in my hand, cold and slimy with brittle
shards. A snail. I flicked it from my fingers and heard it
stick to the wall.

I was outside. In an outhouse; a shed, an old garage
maybe, not a stable, no stable smell. Total darkness. Faint
odour of creosote and dampness. Sweet and sour smell of
dying vegetation.

Dreadful headache. Nausea. The worst of hangovers.

I checked my limbs for soundness, flexed my arms and legs, wrists and ankles, fingers and toes, felt my face and skull through the rough cloth hood, reached hesitantly and hopefully between my legs; everything still there. Freezing cold but alive and, from what I could tell in the dark, healthy. Apart from the headache which was of pounding intensity now. Must have been the ether. No bumps on the head. No signs of him having hit me.

The wind gusted again sending an icy slice down my left side. My teeth chattered. Had to get my body off the floor. I turned slowly in the direction of the padlock till I lay on my front. Tried pushing myself onto my knees but the chain was anchored low down. I felt for where it looped round the wood. There was very little play but I began working it slowly upwards. The strain on my left shoulder muscle meant I had to stop and rest every minute or so but eventually I made it to my hands and knees. The exertion warmed my head inside the hood. The rest of me shivered. I rested.

As full consciousness came back it scared me into immobility. Maybe I could lift the bench and free myself. Maybe out there in the darkness there would be a hammer, a chisel, a crowbar or something within reach to break the chain links, to free me.

But I was afraid to stretch out and feel for them in case nothing was there, terrified to haul at the bench in case it didn't move . . . Then, there would be no escape. No survival. I would be here when he came back with the gun.

Chapter One

It all started two weeks ago on the first Saturday in March. I was sitting in the jockeys' changing room at Haydock Park knowing that by dusk my riding career would be over once and for all. This was my first season back riding after losing my jockey's licence and serving a five year ban. Last time round I'd been Champion Jockey . . . The memories made it worse.

Before deciding to quit I'd been agonising for weeks, as though it were a complicated equation. It was simple. Only one factor mattered: I wasn't earning enough to feed myself. I owed money to banks, garages, saddlers and my landlord . . . and Jackie, my girlfriend.

My credit had run out. It was time to find a proper job and pay off the debts. Time to leave the only career I'd ever known, riding steeplechasers. The most galling thing was that I was good at it, one of the best.

Still, owners and trainers had chosen to ignore that. Maybe they were taking revenge, paying me back for past sins. Whatever, there wasn't a damn thing I could do about it.

I looked around me. One thing I wouldn't miss was these cold gloomy corners. The pecking order in the changing room classified me fourth division now, along with eight or ten others, all has-beens and never-will-bes. Our own little clique, losers one and all but too terrified to admit it. So we buoyed ourselves with empty banter

and hollow camaraderie, scared to let the facade drop
exposing big failures, small lives.

I was here for one ride, a no-hoper in the novice hurdle.
As soon as the race was over I would shower, change and
leave the racecourse for the last time. I could probably sell
my boots and the two saddles for the price of one month's
rent. On Monday I'd start looking for something else.

The changing room was beginning to buzz with jockeys
and valets preparing for the day's racing. It was Greenalls
Gold Cup day, the last major meeting before the Cheltenham Festival. As usual there was a quality field for the
big 'chase. I heard someone say the favourite, Cragrock,
was a certainty. Rewind the tape five years and I'd have
been riding it.

I couldn't stand any more of the happy chatter and the
atmosphere of anticipation. My ride was two hours away.
There was no need for me to stay in here till then so I got
up and headed for the door.

Things went suddenly quiet among the group over to
my right, eight or nine jockeys in various stages of
undress. Con Layton's Irish accent rose from their midst.
'And did yer mammy iron your nice clean underpants for
you before you came out? I'll bet she still wipes yer little
bottom too? Is that right . . . ? Come on, don't be shy,
you can tell yer Uncle Cornelius . . .'

I could only see the back of Layton's head. Stepping to
the side and squinting through someone's crooked elbow
I saw the reddening face of Layton's latest target, a kid
named David Campbell Cooper. The boy was only nineteen but already had the makings of a top jockey. Well,
he had the skills, whether or not his heart was in it was a
different matter.

He was a quiet kid, didn't mix and didn't speak much,
mostly I suspected because he was painfully self-conscious
about the distinct 'th' for 's' lisp which made his upper-class accent sound staged and effeminate.

There were a couple of strained chuckles from Layton's audience as they watched him tormenting the boy. The Irishman wouldn't be doing it just for fun. Young Cooper had a fancied ride against him in the big race, this was Layton starting to psyche him out.

Layton had built himself a reputation not just as a bully but as a genuine 'hard-man'. He was also a crook who arranged and rode in fixed races. In the jockeys' table he was around second division and made a nice living one way and another. Of the other lads, the smart ones avoided him and his schemes, the not so clever got sucked in and bled dry.

Since I'd come back I'd had little to do with him, though he had thrown the occasional taunt in my direction just by way of keeping his hand in. I'd had more things to worry about than rising to the bait.

He was stooping close to young Cooper now, face to face. He said, 'D'ye still sleep with yer mammy?' It came out as Layton meant it to, dirty, salacious. The boy's flushed face was rock-still but he couldn't hold Layton's gaze any longer. His eyes, begging without hope for someone to intervene, flitted sideways and upward at the ring of faces watching him.

Layton said, 'What does yer mammy look like with no clothes on?'

Tears welled in the boy's eyes. No more chuckles from the audience. A couple turned away shaking their heads. The whole room was silent waiting for the boy's reaction. Some of them would want to step in but they knew the kid had to handle it himself if he wanted to survive. He was learning how hard a world it was.

Enjoying the boy's humiliation Layton said, 'Come on, son, what does she look like? All the lads would like to know.'

I was standing twenty feet away. I said, 'That how you get your kicks, Layton?'

Everyone turned. Layton pushed through them and walked towards me. Young Cooper looked at me unable to hide the gratitude and relief in his eyes.

Layton stopped six feet from me. About five seven he had reddish-brown hair tightly waved, coarse and wiry like steel wool. His ice-blue eyes were close-set below thick eyebrows which met above his hawk-nose. His white T shirt was blotched with water stains and he held on to the ends of a yellow towel which hung round his neck. He said, 'A voice from the gallery, Malloy . . . I didn't quite catch what you said.'

'I said is that how you get your kicks? Is that what turns you on, getting young boys to talk about their mothers? Or is it just the bullying that gives you the big charge?'

It was Layton's turn to redden. 'You sayin' I'm a bully, Malloy?'

'Either a bully or a pervert, take your pick.'

His fists balled, jaw muscles clenched, eyes went cold but I could see he wasn't sure what to do. It must have been the first time in years someone had stood up to him, challenged him. Even worse, he didn't know the strength of his opponent.

If he got into a fight now he could, for all he knew, come out with a broken jaw which, apart from the loss of face, would mean he wouldn't be riding for a while.

Feet apart, hands by my sides, I stood calmly staring at him, watching him try to make a decision. Though I'd told no one yet that I was quitting he knew if it came to a brawl that I had much less to lose.

His hands relaxed and he clasped them behind his back and put on a sly little smile. 'You've an awful insolent mouth on you, Malloy.'

'I can live with it. Better than a mind like a sewer.'

He was realising he wasn't going to win any battle of words either. Taking a couple of steps towards me he

leaned forward till I could see the tiny blue veins in the whites of his eyes. He said, 'You and me must get together some time soon.'

I held his gaze. 'Any time.' I said, 'Just give me a couple of days' notice so I can arrange a vaccination.'

A few giggled at that and there was one outright laugh and I saw in Layton's eyes that he knew he had to do something. With our faces still so close I guessed it would be a head-butt and I moved just as he tried it, stepped aside as he over-balanced and put his hands up to stop himself falling forward.

I hit him sharply in the side just below the ribcage then again in the kidneys. He grunted and went to his knees. I stayed behind him, grabbed the towel from his shoulders, looped it around his neck and pulled a tight stranglehold while I stood on his left calf to stop him rising.

He gurgled, clutching at the towel, trying to get a finger-hold. I leaned close to his ear. 'How does it feel, Layton? What's it like to be on the receiving end?' I jerked the towel tighter and his tongue came out, his eyes watered.

I let go suddenly and he slumped forward, his head on the bench, saliva dripping from his gasping mouth, glistening on the dark tiles. I stepped away. There were maybe twenty people looking on, most watching me, some staring at Layton.

I turned to leave and heard Layton trying to rise. Looking round I saw him sprawled against the bench now face up, still breathing hard but glaring at me. 'You're a fokking dead man, Malloy,' he hissed.

'Top marks for perception,' I said.

Layton looked puzzled as one of his buddies, Meese, helped him away to the toilets.

The buzz of conversation resumed. Colin Blake came up and squeezed my arm. 'Nice one, Eddie, but you ain't done yourself no favours there, mate.'

I smiled at him. 'You'd be surprised.' Unwise as it may have been the confrontation had improved my self-esteem, though I wasn't sure how much of the bravado had come from the knowledge that after today I would never be in a changing room with Layton again.

On my way out a couple of the lads slapped my back and said well done. I almost felt as if I'd won a race.

In his father's red and luminous yellow colours young Cooper was sitting on the scales, weighing out for the first race. Still embarrassed, he glanced at me and I could see that his discomfort now stemmed from the realisation that he'd had to be rescued, that he couldn't cut it himself.

Not wanting to make him feel obliged I smiled briefly and walked on, but he stuck out a hand to grip my arm as I passed. I stopped and looked down at him; dark hair, deep fringe, dark eyes, pale smooth complexion, he said, 'Thank you,' avoiding the shortened version so he wouldn't have to pronounce the 's'.

'Forget it,' I said. 'Good luck today.'

He smiled weakly and nodded, causing the scale needle to bob between ten stone ten and ten twelve. I left him with his own troubles and took mine outside.

The rain had stopped though just for a breather judging by the heavy grey sky. I stood by the rail of the parade ring watching heavy drops splash to the ground from the big trees in the centre.

The oval horsewalk was empty but the horses for the first would soon be in and the crowds would form around the ring to watch them parade. Then the bell would ring in the changing room and the jockeys would come out and make their way through the admiring throng like gladiators heading for the arena.

They'd huddle with trainer and owner and friends and talk tactics, make plans. Then they'd mount, slip their feet into stirrups, grip reins, pat necks, whisper meaningless

words of reassurance to the horses as they were led out; they'd be smiling and confident, staring straight ahead above the crowds, feeling that tight little thrill that comes from being different from the masses, from knowing that among the millions who love racing you are one of the main players.

And I wouldn't be there.

Not after today. And that gut-sick feeling of hopelessness came back and I suddenly knew what drug addicts must feel like when someone tells them there's never going to be another fix.

I don't know how long I stood staring. In front of me were trees, wet grass, white rails but lost in my own misery I saw nothing and when someone touched my elbow and spoke my name I turned slowly as though in a dream.

Her face was thin, hair dark and luxuriantly thick, eyes brown and distinctly oval, good mouth with well-shaped lips, my height, she looked at me. 'You okay?'

I nodded, dredging up a half-smile. 'Sorry, I was miles away.'

She said, 'Carter told me what you did to Layton. I just wanted to say I wish I'd been there.'

Lisa Ffrench was being pretty forthright. I didn't know her much beyond saying hallo. Her job barred her from 'consorting' with jockeys and she was probably leaving herself open to criticism even talking to me now. Lisa was a stenographer. She worked for The Jockey Club, noting, as in a law court, everything that was said during Stewards' Inquiries.

I shrugged. 'I didn't really *do* anything . . . just put him in his place.'

'Well and truly, the way I heard it.' Her smile was wide, approving.

I said, 'I take it you're not a member of his fan club then?'

'Watched him lying through his teeth too many times . . . and sucking up to the Stewards.'

I nodded, anxious to be alone again so I could be as miserable as I wanted. I said, 'Well, it won't take him long to bounce back, nasty as ever.'

'No doubt, but his ego will stay bruised for a while so you'd better watch yourself.'

'Shouldn't be too hard. This is my last day.'

'Last day at what?'

'Race-riding. I'm quitting.'

She looked puzzled, her long thin eyebrows knitting a little frown. 'Why?'

'Because I can't make a living at it any more.'

She shook her head slowly. 'That's tough. Bad luck. You're a good jockey.'

'You think so?'

She nodded.

I smiled ironically. 'Pity you don't own a string of twenty.' I looked away again across the parade ring expecting her to politely excuse herself before the conversation got embarrassing. But she stayed. 'What're you going to do?' she asked.

I shrugged. 'Dunno, but I know what you'd better do before your bosses see you talking to lowlife like me.'

She said nothing for a while but I was aware of her looking at me. Then she said, 'Is it safe to leave you?'

Puzzled, I turned towards her again. She was still smiling. 'I'm scared in case you overdose on self-pity.'

My smile widened slowly till it was as bright as hers, then she turned and headed for the weighing room walking athletically in her flat shoes, skinny bottom swinging in her tight, checked, knee-length skirt, shoulders straight under the pads in her short matching jacket.

I watched her disappear through the door. Two minutes later she came marching back, making straight for me again. Half surprised, half apprehensive, I waited. She

approached, her eyes on me from a long way out, a look of triumph on her face.

When she reached me she offered a piece of information that could save my career and ruin hers.

Chapter Two

'Why are you doing this?' I asked.

'Because I don't want you to quit.'

'What does it matter to you, you don't even know me?' It sounded more hostile than I'd meant it to and she raised her hands in surrender and took a step back. 'Okay, okay, sorry for interfering, do what you like.'

I tried to look apologetic. 'Look, Lisa, I'm sorry, I didn't mean to sound ungrateful. I appreciate what you're doing – we hardly know each other . . .' I tailed off rather lamely.

She stood trying to figure me out. The wind caught her heavy shoulder-length hair and lifted it to show a small gold ear-ring. Her brown oval eyes told me her patience was waning. She said, 'Fine, go and talk to Barber then. Good luck.' She turned and walked away with that confident head-up stride.

Hubert Barber trained Cragrock, the favourite in the big race. His stable jockey, Tommy Gilmour, hadn't turned up and if he didn't appear in time Barber had no plans to seek a substitute. Lisa had overheard him tell the Clerk of the Scales confidentially that he planned to withdraw the horse.

She'd just been trying to persuade me to approach Barber and ask him to run the horse and let me ride.

I had ridden for him a number of times during my Championship season and we'd got on well together but he'd never offered me anything since my comeback, though I'd never pushed myself with him.

Watching Lisa disappear into the crowd I thought, what the hell, I might as well try. With no confidence and little hope I went to look for Barber.

I asked around and someone told me he was at the main gate. I found him outside it shuffling impatiently, peering at cars coming in off the main road, squinting into taxis as they pulled up.

Barber was an easy man to recognise: six two, heavy, maybe eighteen stones, big red nose, prominent ears, moist blue eyes and a clump of pure white hair tucked under a tweed cap. Superstitious like many racing folk, he wore the same huge army-issue overcoat he'd worn when he trained his first winner. Just as well he only trained jumpers as it would be pretty hot under there in July.

'Mister Barber,' I said. He turned quickly, suddenly hopeful, but his features sagged when he saw it wasn't his stable jockey.

'Hallo, Eddie,' he said gruffly then went back to scanning incomers who were becoming scarcer as the first race drew near. Few vehicles coming now, just some stragglers hurrying on foot from the car park.

I was unsure of what to say, how to put it. I wasn't much good at asking for rides at the best of times and there had been so many refusals in recent months that my confidence was shot to pieces. The fact that this was my last gasp didn't make it easier.

'Mister Barber, I heard Tommy Gilmour hasn't turned up.'

He gave me his full attention. 'Who told you that?'

'Well, we sort of noticed it in the weighing room,' I lied.

'Any of you lads see Tommy last night?' he asked.

'I don't think so. Nobody mentioned it.'

He stared down the long drive again and said, 'Can't understand it. He's always been a hundred per cent reliable.'

'It's not like him,' I agreed. 'Have you rung his hotel?'

'Rang his hotel, his house; the owner's been ringing his bloody mobile phone for the past hour.'

I let him scan the road for a few seconds more then said, 'Mister Barber, if he doesn't appear, have you thought about a replacement?'

He looked down at me, blue eyes watering in the wind. 'Eddie, I've thought about nothing but a replacement but the horse's owner won't have it, she wants to withdraw.'

'Why?'

'Because the silly cow's convinced that nobody but Tommy can win on the horse. He's a difficult ride and takes a bit of knowing but we've had a right few quid on ante-post, her husband and me, and we're desperate to run him.'

He really got going then, gesticulating, jerking at his cap. 'She's a nice lady, Loretta, but she's wrong on this one. Thinks because Tommy is Champion Jockey he's a stone better than the rest of you. Someone else rode the horse last year and he fell and didn't get up for five minutes, Loretta was hysterical, threatened to take the horse out of training altogether. Crazy woman.'

'Where is she now?' I asked.

Barber dabbed at his big nose with a hankie. 'Back in her box. Paul, her husband's trying to talk her into accepting a substitute but he's fighting a losing battle. I had to get out of there before I strangled her.'

I looked up at him. 'Do you think she'd accept another Champion Jockey as replacement?'

He stared down at me. I shrugged, 'Okay, so it was five years ago,' I said, 'but it's worth a try.'

Still morose, he shook his head then suddenly his eyes

lit up. 'You might be right, Eddie! You might be right! Come on!'

Checking his watch he turned and hobbled back into the course. An accident a few years back had left him badly lame in his right leg. Barber always claimed it had happened when he came off a horse on the gallops but Muriel, his wife, said he broke it when he 'fell down the stairs, pissed'.

I walked alongside him conscious of the steep rise and fall of his left shoulder as he tried to hurry through the puddles. The off of the first race had just been announced and the commentary pulsed through the speakers. Barber, face beaming, kept saying quietly, 'The very man! The very thing!'

He told me to wait by the weighing room as he disappeared into the main stand.

I waited, trying not to hope too hard. Within five minutes Barber hove back into view, his face telling me all I needed to know. Smiling wide he slapped my shoulder and said, 'We're back in business! I'll send someone along with the colours and I'll see you in the paddock.'

Stunned, surprised, delighted, I grasped his hand. 'Hubert, I know it's an old cliché but this means a hell of a lot to me.'

He gripped my forearm with his free hand. 'Me too,' he said, 'me too. Listen, do me one favour, Eddie, try and make sure the TV cameras don't catch your face before the race starts.'

I stared at him. 'Why?'

He smiled. 'Just do it. I'll explain later.'

It took me a minute to figure out what he'd done, then I knew – if I lost Barber would be in deep trouble with Loretta Whitehead.

Emotions bubbling, brain buzzing with plans and hopes, immediately high on the prospects of showing thousands of racegoers and millions of TV viewers that Eddie

Malloy could still cut it I strode back into the changing room, grabbed Tom, my valet, by the shoulders, shook him and said, 'I ride Cragrock in the big one!'

He stared at me. 'By the looks of you you'd think you'd already won it!'

Wearing green and blue colours, Bill Brandon, one of the veterans, saw my smile as he passed and said, 'You look as if you've won the pools, Eddie.'

I fought to contain my excitement. 'Hubert Barber just asked me to ride the favourite in the big race.' I had tried to say it calmly but it came out loud and boastful. Most of the jocks heard me.

Bill looked puzzled. 'Where's Tommy Gilmour?'

I shrugged. 'Hasn't turned up. They weren't going to run him but they've had a few quid on and decided to have a go.'

'Good luck to you, then,' Bill said ungrudgingly and I took it at face value and smiled. Then Con Layton's furtively soft Irish tones came from behind me. 'Gilmour could handle that horse, Malloy, but you couldn't ride one side of him. You'll make an arse o' yersel.'

I turned to face Layton, it hadn't taken him long to recover from our earlier scrap. I stared at him and got back the usual taunting look from his small, pale, close-set eyes. It would have been better to let it pass, the last thing I wanted was a running feud with Layton. But my spirits were high and my blood was up. Besides, I hadn't had much to celebrate all season so I wasn't going to let this creep sour it for me.

I said, 'Well, you'd certainly recognise an arse before most people, Layton, since you see one when you're shaving every morning.'

Everyone heard. The place went silent. Most of the guys watched Layton who'd lost his mischievous look and was glaring at me coldly. He spoke, softening his tone, trying to sound menacing. 'Pretty full of yourself, Malloy,

on the strength of one good ride, ain't you? Pretty full of
yourself for a has-been.'

I smiled warmly just to irritate him. 'I'd sooner be a
has-been than a never-was.'

'Listen, Malloy –'

'You listen! How long does it take you to learn a lesson?
How many second prizes have you got to get?'

Realising he was quickly losing this round too he was
sensible enough not to risk further humiliation. Obviously
raging, he growled, 'You'll get yours, Malloy!' and
marched out. One of his sidekicks, Ben Meese again, a
swaggering little runt with bad skin, tried a bit too theatri-
cally to fill the brief silence by pointing the end of his whip at
me and saying, 'You'd better be *very very* careful, Malloy.'

Taking two strides towards him I bent over till our noses
were almost touching and said, 'Meese, if I'm not afraid
of the organ-grinder, what chance has the monkey got?'

He didn't care for that nor for the burst of laughter
from the lads. He reddened, glared at me with hate, then
turned and whacked my saddle hard with his whip before
scuttling away after Layton.

Ten minutes before the off three of us stood in the
paddock feeding off each other's tension. I was on edge,
aware it was my big chance. Barber's money was on the
line along with his judgement in letting the horse run.
Paul Whitehead had a big financial stake too and he stood
close as Barber gave me riding instructions, Paul repeating
them, nodding, tugging at his ear-lobe.

'Where's Loretta?' I asked.

Barber said, 'Eh, we persuaded her to watch it on telly.
Muriel's under instructions to keep her occupied.'

I smiled up at him. 'You told Loretta Tommy had
arrived, didn't you?'

Barber said, 'Ask no questions, hear no lies. A Champion Jockey's a Champion Jockey. Just get out there and
ride like you used too.'

When the bell rang for us to mount it was a relief to be legged up onto the big sweating bay gelding. Looking down on the two troubled upturned faces I smiled and told them not to worry. The blonde stablegirl led us out of the paddock towards the racecourse.

Cragrock's lass let him go and the big horse took a fierce hold of his bit and dropped his head, wrenching the reins from my hands so quickly the friction almost burned my fingers as I subconsciously relaxed them till I felt the buckle end. We broke into a loping canter and with his nose almost hoovering the grass he headed for the start.

'You'll have to do better than that,' I told him and his ears flicked back, listening. I spoke to him quietly and confidently all the way down and as we approached the gate I played the bit in his mouth, pulling, slackening, pulling and he responded sweetly by slowing to a trot. Easy money.

I reached forward to pat his neck and, sensing a hand off the reins, he suddenly dug his toes in and whipped round. On my way out of the saddle I grabbed at the plaited mane as my heel caught under the saddle flap and that was all that saved me from falling off.

Cragrock, smiling inwardly no doubt, trotted on with me hugging his neck and making undignified efforts to push myself upright again.

Under control once more he walked calmly and obediently forward for a look at the first fence then turned and trotted quietly back to join the others at the start.

Fred Harbour, the assistant starter, moved among us checking girth straps which always became loose as horses stretched on the way to the start. Fred was an ex-jockey staying in touch with the game as best he could. Accumulated injuries had forced him into early retirement. Fused vertebrae and oft dislocated shoulders had slowly curled his nine-stone body up till he looked sixty rather than forty.

It was the horses he loved; he spoke little to the jockeys, resenting the fact that he wasn't one of us any more. He moved towards me and I pulled Cragrock to a halt. Fred twanged the girths to test for slack. 'How are you doing?' I asked.

'Okay.'

From up here you only ever saw the top of his cloth cap. His injuries made it difficult for him to straighten his neck. Fred grunted as he strained to get my girths one hole tighter then, head still down, he said, 'Watch yourself, I think Layton and Meese are going to try and put you out of the race.'

It was the first time he'd spoken more than two words to me. 'Thanks,' I said. He didn't acknowledge, just patted Cragrock's neck and moved on. I looked around. The others circled me, chatting, trying to discover each other's tactics, who was going to make the running, who would be dropping out early. Layton and Meese were together. Layton laughed harshly, rolling his head back. Meese smiled up at him.

The starter called us into line. I moved Cragrock towards the rail, his head just behind the starting tape. Someone barged up my inside, shoving me to the right. I glanced across. It was Layton, pale smiling eyes looking watery behind his goggles. I glimpsed to my other side. Meese was there, smiling too.

They knew Cragrock had to be held up in the middle of the field and they'd obviously decided to waste no time in trying to intimidate us. I had a little surprise planned.

Chapter Three

I watched the starter as he looked across waiting for as straight a line as possible. His fingers tightened on the starting lever and as he opened his mouth to call 'Okay, jockeys!' I kicked Cragrock hard in the belly. The tape flew up, Cragrock's ears pricked, Layton cursed and after the first six strides we were four lengths clear of the rest.

Cragrock was confused. Used to his jockey fighting to hold him back, his ears flicked like antennae as he tried to figure out why he was being not only given his head but pushed along. He was still thinking by the time we reached the first fence and he took off a stride and a half too soon but we sailed over and landed just as far the other side, balanced and running.

We went ten lengths clear.

Coming to the second, his blood was up. Going too fast. No time for adjustment. He took off way too soon. *Jesus!* His front hooves barely cleared it. His hind legs hit the fence smashing birch twigs out like feathers from a shot pheasant. I sat back expecting him to pitch forward but the effort of the leap and staying upright brought only a short grunt from him as he sucked in air trying to regain full steam.

Before he could, I took a determined hold of the reins and managed to break his stride. He thought for a second about fighting then accepted and slowed to the slightly

easier pace I wanted. We were beginning to get an understanding.

His initial exuberance gone, Cragrock settled to a
steady pattern, his easy stride beating out that rhythmic
thud on the turf, all the more noticeable in the eerie
silence afforded a front-runner. Each leap brought a brief
suspension of the hoofbeats and another fix of the exhilaration which had made an addict of me from the beginning.

I was getting paid for this.

We'd travelled a circuit and nothing had got near us but
if we kept up this pace Cragrock would tire. I needed to
ease him down and as soon as I thought it he understood
and dropped half a gear, totally in synch with me now,
relaxed, enjoying himself as we set out on the second
circuit.

As we approached the last in the back straight, four
from home, they came after us. It sounded like a group
of three. Ten strides from the fence Cragrock sensed them
closing on him and suddenly his rhythm altered and he
guessed at the take-off. There was nothing I could do . . .
At full stretch I saw the birch coming up fast to meet
us . . .

We ploughed into the guts of the fence. Cragrock's
shiny black front hooves were momentarily higher than
his head as he stretched trying to save himself then came
that awful vacuum as his half-ton body hit the tight packed
birch . . . The weird feeling of being in a snapshot, waiting
for the punch of the momentum to catch up.

As always, it did.

And it smashed Cragrock onwards and downwards,
thumping the air from his lungs in a long despairing rasp.
A fraction of a second before I was catapulted forward I
saw a blur of bay, chestnut and grey horseflesh flash past
in a graceful arc. Cragrock, still doing everything to stop
himself crashing into the ground, was trying desperately
to get a leg out and the effort caused his big frame to

buckle then straighten under me throwing my legs and backside higher than my head as my face was forced into his mane. No brilliant recovery by Malloy, I was on my way out over his head when suddenly he found a foothold, got his undercarriage down, then scampered along like a crab before raising his neck, belting me in the face with his head and pushing me, inadvertently, back into the saddle.

Stunned and bloody-nosed I tried to collect my senses as the horse found his stride again and galloped on. My head cleared. Three to jump. We lay fourth, seven lengths behind the third, twelve off the leader. But Cragrock, surprisingly, was getting his second wind, running on again. He rallied as we rounded the bend into the straight. Ahead of me three pairs of white breeches pumped in unison.

Because of their crouch I couldn't see the colours but you get to know a rider's style and build. One of those in contention was Meese who had weightlifter's thighs.

I pushed on and we'd got the deficit down to five lengths when, halfway round the turn, Layton ranged alongside me, his almost toothless grin telling me he still thought he had plenty of horse under him. The running rail was on my left, Layton on my right. He moved his horse, Machete, a big powerful grey, across to lean on us. Cragrock hadn't much fight left.

'Layton! You bastard!' I hissed.

He looked across, boring harder into us now and spat at my face. The wind carried the gob and it splatted greasily on my goggles as we were forced into the rails. The white plastic shattered sending out a spray of shards. Cragrock broke stride and Layton, laughing, eased his horse away and kicked on towards the third last.

Panting with rage and frustration I pulled my smeared goggles down and hauled Cragrock off the rail, though I knew the race was lost. Much to my surprise Cragrock was quickly back on an even keel as we approached the fence. He met it on a beautiful long stride, landing far out on the other side, feeling as though he'd never left the ground. After going at such a hectic pace maybe the enforced breathers he'd had through the mistake and Layton's interference had actually helped him.

I was closing though Meese was obviously travelling best of the four in front. Layton, seeing his friend creep through on the rail as they rode for the second last fence, eased his horse right-handed, squeezing the chestnut in the middle onto Meese's bay as they all took off. Unbalanced, the bay scrambled over then disappeared from view; he was down. Layton would be laughing, knowing that, wronged or not, Meese would back him if there was a Stewards' Inquiry.

Cragrock now two out, in lovely stride again; soaring over I looked down and saw Meese lying under the rails as his horse struggled to his feet.

Up ahead, although he made an exaggerated play of trying to straighten him, Layton's horse continued to hang right, intimidating the little chestnut alongside him.

We were three lengths off them, still closing but feet at a time now rather than yards. It didn't look like we'd make it unless the pair in front blundered.

With Layton still squeezing out his rival they were both flat to the boards and drifting right coming to the last, close together, leaving me more than half the fence. Layton met it dead right. His challenger finally chickened out putting in two short strides, losing his impetus.

Cragrock met it in his normal stride pattern, jumped with no wasted effort and landed running at Machete's quarters. Layton, for the first time, looked over his left shoulder. His pale eyes widened and he mouthed a curse as he saw me. I smiled.

He knew he was in trouble. The run-in at Haydock goes around the open ditch which means that after you've jumped the last you have to tack across quite sharply to the left to avoid the wooden gates dolling off the fence. Layton, obviously expecting no challengers from behind, had left himself an even tighter angle to get out of trouble through squeezing out the others.

The angle became dangerously acute the nearer you got to the gates. Layton hauled violently at his horse, trying to pull him left.

Machete was tired. So was Cragrock. Both breathing hard, sides heaving, muscles straining, nostrils flaring as they snorted huge lungfuls of air.

I was running out of energy too, panting as I scrubbed and pushed.

But Cragrock was running straight. Machete, with Layton pulling hard on the left rein and desperately hitting him down the neck and shoulder, was totally unbalanced.

And the black and white dolls were coming closer.

I was a neck off him which gave him a few final seconds of hope before he realised he was trapped. They hit the first gate and by the sound of his curse and howl, Layton's right leg had taken the full impact. He hit the next three like skittles, only they didn't fall down.

He stopped riding. I went a length up, opening the trap and sensing Machete behind me hanging wearily to his left. I felt a pang of sympathy for Layton's brave horse but none for him.

The race was over. I eased Cragrock past the post becoming aware for the first time of the roaring crowd.

Glancing round at Layton as we pulled up I saw him slip his feet tenderly from the stirrups. His right boot was torn, blood dripping from the toe staining his horse's foreleg.

As we came back in along the horse-walk my breath mixed in the chill air with the steam rising from the gelding. I was blowing almost as hard as he was. But I was

elated. A couple of hours ago I'd been almost suicidal,
now I'd won one of the biggest races of the season and
beaten Layton at his own game.

Cragrock's blonde stable girl, cheeks rosy and eyes shining, came running to meet us followed at a measured
hobble by Hubert Barber. I consciously took a few lungfuls of air hoping to steady my breathing before the trainer
saw how unfit I was.

The delighted girl grabbed the reins, kissed the horse
and reached up to squeeze my hand. Her natural joy and
enthusiasm gave me a sudden unexpected moment of
peaceful happiness, contentment . . . something I hadn't
felt for a very long time.

The crowd was three or four deep down the rails to my
left, close enough for me to trail my whip along if I'd
wanted, knocking off all their hats. The odd shout of 'Well
done, Eddie!' rose from their ranks moving me to touch
my cap and nod in acknowledgement.

Barber's face showed a mixture of relief and annoyance.
He said, 'What were you two silly bastards up to?'

'All down to Layton,' I said. 'He tried to do a proper
job on me on the home turn. There's bound to be an
Inquiry.'

Barber said, 'And you tried to get your own back! On
the bloody run-in of all places!'

'I held my line, Mister Barber, that's all. Layton can't
complain about that.'

Still looking surly he said, 'You shouldn't have
retaliated.'

'If I hadn't you'd probably be leading in the second.'

That seemed to cheer him slightly. He nodded then
looked up at me again. 'Other than that,' he said, 'you
rode a bloody brilliant race . . . despite changing my
orders!'

I smiled and shook his hand. 'Thanks.'

We walked in towards the winner's enclosure to the

cheers of a big crowd. God, I'd forgotten just how sweet it was.

Struggling now to keep up, Barber cried, 'Hey, whoa!' and grabbed at the reins to slow the horse. 'I'm the bloody trainer remember, you might at least wait for me!'

Cragrock's lass turned and looked at me and we both laughed. As we entered the winner's enclosure the loud-speaker's message of 'Stewards' Inquiry', although expected, turned the welcoming cheers of the crowd into sighs of disappointment.

Barber, seeing his stake money once more in jeopardy, looked worried. 'I don't need this, Eddie. Don't need it,' he said as we stopped in the winner's berth. 'I've had enough hassle for the day.'

I dismounted as the large crowd, unsure of the final outcome, applauded half-heartedly. I undid the girths and the saddle pad squeaked keenly as I drew it from the back of the sweating horse and hung it on my arm. Turning to Barber I smiled confidently. 'See you soon for the presentation,' I said.

'Let's hope so.'

Con Layton sat smoking in the corner of the changing room, his feet up on the bench, half-dried blood crusting round the tear in his right boot. A valet said, 'Better get that seen to, Con.' Layton, smiling at me, said to him, 'That's evidence in the Stewards' Inquiry. You wouldn't be wanting me to cover it up.'

I sat down across from him but near enough, I hoped, to appear menacing. If he was bothered he didn't show it. My cold stare met with a smug smile and a blown smoke-ring which broke up as it looped and twirled like a tossed coin.

Between smoke-rings the smug smile stayed fixed on his thin lips. When he spoke he didn't look at me. 'What're you starin' at, Malloy?' His tone suggested not so much a challenge as a general inquiry.

'I'm trying to work out why you think the little arguments we had earlier make you think you've got the right to try to kill me.'

He smiled. 'Ah it's a big bad world out there, Malloy, where clever words are of no use to you. You must learn to be tough.'

I leaned forward, elbows on knees. 'I think I'm tough enough to handle an idiot who blows smoke-rings that are bigger than his brain.'

The smile disappeared as he turned slowly to stare at me. 'Malloy, you've an awful smart mouth.' Then he flicked the burning cigarette end straight at my face.

I ducked then got quickly to my feet ready to lunge at him. Layton was rising to meet me when a stern voice brought us up short. 'Malloy! Layton!' We turned. One of the Stewards' Secretaries stood at the door. Neither of us was sure how long he'd been there.

'Come with me,' he said, 'the Stewards will see you now.'

Like a frustrated child I considered shouldering Layton aside and marching out first but I decided I'd rather have the bastard in front than behind me. Waiting for him to take the lead I glowered at Layton from a height advantage of no more than an inch. His mean mouth smiled but his cold pale eyes were hard. 'Malloy,' he said, 'you'd better hope they warn you off again . . . You're a marked man.'

He headed for the door. I fell in behind and said, 'Listen, if you so much as come within spitting distance of me in a race again I'll break your legs.'

'What was that, Malloy?' asked the Stewards' Secretary.

'Nothing, sir, I was just asking Mister Layton if he was riding in the next.'

'Neither of you will be riding in the next if you keep the Stewards waiting much longer!'

The Stewards' Secretary was a tall man, maybe six

three, but very thin. His shoulder blades swung at our eye level as we followed him. His name was Claude Beckman. He stopped outside the Stewards' room and told us to wait.

Beckman knocked, turned the handle and took his trilby off as he went in, closing the door behind him.

We stood in silent animosity. This was my first Stewards' Inquiry since coming back. Nothing would have changed. Behind the door Beckman would be briefing the Stewards' panel, re-running the video of the incidents in question, telling them where he thought the fault lay.

The Stewards were unpaid local volunteers, mostly of 'good breeding', lovers of racing no doubt but many of them not as well versed in race-riding techniques as they should have been, considering our livelihoods often depended on their decisions.

Beckman was a paid official as were the other Stewards' Secretaries. They were appointed because of their in-depth knowledge of racing and had often ridden them-selves, though mostly as amateurs. Their job was to help the Stewards reach a fair decision. Many Secretaries were from military backgrounds. Far too few were ex-professional jockeys, who did the best job of all. But the Stewards tended not to trust the ex-pros and preferred the principle that new brooms sweep clean. Though old ones, I thought, glancing at Layton, knew where the dirt was.

We waited in silence. Few of us like Inquiries. You're made to stand in front of the panel like naughty school-boys while the Stewards address you by surname only and warn you to speak when spoken to.

They called us in. Layton went first, limping theatri-cally. Beckman, impatient, nodded at us to move quicker. The room was almost square; high roof, tatty decoration, poor lighting and bad ventilation judging by the musty smell from the shelves of books on the wall to my left. A nicotine film covered the once white ceiling and two big oil paintings.

Two men and a woman sat behind a long table. The Stewards. I knew them: Lord Cumbenauld, the Chairman, about sixty, thick white hair, tortoise-shell glasses, three-piece tweed suit with fob watch in waistcoat.

On his left was John Carnduff, a young Manchester businessman recently appointed joint master of the Wynstay Hunt. Dark curly hair, not bad looking though he'd collected a sizeable pink scar across the bridge of his nose since I'd last seen him.

On the Chairman's right was the Honourable Clarissa Cover who bred and raced jumpers with some success. Mid-fifties maybe, fair hair, elegant bone structure; she wore a royal blue dress with big gold-coloured buttons. Under the table her legs were crossed. I wondered if she knew her slip was showing.

Sitting off to Miss Cover's right, fingers poised over a grey machine, was the stenographer, Lisa Ffrench. I watched her from the corner of my eye. She didn't even glance up.

Beckman was looking down at us now. He was fortyish, prematurely bald in so perfect a ring above the fair Friar Tuck fringe it looked like his head had swollen through the circle and would go down again after ice-pack treatment. He spoke. 'We are here to inquire into careless riding in the last race. You will both answer the Stewards' questions truthfully and without the usual tiresome embellishments.'

Video evidence during inquiries often pin-pointed the main culprit but when guilt wasn't clear it tended to be the more articulate jockey, the best salesman, who won through. Embellishment was understating it, often it was pure fiction, but it was part of the trade, something you tried to learn along with the other skills.

Lord Cumbenauld cleared his throat and asked us to

explain our actions on the final bend and after the last. Layton got in first, bowing and scraping and, as expected, lying. He blamed the problems on his horse hanging badly.

I disputed it and told them it was deliberate. Layton, who'd been chummily calling me Eddie, acted horrified at this claim. The Stewards looked unconvinced.

'May I suggest we see the film, sir?' I said. Every race is filmed both from a camera patrol and from a head-on view in the straight. It wasn't often that film evidence was badly interpreted and I was confident the panel would find in my favour as soon as we'd seen it.

The Chairman glanced up at Claude Beckman who reddened slightly as he said to me, 'It is not a jockey's place to decide when a film should be viewed, that decision rests with the Stewards. Unfortunately, in this instance, we've had a technical problem which means the film will not be available. This case will be decided on the evidence of our own eyes and the testimony of those involved.'

Pompous bastard.

I noticed that Lisa Ffrench's fingers went silent on her keyboard before Beckman finished speaking. I glanced at her. She looked bewildered for a second as she stared at Beckman before tapping in his last few words. I looked back at him. The flush, now colouring his scalp, had deepened slightly.

They listened for another five minutes as we put our cases: I as quietly and sensibly as I could and Layton increasingly dramatically as he felt the verdict slipping away (at one point he asked if he could sit down as his injured foot was killing him).

They sent us outside again and closed the door while they made their final decision. I'd been confident going in, that the video evidence would clear me. With a less sensible and knowledgeable panel I'd have been having severe doubts by now but I knew that the main thing in my favour was Layton's reputation. Many of the Stewards were convinced he was a crooked bastard, they just couldn't prove it. I didn't think they'd be doing him any favours. I expected to be called in and exonerated within a minute or so.

Five minutes later we were still waiting. Jocks were weighing out for the next. The officials were waiting to present the prize for the Greenalls. People were getting worried. I was one of them.

The door opened and Beckman motioned us back in. He didn't look pleased. We stood in front of the panel trying to guess from their faces. Deadpan.

Lord Cumbenauld spoke. 'Without video corroboration we've had to take both your stories with a large pinch of salt and have made our decision on our own' – he glanced, rather coldly I thought, at Beckman – 'and Mr Beckman's recollection of the race. There is no doubt, Malloy, that you made the best of the situation after the last and that you had no intention of allowing Layton a clear run. However, you did keep a straight course and we've decided that Mister Layton's problems were of his own making. The result stands.'

I heard Layton breathe sharply through his nostrils. I smiled at the panel and said, 'Thank you.' The Chairman nodded and as we turned to leave said, 'And Layton, since your injured foot is causing you so much pain we've also decided that you must pass the doctor before riding again.'

Layton cursed. I managed to suppress my laughter till I got outside where Layton went through his full repertoire of bad language and left me in no doubt that I had an enemy for life.

By the time I'd been introduced to Loretta Whitehead at the trophy presentation she'd already forgiven Barber and her husband for deceiving her by saying Tommy Gilmour had turned up just in time. She looked of Latin stock with soft tinted skin though she wore the most horrendous silvery lipstick I'd ever seen. But she was charming and promised me more rides and invited me back to the box for a drink. I said I'd come straight after my ride in the next race and hurried off to get ready.

Pulsing with energy, feeling great, I changed into the black and red colours of my next mount pausing only to shake hands and accept congratulations from the lads, especially the little team in my own corner all of whom were now buzzing. If there was hope for one of us there was hope for all.

Amid the laughter and horseplay and leg-pulling I felt as good as I had for five years. Gradually, over ten seconds or so, I was aware of the room becoming steadily quiet. From near the door down to where we were the noise just sort of dried up like taps being turned off.

Along with everyone else I looked up towards the main door. Bob Carter, the senior valet, a big imposing man, stood there white-faced, mouth open looking at us, though his eyes were almost blank of expression. When there was complete silence Bob said, 'The police just found Tommy Gilmour's body. He's been murdered.'

Chapter Four

A jogger had found Tommy's body in thick woods about a mile from his hotel. He had been shot between the eyes. No further details were available.

Despite the bright colours we wore it was a morbid group that filed out to ride in the next.

Having been away from racing for five years I hadn't known Tommy Gilmour that well but I knew he was a nice guy, a good solid pro who'd worked hard for the breaks. A quiet family man, he didn't socialise much and had, through choice, no close friends though he was liked and respected by everyone.

As we lined up at the start my own feelings were confused. I was the only one who'd benefited from Tommy's death which, to me, meant I should have felt dreadful. But I didn't.

Sure, there was a sadness for him and I tried hard to multiply it, but I couldn't make it overcome the pleasure I still felt from winning, the new hope that was there, the heartless pragmatism that was hatching plans to try and take Tommy's place at Barber's.

The least I should have been able to find in compensation was a large helping of guilt but I couldn't. It was then that I realised how desperate I must have been these last few months, how much my character had changed, how right Jackie had been about me.

Jackie . . . I hadn't even phoned her with the good

news. Maybe she'd have seen it on TV. God, I hoped not, that would make things even worse. I resolved to ring her as soon as I got back in.

The starter raised his flag, the rain took it as a signal to begin spitting at us again and we raced off into the gathering gloom.

Mine finished a distant seventh and I dismounted the weary sweating chestnut and headed for the warmth of the weighing room. The feel of stones through my paper-thin bootsoles reminded me that I hadn't even done enough riding this season to toughen my feet. Well, maybe it would all change now. Maybe today would be the turning point.

Halfway across the wet tarmac I became aware of someone coming at me from right angles. He was in a hurry. A couple of strides from me he said, 'Eddie Malloy?'

I stopped. 'That's right.'

'Good. Can I ask you a few questions?'

He had a notebook but I didn't recognise him as a racing journalist. 'What about?' I asked.

'Winning the big race.'

'Sure.' I could use all the publicity I could get.

He said, 'How does it feel to have won under such circumstances?'

I looked at him: big guy, fat, hatless, serious looking, glasses slipping down his nose. 'Under what circumstances?' I asked.

'The murder of the bloke who was supposed to ride the horse, you know, Gilmour, Tommy Gilmour.'

'Who do you work for?' I asked.

'*The Globe*. Big circulation.'

Among those that liked sleaze with Sunday breakfast, I thought, but I would have to give him an answer. 'I feel terrible for Tommy and his family, we all do but we're professionals with a job to do and the only satisfaction I take from the race is that I did my job well.'

'But it takes the shine off, is that what you're saying?' He looked at me, smiling and nodding in that inane way that reporters think encourages you to talk.

'Of course it takes the shine off! You don't see anybody celebrating, do you?'

He was scribbling. 'Why would anyone want to kill Tommy Gilmour?'

Jeez. 'How should I know? Why don't you find the guy that did it and ask him?' I stepped past him and headed for the weighing room. Undaunted, he fell in beside me and asked, 'What do you think of the guy that did it?'

I stopped and glared at him but he just stood, pencil poised, like a robot waiting for the next component. I said, 'What do *you* think of him? . . . He must be a lunatic!'

He nodded. 'And do you think he'll strike again?'

'If he does I hope you're there to witness it first-hand, which should save you asking people silly questions.'

I left him looking puzzled on the steps.

I showered and changed before heading home. The victory party had, understandably, been cancelled. Any celebration would have been veiled by a shroud as cold and heavy as the one covering Tommy Gilmour's corpse.

I pushed thoughts of Tommy from my mind and decided to pick up a couple of bottles of champagne on the way home and surprise Jackie. God, it would be surprise enough for her to see me come in with a smile on my face. I'd tried to ring her before leaving the course but the line was engaged. At least that meant she hadn't left me.

We lived in an old hunting lodge in Leicestershire, leased to us by Henry Kravitz, an owner I rode for occasionally. He'd been very understanding about the rent, which was just as well.

The lodge lay in flat countryside about three hundred yards off the main road. The wide drive leading to it was uneven and badly pot-holed in places. I bumped along it in the darkness, pulling up quietly by the side wall of the building.

The only light through the windows was from a lamp in the living room. Softly I turned the handle on the big heavy door. It was locked. That wasn't like Jackie. I felt for my key.

When I closed the door behind me and heard the perfect silence I knew she'd gone. The phone was off the hook. The note was under the lamp, her big looping handwriting in a pool of yellow light. 'I looked in the mirror, Eddie, and a thirty-five-year-old woman looked back at me. You were killing me. I didn't know it till this morning and maybe you didn't know it but it was happening. I just want to be twenty-three again. I don't have to be happy, I just want not to be dying . . . Jackie.'

Over the top as usual, typical Jackie. I smiled and folded the note, letting it flutter back onto the table. She had an awful temper and became overwrought about the smallest things. Then she'd recover and go the other way, smotheringly loving. The mercurial highs and lows had troubled me at first but I was just about getting used to them. Confident she'd come back in a day or two I poured a drink and flopped into the chair and thought back on our nine months together.

Last summer, Jackie had saved my life, literally. I'd been helping The Jockey Club Security Department in a criminal case and rather carelessly found myself at the wrong end of a gun.

Just when I'd given up on the cavalry Jackie appeared, shotgun in hand, and persuaded the guy to behave. We'd already fallen in love before it happened but the danger of that moment, the relief, it sort of turbo-charged our affair and we lived and loved on the potency of it for months afterwards.

I sat in the pale lamplight, in the cold of that big twelve-roomed house, and listened to the silence. I'd grown so used to Jackie fussing around me usually in an effort to cheer me up after another bad day . . . but the silence, the peace . . . I found surprisingly welcome, a tiny gladness that I was alone again as I'd been for most of my life.

Then I felt guilty. She hadn't much money, where had she gone? Back to her mother in Ireland? Did she have the fare? I could ring her there . . . maybe best to wait a few days. Till we were missing each other intolerably . . . be easier then.

Get busy now. Take your mind off it.

I put the champagne in the fridge and a cheap curry in the microwave, shovelled the ashes from the fireplace and set some new logs burning, steeped a couple of shirts in the big white sink, ate the curry then poured a large whisky and settled down by the fire to scrape the mud from my boots and shine them up. I switched off the lamp and rubbed and polished away rhythmically in the glow of the flames which reflected and danced in the folds of leather and warmed the whisky's colour to coppery gold.

Two hours and three drinks later Jackie was still on my mind twisting me between worry about where she was and anger that she'd gone. Surely I hadn't become that hard to live with? Most of the time I'd tried to be philosophical, tried to shield her. Okay, so once or twice there had been totally black despair when I couldn't see any way out . . . maybe I'd dragged her down too deep . . .

Still, she'd be back. As soon as she heard the good news she'd be back. I drank again, cursing her silently for making me 'celebrate' alone, for turning the festival into a wake.

Melancholy was taking a stronger hold than the alcohol and I decided I'd be better off asleep than sitting alone feeling sorry for myself in this big bloody dungeon in the middle of nowhere.

As I got out of the chair the phone rang. It was Lisa Ffrench.

'How'd you get my number?'

'Mutual friend,' she said. 'You heard about Tommy Gilmour?'

Something in her tone put me on the defensive. 'Yes,' I said, 'I couldn't believe it.'

'Nor can Susan, his wife.'

'You've seen her?'

'I'm with her now. At her house. I came straight here from Haydock. She's under heavy sedation.'

'I didn't realise you knew the Gilmours.'

'I knew Susan before she met Tommy. We were at school together.'

I hesitated, awkward. 'I'm sorry,' I said, 'it must have come as a hell of a shock . . . they've got a couple of kids, haven't they?'

'One's four, the other's only two. We haven't told them yet.'

We?

'God help them,' I said.

'If there was one, He would've helped them before their daddy got shot, don't you think?'

'Maybe.'

'*Maybe?*'

Shit . . . What did she ring for, an argument about religion?

I said, 'Lisa, if you want to be mad at someone, go ahead, I owe you one.'

'I'm sorry,' she said, 'I didn't mean to snap.'

'It's okay.'

Calm again she said, 'Listen, did you hear any rumours about Tommy, about the murder?'

'Not a thing. All anybody could say about him was that he was a nice guy. I don't think anybody even knew him that well.'

She said, 'I heard it might have been something to do with someone trying to stop the horse running because there'd been a big ante-post gamble.'

I considered it, knowing that bets placed prior to the day of the race were lost if the horse didn't run.

'A bit drastic, I'd have thought,' I said. 'It would have been easier to nobble the horse than kill the jockey.'

'Did you know the horse had been under a twenty-four hour guard for weeks?'

'No, I didn't.'

I interpreted her silent pause as, Well you don't know much, do you? Then she said, 'Anyway, I heard that rumour today from one of the Stewards. I'm going to tell the police about it.'

'Have they been to talk to, uh . . .'

'Susan.'

'. . . Susan, yet?'

'They wanted to but I told them she was unfit. They're coming in the morning.'

'Best tell them then,' I said lamely.

'Yes. But will you keep your ear to the ground for me, let me know if you hear anything about it?'

Jeez, not happy with fixing rides for me, now she wants to solve murders.

'Sure,' I said.

'Okay, I'll give you my number here and my number at home. You'll catch me at one or the other if we don't meet on the racecourse.'

I found a pen and scribbled the numbers.

'By the way,' she said, 'you know in the Inquiry today when Claude Beckman said the video wasn't available . . .'

'Yeah, technical problems.'

'Not when I saw it there weren't.'

'You saw the tape?'

'I saw Beckman watching it before the Stewards arrived.

He hadn't heard me come in and as soon as he realised I was there he switched the VCR off and muttered something about a faulty tape.'

'Did he tell the Stewards beforehand it was faulty?'

'I didn't hear him.'

'He must have, 'cause they didn't look surprised when he told me . . . though you did.'

'I know.'

I said, 'Maybe it was faulty in places you didn't see.'

'I don't think so. I think Beckman's got it in for you in a big way. He was really having a go before you came in, trying to convince the panel you were to blame and should be disqualified. And when you were cleared he was absolutely fuming.'

'Any idea why? Why he's got it in for me, I mean.'

'I thought you might know.'

'Haven't a clue. Hardly know the guy.'

'Well, you'd better watch out.'

'I will, thanks.'

'Okay, ring me if you hear anything, will you?'

'Sure and . . . Lisa, thanks for today, for pushing me towards Barber.'

'That's all right.'

'No, I mean it. I wouldn't have done it myself. Confidence was gone . . . shot to shit.'

Lisa said, 'You've had a few bad breaks, you just needed a boost.'

'Maybe.'

'Look, Eddie, I've got to go, the baby's crying.'

'Okay. Goodnight.'

She hung up.

When I realised I'd written her phone numbers on the back of Jackie's goodbye note I felt a sudden pang of guilt, of unfaithfulness.

I sat down. It took me ten minutes to finish my drink. Nine of them were filled with thoughts of Lisa and what

she'd said. Jackie crowded back in for the last one and as
the wind picked up outside I imagined her wandering in
the darkness or huddled miserably in the corner of some
bus shelter. Too much booze, Eddie, time for bed.

I rose next morning and dressed quickly in the cold damp
room. After a restless dream-filled night I was looking
forward to hot coffee and maybe some good publicity in
the papers, though I knew Tommy's murder would take
the headlines.

I jogged along the hall and as I approached the foot of
the stairs I noticed an envelope on the mat. Unless the
Royal Mail had started a Sunday service someone must
have delivered it by hand.

Maybe it was from Jackie.

It was heavy. 'Malloy' was written on the front in neat
block letters and I ripped it open as I walked to the
kitchen. Inside was a thin racing diary. Tucked between
its pages were two pieces of paper: one was a cutting
from a morning newspaper headlined, Champion Jockey
Murdered. A section of the text had been highlighted in
bright yellow: 'Malloy said that the killer must be a
lunatic.'

The other piece was plain white; printed in block letters
was: 'News for you – the lunatics have taken over the
asylum.'

Below that was: 'Numbers 32:23.'

I skiffed through the diary. It was Tommy Gilmour's.

Chapter Five

My first thought was that it was a sick joke. Layton maybe, still mad from yesterday, trying to wind me up. But how the hell would he have got hold of Tommy's diary?

I put the kettle on.

How did this guy, whoever he was, know where I lived?

Steam from my coffee condensed on the cold glass as I stood by the window watching wraiths of mist glide slowly among the wet trees. The note, though cryptic, was obviously meant to be at best a warning and at worst a definite threat. If it was genuine then for my sake as much as Tommy Gilmour's I had to call in the police.

If I reported it and it turned out to be Layton or someone winding me up then I'd be laughed out of the weighing room. So what? It wouldn't be the first time I'd been made to look foolish.

Indecision. I didn't want to over-react. Maybe I should ask McCarthy's advice. He worked for The Jockey Club Security Department. We'd helped each other in the past. I found his number in my diary. He was out. I left a message on his answering machine asking him to ring me.

A thick fog came down, wrapped itself around the house and stayed there all day. I spent a couple of hours on the newspapers, searching vainly for some decent publicity but they'd all homed in on Tommy's murder.

The racing writers mourned him and wrote warm obituaries, while the tabloid hacks speculated on the motive.

None offered anything concrete. A police spokesman said the forensic boys were taking Gilmour's hotel room apart and stripping down his car in search of clues. They appealed for anyone they thought could help to come forward.

Should I be coming forward with the note and the diary? I'd tried to forget about it, pushed hard a few times to get it out of my mind but it came arcing back, like a kid on a swing demanding attention, and stayed nagging at me all day. If the note had come from the killer then there would be a chance he'd also left one at the murder scene. It would give the police useful corroboration.

I decided to wait till I'd heard from McCarthy but by seven he still hadn't returned my call. I rang the police.

They asked if it would be convenient for someone to come round for a statement as soon as possible. Asked when that would be, the bloke said he'd get a local man who would then pass the stuff on.

The cop turned up an hour later; DS Latimer, local CID, young but world-weary in that practised way that says, Even though I'm only twenty-eight I've seen it all. Surrogate detection obviously didn't appeal to him and he quietly sipped coffee, wrote down my brief statement, took the diary, notes and envelope and told me one of the Manchester boys would get back to me.

I thought about calling Lisa but the prospect made me feel like a kid running to the teacher with a secret hoping for a pat on the head. The girl was too competent.

As dusk fell around the silent fogbound house all the supposings and what-ifs jockeyed for position. If no one could think of a motive for Gilmour's murder who could say there wouldn't be another victim? Maybe the killer was a mad punter who'd lost money on Gilmour's horses . . . Supposing he backed one of mine tomorrow or the next day? I could be riding for my life without even knowing it . . . No, that was ridiculous.

The evening dragged on. The fog crept quietly around the house looking for a way in. Sundays are never my best days anyway but this was a real bummer. I stopped reading, switched on the radio . . . choirs singing hymns that made my soul feel even heavier. I had spoken to no one except Lisa since leaving the racecourse yesterday.

Jackie came into my mind again. Young pretty feisty determined Jackie. She of the auburn hair and hazel eyes, the freckles and the squint-toothed smile. And I wondered again where she was. Why hadn't she phoned?

Hubert Barber yanked me out of my depression around seven o'clock when he rang. He was still pretty shocked about Tommy and I sympathised as he reminisced for a while but when he asked me to ride three at Leicester for him next day and two at Sedgefield on Tuesday I had to suppress a whoop of delight. I poured a large whisky to celebrate, toasted my ghostly flickering reflection in the mirror above the fireplace and had an early night.

I travelled home from Sedgefield on the Tuesday with a winner and a third to add to my two winners at Leicester the previous day. Barber's stable was in cracking form and I'd got in with him at just the right time. Apart from missing Jackie I was happier than I'd been for years and still finding it tough to feel guilty about it.

Maybe if I'd known Tommy better I'd have felt worse but the reality was that his death had given me a good break, a new chance. I had to snap it up without agonising over it but maybe I was making too good a job of that. People were beginning to react.

A couple of the other jockeys, ones who would normally have passed the time of day, had ignored me completely at Sedgefield. I could live with that but on the way to the car park three potential sources of rides, two owners and a trainer, had walked straight past without acknowledging my greeting which was the equivalent of slamming the door in my face and double-locking it.

I knew some people were pissed off about me getting Gilmour's rides but these reactions just didn't tie up. Race-riding is a hazardous occupation and injuries are common. If something happens to a jockey someone else takes his rides. That someone else could easily break his neck the following week, letting in another substitute. It's a tough game and racing folk normally accept that. Somebody had to take Tommy's rides. These guys were acting as if I'd murdered him myself.

I still hadn't contacted McCarthy to discuss the note and the diary. We kept missing each other, leaving messages. I'd left one last night telling him exactly when I'd be at home and where I was racing for the rest of the week.

It was dark when I got back and the house was cold. I switched on two lamps, built a fire and pushed a three-hundred-calorie packet meal into the microwave. Normally I could eat what I wanted and seldom had weight problems but I found the diet meals palatable and convenient.

I closed the big curtains and poured a drink. When the oven bleeped I emptied a rather weary looking lasagne onto a plate, turned on the big 1950's Bush radio in the corner and sat down to listen to the news as I ate.

Ten minutes later I switched the radio off, slung a few more logs on the fire and sat in silence to go through the next day's runners at Southwell. Chris Brytham, a trainer I hadn't ridden for before, had booked me to ride two and, being back in the public eye a bit, there had to be a chance of picking up a couple of spares. Things were looking up. I felt comfortable and relaxed.

I must have dozed off. I woke convinced I'd heard a noise outside. Sudden thoughts of Tommy Gilmour, the note, and the memory of some unwelcome clashes I'd had last year with villains caused a surge in my gut. In stockinged feet I moved quietly towards the window and listened.

Through the crackle of burning logs I heard the clunk of a car door closing and the crunch of boots on gravel. A few seconds later the heavy doorknocker fell like a pinball hammer, pounding an echo along the oval hall. Whoever was calling had no intention of surprising me . . . . Then again maybe Tommy Gilmour had thought the same.

Hanging by a piece of string from the coat stand in the hall was a metal baseball bat I kept. Unhooking it I moved behind the door as the knocker fell again. 'Who is it?' I asked.

'Eddie? It's Mac . . . Peter McCarthy.'

I wasn't sure. It didn't sound like him. McCarthy had played a big part in my comeback. Almost six years ago I'd been Champion Jockey till I'd lost my licence after being falsely implicated in a doping ring. After I'd served a five-year ban McCarthy, a Jockey Club Security man, had recruited me to help him catch the guy who'd framed me. We caught him, I got my licence back and McCarthy got promoted. Maybe I was still drowsy but I wasn't sure it *was* Mac on the other side of that door. I listened . . .

'Come on, Eddie, stop messing about, it's bloody freezing out here. Let me in.'

That was Mac.

Still wearing coat and scarf he sat by the fire. The glow haloed his dark curly hair. Pulling a small container from his pocket he grimaced as he popped two sweeteners into the mug of coffee I'd just handed him. 'Hate these damn things,' he said. 'Always leave a bitter taste.'

'How's the diet going?'

'Lost seventeen pounds but it's killing me. Jean won't give me a break. Not even at weekends.'

'Good for her.' Jean was his wife who'd recently decided

that after fifteen years of marriage to a slob she was going to do something about it. McCarthy's boss at The Jockey Club was retiring soon and Jean was determined that Mac would get the post when it came up. She had set about decreasing his waistline and improving his table manners (he was a habitual belcher though he claimed it was a medical condition).

McCarthy was forty-one years old, six two, fifty pounds overweight and bloody good at his job. It was Mac who'd persuaded his bosses that I could help them break the doping case, though his motives at the outset were not completely selfless; I took the chances, he got the glory.

Sipping his coffee he glanced around the room. 'Nice place,' he said.

'Cold place. You ought to try sleeping in it.'

'Buy yourself a hot-water bottle from Saturday's prize money.'

'Maybe I will.'

We chewed the fat a while. He asked about Jackie. I told him. He sympathised.

Although mildly surprised that he hadn't simply called me to find out why I wanted him, I assumed McCarthy had come to discuss the messages I'd left on his machine. But I saw from the glint in his eye that he wasn't here just for that, he was up to his old tricks again.

McCarthy enjoyed playing a silly game which might have been called Guess Why I'm Here. Most people when they get a bit of news or have some supposedly 'secret' information can't wait to pass it on. Not Mac. He hoarded these little nuggets like a miser hoping people would prod and dig and sweat till they'd winkled them out. This annoyed me intensely and he knew it. He smiled as he watched me waiting.

'What was it you wanted to talk to me about?' he asked.

I played him at his own game. 'Tell me what you wanted first.'

He tried the open, innocent face. 'What do you mean?'

'Mac, it's half-past eight. This place is a three-hour round trip for you. You didn't come just to find out what I wanted, you could have done that by phone.'

'I tried and couldn't get you! Anyway, I was at a meeting in Nottingham so it was no problem dropping by.'

I was almost believing him but he couldn't resist that little knowing smile which gave him away. I sighed. 'Mac, you know this pisses me off, why do you keep doing it?'

'What?'

'This little girl's game of I know something you don't know.'

That got him. 'It's not a little girl's game, it's a matter of judging the proper moment, saying the right thing at the right time.'

'Come on, Mac, you love it!'

He got huffy and serious looking. 'I'm working on the Tommy Gilmour case.'

I didn't answer. Something was creeping into his eyes that I didn't like . . . expectation. 'And?' I asked.

'I wondered . . .'

'Wonder all you like, Mac, but leave me out of any little scam you've got planned. I've told the police what I know, done my duty as a citizen and all that.'

He played the wounded look. 'Eddie, I know you want to get on with your career, there's no way I'd ask you to get involved in anything that didn't concern you.'

'Good. What can I do for you then?'

'Re*lax*! I just wanted to ask you a few questions since you were indirectly involved.'

I bristled. 'How do you work *that* out?'

'Well, you got Gilmour's ride in the Greenalls, didn't you?'

'What the hell is that supposed to mean?'

'Take it easy, Eddie, I'm not accusing you of anything.'

'What *are* you doing then?'

'I'm only stating a fact. When Gilmour disappeared you got the mount.'

'So?'

'Who offered you the ride?'

'Nobody. I asked for it. I asked Hubert Barber if I could ride.'

'When did you speak to him?'

'Just before the first race.'

'Did he mention that the owner initially wanted to withdraw?'

'Mac, how is all this relevant?'

He half sighed, half blew on his coffee. 'It probably isn't but I have to start somewhere. I've got nothing.'

I wondered if the police had told him about my special delivery on Sunday. I said, 'Okay, Barber did say that Loretta Whitehead was thinking of withdrawing the horse but her husband, with Barber's help, persuaded her to run. They'd had a few quid on ante-post.'

McCarthy, pudgy cheeks reddening now from the heat of the fire, looked troubled. 'That's the only possible motive I can think of, the betting side, someone trying to stop the horse running, but it seems too desperate, too extreme.'

'I think you're right, Mac. Killing the jockey wouldn't have guaranteed anything. It's too easy to get someone else to ride.'

'But maybe they planned on that, knowing Cragrock was such a difficult ride maybe they didn't care who rode him so long as it wasn't Gilmour. Christ, every time Cragrock won this season the papers were full of how nobody but Gilmour could have won on him.'

'Yeah, the Press boys did Tommy a real favour there, eh?'

McCarthy shook his head slowly. 'Poor bastard. His wife's taking it really bad, you know.'

'Been to see her?'

He stared at the flames. 'Haven't had the bottle to . . . I must do it soon.'

I nodded in sympathy. 'You checked out the betting side?' I asked.

'Checked it all the way back. No bookmaker was consistently offering Cragrock at a higher price than his competitors and nobody had any substantial liabilities on the horse. Barber and his owner had some biggish bets but they'd already told us that. There's virtually nothing to support the betting side as a motive for Gilmour's murder.'

'Just as well you've been up there before, Mac, you're going to need the experience.'

Puzzled, he looked at me. 'Up where?'

'Shit creek without a paddle.' I went to get a drink.

He called after me, 'I might not be the only one in the canoe, Eddie.'

The quiet, very personal tone of the comment made it clear to me even before I turned to look at him who he thought his travelling companion might be. He knew something and was trying like hell not to smile. I sloshed whisky into a glass and went to sit down, determined not to play his little game. If he had an ace up his sleeve I wasn't going to unbutton his cuff looking for it. He read me and thought he'd change the subject for a while.

'What about Saturday's race, Eddie, I heard you got a bit of a rough ride?'

I nodded. 'Con Layton and one of his cronies. Nothing I couldn't handle.' I told him about our confrontation in the changing room and how the Irishman had lied at the Inquiry.

'You want to watch Layton,' he said, 'he is your original nasty piece of work.'

'So they tell me.'

'His party trick is biting the necks off beer bottles and swallowing lit cigarettes.'

'That just about sums up his mentality then, doesn't it?' I said.

'Maybe, but he's a wily bastard. We've been watching him for the past two years, trying to catch him at one of his dodges. He can be smart when he wants to.'

'As long as he's smart with someone else and not me I won't be too bothered. I'll be happy to be left alone to pick up my career.'

He gazed at me. I looked away, staring into the fire, and he said, 'That means left alone by me as much as Layton, doesn't it?'

I gazed at the flames a few seconds longer then looked up at him. 'Mac, the reason I helped you last time was to get my licence back. Okay, sometimes it was great playing detective but when I found myself on the receiving end of beatings and scaldings and threats, when I had to deal with idiotic cops and junkies and psychos it kind of started losing its attraction . . . And on top of everything else I was shit-scared most of the time.'

He smiled at me. 'But you got the job done, you were good.'

'Mac, you know what the bankrupt Chinese stamp collector said, don't you? . . . Philately will get you nowhere.'

'So you're going to sit this one out?'

'If it's all the same to you.'

He sipped his coffee and took on his grave face but somewhere behind those dark eyes, devilment glinted. The ace-up-the-sleeve look was back. 'I don't think you'll be able to, Eddie.'

He loved this.

'Out with it, Mac.'

'I was at Windsor yesterday . . . There was a rumour going round, one I first heard on Sunday evening.' He paused, drank . . . the bastard.

'And?' I said.

'They're saying you had Tommy Gilmour murdered.'

Chapter Six

I stared at him, conscious of holding my breath. 'You're winding me up, Mac.'

He shook his head. 'Wish I was.' He looked serious but I couldn't believe what he'd just said.

I watched him closely, still half convinced he was joking. I said, 'Come on, why would *I* want Tommy dead?'

He watched me, trying to judge what to say and how to say it. 'They're saying you did it to get his rides.'

My head went back as a slightly manic laugh escaped me and, relieved, I lifted my drink and slumped easily back down into the chair. 'Is that all?' I asked. 'Is that my sole motive for having Tommy Gilmour murdered?'

He shrugged. 'As far as I know.'

'Well that's all right then.' I held my glass up and said, 'Cheers.'

McCarthy stared at me. 'Eddie, look, you could be in very deep trouble here.'

'*Mac!* For God's sake, it's too ridiculous for words, you should know that.'

'Eddie, I know that and you know it but you can't just write it off so easily for others, for people that *don't* know you.'

I couldn't believe he was pursuing it. 'Look, I'm a jockey. I ride horses for a living. I go racing, then I come back to this big house and eat and sleep then go racing again. I'm a jockey, not a bloody Mafia-man!'

He was irritated. 'So people are supposed to just ignore your criminal record, your history of violence?'

'My *history* of violence, as you know, is confined to kicking the shit out of the guy who framed me which, as you also know, was what earned me my criminal record, so stop exaggerating.'

'What about almost ripping the throat out of Stoke's two men with the barbed wire?'

'It was them or me as you well know!'

He squirmed a bit. 'I'm only trying to play devil's advocate, Eddie. These are serious allegations.'

'Mac, I just can't accept that. Anybody with half a brain would laugh you off the racecourse if you repeated all this to them. Me having someone murdered just for his rides? What do I do if Barber's horses go down with the virus, murder someone else?'

'You're laughing. Didn't you read about that woman in America who's supposed to have had a football cheerleader killed so her daughter could replace her on the team?'

'Yeah, well that's America for you, Mac, but we're talking about little old England.'

McCarthy put his cup down and hauled himself out of the chair. 'Well,' he said, 'you're obviously determined to write this off without any more thought.'

'It doesn't deserve any more thought,' I said, standing up and putting my glass on the marble mantelpiece. 'Who started these rumours anyway?'

He shrugged. 'I don't know.'

'Well who did you hear it from?'

'Half a dozen people.'

'I don't believe it . . .' Resting my elbows wearily on the mantelpiece I cradled my head in my hands. Then, remembering the note and Tommy's diary, I told him about them.

'Who sent them?' he asked.

'How the hell do I know? They were meant to look like they'd come from Gilmour's killer. That's what I rang you about.'

'You think it was meant as a threat?'

'Or a warning . . . If it's genuine.'

'Why would he warn you?'

'Maybe he was upset at me calling him a lunatic.'

Mac shut his eyes and frowned deeply. ' "The lunatics have taken over the asylum . . ." ' he mused, then, 'What do you suppose the numbers meant?'

'Haven't a clue.'

'What were they again?'

'Thirty-two and twenty-three.'

'And they mean nothing to you?'

'Not a thing. What struck me as curious was that he'd written the actual word *numbers* before the figures themselves.'

Eyes still closed, Mac shook his head in defeat. 'Beats me.'

'Shouldn't the police have told you I gave them this stuff?'

'In theory, yes. It seldom works in practice.'

'But you will make sure the rumour-mongers get to hear about them, the note and the diary?'

Massaging his face with his big hands he looked at me. 'Think it'll make any difference?'

'It had better!'

He shook his head. 'Eddie . . . If they think you're guilty of something they'll just see this as some attempt at a cover-up.'

'By who?'

He raised his eyebrows. 'By whom, Eddie.'

'Spare me the grammar lesson, Mac, I've got better things to worry about.'

He shrugged. 'Just trying to cheer you up.'

'Well cheer me up by telling these idiots they're talking

rubbish. And if they think I'm forging notes and stealing diaries to give myself an alibi, well . . . look, I'll tell you what, just give me their names and I'll have a little word myself.'

Mac said, 'Come on, Eddie, everyone who *knows* you will know the rumours are nonsense, I've –'

'Listen, just note the name of the next person you hear it from or tell them to contact me direct.' I was getting angry. Mac could see it. He paused, watching me, hoping I'd cool off. I didn't.

By way of closing the subject I marched across to the drinks cabinet and poured myself a large defiant whisky. 'Cheers,' I said coldly to McCarthy.

He looked at me. 'So you don't want to help in tracking this guy down?'

'This is what all this is about, isn't it?' I said. 'You make me feel threatened, I get involved in looking for Gilmour's killer and you have an easier life.'

He shrugged. 'I'm not denying I could use your help but I think you owe it to yourself to –'

'Look, Mac, don't give me that crap. I'm staying well out of it.'

'Okay.' He put his hat on. I followed him out to the hall and opened the door. 'Sorry you've had a wasted journey, Mac.'

He looked at me from his four-inch height advantage. 'Eddie, I think you're badly underestimating the feeling that could build up if Gilmour's killer isn't found soon . . . Take a minute to look at the full picture from a stranger's point of view, you've been away five years, remember, there aren't that many people around now who know you well.'

He was right about that.

'As far as they're concerned,' he went on, 'you're an ex-champion jockey with a grudge against the establishment for taking your licence away and virtually killing your career. It's your first year back and you're having a terrible season; everybody knows you're up to your eyes in debt and don't look to have any way out. Naturally you're getting desperate.

'As I said, you've got a criminal record, you can be ruthless and you can be violent. And don't forget, who was the only jockey who went and *asked* for the ride on Cragrock?'

He stepped outside. 'Think about it,' he said. 'You've got my number.'

I watched him drive away then slowly closed the door and went and sat on the rug by the fire, head in hands, feeling, suddenly, very weary. The more I thought and worried about what Mac had said the more plausible the rumours seemed.

My mind returned to Sedgefield where a couple of jockeys had ignored me and two owners and a trainer had given me the cold shoulder. I hadn't understood it then. I did now and if those people could believe I had Tommy Gilmour killed anybody could, even Hubert Barber. And if I lost the Barber rides now, I was finished. There'd be no more comebacks.

I didn't get a hell of a lot of sleep.

The 10 a.m. news had just finished and I was ready to leave for the races when the phone rang. It was Chris Brytham, the trainer who'd booked me to ride his two at Southwell. He came straight to the point.

'Eddie, I'm sorry but I'm going to have to cancel those bookings for today.'

Horses were sometimes withdrawn at a late stage for various reasons. 'Aren't they running?' I asked.

He paused and cleared his throat which told me all I needed to know before he answered. 'They are running but . . . well the owner's asked me to find another jockey.'

'Why?'

Another pause, then, 'I'm sorry, Eddie, it's not my decision. If it had been you would have kept the rides.'

It was my turn to be quiet. Brytham tried to fill the silence. 'I was just hoping I'd catch you before you left . . . Save you a trip . . . I'm sorry.'

Everything Mac had said last night was crowding in on me and I fought to stay cool. 'I appreciate the thought, Mister Brytham, but I'll be going to Southwell anyway. And listen, thanks for the call. I can think of a number of people who would have replaced me without even letting me know.'

'I just wanted to tell you it wasn't my decision, Eddie. I daresay you've an idea what it's all about and personally I think it's a load of rubbish. If things weren't so tough I'd tell this owner where to go but . . . well, you know how it is.'

I knew how it was all right, there were too many trainers chasing too few owners. Chris Brytham wasn't the only one having to lick boots.

'Yeah, I know . . . Forget it. Thanks again for the call.'

'I hope it all gets sorted out soon,' he said and rang off.

Me too, I thought, me too.

Well, well, well, it looked like Mac was right. There were people out there prepared to believe these crazy rumours.

Common sense told me to ring Hubert Barber and find out if the stories had reached him and, if so, how did I stand? If Barber pulled the plug I had two choices: hang up my boots and saddle till the police found Gilmour's killer or hang them up and go find the bastard myself. The way I was feeling right at that moment, the latter was very much favourite. Afraid of what I'd hear I decided to put off ringing Barber till later.

I was determined to go to Southwell even if, as seemed likely, I had to stand around all day doing nothing. To stay away would only fuel the rumours. I slung my gear in the car and accelerated viciously down the drive, kicking up stones and dirt from the loose surface.

Pulling out on to the long straight road I pushed the needle up to seventy within a short distance, then flashing headlights glinted in my rearview mirror. Five or six hundred yards behind me was a big white car, police maybe, and I dabbed the brakes to get back to the speed limit.

The car closed quickly and kept flashing. Close now, no police livery, no light on the roof, two men in the front seat. Suddenly, I didn't like it. I pressed the gas pedal smoothly to the floor and got up to ninety. They closed up effortlessly to within a few feet of my bumper, a big white Rover 820, lights flashing, horn honking, the bearded passenger, angry, signalling wildly that I should pull over.

No thanks, pal. I kept going, sweat prickling on my scalp. Who the hell were they? Why was my life so complicated? How come there was never anyone around when you needed witnesses?

At a hundred, steering wheel vibrating in my hands, they pulled out and moved alongside me. I glanced across. The bearded guy was holding something up to the glass. I checked the road and glanced again. It was a small open leather wallet showing what might have been a police badge. Then again it might have been a shiny plastic token from a box of cornflakes.

We were only a couple of miles from a village and if I could hold out that long at least there'd be someone around when I did stop. My two friends had other ideas and as they quickened past they crossed in front of me and steadily applied the brakes.

Ramming them was an option but not a very good one. It was unlikely to do enough damage to stop them and if it was the police I'd be even deeper in the shit. Braking suddenly, as hard as safety allowed, I skidded to a halt at the edge of the road.

The Rover stopped fifty yards in front, reversed thirty and stopped. Both men got out. So did I and I stood by the open door watching them come towards me. They wore shirts and ties and walked like cops and they also had that look about them of trying to remember whose turn it was to do the wisecracks. The honour fell to the clean-shaven one, the driver. Stopping by the front bumper he said, 'Mister Malloy, is it?'

'Who's asking?'

At arm's length he held out his little wallet. 'Detective Sergeant Kavanagh.' Tall, fair hair, blue eyes, the gauntness of his face highlighting the small scar on the ridge of his right cheekbone; white shirt, navy tie, dark trousers, black shoes . . . dressed like a cop. I stepped forward and looked at his credentials without taking the wallet from him. The name was right but for all I knew the card could have been turned out that morning on an Acme printing set.

'This is Detective Sergeant Miller who was rather having doubts about your name for a few minutes. We knew it began with M-a . . . and I was pretty sure it was Malloy but my colleague here swore it was Mansell.'

Very droll. At least it told me they were genuine cops who had read up on their motorist gags before leaving the station.

'I'm afraid,' I said, 'that when a big car with no markings comes buzzing up my arse at a hundred miles an hour it tends to make me a little nervous.'

Kavanagh smiled and said, 'Now with your background, Mister Malloy, I can understand that.'

'Good,' I said, ignoring the jibe. 'Now what can I do for you?'

'You can come and join us in the nice warm car out of this nasty wind. We just want a little chat.'

'I don't mind the chat but I'd just as soon have it out in this nasty wind if it's all the same to you.'

He smiled again. 'Fine.' Then turned to his mate. 'Eric, how'd you like to get my jacket from the car?' The dark, bearded one stalked off silently and came back with a corduroy jacket round his shoulders and a puffy, brightly-coloured casual jacket over his arm. Kavanagh pulled the jacket on; sky-blue with red and yellow diamonds, purple epaulettes and green toggles; I'd seen quieter jockeys' silks.

Fiddling with the zipper of his jacket Kavanagh smiled and said, 'Where were you last Friday evening?'

Chapter Seven

'Was that when Gilmour was killed?' I asked.

'Maybe you can tell me that,' Kavanagh said.

'I had dinner with some friends,' I said.

'Where?'

'Southport.'

'And after that?'

'Had a drink in the bar of the Castle Hotel and went to bed.'

'Alone?'

'That's right.'

'What time?'

'What time did I go to bed?'

He nodded.

'I don't know, somewhere between eleven-thirty and midnight.'

'What time did you have breakfast?'

'Eight o'clock.'

'So between midnight and eight you have no alibi?'

'Alibi for what?' As if I didn't know.

Kavanagh grinned apologetically. 'Sorry, poor choice of words. What I meant was nobody can account for your whereabouts between midnight Friday and 8 a.m. Saturday.'

'I told you, I was asleep.'

His smile dropped and his bony face suddenly looked cold and sinister. 'You told me you were asleep alone which means no one was with you which means you might be in very deep trouble.'

The serious look was supposed to make me nervous but he was bluffing. I shifted my weight, resting a foot on the sill of the open door. 'Listen, Mister Kavanagh,' I said, 'I'm going to Southwell races. I would very much like to get there in time for the first race. You've chased me along the road at a hundred miles an hour scaring the shit out of me in the process, you're firing questions at me like I was on Mastermind and now you're threatening that I might be in trouble. Haven't you forgotten something? You still haven't told me what the hell this is all about?'

Miller, the bearded one, spoke for the first time. 'Stop being a smartass, Malloy, you know fine what it's about. Maybe instead of going to the races you'd like to turn your car around and follow us back to the station, we can explain everything there.' The dark beard on his pale skin was thin and well tended, his hair was slicked with gel, though a long tendril had worked loose by his right temple and was swinging in the wind.

'You asking me or telling me?' I said.

Kavanagh spoke. 'We're asking you, Mister Malloy, asking you nicely.'

'Then you won't mind if I decline, just as nicely.'

They weren't pleased. 'Look,' I said, 'I know all the garbage that's being talked on the racecourse and I'm just as anxious as you guys to clear it up. I don't mind in the least giving you what you need. I'll sit and talk all night if you want but right now you've caught me at a bad time. If I don't turn up at Southwell today all the assholes who are already talking will say I've gone to ground. Contact the local CID, they've already taken a statement from me, then if you still want to speak to me I can meet you somewhere after racing.'

I deliberately didn't mention the note and diary in case they led to further questioning.

Kavanagh looked at Miller who kept looking at me. I pressed on. 'Look, put yourself in my place. What would you do? I've got to turn up at Southwell. Tell me where you guys are based and I'll come and see you after the races. I'll drive straight there.'

Miller wasn't happy but Kavanagh said, 'We're at the Griffin Hotel in Leicester.'

I nodded. 'I know it. I can be there around eight.'

Kavanagh's smile came back. 'We can have a nice cosy dinner.'

I half smiled, but didn't reply. Kavanagh headed back to the car. Miller glared at me. 'You'd better be there, Malloy.'

I smiled just to annoy him. 'Wouldn't miss it for the world.'

I got back in the car and Miller went to join his partner. As I pulled out to pass them Kavanagh stuck his head out of the window and motioned me to stop. I pressed the button and the passenger window slid down. Kavanagh was smiling big now and shouted, 'Any tips for today?'

My eyes said to him, cheeky bastard, and he laughed as I drove away.

Acting normal at the races was not going to be easy, especially as I now had no booked mounts. Hanging around scavenging for spare rides didn't appeal to me at the best of times. Now that people would be finger-pointing and bad-mouthing me behind my back I found the prospect even less endearing.

Standing by the door of the weighing room I watched the comings and goings of a sparse crowd. Small track, cold day, midweek meeting, moderate horses – they'd be lucky to get five hundred through the turnstiles. They were really only racing for the benefit of the off-course betting shops throughout the country who paid a levy to make it worthwhile for the racecourse. Those of us at the sharp end scratched around for slim pickings and dreamt of better days.

At the approach of anyone I recognised I subconsciously stiffened, waiting to see if I'd be acknowledged or ignored. Everyone I knew spoke or nodded though some held eye-contact a bit longer than normal as though hoping to discover something. Others grunted and avoided looking at me at all. The word was definitely out and some, undoubtedly, had their suspicions.

Feeling out of place in suit, shirt and tie I moped around the changing room as jockeys and valets busied themselves with colours and saddles and boots. From the general odour a keen nose could pick out deodorant, leather, saddle-soap, liniment, sweaty socks . . . All was hustle and bustle. Except me. I went outside again.

Just after the second race I watched Bobby Watt, a trainer I used to ride for, hurrying across the parade ring. 'Eddie!' he called as he approached. He looked anxious.

'Mister Watt,' I said. 'How are you?'

'In the shit. You don't ride in the fourth, do you?'

'No.'

His narrow flushed face below red thinning hair was tense, his eyes almost pleading. 'Will you ride mine?'

I didn't know what it was, it could have been a bad-legged, one-eyed dog with no brakes or steering but I wasn't turning it down. 'I'd be glad to.'

'Great, I'll be back in five minutes.' He scampered off towards the weighing room. A forty-five minute final deadline was enforced before each race for the declaration of jockeys; I reckoned Watt had about three minutes to declare me for his horse.

Pulling out my racecard I checked its name: White Hart, due to be partnered by Mr D. Campbell Cooper, the kid Layton had almost had in tears on Saturday. Young Cooper had been pushed into the game by his multi-millionaire father who was, I'd heard, a major pain in the arse. Daddy, apparently, was trying to buy success for the boy and had twenty horses in training. White Hart was one of them.

So why wasn't David riding it? I checked to see if he'd had a fall in either of the first two races; nothing, no booked mounts other than this one. Maybe he was sick.

Bobby Watt came back, moving at a more sedate pace. 'You make it okay?' I asked.

He nodded. 'Just. Clancy's got the colours.'

'Fine,' I said. Clancy was a valet. 'What's happened to young Cooper?' I asked.

Watt produced a cotton hankie from his trouser pocket, wiped his flushed sweaty brow and tucked the hankie away again. He raised his eyes to look at me. 'Campbell Cooper, if you *don't mind*. As his father would say.'

I smiled at his gruff mimicry. 'So where is the kid?' I asked.

Watt shrugged. 'Nobody knows. He hasn't turned up. His old man's going crazy.'

Immediate uncomfortable thoughts of Gilmour. I tried not to let it show. 'Has he done this before?'

'Not turned up for a ride? Never. Keen as mustard. Well, once he's on a horse he is, otherwise you wouldn't know he's alive, especially when his old man's around. Poor kid's scared to breathe in case he gets a bollocking.'

'Where is his father?'

Watt nodded towards the main stand. 'In the Owners' and Trainers' Bar. He's been ringing the kid's carphone for the past hour solid.'

I wondered if Cooper senior had heard the rumours yet. 'Does he know you've asked me to ride?'

'Does it make a difference?'

'Not to me it doesn't, but depending on what he's heard . . .'

'You mean that crap going round about you and Gilmour?'

I nodded. He smiled, showing small discoloured teeth. 'Load of bollocks and everyone knows it!'

'Everyone?'

'Anyone with any sense.'

'I wish I had your confidence but I can do without the publicity of taking another ride from a jockey who's disappeared.'

Watt patted my shoulder as we turned towards the weighing room. 'Don't worry about it, his car's probably broken down or he's dirtied his nappy or something.'

Half an hour later I had the misfortune of meeting the boy's father. I'd always considered the stories about him to be grossly exaggerated. I was wrong. Cooper had made millions in the hotel and property business and he believed that his money meant he could do and say as he pleased to anyone at any time. People said that he had no ambition to be liked and he delighted in being rude and aggressive.

The clouds had cleared and a watery sun hung over the parade ring where little groups of owners, trainers and jockeys stood chatting, corralled by their circling horses. Everyone was well dressed and reasonably sober.

Just to prove that no one dictated what Jack Cooper wore to the races he came striding across the lawn in jeans and an open-necked denim shirt. He moved fast in a straight line towards us, pinched, high-cheekboned face grim and determined looking. I glanced at Watt; he looked nervous and whispered, 'Shit, he's in a temper!'

Cooper stopped in front of us; early fifties maybe, light-brown hair suspiciously short of grey, dark eyes, my height but leaner, wiry. I was struck by his skin texture: very thin, almost parchment-like on his face, few obvious wrinkles but you knew that when he got round to smiling they'd appear suddenly like a concertina opening.

Watt said, 'Jack, this is Eddie Malloy.'

Smiling, I held out my hand. Cooper ignored it and

leaning at me like a Regimental Sergeant Major he said, 'Watt says you're a hotshot. You'd better be. You get one chance with me, that's all. I've had a very big bet here . . .' – he jabbed a finger at me – 'so *don't screw up*!'

Nice to meet you too.

Watt said, 'Eddie's good, Jack, he won't let us down.'

'I'll do my best,' I said through gritted teeth.

Cooper said, 'Do better than your best, Malloy. Win. I've got a lot of money on this horse. You cut slices off his hindquarters if you have to.'

I'd sooner cut slices off you, you bastard. I needed the breaks but not this bad. Calling his bluff I unbuckled my helmet and said, 'I'm a jockey, Mister Cooper, if it's a butcher you're looking for try the High Street.'

Bobby Watt, pulling nervously at his ear-lobe, intervened. 'Eddie, I'm sure Mister Cooper didn't mean –' He was interrupted by a thump on the shoulder which knocked him off-balance.

'Don't fucking apologise for *me*!' Cooper shouted. Among the little cliques around us a few heads turned in our direction. Watt straightened, trying to regain his composure. 'Sorry, Jack, I was only –'

'Shut it!' Cooper barked and turned his attention back to me. 'Are you saying you won't ride this horse?'

'I'm saying if you want me to ride I'll do my best but I won't knock him about if he's struggling.'

The loudspeaker sounded: 'Jockeys, please mount.' Each lad led his horse off the tarmac to halt on the lawn as jockeys moved towards them. White Hart waited about twenty yards away.

Cooper turned to Watt. 'You said this bastard was desperate. You said he'd do what he was told.'

I looked at Watt. He shrugged and half smiled apologetically. 'Well, he was wrong,' I said. 'Now do you want me to ride this horse or will I go and take these colours off.'

Cooper sneered. 'The Stewards would fine you for refusing to ride.'

'Not if I told them the reason.'

'You wouldn't dare!'

I didn't reply, just stared back at him, poker-faced. The skin around his eyes creased as he squinted at me, trying to weigh things up but he knew I had him. A substitute at this stage wouldn't be allowed. If I didn't ride, the horse didn't run and the Stewards would want to know why. Also, Cooper wouldn't have the chance to land his big bets.

The others were mounted and preparing to leave the parade ring. White Hart's lad was looking anxiously in our direction. Cooper said, 'You think you've got me by the balls, Malloy.'

I nodded. Watt was almost wetting himself, already picturing a horsebox pulling up in his yard to remove Cooper's horses.

'Get on the horse!' Cooper said bitterly.

Knowing it would be my last ride for him anyway I pushed my luck and said, 'What's the magic word?'

'What did you say?' Cooper hissed.

'What's the magic word to get people to do what you'd like them to do?'

Face reddening, eyes bulging, neck veins straining he slapped his fringe away from his forehead. 'Malloy! If –'

'Ah ah.' I smiled, determined now, nothing to lose. 'The magic word?'

'*Please!*' He spat and strode off, steam-driven, across the parade ring. Laughing quietly I walked towards the horse. Watt, pale now and sweating so much his hair was damp, followed me shaking his head and saying again and again, with different inflexions each time, '*Jesus Christ Almighty!*'

Although six to one with the bookies the horse was clearly the best in the race. Watt must have been cheating with him all season to get such a decent price. We were going easily throughout and could have won by ten lengths but I decided to give the bold Mister Cooper a few palpitations by holding my challenge till the last few strides before winning cheekily by a head.

Cooper met us in the winner's enclosure. You'd have thought his winning bets would have cooled his anger a little but he was still bubbling at high temperature. The sparse crowd's applause as I dismounted couldn't drown his words: 'Get weighed in and get those colours off, you'll never wear them again.'

Undoing the girths I glanced sideways and said quietly, 'Mister Cooper, my memory suffers when people don't talk nice to me. Sometimes makes me forget to do things like weigh in.'

Every rider has to report to the scales after each race and have the Clerk check that he's come back with the same weight he went out with. If I failed to do that it meant automatic disqualification, all bets lost.

Until I weighed in I still held the whip hand. Cooper had forgotten that. Instead of trying to be polite he reverted automatically to threats. 'Malloy, you don't weigh in I'll make sure you never ride in Britain again. I might even fix it so you never fucking walk again.'

Saddle across my arm I sidled up to him. The crowd probably thought we were exchanging pleasantries. 'Listen, Cooper, I'd have thought a smart man like you would have twigged by now that I don't like being threatened. It doesn't scare me . . . just rubs me up the wrong way, winds me up. Now you might think that 'cause you've got tuppence less than Sheikh Mohammed it buys you the right to abuse everyone you meet but it doesn't cut any ice with me. I need the rides and I need them badly but if all the owners in racing slithered out of the same hole as you I'd go and shovel shit for a living.' Leaning close to his face, I said, '*Comprende?*' I didn't wait for a reply.

Not weighing in would have sorted Cooper out nicely but it would also have deprived me, and hundreds of honest punters, of a much needed winner, so I did my duty.

I hung around till the last race looking for more rides but interested too in whether or not Cooper's son would turn up safe and well. By the time I left he hadn't and I consoled myself with the thought that if, like Gilmour, he was found murdered at least they couldn't accuse me of trying to curry favour with his father.

Reviewing the day as I drove home I should have been depressed. Still no word of Gilmour's killers, the rumours about me were obviously gathering pace and to top it all I'd lost another good source of rides in Jack Cooper.

But I felt fine. My run-in with Cooper had given me back a lot of self-respect, something I'd been pretty short on during the past five years. So I'd lost a few rides, what the hell? I felt as good about myself as I had in a long time and I'd forgotten how much that meant to me. And I'd ridden a cheeky winner, boosting my already growing confidence.

On the way to Leicester to meet Starsky and Hutch I stopped off home to dump my gear. The phone was ringing as I went in and I scooped it from its cradle. Hubert Barber was calling with bad news.

Chapter Eight

Barber said, 'Eddie, something's come up, we need to talk.'

His tone was serious so I didn't need three guesses. 'Sure, Mister Barber, I'm free just now.'

'Not on the phone. You're at Stratford tomorrow, aren't you?'

I took a deep breath. 'If you still want me to ride those three horses, I am.'

'Can you meet me in the car park around half eleven? You know my car, a blue Range Rover.'

Rides neither confirmed nor denied.

'Mister Barber, can I ask if this is about . . .'

'I'd sooner we discuss it tomorrow, Eddie.'

Fine. One more try. 'Is it worth bringing my riding gear?'

'Bring it. See you tomorrow.'

I hung up. At least I wasn't jocked off. Yet.

On the drive to Leicester to meet the two cops I forced myself to accept that my three rides next day would probably be my last for Barber. He wasn't the type to sack me because of a few rumours. Either he'd heard something else or his owners had said they didn't want me. I decided it was time I took things more seriously.

The Stockwell lounge in the Griffin Hotel was big, high-ceilinged, softly lit, had inch-deep carpet pile and red velvet curtains the height of yacht sails. Spotlights shone on a four-tier display of fancy liqueur bottles behind the long, polished wooden bar. The place was about a third full, maybe thirty people. Their conversations hummed just above the tone of the music.

Miller and Kavanagh sat in the corner where the crimson curtains provided a quiet backdrop to Kavanagh's sweater of multi-coloured squares. The guy certainly liked to be noticed. When he saw me approach he smiled in a way that said here comes this evening's amusement.

I nodded and sat down. Kavanagh kept smiling. Miller glowered. No fancy duds for him; dark blue cotton shirt and black slacks.

'You made it,' Kavanagh said.

'Told you. I'm anxious to co-operate.'

His blond head nodded slowly, easing the smile a few watts. 'Sure,' he said. 'Have you eaten?'

'I grabbed a sandwich when I dropped my gear off. I'm okay.'

'Good.'

Kavanagh bought a round of drinks then they both got to work on me. Skirting around at first, messing about, trying to make me believe they had proof I was involved. After half an hour they saw I wasn't biting and got on with the direct questions, all of which I answered as honestly as I could. Four drinks down the line it was obvious they had nothing to go on though they weren't happy about admitting it.

I said, 'Can I ask a few questions?'

'Ask away,' Kavanagh said.

'Have you spoken to the local CID?'

Kavanagh nodded. 'They told us about the note you said you'd got.'

'What do you mean, I *said* I'd got? It was pushed through my door early on Sunday morning.'

Miller said, 'Who pushed it, you?'

'Come on! Have you guys seen the note? If I was cooking up a story I think I'd have come up with something a bit more credible than that.'

Kavanagh smiled. 'Seems pretty credible to me.'

I said, '*You* think it's genuine then? You think the killer wrote it?'

'I'd say it's odds-on the killer wrote it,' Kavanagh said.

I turned to Miller and said, 'So?'

Kavanagh said, 'Doesn't mean to say you're not the killer, Malloy.'

'Oh, come on! What about the diary?' I said.

'What about it?' Kavanagh asked. 'Who'd be most likely to have a murdered man's diary . . . the murderer?'

'Exactly!'

'So who had it, Malloy? You did.'

I looked at him. He was still smiling. I shook my head. 'I'm pissing in the wind with you two, aren't I? It's a complete waste of time.'

Miller said, 'It's you that's wasting our time, Malloy.'

Trying to contain my anger, I said, 'No. You bastards are wasting my time and your own. Gimme your boss's name, maybe he'll give me sensible answers to my questions.'

Unfazed, Kavanagh said, 'What questions?'

'Questions like, Was a note found on Gilmour?'

'If it was it doesn't really help *you* out, does it?'

'Did you find a note on Gilmour? In his car? In his hotel room?'

Kavanagh said, 'What do you think, Eddie? Would you bet on it? What d'you reckon the odds would be?'

'I'd reckon it was long odds on. If the same guy that wrote my note murdered Gilmour then I'd say there'd be every chance he'd have left one. Somebody that thinks that way, well . . . well it's just what I think he'd do.'

Miller said, 'He didn't.'

I turned to Kavanagh for confirmation. He nodded and said, 'That's right.'

I said, 'He didn't leave one or you guys didn't find one?'

Miller gave me one of his cold looks. 'He didn't leave one.'

I stood up and put my jacket on. 'I don't believe that. I don't think your people looked hard enough.'

Miller glared up at me. 'Malloy . . . we don't give a fuck what you think.'

I said, 'Well that's been pretty obvious since I sat down. Now, if you don't mind, I'll say goodnight.' I edged my way around the table, saying, 'I'll ring your boss tomorrow, see if I can get any sense out of him.'

Miller raised his legs, resting them on Kavanagh's seat, blocking my way. I looked down at him, his chin resting on his knuckles, gold pinkie ring gleaming in his dark beard. His eyes swivelled upwards as he bit at the loose flesh between thumb and forefinger; the guy thought he was Vincent Price. He said, 'Be sure and tell him how kind and considerate we were to you.' I stepped over his legs and went home.

Though it was eleven-thirty when I got in I was anxious to find out if young Campbell Cooper had surfaced. I rang Bobby Watt, the trainer, who, after moaning about the way I'd talked to Jack Cooper earlier, told me that the kid arrived home around eight. He'd got lost walking along some country roads after his car broke down. No sense of direction, Watt said. I was beginning to know the feeling.

I'd just pulled the cold bed-sheets over me and was reaching to turn out the lamp when the phone rang. Ten past midnight. I hurried downstairs. It was McCarthy. No apology for the late call. 'You saw Kavanagh and Miller tonight.' A statement.

'That's right,' I said.

'You talked about the note and the diary,' Mac said.

'Mac, did you get me out of bed to tell me what I did tonight?'

'I've just been speaking to their boss.'

'Kavanagh's and Miller's?'

'He rang me. They should have told you not to mention the note to anyone.'

'Well, they didn't.'

'I know. They've had a bollocking. But Inspector Sanders wants to make sure you don't discuss the note with anyone till we know a bit more about it.'

'Tell Inspector Sanders that doesn't quite fit in with my plans. I'm meeting Hubert Barber in the morning and unless I can convince him I had nothing to do with Gilmour's murder then I ain't going to be riding for him any more. I need to tell Barber about the note.'

'Eddie, this could mean the difference between catching the guy or not.'

'Too bad.'

'Come on, Eddie . . .'

I stayed silent.

Serious now, Mac said, 'Eddie, the note's *sub judice*. If you discuss it or comment on it in any way you're breaking the law.'

'Mac, gimme a break with all the official crap.'

'Sorry, Eddie. Sanders said to ask you nicely then to tell you your feet won't touch the ground.'

'If I can't talk about this note, the ground's the only thing my feet *will* be touching. They certainly won't be in a pair of stirrups!'

'Eddie . . .'

I hung up. Bastards. They had me all ways.

I lay awake for a while, the anger still bubbling. I wished Jackie were here . . . Selfish, I just wanted someone to moan to. I tried to rationalise. Maybe telling Barber about the note wouldn't serve much purpose; I didn't even have a copy to show. He'd probably think I was making the story up in desperation. And, if Inspector Sanders was taking the note that seriously it had to be a good sign for me. Why the big hoo-ha about the note anyway? I'd have thought the diary was more important.

It was dull and drizzly as I pulled up next to Barber's Range Rover in the members' car park at Stratford. Through the rain-covered windshield Barber's head with his icing-white hair was like a melting pudding though when I got in his features looked stern.

'You've got your lights on,' I said.

'Thanks.' He flicked a switch. 'Good trip?' he asked.

'Seen worse.'

He turned face-on, looking solemn. 'Have you heard these rumours about Tommy?'

'I've heard I'm supposed to have had him killed.'

He stared at me for a long time. Maybe he was waiting for me to glance away or look nervous. I held his gaze. He obviously wanted to trust me. The prospect of having to interrogate me didn't sit well with him. I tried to make it easier.

'Hubert, listen, you don't owe me anything. You're as entitled as anyone else to be suspicious. Ask whatever you want, I won't take offence.'

He sighed, hung his head and ran his fingers through his hair till it stood up like Tintin's. 'I don't want to ask you questions. I don't feel I have to. I've always considered myself a fair judge of a man and I think this whole bloody thing is a piece of nonsense.'

'But?'

He looked at me. 'Some of my owners are getting a bit windy.'

'They don't want me on their horses.'

Looking uncomfortable and apologetic, he said, 'It's one chap in particular, been ringing the others up, getting them at it.'

'Who?'

'Jack Delaney. I don't think he has anything against you personally, he's just a bit of an old woman, listens to too much gossip. He keeps saying he's got inside information on you from the Stewards' room.'

'Like what?'

Barber shrugged. 'I don't know. Delaney just keeps saying, trust me. He's pretty close to one of the Stewards' Secretaries, Claude Beckman.'

It was Beckman who'd given me a tough time in the Inquiry after the Greenalls. Beckman who'd withheld the race video. 'What's Beckman saying about me?'

'I don't even know if it is Beckman, Delaney won't say.'

'Maybe I should talk to Delaney.'

'No. Leave it just now. I've persuaded them to hold off for a week to see if the police come up with anything on Tommy.'

'So I'm still riding for you?'

He nodded.

'Till when, this time next week?'

'Next Thursday morning.'

'And if my name's cleared before then?'

He smiled. 'You'll be riding for me for as long as you keep riding winners.'

I looked at the big open face, knowing how hard he'd probably had to fight to keep me riding. Offering my hand, I said, 'Thanks, Mister Barber.'

He shook it. 'I'm only sorry it's worked out like this, Eddie.'

'Forget it. I'm sure something'll turn up in a week.'

'Hope so.'

Opening the door I stepped to the ground. 'See you later, Mister Barber.'

'Eddie . . .'

I looked at him.

'. . . we've decided to run Great Divide in the Gold

Cup . . . If the police find Tommy's killer by then, you ride.'

I smiled, nodded, didn't know what to say. Pushing the door closed I raised a hand in acknowledgement and saw Barber's smile widen.

The rain had weight behind it now and I sat in my car listening to its rhythm on the roof and thinking about a week today. The Cheltenham Gold Cup was the biggest steeplechase of the year and Great Divide had a real chance of winning . . . Jesus, that would put me right back in the big time. I decided it was time the police had a little assistance.

Barber's three horses gave me a winner and a second. My last ride, in the fourth, was unplaced. There was little chance of picking up a ride in the last two so I changed and rang McCarthy.

His haughty secretary told me, 'Mister McCarthy's in France.'

I left a message. He rang me just before nine that evening.

'Why didn't you tell me last night you were going to France?'

'I would have if you hadn't hung up on me.'

'Yeah, sorry about that, I was mad.'

'I guessed. You didn't mention the note to Barber?'

'Didn't mention it to anyone.'

'Good. I'm sure it's the best way forward.'

'Mac, are you still interested in having my help on this?'

'Of course! Have you decided to come in?'

'Nothing else for it. Until this guy's caught it doesn't look like I'm going to have much to do anyway.'

We arranged to meet at Sandown next day. I spent half the evening going through cuttings in the offices of the *Gloucester Crier*. I knew their racing reporter, Guy Webster, quite well and he'd been happy to help. Gilmour, an Irishman, had lived in Gloucester since getting married seven years previously. A local hero, there were numerous articles on him, most written by Webster and most churning out the same adulatory stuff. I found nothing to suggest why anyone should want to kill him.

Webster had gone to the pub and left me to it, though I had strict instructions to return the cuttings to Benny in the Library. Benny, well past pension age to my eye, was small, thin, bald and doleful looking. He took the folder from me. 'Find what you wanted?'

''Fraid not.'

He moved away between the racks and slid the folder back onto its shelf. I called after him, 'Tell Guy Webster I said thanks, will you?'

He nodded, turning. 'Was it Webster's stuff you were going through?' he asked.

'Yeah, some articles on Tommy Gilmour.'

'The bloke that got murdered?'

'That's right. Did you know him?'

Benny stuck his hands in the pockets of his brown cardigan. 'I didn't myself but Webster knew him well. Gilmour was the reason he got his job here.'

'How come?'

'The previous bloke wrote a story on Gilmour and it got spiked. He took the hump and walked out.'

'Spiked?'

'Binned. They didn't print it.'

'Why not?'

He shrugged. 'Dunno.'

'What was the reporter's name?'

He frowned and looked at the ceiling. 'Can't remember. Funny name it was . . . but I can't remember. Scotch guy, hadn't been here long. Fancied himself as a bit of an investigative journalist, know what I mean? Watched too many TV programmes.'

'But he wrote about racing?'

Benny nodded then settled down at a small bare table,

opened a yellow tobacco tin and started rolling a cigarette. 'He'd only done a couple of pieces when he left.'

'Why did he get so upset about one story not being printed?'

He shook his head, frowning as he concentrated on an even spread of tobacco. 'Don't know. All hush-hush.'

'You must have heard a whisper of what the story was about.'

The tip of his tongue came out and he drew the thin paper along, sealing it, put the cigarette in his mouth and stood up patting at his pockets. 'What did I do with those matches?'

I waited. He found them and lit up, then said, 'I think it was something to do with the IRA.'

Chapter Nine

The name of the guy who resigned over the Gilmour article was Johnny Angell. Webster, the reporter who took over from him, remembered it because it was unusual. Webster was sure he'd gone back to Glasgow to work for a Scottish paper and, no, Webster wasn't aware of the contents of the 'IRA article' so he couldn't help me. I didn't believe him but I didn't press it.

After a few phone calls I tracked Angell down on a Glasgow number, or at least his answering machine. I left my name and mentioned Tommy Gilmour's.

My one ride at Sandown finished unplaced and I didn't hang around the weighing room long afterwards. It had been a while since I'd ridden this far south but the rumours would have reached here all right and I didn't know how I'd be treated. The southern jockeys tended to venture north only when there was a big meeting and I hadn't seen many of them for a few weeks.

Most spoke to me though none mentioned Gilmour. A couple of times when I saw two or three of them close together in the changing room I imagined they were whispering about me but paranoia is one of my failings. It would have helped to be able to talk to them about it, maybe someone could have told me something significant. But until the rumours died down any questions from me were bound to be viewed with suspicion.

I was hoping McCarthy would have something for me

to work on but he didn't. We sat in a little office-cum-store-room which was uncomfortably warm and smelled like it hadn't been aired for years. McCarthy, sweating, tried to open a small window but it was jammed with dried paint. He took off his jacket, loosened his tie and sat down, his belly straining at the buttons on his white shirt.

'Thought you had clout,' I said. 'Couldn't you get a better place than this?'

'It's not mine. We don't have an office on-course you know, we've got to take whatever's free.'

'Only winding you up, Mac.'

He didn't smile.

'So the police have got virtually nothing to go on?' I asked.

'Not a jot. Most murders are domestic, committed by someone known to the victim. If they can't pin it down within that framework it gets pretty tough for them.'

'Hence the reason they've been hassling me.'

'I wouldn't take it personally.'

'You would if you were the one getting hassled.'

'Don't get paranoid, Eddie.'

'You know the saying, Mac, just because I'm paranoid doesn't mean somebody isn't following me.'

Eyes to the ceiling he grimaced then said, 'We've got to work out where we go from here.'

I hadn't told him about Gilmour and the supposed IRA story. I wanted to speak to Angell before the police did to save any more of the *sub judice* crap. I said, 'I think you should ask Inspector Sanders to run his fine tooth-comb over Gilmour's belongings again. His car, his clothes and bags, his hotel room . . .'

'What for? It's all been done.'

'Because until such times as it is proved otherwise I'm assuming the note I got came from Gilmour's murderer. And, as I said to the cops, a guy who writes cryptic notes for one quite probably does for all, it's part of his modus operandi.'

'I don't disagree with you, Eddie, but they've looked and can't find.'

'Tell them to look again.'

'I'll try.'

'Wasn't there anything else?' I asked. 'I mean, do they know the exact gun model? Was he only shot once? Had he tried to fight back?'

McCarthy, sweating freely now, said, 'They found ether in his lungs. His right leg had been broken at the knee.'

'*Had* been broken or was broken in the struggle?'

'Broken deliberately, they think, by a heavy blunt instrument, just a few minutes before he died.'

Frowning, I looked at Mac. 'What the hell would the guy want to do that for?'

Mac shrugged. 'Who knows? Maybe Gilmour was fighting back?'

'So why didn't the guy just shoot him?'

'Dunno.'

'I mean, if he wanted to make Gilmour suffer for some reason why not break his leg a couple of hours before shooting him?'

'Eddie, I don't know. I wish I did know.'

'What about the ether, can't the forensic boys trace the source?'

'Ether's ether. Tell me a brand name that you know.' Mac ran his shirt-sleeve across his hot wet brow. 'God, I'll need to get out of here.'

'Lose some weight,' I said; 'you wouldn't sweat so much.'

'Give me a break, you're as bad as Jean.'

'Did I ever tell you that story about the country hick who became an American football star?'

'The one where he says, Gee, you sure don't sweat much for a fat broad?'

'I told you it.'

'More than once.'

'It's a true story, you know.'

'Apocryphal, Eddie, apocryphal.'

'Bless you.'

'Very funny. Are you ready?'

'As I'll ever be.'

I smiled. Mac got up and reached for his jacket. He said, 'You're pretty jaunty for somebody who's sure he's holding a threatening note from a murderer.'

'I'm hoping to get him before he gets me.'

'Well you'd better hope he doesn't have that Beretta stuck in his waistband.'

'I'll be careful.'

We went out into the cold March wind and Mac sighed and told me that was better. Together we walked to the car park.

I said, 'Have you seen Mrs Gilmour yet?'

'I'm seeing her on Tuesday.'

'Have the police spoken to her?'

'Of course.'

'Bet they didn't ask if Tommy got a strange note in the post during the past few weeks.'

Mac, flush-faced, looked at me. 'I'll find out.'

On moonless nights the darkness was so complete around the lodge I needed a torch to walk the few steps from the car to the front door. Without one I'd have felt my way forward, arms outstretched. It gave me a lot of sympathy for the blind.

I got in and switched off the torch, leaving it by the door so I'd remember to take it with me tomorrow. As I clicked the light-switch in the sitting room the bulb flashed and popped. Blackness. The light on the answerphone, winking frantically, had the room to itself. I got the torch again and found another bulb in the kitchen.

I made coffee and a sandwich and pressed the play button on the answerphone. Johnny Angell's gruff Scottish voice told me I'd probably get him if I rang in the morning before ten-thirty.

Next morning, at nine twenty-five, after his phone rang a dozen times, I spoke to the man himself.

He complained good-naturedly about me getting him out of bed on a Saturday morning. I apologised and told him I was a friend of Gilmour trying to help find his killer. I didn't mention the note or the racecourse rumours. Angell remembered the article and the editor who'd spiked it and him he cursed roundly though without malice.

He told me the piece was based on the fact that Gilmour, at one time, was held for twenty-four hours by the police at Fishguard under the Prevention of Terrorism Act. No charges were ever brought and though Angell dug deep into Gilmour's background the best he could come up with was that Gilmour's cousin, a suspected IRA member, had spent two years in Long Kesh internment camp.

I asked him if he thought there could be any terrorist connection in Gilmour's murder.

'Doubt it,' he said. 'But anythin's possible these days.' His reporter's nose sniffed around for a while as to why I was so interested. I told him I was simply a friend of Tommy's trying to make sense of it all. I'm not sure he believed me.

Where to next? The kitchen for more coffee was the best I could come up with.

Cradling the hot mug I sat, knees up, in the bay window. It was a fine, bright morning. I noticed for the first time the new buds on the line of trees that stretched away from the dry-stone wall across the road. Spring. Already. Three days till the start of the biggest jumps meeting of the year, the Cheltenham Festival. Five days till the Gold Cup. Five days for Gilmour's killer to turn up or I wouldn't be riding in the race.

I wondered what he was doing right now, the killer. Writing his little notes? Oiling his gun? Choosing his next target?

I sipped coffee. Where next, Eddie?

There had to be another note. Had Mac persuaded the police to look again? Where were Gilmour's things, his clothes and stuff? Maybe they'd been returned to his wife. Would she let me search through them? What about the hotel room, maybe I could get in there for a look around? Maybe if McCarthy introduced me to this police inspector it would help.

I rang him. He said it couldn't do any harm and that he'd arrange a meeting. Soon, I told him, then asked for Mrs Gilmour's telephone number.

Then I remembered Lisa Ffrench. She was a good friend of the Gilmours. It would be easier if she could arrange the meeting with Susan Gilmour. I rang and caught Lisa just before she left for Chepstow races. I told her what I wanted and asked her to phone Mrs Gilmour.

'No need. She'll be happy to see you. Come this evening.'

'Are you sure? I mean, is she up to answering questions?'

'Susan will do what she has to to help find Tommy's killer.'

Lisa it seemed was happy to be confident on behalf of others.

'Maybe,' I said, 'but I would feel more comfortable if you speak to her first, ask *her* if she wants to see me.'

'Okay, okay! I'll ring her from Chepstow. If there's a problem with it I'll contact you at Doncaster. Otherwise, I'll see you when you get there this evening. You know where Susan lives?'

'No.'

'Got a pen?'

*   *   *

At Doncaster I rode a winner and a third, got kicked in the butt by a horse, causing much hilarity in the crowd around the winner's enclosure, was snubbed by a couple of owners I knew and slagged off by Layton in the changing room. Just after four o'clock, nursing a badly bruised buttock, I limped out of the course and pointed my car in the direction of Burford in Gloucestershire.

The Gilmours' house sat in a garden of about an acre, the front lit by two ground-mounted floodlights on the lawn. A lattice of iron framed the door giving the climbing roses a thornhold. I rang the bell and moved around nervily.

I was no good at small-talk at the best of times and felt awkward at the prospect of meeting this woman, still grieving badly no doubt.

God, she was entitled to grieve. Tommy had only been dead a week. I hoped the doctor had given her something . . . I hoped the children wouldn't be there.

Behind the door, heels clicked, coming closer. I took a step back and stuck my hands in my pockets then took them out again. The door opened and the lawn lights behind me glowed on Lisa's face.

It was the first time I'd seen her wearing make-up. It made a difference, took away the boyish look. I'd only ever seen her wear business suits and white buttoned-up blouses. Tonight she had on a thick pale-blue V-neck sweater embroidered with flowers above a long floral skirt. She smiled. 'Hallo, Eddie.'

'Lisa . . . hallo! Everything okay?'

She nodded. 'Come in, Susan's expecting you.'

Catching a slip of her perfume as she turned, I followed her down the hall. Along the darkest part her figure, skirt swinging, was silhouetted against the rectangle of yellow light from an open door at the bottom. Turning her head she said, 'You found your way all right?'

'Eventually. I'm not the greatest navigator in the world so I usually leave plenty of time.'

'Very wise.'

We went through the open door into a kitchen painted deep yellow. 'Susan,' Lisa said, 'this is Eddie Malloy.' She got up from her chair at the big pine table; blue eyes, sharp nose and chin but attractive with her blonde hair gathered in a neat bun arranged between small pearl ear-rings. A gold chain hung on the line of her collarbone over a fine polo-neck of black angora which was tucked into fawn trousers. Mid-to-late-twenties, slim and small. She leaned across the table offering her hand. Stepping forward, I took it. She smiled and sat down.

I felt uncomfortable, inexperienced in the social niceties, if that's the right word, of bereavement. Just then I didn't want to be a twenty-eight-year-old jockey, I wanted to be a seasoned fifty-year-old who could offer words of comfort and understanding.

I said, 'I do hope this isn't inconvenient for you. Lisa said it would be okay.'

She looked up at Lisa and smiled. 'Of course,' she said, 'I'm fine.'

Lisa reached forward and squeezed her friend's shoulders affectionately.

'Would you like a drink?' Lisa asked me.

'Coffee, please, just black.'

'Susan?' Lisa asked.

'A cup of tea would be lovely,' Susan said.

Lisa filled the kettle. Susan, trying a brave, tired smile, looked at me, her sad blue eyes red from crying. This was not going to be easy.

'I was terribly sorry to hear about Tommy,' I said. She nodded, still trying to smile. I went on, 'We all were. I've never seen the weighing room so quiet . . . so shocked. I wasn't particularly close to Tommy, but I rode against him a few times and he was one of the best jockeys I've seen . . . He was a good sportsman too, a gentleman.'

She nodded, looking down at the table-top. 'Thank you,' she said quietly.

'How are the children?' I asked, not knowing how much to dwell on it but not wanting to appear embarrassed by avoiding the subject.

She clasped her hands and said, 'As well as can be expected, I suppose.' She smiled and I thought she was going to leave it at that, a polite response to a polite inquiry. But then she said, 'Sally's been very subdued, almost withdrawn, until yesterday, when she clung to me all day, wouldn't let me out of her sight.'

'Sally's the oldest?' I asked.

She nodded. 'Four.'

Lisa, pouring hot water, said, 'Susan, Sally's reactions are quite natural, you mustn't worry.'

Susan, almost tearful now, looked across at her and said, 'She came to my room at two o'clock this morning to see . . . to check' – she paused, biting her lip – 'that I wasn't dead.'

Lisa came over, sat down and took Susan's hand. She spoke softly, soothingly, 'That's perfectly natural, Susan. She feels insecure, doesn't understand how Daddy can be there one day and gone the next. She's checking on you to reassure herself and it shows she's behaving naturally. You'll probably find she'll carry on that way for some time.'

Susan, tears beginning to spill now, gripped Lisa's arm and said, 'But it's so hard being strong for the children when I feel so fragile.'

Lisa resisted giving further practical advice and reached out to stroke her friend's hair. What was left of Susan's reserve disintegrated and came out of her in a long involuntary moan as she slumped forward, head in hands, and started sobbing in that breathless broken way that told me she was powerless to stop.

Lisa helped her to her feet. I got up and said, 'Is there

anything I can do?' Lisa, cradling her friend's head on her shoulder, moving her slowly towards the door, looked at me and said, 'We'll manage. If you wouldn't mind excusing us for a few minutes.'

'Of course,' I said.

'Help yourself to coffee. I'll be back soon.' She smiled, cool and coping, practical but sympathetic. I was getting to like her. I heard them go upstairs, Susan's sobs muffled in her friend's shoulder then fading to a whisper as a door closed behind them.

I felt a mixture of frustration that I hadn't had a chance to ask Susan any questions and a slightly guilty relief that Lisa had been here to take her away when she broke down.

Standing drinking coffee I looked around the kitchen: a few narrow exposed beams, wicker baskets of different sizes hanging from the walls, four pot plants standing on the deep window-sill, two pictures of country scenes, baskets of fruit and vegetables, a terracotta pitcher, an apron hanging by the sink . . .

I heard a child's cry from upstairs, 'Muuummy!' A door opened and closed and I heard Lisa say, 'Sshhh, darling . . .' The rest of her words were too faint to make out. I sat down again at the pine table, the surface scarred and notched by years of family use . . . family . . . Not much of a family now with Tommy gone. I felt more sad at that moment than when I'd heard of his death. Sad and guilty, finally, that I was the only one who had benefited from it.

And I was here tonight for my own ends, not for Tommy or Susan or their children, just for me . . . to protect my shitty little career, to get myself back in the limelight, to be a big shot again . . . Jesus Christ, I hated myself. Right at that minute I considered myself a lower form of life than the guy who'd killed Tommy.

I hadn't heard Lisa come back. She was looking down

at me. 'Are you all right?' she asked. I looked at her. A lie would have been best but would have made me feel even worse later, so I said, 'I feel bad about coming here. Lousy. I shouldn't have done it.'

'Don't be too hard on yourself, Susan's emotions are rubbed raw at the moment, she can break down for any reason.' She went to the sink. 'More coffee?' she asked.

'No, thanks.'

She poured herself one and came back to sit across from me. 'You wanted to ask Susan some questions about Tommy,' she said.

I nodded. 'But I'm not so sure it's such a good idea any more.'

'Why not?'

'Because it was for my benefit, not hers.'

'How come?'

She seemed genuinely curious, elbows on the table, leaning towards me, brown eyes concentrating. But I was reluctant to go on. There wasn't a short way of telling it. 'I'll tell you some day when you've got a few hours to spare and less on your mind.'

She said, 'I'm not going anywhere. Susan's sleeping, I gave her a sedative, and the children are watching television upstairs.' Without taking her eyes off mine she raised her cup and sipped, looking at me with an intensity I found almost disconcerting. I said, 'There are some rumours going round the racecourse –'

She interrupted. 'About you and Tommy . . . I've heard them.'

That caught me. 'Did you tell Susan?'

'No.'

'Why not?'

She shrugged, opening her hands. 'Because they're probably a load of nonsense.'

'*Probably?*'

She shrugged again, smiling. 'Well *I* would bet on it.'

'Very kind of you,' I said, half sarcastically.

'Don't mention it.'

I pressed on. 'Look, the real reason I came here tonight . . .' That intensity was back in her eyes, totally attentive, equally seductive, very off-putting.

'I'm listening,' she said.

'To save my own skin, my career. To help kill these rumours about me and Tommy 'cause if I don't nobody's going to give me any rides.'

No reaction.

I went on. 'I came here because after another taste of the big time at Haydock last Saturday I remembered how much it meant to me. I'm not giving it up. It's my last chance and whatever it takes to make it this time I'm going to do it no matter the cost to anyone else. Now, sure, I'm sorry for Tommy and for Susan and the kids but I came here tonight to solve my problems not theirs.'

She looked at me for a while then said, 'It's your life, you've got to make the best of it.'

'Mmm. Maybe.' I sipped the dregs of cold coffee to shut myself up. I felt like saying a lot more but Lisa had troubles enough with the family upstairs without being Mother Confessor to a jockey on a guilt trip.

I changed the subject so we could talk about her for a change. She'd known Susan since schooldays and obviously cared very much for her. She was Sally's godmother and had holidayed with the Gilmours a few times. After eighteen months in America working as PA to a magazine editor in Atlanta her work permit expired and she'd come back to Britain.

'To the boring old Jockey Club,' I said.

She smiled. 'It's all experience.'

'You don't plan to make a career of it then?'

'No way.'

More through politeness than a wish to probe she asked me about my life outside racing. I told her bits and pieces but left out some of my experiences over the last five years like the eighteen months I'd spent in jail and the three years living rough in a caravan breaking rogue horses for a dealer with the scruples of a timeshare salesman.

She was relaxed and confident, easy to get along with and could be immensely attractive when she looked at you as if you were the only thing that mattered in the world. With Jackie still on my mind the last thing I needed was to tumble into another relationship, though I may have been flattering myself.

We chatted on aimlessly but comfortably till I'd finished another coffee and I decided it was time to go.

Lisa said she'd ask Susan for the answers I needed and promised to keep her ears open on the racecourse. She walked me to the door.

The grass sparkled wet below the lawn lights which cast a cosy glow on the house with its climbing roses. You'd have thought there was no nicer place to be on a cold rainy March night if you didn't know about the sadness inside.

'Lisa,' I said, 'I know everyone says this but tell Susan that if there's anything I can do to help she must get in touch.'

She looked at me for a few seconds then said, 'Thought you were only in this for your own good?'

I shrugged. 'Thought I was.'

She smiled and said, 'The best thing you can do for Susan is find the bastard that killed her husband.'

I nodded. 'Ring me,' I said.

'I will.'

I was hoping she'd go inside but she watched from the step and noticed the limp I'd managed to disguise all evening. She called after me, 'You're limping, what happened?'

I turned and, walking backwards, I said, 'Got kicked in the buttock by an ungrateful horse.'

She stood in the light of the doorway, sleeves up, arms folded, skirt billowing in the draught. Smiling, she said, 'Never seen a bruise in the shape of a horse-shoe.'

Resisting the come-on and still moving away I said, 'It looks sort of like an upside down heart.'

'A broken one?' she offered.

'That's right,' I said, out of her sight now in the darkness, 'only it heals quicker.'

Chapter Ten

Detective Inspector Sanders had agreed to meet McCarthy and me on the Sunday if we didn't mind driving up north. He was just about the handsomest man I'd ever seen: six feet two, maybe fifty, but athletic looking with short iron-grey hair and matching moustache, perfect eyebrows, square jaw, highish cheekbones and eyelids that always looked one-third closed over his brown eyes. I'd bet he'd had some women trouble in his time.

He led us into his office which was immaculately clean and tidy and smelled of polish. A vase of mixed carnations sat on a full bookcase, and above his big desk hung a picture of Sanders shaking hands with the Prime Minister. Sanders took my coat and hung it on a wooden stand in the corner. He wheeled two big comfortable seats up to his desk for us then a young policeman brought a silver tray with tea on it.

Sanders, smiling, thanked the kid then, anxious to promote his 'I may be a bigshot who looks like a movie-star but I'm really just one of the boys' image, he poured tea for us, insisting that he did the milk and sugar too.

After the usual niceties regarding the trip and how busy the M6 was these days he chatted with Mac about his boss at The Jockey Club. I don't know if McCarthy picked it up but Sanders struck me as being pretty interested when Mac mentioned his boss was retiring soon.

McCarthy explained about me and how I was involved

and Sanders, finger and thumb stroking his moustache in opposite directions, smiled and nodded, sharing his attention between Mac and me as he listened.

Sanders said to me, 'I believe you've met two of my men, Kavanagh and Miller.'

'I've had the pleasure twice,' I said.

'Good policemen,' he said.

'*I* was impressed,' I said.

He nodded, missing the sarcasm. 'And you're giving The Jockey Club some help on this one from their side?'

Which meant be a good boy and stay out from under our feet. Mac and I glanced at each other and I said to Sanders, 'I've got a vested interest as you probably know but we were sort of hoping that the police and The Jockey Club could work together.'

He straightened and tilted his head back slightly and said, 'Of course. We'd be glad to have any input from you.'

Mac, to his credit, stepped in. 'Absolutely, Inspector, but we would be looking for reciprocation. Two heads, after all, are better than one, even if they're sheeps' heads, that's what I always say.'

Sanders just stopped himself from frowning. I don't think he cared for the farmyard comparison. Just as well McCarthy hadn't made it pigs. The Inspector finally dug up a condescending smile and said, 'We'll help wherever we can.' Which meant whenever he saw fit to throw us a few morsels.

I said, 'Inspector, can I ask if you've had a chance to go over Tommy Gilmour's things again?'

'Ah,' he said, 'in search of the elusive note?'

I nodded.

'If your involvement with this case lasts any great length,' he said, 'I think you'll find that I have one of the most thorough and professional teams in the country.'

'I don't doubt it,' I said, 'but you wouldn't expect them

to be perfect, would you? Something could have been missed first time round.'

He considered me. The smile was still on his mouth but his eyes hardened as I watched him. 'I don't think so, Mister Malloy, but I'll bear your suggestion in mind.'

I sat up, leaned forward and said, 'Inspector, I hate to be a nuisance but I'm convinced there's a very strong chance that there is another note. Would you have any objection to me going through Gilmour's things? His car, hotel room?'

He looked at this pest across from him long and hard. I could sense Mac beginning to shift around nervously. Sanders said, 'I don't think that would be a good idea right at this moment.'

'With respect,' I said, temper rising, 'I don't have a lot of time to waste. Unless I can do something by Thursday morning to prove I was not involved with Gilmour's death then I can probably say goodbye to what remains of my career.'

That made his eyes smile again. He said, 'You have my sympathy but *my* career depends on catching criminals not rehabilitating jockeys back into the community.'

Police-speak for helping ex-jailbirds and he knew I knew it. I didn't see much point in humouring him or trying to be Mister Nice-Guy any more. I said, 'Well, I hope I have the chance some day of influencing *your* career.'

He smiled, happy in victory. 'I do think that's most unlikely, Mister Malloy.'

The meeting ended shortly after that with Sanders, courteous again, accompanying us to the main door. Half-way along the corridor I realised I'd forgotten my coat and went back for it.

It was a cloudy and dull afternoon with rain threatening as we made our way back towards the M6. Mac's car was at my place. I was driving.

'Well,' I said, 'bet that was worth coming all the way from Lambourn for?'

Mac was gloomy. 'The only decent bloody meal Jean cooks these days is Sunday lunch. To think I missed it to sit listening to that pompous bastard . . .'

'Isn't he a prick? How do these guys get the jobs? I can't believe it!'

'You did your usual, Eddie, wound him up. I suppose he might not have been so bad if you hadn't.'

'What'd you expect me to do? He's sitting there as though he has all the time in the world to catch this guy. What am I supposed to say, I'll come back next week and see if he feels any more like co-operating? Come on, Mac!'

'You'll have to learn some diplomacy.'

'Bollocks.'

'Enough said.'

We travelled in silence for a while then I teased him about Sanders showing a keen interest in the fact that Mac's boss was retiring soon.

'You know these inspectors,' I said, 'come up the hard way, working-class northern lads, wouldn't he just love a top job with The Jockey Club.'

'Naah, can't see it, Eddie,' Mac said without conviction.

'Well, I wouldn't be so sure, you know how much value they put on these ex-security types . . . Police Inspector? Sky's the limit in my book.'

He went even quieter after that and between that and his missed lunch moped for so long it took him a while to realise we were travelling in the wrong direction. It had been raining twenty minutes when, spotting a roadsign through the swinging wipers, he said, 'Eddie, you're going the wrong way.'

'I know.'

'We want to go south.'

'Not yet we don't.'

He caught the determined tone in my voice and said wearily, 'Eddie, where are we going?'

'To a place that does a very nice lunch. And if you promise not to moan at me too much I won't tell Jean you broke your diet.'

'I haven't.'

'You will.'

The Green Manor Hotel was only a couple of miles from Haydock Racecourse. It was the last place Tommy Gilmour had stayed, the last place he'd been seen alive. As I turned the car through the gates, tyres crunching across the gravel, Mac said, 'Please tell me you're not planning what I think you're planning.'

Swinging the car into a parking spot I killed the engine and smiled at my fat, hungry, dismayed companion. 'Needs must when the devil drives, Mac.'

He moaned softly and got out.

McCarthy ordered lunch while I found a phone and called Lisa Ffrench.

Over thick, grilled fillet steaks (cream-sauce for me, none for Mac) McCarthy tried to convince me it wasn't a good idea to try to get into Gilmour's room.

'It might not be a good idea but I'm going to do it and if I don't find anything I'm going back to Tommy's house tonight to check out his car and his personal gear.'

'The police will still have that stuff.'

'Uh-uh,' I mumbled, mid-chew. 'They sent it back to Mrs Gilmour last Friday.'

Lisa had just told me that but it was best if Mac didn't know she was involved.

He shook his head. 'There's no way they'll let you into Gilmour's room.'

'Want to bet?' I smiled.

'You've got one of your stories cooked up,' he said.

I shook my head. 'Better than that.'

He saw the mischief in my eyes and said, 'I don't think I want to know.'

I chuckled. 'How's your steak?' I asked.

He cut himself a large corner of the meat, squeezing a trickle of blood onto the plate. 'It tastes great,' he said, 'it's the indigestion that's worrying me now.'

'Relax,' I said, 'I'll make sure you come out squeaky clean.'

He said, 'I make a point of being wary of people who advise me to relax.'

'Could've been worse . . . I might have said, *trust me*.'

He chewed in silence till his curiosity got the better of him. 'How do you plan to get into the room?'

'You still got that nice big fountain pen you carry around?' I asked. Puzzled, he nodded slowly. 'Can I borrow it a second?'

'What for?'

Reaching into my jacket pocket I took out a piece of folded paper and pushed it across to him. He put down his fork and shook it open with one hand; it was blank except for the official heading of the Greater Northern Police Force. McCarthy closed his eyes for a few moments, his head sinking steadily.

When he looked up again I smiled and said, 'Remember when I forgot my coat?'

McCarthy held the sheet between tips of thumb and forefinger. 'You *stole* this from Sanders' office?'

I shrugged. 'It was lying around. I was tidying up.'

'*I* didn't see anything lying around.'

'Top drawer, right-hand side,' I said, smiling.

Eventually I persuaded Mac to lend me his pen. He gave it to me with his ritual 'I am washing my hands of this' look.

Leaning on the wine list I wrote: 'To the Duty Manager, Green Manor Hotel, St Helens. The bearer of this letter, Mister Edward Malloy, is on temporary secondment to

The Jockey Club Security Department. I would be grateful if you would allow him access to the room occupied on Friday 1st March by the late Thomas Gilmour. Further, I would ask that you and your staff co-operate with Mister Malloy in any questions he may ask. If you wish to discuss this please feel free to contact me on the above number.' I signed it 'Inspector Eric Sanders'.

'Want to see this?' I asked McCarthy.

'No, thanks. If you screw up, you're on your own.'

'Mac, whatever happens, you know I wouldn't drop you in it.'

He got up and said, 'I'll be in the bar.'

I was wearing my only suit: navy, double-breasted, two hundred and fifty quid's worth, along with a white button-down shirt, navy and wine floral tie and black shoes. Clean shaven and sombre looking I handed the note to the duty manager whose badge said his name was Christopher Cheeseman.

His hair was blond, straight and very fine. His blue eyes above pudgy cheeks read the note then without looking up he said to the girl behind the desk, 'Anyone in two-ten, Joanna?'

Joanna punched a few buttons on her keyboard and said, 'No, Mister Cheeseman.'

'Would you hand me the key, please?'

She did and he smiled and asked me to follow him.

The room wasn't that big: two single beds, wardrobe, trouser press, chair, writing desk, television, mirrors, kettle with tea and coffee stuff. I started at the window end, working through the desk drawers, wardrobe shelves and base, the floor, skirting boards, under the beds, methodically checking the least likely places, trying to cover every inch.

The telephone table; nothing stuck under the 'phone. The table had one narrow shelf, dark and quite deep with nothing, apparently, on it. On my knees I reached to the back of it and felt a book. I slid it out: the Bible. Holding the spine parallel to the floor I shook it, riffling the pages with my right hand. A card, a white card with writing on it fluttered to the floor.

I bent and scooped it up. It said: 'This Bible was placed here by the Gideon Society.'

Shit.

I put the card down then noticed something written on the back. Picking it up again I saw the same neat block writing that had been on my note in the same black ink. It read 'Hebrews 9:22.' It took me a few minutes to find the quote. It was: 'Without shedding of blood is no remission.'

It gave me a surge of elation. I had the proof I needed that I had nothing to do with Tommy's murder. It let me off the hook, left me free to ride *all* of Barber's horses including his Gold Cup runner.

I went and got McCarthy and he rang Sanders who arrived within the hour looking hot and bothered. Kavanagh and Miller, no happier than their boss, followed him up the steps to the front door as we watched from the bar.

McCarthy tried to be amiable but none of them spoke till we reached the room. I told them what I'd done and showed them the Bible. Miller approached and turned me by the shoulders, forcing my hands against the wall.

He searched me then Kavanagh read me my rights and they marched me down to the police car, took me back to the station, threw me in a cell and told me that in the morning they intended to charge me with the murder of Tommy Gilmour.

Chapter Eleven

They locked the door on me at ten minutes to five on the Sunday afternoon. Between then and the next morning I saw no one except the silent cop who brought me a dried-up meal around seven-thirty.

The cell had cream-painted brick walls marked with smudges where someone had tried to clean off graffiti. Curl-edged brown tiles pocked with cigarette burns covered the floor which supported one bed and a chipped wash basin. The place smelled of Jeyes fluid.

I spent an uncomfortable though not particularly stressful night since I was confident I'd be released as soon as Sanders considered he'd given me a big enough fright for pulling the stunt with the headed notepaper. If they honestly still suspected me of Gilmour's murder they'd have been interrogating the hell out of me.

Breakfast in the shape of parched scrambled egg and toast arrived at eight. Kavanagh and Miller arrived at eight-thirty, Kavanagh frowning and tutting at me like a disapproving teacher and Miller wearing his usual aggressive stare. They took me to 'the interview room'.

We sat on metal chairs with wooden seats opposite each other across a table; two against one. Kavanagh talked. Miller clicked a tape-recorder on and also took notes.

Kavanagh said, 'You've been a very silly boy, Eddie.'

'Slap my wrist, then, and send me home.'

Miller's jaws clenched and he stared up at me from

beneath those dark eyebrows. Kavanagh said, 'I don't think you'll be going home for quite a while.'

'Then you'd better charge me with something.'

Kavanagh smiled. 'Where do you want me to start?' he asked. 'Stealing police property? Forgery? Impersonating an agent of the Greater Northern Police Force? Murdering Thomas Anthony Gilmour?'

'Come on, Sergeant Kavanagh, why don't you just admit that you and your boss are a bit peeved that I found something you guys should have found a week ago.'

Kavanagh went cold-eyed and said, 'It wasn't there a week ago.'

There was silence while he waited for that to sink home with me. I smiled and said, 'You honestly expect me to believe that *you* believe I wrote that note myself yesterday?'

He shrugged. 'You said it, Eddie, not me.'

I laughed and sat back, shaking my head. Kavanagh said, 'You were in the room alone, you could have done anything. You gained fraudulent access. You were desperate to get in there.'

'I was desperate to get in there because as I kept telling *you*, your boss and anyone else who'd listen there had to be a note. You people were too pig-headed to go and look again. I was the one taking all the shit, what did you expect me to do, sit quiet and watch my career run down the drain?'

He waited, knowing he was getting me riled then said, 'Did you ask McCarthy to come to the room with you?'

'You know I didn't or you wouldn't be asking.'

'Why didn't you?'

'Because it wasn't his problem.'

'He's in charge of the case for The Jockey Club.'

'McCarthy does things his way, I do things mine. In theory, with the letter and stuff, I was breaking the law, if I'd pushed Mac into it too his employers wouldn't have been pleased. I can take my chances. I've no one to answer to.'

He smiled. 'Except us.'

I sighed in frustration. He said, 'Convenient that McCarthy wasn't with you. Did the hotel manager ask if you wanted him to wait in the room?'

'You obviously know damn well he did.'

'But you sent him away.'

'Look, Kavanagh, you know this is a load of crap. I'm not going to answer for every little thing I did yesterday.'

'You're above the law now, are you?'

'I'm above being wound up by people like you. This makes your Monday morning, does it? Helps beat the depression of coming to work?'

'We're just trying to do a job, Malloy.'

It was obvious the tape-recorder was on, Kavanagh talking official and acting all hurt. First chance they got outside of this room they'd be back to their smartass remarks and threats.

I said, '*Trying* is the right word 'cause you haven't been too successful so far, have you? Doubting my word on the note, missing the one in Gilmour's Bible . . . Now you're trying to hide your embarrassment, trying to turn the screw on me with all this nonsense, it's bloody pathetic! You *know* I had nothing to do with Gilmour's murder! So does Sanders! But you're obviously going to take whatever childish satisfaction you can get by messing me around as long as possible!'

Kavanagh tutted, 'Sounds like the bluster of a guilty man to me.'

He had me well on the boil and I had to fight to keep control. I was tempted to goad him with missing Gilmour's potential IRA connection too but it would have meant a grilling for Susan Gilmour who would never stand the strain. I also kept my mouth shut about my booked rides at the Cheltenham Festival which was twenty-four hours away. I had to be out by early next morning both to keep my rides and to avoid making the headlines.

The way things were going it didn't look likely and I didn't want to give them any more to gloat over than they already had.

Kavanagh kept at it for two more hours, trying to wear me down, trying, supposedly, to get a confession, though I was convinced his heart wasn't in it; he knew it was a sham as much as I did. I tried to persuade him I'd do him much more good on the outside than in here but he ignored me, just kept pounding away at the same points.

I had an idea. 'What have you done with the note?' I asked.

Kavanagh said, 'It's gone to forensic . . . with your fingerprints on it.'

I said, 'It's also gone to forensic with ink that's at least a week old.'

Miller glanced up at Kavanagh; Kavanagh looked at me. 'I'm not sure they can test for that sort of thing,' he said.

'Well, either you can go and find out or you can get me a lawyer and he can find out.'

Miller stopped the tape and they took me back to my cell.

At twelve-thirty the silent cop brought a salad lunch but wouldn't answer my questions as to where Kavanagh had got to. Nobody came and throughout the afternoon my frustration grew; I had to be out for Cheltenham tomorrow.

By dusk my patience had run out and I stood at the bars shouting till someone came; it was a dark-haired, one hundred and sixty pound WPC who looked as if she'd had as bad a day as I'd had.

She stared at me. 'What's the problem?' she asked.

'I want to see Kavanagh.'

'Well you're out of luck, he went home an hour ago.'

'You're kidding.'

'Not my style. Had my sense of humour surgically removed when I became a cop.'

'Did he mention me?'

'What's your name?'

'Eddie Malloy.'

'Not to me he didn't.'

'Is Miller still here?'

'I doubt it.'

'Would you mind checking?'

She put a hand on the bars, leaning on her big straight arm, and looked at me.

'Please,' I said, 'it's important.'

She said nothing, turned and went back the way she'd come.

Half an hour later, sitting on my bunk, I heard a key turn in the heavy lock of the door at the end of the corridor then the click of heels moving at a slow pace. I got up. The moving face was blurred by the bars. It was Sanders, the Inspector himself.

I stepped back as he opened my door and came in. He didn't bother locking it again. I guess he thought not even Eddie Malloy would have the temerity to try to escape while he was talking.

'Sit down,' he said.

I sat on the bunk. Trying to be cool he moved languidly to the wall, put his back against it, hands behind his buttocks, and raised a boot-heel, resting it on the brick. His heavy five o'clock shadow made his handsome face even more macho looking.

'How are you?' he asked quietly.

'How do you think? Pissed off.'

'Smart fellow like you? I'd have thought you'd find something to occupy your mind.'

Kavanagh must have told him I was easily wound up so I didn't answer. He said, 'I hear you've been making recommendations to our forensic boys. Aren't you happy just telling CID how to do *their* jobs?'

I stared up at him. 'Look, Inspector, I know and you know you're just holding me here out of spite. Let me out now and we'll forget it, I won't register a complaint.'

He raised his fine eyebrows. 'Blackmail, is it? . . . What next, bribery?'

Hopeless. I sighed, shaking my head. 'I asked for a lawyer more than seven hours ago.'

Easing his pelvis forward he released his hands and brought them round, folding his arms, knee still pointing at my face. 'Why would you want a lawyer? You haven't been charged with anything.'

Straining for a level voice, I said, 'Let me go, then.'

'Can't. I expect to charge you with Gilmour's murder as soon as we have the results from forensic.'

Resisting the urge to blow my top and have the same conversation I'd had twenty times with Kavanagh, I said, 'When do you expect to have them?'

'The results?' Eyebrows up again, head tilting sideways, 'Tomorrow evening maybe, possibly Wednesday.'

'You can't hold me that long without charge.'

'If I have a word with a friend of mine at the DPP's office I think you'll find, Mister Malloy' – he pushed off the wall and stood up straight – 'that I can.' His perfect white-toothed mouth smiled derisively down at me.

I glared at him. 'You know you're playing a game here. You know you'll have to let me go as soon as those results come through.'

He kept smiling. 'I wouldn't be quite so sure of that if I were you.'

I stood up. He was still three inches taller than me. I moved a pace closer to him and said, 'That means you're trying to fit me up.' His smile vanished. *Got him riled.* I followed through. 'Is that where Kavanagh and Miller are now, out doing a little bit of fabricating evidence?'

His jaw muscles flexed then he said quietly, 'Don't keep that sort of talk up too long in here.'

I smiled. 'Truth always hurts, Inspector.'

He took a step forward. I stood still. Our faces were a yard apart. You could tell just by his eyes how angry he was, then I noticed his right ear beginning to twitch. It was very slight but enough to pull his eyebrow marginally out of alignment each time. Boy, was he mad. Boy, was I happy about it. He turned and went out, locking the door.

He went down the corridor considerably faster than he came up it. I sat smiling perversely, knowing Sanders would still be doing his best to re-bury my resurrected career. Stuck in this cell, I wasn't even going to be at the wake.

I lay in the darkness staring at the ceiling, fidgeting uncomfortably as the cheap bed-springs bored into my back. Trying to be philosophical, practical, I wondered how I could contact McCarthy, ask him to get in touch with Hubert Barber to tell him I wouldn't make Cheltenham and he'd have to get someone else. Someone else who'd probably take over from me the way I'd taken over from Tommy.

Maybe Mac could get me a lawyer. A good one. Somebody who could get me out for Wednesday. Surely Barber would forgive me missing one day? What about his owners, though? What would they be saying? I was certain to be in the papers.

Sleep was miles away. Thoughts bounced around my brain so fast I had to make conscious efforts to calm myself. Why does everything seem so much more acute at night when you're lying awake?

High in the wall was a small window, the glass so thick it was almost opaque. The blurred bright ball behind it could only be a full moon. I watched it. The same moon that was hanging over Cheltenham racecourse, over Susan Gilmour's house, over Lisa Ffrench.

I wished she were here with her cool, unflappable practicality, her dark-eyed intensity . . . That was the last thought I must have had because I dreamt about her.

The same window showed daylight when I woke up with what was becoming a familiar soreness in my muscles from the bad bed. It took me ten seconds to realise where I was and I'd just pulled my thoughts together when I heard the key turn in the corridor door. I prayed it would be Kavanagh. I reckoned I'd a reasonable chance of getting through to him, persuading him to let me make a call.

It wasn't. It was the silent breakfast cop, tall and skeletal, an inch gap at the throat of his shirt, his bony wrists like pistons coming from his cuffs as he laid the tray down. I asked him to get Kavanagh for me, or Sanders or even Miller. He just stared back. I pleaded with him to call McCarthy. Eventually he spoke. Shrugging his narrow shoulders apologetically he said, 'I'm sorry, mate, I can't.'

It didn't help but at least it proved he was human. I was beginning to think he was a walking cadaver.

I paced the cell slowly, dragging the minutes and seconds behind me. They'd taken my watch but every time I turned towards the door I saw through the bars the big black clock high on the wall.

I tortured myself with thoughts of Cheltenham, the biggest National Hunt meeting in the world. The place where it was an achievement for owners, trainers and jockeys even to have a runner. Where riding any winner over the three days left you a memory that lasted years. To be connected with the winner of one of the two major championship races was to bask in the glory of it for the rest of your life and be spoken of, even after death, as the man who rode, owned or trained a Gold Cup or Champion Hurdle winner.

Forty thousand or so racegoers, some from halfway round the world, would be on their way to the course now in cars, trains, buses, on foot . . . those in helicopters would look down on the others converging from all directions like people who'd found the end of the rainbow and were certain the gold was there.

I tried to drive it away, think of something else, but I couldn't. The clock hands crawled to eleven-thirty. At the course, horses would be coming down the ramps out of their boxes, looking around, ears pricked, excitement building, knowing why they were there, walking off towards the stables, coats gleaming, muscles showing hard and smooth, fit to run for their lives.

The crowds would be buzzing, moving past shouting news vendors, heather-pushing gypsies, cockney ticket touts. They'd be queuing for racecards, filtering down to look at the course or striding determinedly towards the bars which would be full of people and noise and anticipation, whisky fumes, champagne bubbles and cigar smoke.

Bookmakers would be setting up their stands, opening satchels, counting money into them, paper money, thousands of pounds. They'd be cleaning boards, sorting racesheets, smoothing the pages of their big fieldbooks, bantering among themselves, boosting collective morale knowing they were seen by almost everyone else there as 'the enemy'. Only a hundred or so of them against forty thousand but favourites for victory even though all they had for ammunition was luck.

Ten to twelve.

The main players would be gathering around the glass-fronted weighing room: Jockey Club members, millionaire owners, movie stars, pop singers, maybe even some of the Royal Family; trainers, jockeys . . .

Jockeys . . . They'd be discussing prospects, exchanging

information, formulating plans, enjoying that delicious high of anticipation that can only be savoured before your first ride of the day, before the disappointment of a loser or a faller snuffs it out.

I sat down on my bunk almost crying with frustration. Then I heard that key turn in the door in the corridor.

Two sets of footsteps. I looked up. The leader was a cop I hadn't seen before. McCarthy was behind him looking serious. The cop opened the door and went away without locking it. McCarthy stared at me, still unsmiling, as I stood up.

'What is it?' I asked.

'Come on, you're out.'

Out? 'How come?'

'Good news and bad news.'

I waited.

He said, 'You know Dermot Donachy?'

'The Irish jockey?'

Mac nodded.

'What about him?'

'They found him dead last night. Same gun that killed Gilmour, same modus operandi.'

'Jesus!'

'The manager of a Cheltenham disco discovered his body in the toilets.'

I looked at the clock: five to twelve. Grabbing McCarthy's arm I hauled him through the door. 'Come on, I can still make Cheltenham. You can tell me the rest later.'

Sanders didn't come to say goodbye, nor did his two wise monkeys. We stood at the desk waiting for the tortoise-slow sergeant to get my things together. A thought occurred to me and I said to Mac, 'Did they find a note on Donachy?'

Solemn faced, he looked at me. 'Yes.'

'A biblical quote?'

'They think so. Too much blood and brains on it to be certain just now . . . The note was rolled up and stuck into the exit wound in his head.'

Chapter Twelve

We left the station at twelve-ten. Cheltenham was one hundred and twenty miles south and the first race was two-fifteen. I had a mount booked in the two-fifty but would have to be there at least half an hour before that. McCarthy offered to drop me back at the Green Manor Hotel to pick up my car.

'Mac, we don't have time for that! Get on the motorway and get your foot down.'

'Come on, Eddie, you've got no chance of making the second race.'

'We'll make it if you drive fast enough.'

'Even if the motorways are clear we'll never get through the jams around the course.'

'Let's worry about that when we get there.'

He looked across at me and said, 'No way am I driving at a hundred, I've already got a speeding ticket.'

'Fine,' I said. 'Pull over. I'll drive.'

He grimaced. 'You're not insured, Eddie.'

'Mac! I've just spent the last two days locked in a cell wondering if I'm going to be charged with murder and you're whining about speeding tickets and insurance! It's the Cheltenham Festival, for God's sake, and I've got the biggest break this side of my comeback! If you're not going to let me drive then I'll get out now and find some other way of getting there.'

He stopped and got out mumbling something about

being sorry he ever got involved with me. I slid across behind the wheel and did everything through the city traffic except loop the loop.

We hit the motorway, moved into the fast lane, and I pushed the needle of the big Peugeot up to a hundred and twenty, flashing the slowcoaches in front to move over. I prayed for a clear run; no roadworks, no hold-ups, no police.

Mac didn't speak much during the journey, more, I think, out of self-preservation than anything else – he didn't want to break my concentration.

M56, M6, M5, few delays, no police patrols. Thank you, God. We left the M5 at Junction 10 and immediately hit a three-mile tailback. It was one forty-five.

McCarthy looked at me with an ill-disguised smugness that said, What are you going to do now, bigshot?

I got out, removed my jacket and tie, threw them in the back and said, 'See you at the course, Mac.' Since I hadn't been riding enough to keep fit I'd been doing a lot of running and had turned in some reasonable times in the fields and lanes around the lodge. Leather shoes weren't the lightest footwear for it but the grass on the verge showed some give and I soon built up to a nice pace.

I drew my share of laughter and comments as I passed along the crawling line of car-bound racegoers. Their exhaust fumes didn't help my breathing.

It was a fine crisp day with just that hint of warmth that you know will disappear as soon as the sun starts sinking. I built a good rhythm and could have been enjoying it if I'd had time.

Hard pavement now beside the dual carriageway. My feet were beginning to hurt. Three long rows of vehicles queued at the traffic lights about a mile from the course. Five back from them on the inside was a long-haired, leather-clad motor-cyclist revving a big Harley. I stopped

in front of him. He looked at me and eased off the throttle.
'You know where the racecourse is?' I asked.

'Yes, thanks.'

Very funny. 'I'll give you thirty quid to take me
there.'

'Jump on.'

We roared past the rest of the traffic on the outside and
were at the Owners, Trainers and Jockeys Entrance five
minutes later. Sweaty and windblown I must have pre-
sented a pretty wild picture to Hubert Barber when I
found him by the weighing room.

'Where have you *been*?'

'It's a long story, Mister Barber, can it wait?'

'I suppose so,' he said grudgingly.

'I'm sorry,' I said, 'but I've got no kit with me. I'm
going to have to dash off and make some arrangements.'

'Go on then, I'll see you before the race.'

Before turning away, I said, 'Did you hear about
Donachy?'

He nodded, grim-faced.

'Am I in the clear?'

He paused.

I waited.

'Ride me a winner and I'll tell you.'

I didn't. We finished fourth of fourteen in the two-mile
Arkle Chase but the horse, Leandering, ran up to his best
form and gave me a brilliant ride round, flying every fence
and turning into the straight in line with the leaders only
to weaken up that long climb to the post.

Barber came hobbling to meet us. The pre-race tension
now gone, his face told me he was more than pleased with
the performance. 'You've got yourself a horse for next
year,' I told him and he smiled and clapped Leandering's
foam-flecked shoulder.

McCarthy sent in my jacket and tie with one of the
valets and the clink of car keys in the pocket reminded

me I had to arrange for the car to be picked up. I made a few calls.

Two dozen commercial helicopters were parked in the centre of the course and one was owned by a friend of mine who was based in Cheshire. He agreed to drop my car keys off at the Green Manor Hotel that evening.

I knew two northern jocks who were due down tomorrow for one ride each. They usually travelled together but agreed to separate at St Helens so that one, Martin Craig, could drive my car.

I found Barber then and asked again if I was in the clear with his owners. He told me that since they'd only heard the news this morning they hadn't had a chance to discuss things yet but he didn't see it being a problem. I told him what had happened since Sunday and he said that was a hell of a way to get myself an alibi for the latest killing.

Donachy had been based in Ireland and seldom rode here so his murder made nowhere near the same impact in the changing room as Gilmour's had, though some of the lads were clearly uneasy since no motive had been established.

The killings, like it or not, added further drama to the Festival and as the day wore on and people moved around, meeting friends, drinking, exchanging gossip, embellishing tales, boasting of Irish contacts, theories became rumours and rumours became facts. In the end I must have heard a dozen different versions of what 'really' happened.

None mentioned the biblical notes.

The favourite story was that Gilmour and Donachy had reneged on 'arrangements' to give the IRA information on planned betting coups. Someone said Gilmour had been 'knee-capped' before being shot. I thought back to Johnny Angell's IRA story on Gilmour and I wondered what angle the police were taking.

Another theory was that the guy was a lunatic killing jockeys at random. He'd done two Irishmen in a row just to lull the English boys into a false sense of security. He'd get one of *them* next. This set a couple of the lads flapping a bit. Many racing folk are superstitious and when people talk of random selection they're talking about fate. Come the end of the day there were some worried faces in the weighing room.

My ride in the fifth finished down the field and there had been a few nasty spills in the race. As dusk fell I was happy to be sitting safe in the changing room, showered and smelling nice.

There were six of us, all winnerless on the day but drinking chilled champagne courtesy of Kenny Taylor, third top rider this season, who, about three hours previously, had kicked home his first Champion Hurdle winner. Kenny had gone on to the owner's celebration party but he'd left us half a case of bubbly.

We slouched on the benches. I knew most of these guys well, journeymen jockeys who would probably never be champions but would, with luck, stay in the bottom reaches of the top twenty.

Blake and Mason were smoking cigarettes, Garvie, who often smoked pot, had settled for a big cigar. McEnery and Carlin were poking unenthusiastically at a layer of dog-eared salmon sandwiches. I had the evening paper with tomorrow's runners but couldn't concentrate.

'Eddie!' Someone kicked my foot. It was Garvie. 'You deaf?' he asked. 'Let's see the paper.'

I passed it over. Mason crossed his size five feet on the table, laid his semi-bald head back and blew smoke to the ceiling. He said, 'Penman's horse is a fuckin' certainty in the first tomorrow.'

Without looking up from his studies, Garvie said, 'Not even if it started now!'

Mason smiled. He knew Garvie fancied his own mount

in the first, thought it his best chance of the meeting. Mason loved winding people up.

'Don't tell me you fancy yours?' he said. Garvie twigged what he was up to and didn't bother replying. Mason slagged his horse off for another minute or so then gave in when he realised Garvie wasn't taking the bait.

They bantered on while I considered what to do next. Barber still hadn't given me an answer on future rides but I was fairly sure he'd continue to use me. I was to ride Great Divide in the Gold Cup on Thursday, that I did know. But what should I do about my biblical friend?

Forget him. That was my first decision. As soon as Barber gave me the green light I could get back to riding and leave the detective work to the experts . . . Such as they were.

What about McCarthy? With this second murder, the size of his problem had just doubled, he's going to be well pleased if I tell him I'm pulling out. And Susan Gilmour. And Lisa Ffrench . . .

'Penny for them, Eddie?' Someone was speaking.

'What?'

'Penny for your thoughts.' It was Carlin, weathered face, lined and haggard from years of wasting, creasing now, as he smiled, making him look fifty years old.

'Not worth a penny, mate,' I said.

'You were miles away then,' he said.

'Prob'ly missing that nice cell he spent the weekend in,' Mason said.

I'd told them about it earlier, much to their amusement. Garvie threw the paper onto the table and said, 'Know what I fancy? A good curry. A double-hot vindaloo with extra spice, then some black pepper to top it off. A freezing pint of lager to wash it down and –'

Mason interrupted. 'A pint! You'd need a fuckin' gallon.'

'And it'd still blow your bollocks off,' Carlin said.

Garvie, sucking saliva now as his mouth watered, said, 'Who's for it?'

McEnery, red-haired and freckled, said, 'Not me, I'm afraid. Got to take the wife out.'

Mason said, 'You didn't bring her for the three days, did you?'

McEnery nodded. 'So did Blakey and Carlin.'

Mason turned to them for confirmation and they both nodded sheepishly. Mason shook his head slowly. 'How're we supposed to have a decent night out if you dickheads bring your wives with you?'

Blakey said, 'We've brought them for the last three years; we can hardly tell them now they're stopping at home.'

Garvie stepped in to arbitrate and the final decision was that we'd all go for a curry, wives too. After the meal we went to a club where Mason brought his curry back up in the toilet, apart from which it was a pleasant evening. We had a few laughs and I forgot about Gilmour and Susan and Lisa and the decision I had to make.

One arrangement I hadn't made earlier was somewhere to sleep. Mason told me not to worry, he had twin beds in his room and 'hot and cold running chambermaids'. He offered to smuggle me in. Tired, drunk but as happy and relaxed as I'd been for a while, I accepted gratefully.

Next morning, mildly hungover, I was up and away by seven. I had promised Barber I'd be at the course early to ride my Gold Cup mount, Great Divide, in an easy piece of work just to let us get to know each other.

Though we did nothing stronger than a nice half-speed canter the horse felt and looked in superb shape. Barber had him trained to the minute. We set off to have coffee together both very hopeful for Thursday. Over a light breakfast Barber told me his owners, with the exception of Jack Delaney who still thought I was 'up to something', were now backing him and he'd continue to use me whenever possible.

'Don't worry about Delaney,' Barber said, chewing toast, 'he'll come round.'

'He's the guy that's chummy with the Stewards' Secretary, isn't he?'

Barber nodded. 'Beckman, I think his name is.'

'I'd like to know what he's got against me.'

'Forget it. He's an old woman.'

I sipped coffee. It was old women who spread gossip and I could do without any more. I'd have to see what I could find out about Mister Delaney.

I spent the rest of the morning drifting around, still undecided about going on helping McCarthy with this murder case or pulling out altogether. A couple of times I picked up the phone to ring Mac and tell him I was out but I put it down again mid-dial.

I walked round the course, trying to clear my thoughts. It was a beautiful spring morning. The ground, with a good covering of grass, was perfect. I set out, hands in pockets, following the white rails away from the stands. A mile and a half lay in front of me and I was determined that when I passed the winning post I'd have made a decision.

The note I'd received didn't really bother me any more. I didn't think the guy was out to get me. But I wished now I hadn't gone to see Susan Gilmour. Not that she'd expect anything of me, I'd hardly spoken to her. But I'd seen what Tommy's death had done to her. I'd heard her child crying for her, wondering if she was still there or if she was dead now too like Daddy.

Worst of all, and I don't know why, was what I thought Lisa Ffrench would expect from me. We'd spoken for a couple of hours that night. Mutual attraction had been part of it but I'd committed myself in a way, promising Lisa that if there was anything I could do for Susan . . .

She'd said, 'Just catch the bastard who killed her husband.'

Maybe I worried too much what people thought of me. Childish and unprofessional, my head told me. You've got a job to do, a career to pursue. No doubt my head was right but my heart said I had a moral obligation to stay with it.

Not only did I reach the winning post without making a decision, I managed to go through the rest of the day still undecided. The only time it didn't niggle me was when I was riding, which was twice, both times for Barber. I finished second on one and ended up involved in a Stewards' Inquiry where Lisa, stenographing or whatever the hell you call it, gave me a lesson on professionalism. I'd gone in expecting at least a smile and came out without her having so much as glanced in my direction.

I had a brief childish urge then to tell her I was pulling out, but it didn't last.

Immediately after the Inquiry I headed for the car park intent on beating the traffic jams.

Outside the weighing room McCarthy fell into step with me and as we went towards the gate he said, 'The forensic boys deciphered Donachy's note.'

'And?'

'Another quote from the Bible: Romans six, twenty-three: "The wages of sin is death".'

I stopped and looked up at him and I knew he had something else to tell me. 'They've had another look at the note I got?' I ventured.

Mac nodded. 'Remember what it said? Numbers, thirty-two twenty-three . . .'

I said, 'There's a book in the Bible called Numbers, isn't there?'

He nodded again.

'What does it say?'

'"Be sure your sin will find you out".'

Chapter Thirteen

The thoughts galloping wildly in my head kept me awake till the early hours. Was I on this madman's hit list? The police thought there was every chance of it. I'd just spent two hours with McCarthy and Kavanagh trying to figure out some connection between the two dead men and me.

Other than the fact that we were all jockeys I could think of nothing. I argued that if I was on the list why hadn't he tried to kill me the day he'd brought the note? Kavanagh said the killer may not have delivered it.

The police were dissecting Donachy's background and when I told Kavanagh my parents came from Dublin he renewed his grip on the 'Irish link', tenuous as it now was. For various personal reasons I didn't like talking about my family and this reluctance stimulated Kavanagh's hunch about some terrorist connection.

'Not in my family,' I argued.

'Not as far as *you* know,' he said, refusing to let it go. Things got heated then and Mac suggested we adjourn overnight.

The terrorist angle resurfaced in next day's papers. One of them had picked up on Gilmour's twenty-four hour detention by the police at Fishguard, the incident Angell had written about. The only person I'd mentioned that to had been Lisa and I was concerned in case she thought I'd dropped Susan in it.

At nine o'clock I rang Lisa at home. She answered, sounding out of breath. 'You okay?' I asked.

'Fine . . . Been out running . . . Just came through the door.'

'Do you want me to call back?'

'No, it's okay . . . have you found something?'

'Not really, I was wondering if you've seen this morning's papers?'

'The bit about Tommy?'

'I just didn't want you to think they'd got that from me.'

'I didn't,' she said. 'I knew it was only a matter of time before they dug it up. So did Susan.'

'Have the Press been pestering her?'

'They might have been trying to but they won't find her . . . She's gone to stay with a friend in France for a few days.'

'Are the children with her?'

'Of course.'

Of course. Silly question.

She said, 'What about you? Are you any further forward?'

I hesitated, then said, 'Put it this way, I've had one or two little adventures since we last spoke.'

'Anything you can tell me about?'

'How much time have you got?'

'If it's to do with Tommy . . .'

'More myself than Tommy, I suppose,' I said.

'Maybe we can meet,' she said.

'Thought you weren't supposed to hang around with bums like me?'

'I'm not but if *you* don't tell, I won't.'

'Okay. How about Saturday night?'

'Sorry, Susan's due back Saturday evening, promised I'd pick her up.'

'Sunday?'

'Depends how Susan is on the Saturday. I'm on vacation for a couple of weeks after that. Can I call you?'

'Sure.'

'Fine.'

Sounded like she was anxious to get away. I felt slightly awkward. Apart from Jackie my contact with women in the past six years had consisted of occasional drunken one-night stands. Developments in sexual/social manners had passed me by. I wasn't confident any more about interpreting signals, positive or negative.

Lisa said, 'I've got to go. Good luck in the Gold Cup.'

'Thanks,' I said lamely as the line went dead.

Great Divide was my only ride of the day and potentially the most important one I'd ever have. Although I'd been Champion Jockey once I'd never ridden a Gold Cup winner. The race is the most prestigious in the jumping calendar. To win it at any stage of your life can give a tremendous boost to your career. In my current situation it could mean the difference between being Champion again some day or ending up a nobody.

All I had to do was pass the post first.

The changing room was alive with jockeys and valets checking and double-checking, shouting, laughing nervously as the tension built.

A number of people send messages of good luck; used to be telegrams, now it's cards or faxes, and Nobby Simpson, one of the valets, was calling names and handing them out. Everybody had at least one. Mine was in an envelope with my name printed in block capitals.

The folded piece of paper stuck together as I tried to open it. I eased the corners apart. The message was typed, the print faint and uneven. It said: 'Vengeance is mine. I will repay, saith the Lord.'

I read it twice, tucked it back in the envelope and shoved it into the zipper pocket of my kitbag. Tim, my valet, approached and started tying the blue silk cap on to my skullcap. 'Ready for it?' he asked. I nodded slowly.

I *had* been ready, now I was trying to control my thoughts. Tim finished, stepped back, looked me over, spun me round by the shoulders, put a playful arm around my neck and said, 'You should've been one of those male models, Eddie. You'd've made more money.'

I smiled, miles away as Tim slapped my back and wished me luck. I'd need plenty of it if this madman was going to try something during the big race. I'd had a written threat once before, warning me to fall off at the first in the Champion Hurdle or I'd be shot during the race. I ignored it and finished third.

Should I ignore this? Should I tell Barber? If I did he might withdraw the horse. Then again it hadn't been a direct threat to do something during the race . . . But why send me it just before the race?

The bell rang signalling time to leave for the parade ring. I had to make up my mind. We filed through the big glass doors on to the verandah where the privileged people stood: trainers, owners, Jockey Club members and their celebrity guests. Smiling, calling good wishes, patting backs, they parted and we moved through catching the mixed tang of expensive perfumes and cigars. We nodded automatically, acknowledging greetings by tipping our caps in that subservient way that became habit all too easily.

As we broke through the pack and entered the parade ring itself the huge impact of the occasion hit me as it always did. Like moving multi-coloured cake-layers the crowd rose away fifty deep up the steps to the right of the huge oval and you could feel, almost physically, their reaction to our entry. No cheers or clapping but a tangible turn of the tension screw that vibrated round the whole arena.

We cut through gaps in the circling horses and split up

to join the tight little groups scattered across the lawn. Owners and trainers savouring the exquisite torture of nervous excitement on what was their biggest day, certainly of the year and maybe of their lives.

Barber stood over a party of six, none of whom I'd met before. He introduced me; only two were the owners of Great Divide, Mr and Mrs Carfax. The others were friends of the family who kept saying, Isn't it exciting. Too exciting for Mrs Carfax whose heavy jowls swayed as she jigged from foot to foot, nervous as a mink in a furrier's.

Just as Barber was telling me he wasn't going to tie me down with definite riding instructions Mrs Carfax hauled at her husband's arm and whispered in his ear. He in turn leaned across to whisper to Barber who said, 'No access to the one in the weighing room, I'm afraid.' The Carfaxes, smiling apologetically, hurried away across the lawn as the bell rang for us to mount.

Barber legged me into the saddle, squeezed my ankle and wished me luck. The blonde groom, Natalie, who'd led me in at Haydock, was almost pulled off her feet as the powerful chaser surged forward to join the others already circling.

Watching on TV during my prison sentence I'd studied the camera angles and favoured shots at Cheltenham determinedly, promising the other inmates and screws I'd give them a wave when I rode in my next Gold Cup.

Face on to the camera at the top of the ring I smiled and tipped my cap and thanked God I was out here riding and not in there watching.

Natalie led the horse round, walking fast, patting his neck regularly. I called down to her, 'Do you get all the good horses?'

She turned, smiling nervously. 'I'm just lucky, I suppose. Divvy's my favourite. You will look after him, won't you?'

I nodded, fighting thoughts of someone out there with

a high-powered rifle. Aiming at a galloping target he was much more likely to get the horse than me.

She turned to me again as we left the parade ring. 'God, I hate this. I wish we could just keep them in the stable and ride them in the mornings. I wish they never had to race. I can't watch. I have to lock myself in the loo.'

I smiled. 'He'll be fine. And you should watch. He's going to be the best in the country, the champion. How would he feel if he thought you hadn't seen him do it?'

She looked at me as though seeing something for the first time. 'I never thought of it that way.'

Throughout the slow parade in front of packed stands my mind was on the note. Why use a typewriter this time? The others had been hand-written. Why no reference to chapter and verse like the previous ones? This had been a direct quotation. The other notes (apart from my first one) had been found with corpses. Why hadn't he waited till he'd killed me?

The girl slipped the lead rein off as we turned and Great Divide lunged forward, getting the run on me and galloping towards the start more quickly than I'd have wanted. My mind back on the job I got him under control halfway down the all-weather strip, a three-furlong chute which channelled the runners away to save vulnerable turf being churned up. The sun came out offering brightness but little heat in the cold wind.

Veterans though our mounts were we all urged them towards the first fence just to show it to them, through ritual rather than necessity. As Great Divide peered over the beautifully built four-foot-six fence something caught my eye.

About a hundred yards beyond the inside rail towards the centre of the course a man in a dark suit stood alone. He seemed to be holding an object at eye-level and my first thought was that he was sighting something. The sunlight glinted on it; something metal. He suddenly noticed me watching him and quickly and surreptitiously slipped whatever it was into the inside of his jacket. He wandered slowly towards us and as he came closer I saw he was wearing a dog-collar.

This, I thought as my stomach lurched, could well be my man.

Decision time again. I could tell the starter and have the horse withdrawn, though if he was determined to shoot me he'd do so much more easily as I stood around waiting for the others to gallop off.

I told myself I was over-reacting. It could be a priest who was simply checking his binoculars. The glint I saw could have been off the lens. Why did he stuff them so quickly into his jacket then? If I asked the starter to have the police pick him up and he turned out to be innocent I'd be laughed off the racecourse.

Circling at the start I looked back to see if he was still there. He was moving away down the dirt-track on the inside of the rails. Which fence would he stop at?

Come on, Eddie, if it is a gun it's only a small handgun; what chance does he have of picking you off as you jump, especially if you stay on the outside of the field? There were only six runners though, not many places to hide.

Girths checked, small-talk finished, starter mounting his rostrum . . . 'Ready, jockeys?' Nobody answers, the lever cracks down, the tapes hiss skywards and we're off in the Gold Cup.

All abreast we made the short run to the first fence at a speed that left little room for adjustment. We landed safely though at full gallop and each of us knew we'd have to settle our horses down a gear or two to survive.

Even a race as prestigious as the Gold Cup can become an enjoyable romp on top-class horses if the ground is good and the field small. The banter was sharp and pretty relaxed. Close together each could hear what the others were saying.

Tucked away in the middle of the group I kept quiet, concentrating on settling my horse. After the fourth jump he was moving in a nice steady rhythm on the bridle, listening to my signals. I eased him back to the tail of the field ready to move up a few lengths on the outside as we came down the hill for the first time towards the fence where the 'priest' stood.

We approached it tightly bunched, which suited me, hoofbeats drumming, arms straining, boots touching . . . I could see the man, his arms resting on the rails, nothing visible in his hands . . . I switched Great Divide to the outside, giving him no sight of me at all. We all jumped it cleanly and galloped away from the danger.

Still in a tight group we set off on the second circuit all still going well and jumping soundly. Five fences out the outsider, a grey horse, began labouring and dropped away as the pace picked up.

The five remaining jumped the next and as we landed, Bomber Harries on the second favourite, Tuscany, kicked away for all he was worth as the rest of us got our horses balanced. Turning down towards the third last where the 'priest' stood, Bomber had gone four lengths clear.

We all glanced at each other knowing that if anyone kicked on after him now we'd be putting our horses under pressure, accelerating downhill where bodyweight alone caused a natural surge anyway, making the fence, which lay two-thirds of the way down the slope, even more dangerous to jump.

Blakey, still swinging along nicely, said, 'He's gone too soon.' I didn't think so. The others, unsure, looked at Blakey again who said, 'I'm telling you, the bastard's gone too soon!'

I thought Blakey was wrong but I knew if I went after Bomber alone my man at the fence would have the clearest target he could have wished for. If I waited to hide on the outside of the other three I wouldn't win the Gold Cup.

Should I blow my career or give this guy a free shot?

I tried to rouse the others. 'You're wrong, Blakey, he's nicked it! We'd better get after him!'

The others, still uncertain, said nothing. Blakey said, 'Believe me, he'll come back to us!'

He was five clear now and still galloping strongly . . . I couldn't throw the race away, I had to take my chances. Changing hands on the reins I kicked my horse in the belly and went after him, out into the open, away from the safety of numbers.

Galloping hard now, long strides, a hundred yards from the fence and the man in black . . . Bomber went over . . . silently I counted down my final strides, the man straightened up from the rails, I crouched lower, the man reached inside his jacket, the big fence came up, Great Divide's quarters coiled, he sprang, the man's hand came out holding glinting steel, I cringed as we landed . . . and the priest drank from a whisky flask.

I almost laughed, the nervous terror evaporating, replaced by a massive surge of vitality. I whooped like a Red Indian and the horse's ears flicked back. I shouted to him, 'Let's go and *win* this!'

Bomber was six clear leaning into the final bend, no sign of him weakening.

We found our rhythm and I moved into auto-pilot as the whip twirled into the cosh position then diagonally down across Divide's quarters. He responded immediately, surging away after Tuscany's black tail as my body ducked and pushed, my pelvis urging him forward.

Tuscany made a mistake at the second last. I set mine up for a long one as we approached and he answered as I'd hoped, flying in a low accurate trajectory that hardly broke his stride. That gained us a length. Tuscany's error had cost him one.

We were only two lengths down.

Both horses were beginning to struggle as we came to

the last, Bomber's, maybe, a bit more than mine. We gained slowly, a foot or so a stride. I was on the inside, a length behind as we came to it. Crouched low, looking between my horse's ears, I could already see the winning post like a tiny gunsight. If we jumped clean we'd just about do it.

As Tuscany rose in front of us Great Divide did too, mistaking the long shadow of the fence for the take-off point. He crashed down through the solid birch knocking any remaining spirit out of himself.

It was over for us and as his loppy ears drooped with exhaustion it was a question of keeping him balanced, keeping him going for second. I looked round but the nearest pursuer was ten lengths back.

Through the tunnel of crowd noise Tuscany crossed the line four lengths in front of us.

I shook Bomber's hand as we returned to the winner's enclosure. I acknowledged the applause, made a meal of the last fence error to Barber and the owners and retreated to the safety of the changing room. The exhilaration at getting safely over the third last had drained away leaving me feeling empty and stupid. My overheated imagination had probably cost me the Gold Cup . . . Me, Hubert Barber, the Carfaxes and young Natalie.

Barber sent a message to the weighing room telling me we'd been invited to join the winning owners at home that evening for a celebration. The Hadleys lived on the Oxfordshire–Gloucestershire border and Barber had scrawled some rather vague directions.

My first inclination was to give it a miss. I was on a hell of a downer and I'd probably just depress people. To me first is first, second is nowhere. I slipped quietly out of the weighing room, while everyone was concentrating on the next race, wandered out into the car park and locked myself in the car for a while.

The sky was clear now but a few raindrops from an

earlier shower clung grimly to the windscreen waiting for reinforcements. I killed them off with one slice from the wiper blade.

I wound the recliner all the way and lay almost flat so nobody passing could see me and spent the next fifteen minutes berating myself for losing the Gold Cup and cursing whoever had sent me the note.

I was sure now it hadn't been genuine, which meant someone was leaking information about the murders. Either the police or someone in McCarthy's department. The more I thought about it the angrier I became.

Thinking McCarthy's people the more likely source of any leak I set off looking for him to have it out. My frustration grew when I couldn't find him. As I stood in the weighing room hoping he'd appear they replayed the finish of the Gold Cup, forcing me to relive the agony of that mistake at the last. Defeat, as ever, looked all the more painful and exaggerated in slow motion.

Tired of waiting for McCarthy I decided to go back to the hotel. Before leaving I had a word with Nobby the valet who'd handed me the typed threat. He had collected all the messages from the secretary's office. None of the girls there could remember who delivered it.

Chapter Fourteen

Sitting in my hotel room I stared out of the window seeing nothing, trying to drive out thoughts of the Gold Cup with questions on what to do next.

Suspicion-wise I was now in the clear so: do I stay involved with the hunt for this guy? *Why should I?* Because you might be on his list. Because you owe it to Susan Gilmour and her children. Because Lisa Ffrench expects you to.

Simple answers. Ample reasons to stay with it. I knew it might affect my career but it would affect it even worse if the murderer came and shot me in the head.

So what next? Another meeting with McCarthy, maybe, find out who was co-ordinating the police work. Donachy had been killed in the south-west, Gilmour, as I knew to my discomfort, in the north. I hoped that plonker Sanders wasn't in charge.

Would McCarthy authorise a trip to Ireland to let me dig into Donachy's background? What if that background turned up an IRA connection too; would I really want to go on? Looking for a madman who was acting alone was one thing, taking on a terrorist organisation was a completely different kettle of piranha.

No, I couldn't believe the IRA had anything to do with it. Leaving Bible notes was hardly typical of their operation. Sure, religion was in there somewhere, but this had to be an individual, one guy.

Shouldn't be hard to find . . . to catch. I'd tracked down the last lot of villains for McCarthy, hadn't I? *Yeah, you were a big success at that, Eddie. They were just about to blow your head off when Jackie stepped in.*

Jackie . . . She'd been gone less than two weeks and I didn't think about her so much. Well, not every couple of hours anyway. The longer I waited before trying to contact her the more difficult it would be. Although I still missed her a lot I was kind of scared now she'd want to come back . . . I knew we'd start fighting again.

I managed to sleep for an hour. When I woke up things didn't seem quite so bad and I decided to accept the party invitation for that evening. At seven o'clock I showered, shaved and changed then headed for Oxfordshire.

Gresham was a big house. It had looked it from the outside and Mrs Hadley, dragging a bunch of us on a conducted tour, made sure we saw every inch of it. The Hadleys had bought it only three months ago and Mrs H. was as proud as a newlywed in a first flat.

About five feet five and thirty pounds too heavy, Annabel Hadley was fighting off middle age with admirable ferocity and no taste.

Bouffant hair dyed platinum blonde, she had small eyes, red cheeks, three chins and ear-rings the size and shape of playing cards which seemed to stretch her sagging ear-lobes like forks pulling at wet dough.

She wore a two-piece red leather suit which cut into her in more places than string does a roll of pork. Her feet were jammed in white stilettos at least a size too small and her right ankle sported a gold chain.

But she was a nice lady. Talkative, maybe, but nice. She led us round. 'Our last place was so small,' she said, 'but this, well, six reception rooms, twelve bedrooms, six bathrooms, two dressing rooms, games room, gymnasium, and the leisure complex, of course. Then there's the tennis court, which is floodlit, incidentally, huge courtyard with stables, twenty boxes, and a *helipad*! Gareth's thinking of buying a helicopter now.'

A pale bemused girl in front of me smiled. 'I'm sure it would come in handy the way the roads are these days.'

We were halfway up a flight of stairs now and Mrs Hadley, puffing noticeably, stopped by a big window and nodded in the direction of the main gate. 'You wouldn't have seen it in the dark but we have a trout lake and the gardens are all landscaped.'

'It's very beautiful,' the pale girl said.

'Sir Edwin Lutyens designed it, you know. It's a Grade Two listed building.'

'It's gorgeous,' the girl said, 'it really is.' And the other half-dozen in our party, anxious to get back to celebrating, muttered agreement.

The place was so gorgeous that when the inhibitions of the partygoers started slipping and the ash began missing the ashtrays, the occasional drink slopping onto the carpets, Mrs Hadley moved everyone away from the expensive furnishings into her 'leisure complex'.

It was a big glass-walled log cabin, the low arched roof supported by huge beams shaped like boomerangs. Underwater lighting showed the cool blue of the tiles in the twenty-five metre pool edged in a border of white. Two blue springboards, one six inches from the ground, the other about six feet, were already drawing admiring glances from potential divers.

A torturous looking black multi-gym lurked in the corner behind two blue exercise bikes. Around the pool were green exercise mats, tropical plants, white sun-loungers and chairs.

The images of a hundred people reflected ghost-like off the darkness behind the floor-to-ceiling windows which were slowly misting over.

Cigar smoke, laughter and the buzz of conversation drifted across the water as people stood around in groups

talking and joking, drinking, flirting. Three men by the
diving boards, jacketless, ties loose, glasses in hands,
started singing.

I knew maybe half the people there, mostly jockeys,
trainers, owners, a few Jockey Club officials and Stewards.
I should have made the best of it, put myself about a bit.
There were some potentially good contacts, solid chances
of some rides in the future if I got them talking on the
right lines.

But the Gold Cup defeat still hung over me along with
the prospect of weeks or months of detective work in
helping McCarthy and I couldn't quite bring myself up to
life-and-soul standards.

I settled on a congratulatory drink and a chat with the
winning jock, Bob 'Bomber' Harries. We sat on loungers
by the pool drinking champagne. Bomber, fair with wide-
set eyes and a pointed chin, looked as if he still couldn't
believe he'd won the big one. His right eye told me he'd
already had his fair share of alcohol.

It acted like a sort of animated breathalyser. The
drunker Bomber got the more his right eye turned
inwards. When sober he could look straight at you but
once he was pissed his right pupil looked like it was trying
to get behind the bridge of his nose. At that moment it
was off at about forty-five degrees but it could see enough
for him to nod over my shoulder and say, 'I think a friend
of yours wants to see you.'

I turned to see Hubert Barber, glass in one hand, cigar
in the other, breaking away from a large noisy group and
limping towards us. Someone from the group called him
back and when Barber ignored him a small man in a navy
suit, tie still done up and yellow hankie peaked stiffly in
top pocket, hurried after him, stopping him by grabbing
his arm.

They were too far off for us to hear what they said but
the little guy was gesturing in our direction and didn't

seem pleased. Barber pulled himself free and waved the
bloke away with a flourish of his drinking hand which sent
half the contents of his glass over the broad leaves of a
pot plant.

I watched Barber walk towards us along the edge of the
pool, listing badly to starboard once or twice and coming
perilously close to extinguishing the cigar clamped
between his lips in a million litres of chlorinated water.

As he reached us I stood up and smiled. He made me
sit down again, then, grunting and blowing, lowered himself to sit beside me. He nodded at Bomber and reached
across to shake his hand, 'Well done, today, well done!'

Bomber nodded, grinning wide. 'Thanks.'

Barber had raised a sweat which stained his white hair
pink at the temples, white stubble grew on his flushed
jaw and whatever the short guy had said seemed to have
annoyed him.

'Eddie,' he said, 'I'd like you to ride for me next year.'

'Sure,' I said, 'I'd be glad to.'

Obviously puzzled, he looked at me then said, 'No, my
stable jockey, I mean . . . Under retainer.'

I sensed Bomber looking at me but I was staring at
Barber. Stable jockey. Retainer. Jesus, the best I'd hoped
for was that he'd still give me a few rides. A retainer
meant security. It meant riding good horses, being able
to turn down bad ones. And with Barber it meant a serious
chance of becoming Champion again . . . In my second
year back.

He said, 'Eddie, what's the problem?'

I became aware I was staring at him like an idiot. 'No
problem,' I said, 'no problem, Mister Barber. I, I just
didn't expect it. Of course I'm bloody delighted to accept!
Brilliant!'

'We'll talk about money soon, get it tied up before the
end of next week.'

'Great.'

He drank what was left in his glass, most of the anger gone from his eyes now. He smiled. 'We'll show that little bastard, Delaney.'

'Was that him?' I asked. 'The one dressed up like a tailor's dummy?'

'That's Jack Delaney.'

'So he's still got a problem with me riding for the stable?'

'Keeps saying you're not to be trusted. Says Claude Beckman told him it's only a matter of time before you're involved in a major fuck-up.'

I said, 'Beckman's opinion's probably shared by about ninety per cent of his colleagues.'

'Well it's up to us to prove them all wrong then, i'nt it?' He raised his glass again not realising it was empty. Bomber, winking at me, got up. 'I'll get you another,' he said.

I said to Barber, 'What was Delaney saying to you a minute ago?'

He looked at me then said, 'Threatened to take his horses away.'

Barber smiled. I waited. He went on, 'I said, what time will your box be coming, Jack, I'll have the horses ready.'

'What did he say to that?'

'Backed down, didn't he? Said he'd give you one chance.'

I nodded. 'How many chances are *you* going to give me?' I asked.

'Think you're going to need any?'

My decision to stay involved in the hunt for Tommy's killer suddenly swooped back into my head reminding me that detective work and trouble tended to be close partners.

Still nobody but me had decided to stay with it. I could easily renege and concentrate solely on becoming champion again . . .

. . . and live a conscience-stricken life of misery.

As Barber waited for my answer I cursed him silently for not offering me the job sooner. 'Mister Barber,' I said, 'before you commit yourself there's something I'd better tell you.'

Chapter Fifteen

Friday morning I set off for Wolverhampton with Barber's job offer still intact. One proviso: if I got involved in anything that affected my riding for the stable I was out. Fair enough. I'd just have to try and keep things separate, minimise the risk. And hope that the police weren't quite as incompetent as they'd seemed so far.

Wolverhampton racecourse wasn't the most pleasant place to look forward to after three days riding around Cheltenham's beautiful Cotswold valley. The Staffordshire track lies in the industrial belt, flat and featureless and bloody cold when the wind blows.

I won the first for Barber on a novice hurdler in which he himself had a half-share. He wasn't at the races, probably sleeping off his hangover.

My next ride, a handicap 'chaser called Hair Trigger, had an excellent chance and had been backed accordingly by his owners, a four-man syndicate. My personal confidence was high and if he got beaten I knew it wouldn't be for want of a good ride.

Standing in the corner of the changing room I pulled the blue and yellow jumper on. The neck was tight and when my head finally popped through Con Layton was standing six feet away smiling at me.

I smoothed my hair back.

'Do you fancy yours here, Malloy?' he asked.

My first thought was to tell him to piss off but I didn't

need another confrontation. I had to keep a good discipline record or Jack Delaney would be saying 'I told you so' to Barber.

'The connections expect him to run well,' I said coldly.

'Ah and I wouldn't like to see them disappointed,' Layton said, still smiling, 'but there's a difference between running well and winning the race.'

A five-horse contest, a small track, it looked like Layton had one of his bent races in mind. Adjusting my breeches and boot-tops I said, 'Look, Layton, whatever your plans are, include me out.'

He sat down opposite trying like hell to reflect some friendship towards me from those small pale eyes. 'Eddie, there's other things in life than riding winners. What about the little luxuries, the things you can't afford with your ten per cent?'

'I'm not interested. Go away.'

'Clarkie will win this and you'll be on the odds to a grand,' he offered.

I ignored him and started checking my saddle and girths. His voice went very cold, all attempts at friendliness gone. 'Malloy, look at me.'

I ignored him.

'*Look at me!*'

I looked at his hard eyes. He said, 'Clarkie wins this race. You get paid.'

I stood up and stared down at him. 'I don't care who wins but mine runs on his merits so you can shove your money up your arse.'

He got up slowly. 'Malloy, it's four against one. Your horse wants holding up so you'll be in among us. If you're going out to do your best then we'll do *our* best to make sure you come back in an ambulance.'

Hard as I tried to be cool he was making me angry. I took a couple of steps towards him and said, 'Look, what did I tell you last time? You or your cronies come near

me during a race and I'll break your fucking legs. Now
move!' I pushed past him and went to weigh out.

The size of the field gave me the advantage, dirty riding
would be hard to disguise. My girths were being checked.
Layton and Clark circled together, talking quietly. The
lack of pre-start ribbing and the subservient expressions
of the other two jockeys clearly signalled their intentions
to bow to Layton's orders.

We lined up. Layton pulled down his goggles and smiled
at me. 'It's make your mind up time, Malloy.'

I glared at him. 'You've had one warning, Layton, that's
all you're getting.'

The starter pulled the handle. The elasticated tape flew
up. We were off.

The immediate objective being to survive, my first
thoughts were to keep plenty of daylight between myself
and the rest, race well wide of them. It should prompt the
Stewards to keep watching me, if nothing else.

Off a very slow pace I raced on their right flank like a
dog herding sheep, my horse enjoying himself free of hassle and flying divots. We just kept popping the fences
nicely, behind and wide of the others.

Onto the second circuit and they quickened the pace,
trying to draw me in, knowing if I wanted to scuttle their
plans I'd have to join the race soon. Equally, if they
continued to crawl along they'd all still be full of running at the finish, making their intentions to fix the result
obvious.

Two couldn't maintain the increased gallop beyond the
third last and I passed them in three strides. Up ahead
Layton and Clark were talking. I was closing fast but the
wind carried their words out of earshot, though you didn't
have to be a chef to guess what was cooking.

Mine, Hair Trigger, was full of running. We could pass
them when we wanted . . . the problem was which route
to take. If I went outside Layton he'd run wide, carrying

me off-course. Up the inside and Clark would have me through the rails. Between them would be suicide.

But they were both coming under a bit of pressure now and in the scramble of the first few desperate strides after landing over the second last they moved apart slightly and maintained the gap trying to tempt me through.

I kicked Hair Trigger forward as if to dive between them but at the last moment yanked his head to the left almost running into the back of Clark's horse.

The first move panicked Clark into leaning right-handed shutting the gap but that left a big opening on the rails. Clark had bought the dummy and Hair Trigger's head slotted nicely into the vacant space on his inside.

'Rails, you thick bastard!' Layton rasped. 'He's gone for the rails! Stop the bastard *now*!'

Violently changing direction on half a ton of galloping horseflesh twice in a few seconds is a lot to ask and though Clark's horse responded I was away, leaving nothing to cushion him from collision with the wing of the last fence.

The shattering crash, Clark's anguished cry and the horse's grunt told me they'd smashed through. Layton's antics had cost him several lengths and his horse was struggling. He drew his whip and laid into the poor beast under him, more to relieve his anger than raise another challenge.

Hair Trigger was so full of running he jumped the last with the energy of a horse going to the start and galloped past the post well clear. As we pulled up I thought briefly of Clark and how badly he might be hurt, then dismissed any possible twinges of guilt. He'd brought it on himself.

As I walked back in 'Stewards Inquiry' boomed from the loudspeakers and I suddenly felt a curious mixture of rage, elation and relief. Layton had been out to cripple or kill me for the sake of a few thousand pounds. Should I take my revenge privately or try to get him warned off?

If I told the Stewards he'd approached me with a bribe

before the race I was sure that would cast a whole new
perspective on the race when they ran the video. Then
again, Layton would just deny it and accuse me of trying
to get out of trouble by smearing him. No doubt the other
three would back him up, though the way Clark crashed
through that wing I didn't think he'd be giving evidence
from anywhere but a hospital bed.

My memory went back to his scream as the horse came
down but sympathy was the last thing he deserved. Or
maybe he did deserve some – maybe Layton had bullied
him into it the way he'd tried with me. Layton might have
had something on him, something on the others too. That
was the trouble, as soon as you accepted a bribe, the first
time you took part in a bent race, somebody had something on you, something they could use to get your co-
operation in the future.

How come Layton always came out without a scratch?
He was a sly bastard . . . maybe a private come-uppance
was just what he needed.

The syndicate who owned Hair Trigger were incensed
that both their horse and their money had been endang-
ered and I had to hold the biggest of them off when he
tried to get to Layton as he dismounted. 'It won't help in
the Inquiry,' I told him. 'Just calm down. I'll sort Layton
out when the time comes.'

As soon as we'd weighed in Beckman came for us. 'The
Stewards' Room, *now*!' he barked. We followed. Neither
of us had spoken since coming back. I'd decided to play
it cool and let the film evidence speak for itself. Accusing
Layton of attempted bribery without evidence was pointless. It was important, too, to let Layton think he was out
of his league with me, that nothing he tried would bother
me. Then he'd slink back into his own division and stick
to people who were afraid of him.

No waiting outside the Stewards' Room this time.
Beckman, who looked pretty angry himself, marched us

straight in and slammed the door which earned him a reproving glance from the Chairman of the Stewards, Simon Fullmore.

I was glad to see Fullmore. He was known as being firm but fair with a sound knowledge of race-riding. Narrow-faced with slate grey hair and blue eyes he was pushing sixty but looked very fit.

The other two Stewards were Clarence Heaton, an amiable old buffer who hated disagreeing with anyone, and John Chalmers, a man I knew little about.

Beckman started by having a real go at me, accusing me of 'disgracefully dangerous riding'. The Chairman shut him up and gave Layton and me the chance to put our sides.

I held my tongue to let Layton spout his story. Predictably, he lied through his teeth saying I'd been cursing at him and Clark, threatening them both throughout the race, telling them I'd had a big bet on my horse (jockeys are not allowed to bet). He said I'd barged into the back of them deliberately approaching the second last, trying to bring them down.

I put my case as calmly as I could despite frequent interruptions from both Layton and Beckman who stared at me throughout with what looked like very sincere hatred. This was the guy who'd tried to screw me at the Greenalls Inquiry and who'd been badmouthing me to Barber's owner, Jack Delaney. What the hell had I done to upset him so much?

Chalmers asked me, 'Why would Layton and Clark want to stop you winning?'

'If you could have been witness to a changing-room conversation between Layton and me before the race you would know, sir. But since I can't corroborate what was said there, it's probably best that I ask you to draw your own conclusions. I was riding the favourite and you may want to bear in mind the results of previous four- and five-horse races on the smaller tracks which Layton and Clark have ridden in.'

I could sense Layton wanting to say something but he couldn't decide whether he'd be dropping himself deeper in it by opening his mouth. The results were in the formbook and he knew it.

Chalmers said, 'Are you saying that Layton and Clark are responsible for fixing races?'

'I'm not saying anything like that, sir, as I can't prove it. I'm sure the Stewards are more than capable of deciphering the results of a series of races without any help from me.'

'Indeed, Malloy,' said Fullmore, 'but I have no wish to repeat yet again that we are here to discuss an allegation of dangerous riding. Much as we may like to take account of previous incidents' – he glanced at Layton – 'we cannot. Have you anything else to say, Malloy?'

'I'd like to see the film, sir.'

'Layton?'

'Just to say, sir, that Malloy is a very dangerous man to be riding racehorses and I think he should be taught a lesson.'

Fullmore said, 'By the Stewards?'

Layton stuttered and said, 'Of course, sir!'

Fullmore said, 'Well thank you for that advice. Mister Beckman, do you have any more questions?'

Beckman looked at me. 'Malloy, do you have any idea where Clark is now?'

'I should think he's on his way to hospital, Mister Beckman.'

Beckman said, 'That's right. He's going there for treatment to a broken arm, concussion and possible internal injuries.'

I said, 'Some people only learn from experience.'

He didn't take that well. 'You don't consider yourself responsible in any way?'

'Not in the least.'

'Listen, Malloy . . .'

Fullmore intervened. 'Gentlemen, I think it best if we adjourn for the moment to watch the film of the race. Malloy, Layton, the Stewards will view the race in private first. Please wait outside.'

Layton followed me out and closed the door. He looked at me with his sly little half-smile. 'When are you goin' to learn your lesson, Malloy?'

'When are *you* going to learn yours? You're never going to get a result out of me and you'll never get one from the Stewards. They all know you're bent. Maybe they can't prove it but they'll never believe a word you say in Inquiries.'

'We'll see,' he said.

'And I'll tell you one more thing, Layton; I'll spell it out since you don't seem to be taking the hints. You don't scare me and you never will. I've gone through more shit in the last five years than you've ever seen and if you think I'm going to let a prick like you fuck things up now you've got a lot to learn. Stick to playing with the second-raters and stay well out of my way.'

He smiled. 'Ah, you've a lot to learn yourself, Malloy.'

We said nothing more till they called us back in five minutes later. Beckman's florid face, his white-knuckled grip on his notebook, told me all I wanted to know.

Fullmore spoke. 'We have looked at the race and the incident in question a number of times and have come to the conclusion that no blame attaches to Malloy. Clark appeared reckless or at best careless and as such was the architect of his own problems. You, Layton, also appeared careless in allowing your horse to bump Clark's and as such you will be suspended from riding for a period of three days from the twenty-fourth of March.'

Nice one.

Fullmore continued, 'The result stands but before you

gentlemen go it is perhaps worthwhile to warn you that the Stewards will be taking a particularly keen interest in future races where you are opposing each other.'

Layton said nothing. I said, 'Thank you, sir,' then glanced at Beckman whose returned stare was hard and hateful. You'd have thought either Clark was his brother or that Beckman was in league with Layton and had just lost a lot of money. I'd have to make a point of finding out a bit more about Mister Claude Beckman.

My mount in the last finished second which, following the two earlier winners, rounded off a good day, all in all. I showered and changed and headed home, stopping off on the way for a meal.

Pitch black when I got home. No moon again. The lodge in total darkness, my headlights swinging on the windows as I bounced along the drive. Car lights off. Black outside. I reached into the glove compartment for my torch and flicked it on, following its narrow beam to the door.

Juggled my keys in one hand. Found the main one. Turned it and went inside. Flicked the hall lightswitch. Nothing. No popping bulb. Stepped into the living room. Reached for the switch there. Clicked it. Darkness. Shit.

I turned back towards the hall and went to the cupboard under the stairs, my beam searching for the main fusebox. Strange smell suddenly. Sweet. Pungent. The beam found the box. Someone had turned the power off. I backed out quickly. The sweet smell was stronger. A cold metal tube pressed against my neck . . . gun barrel. Something on my mouth and nose now. *Struggle. Struggle, Eddie, struggle*. The torch fell . . . rolled noisily along the hall . . . strange shadows. Smell too strong. Consciousness going. Slumping . . . Sweet smell . . . Ether . . . *Jesus Christ, I'm dead.*

Chapter Sixteen

A condemned man now, the events of the past two weeks summarised in my mind leaving just the rest of my life to flash before me.

I'd never thought of facing death anywhere but on the racecourse. I couldn't come to terms with the prospect of dying naked and alone in a freezing shed . . . there had to be some way out . . .

Running my hand up the thick wood I felt the horizontal block where it stopped. I was chained to a bench of some sort. A heavy workbench maybe or an old butcher's block. If I could just lift it and slip the chain clear of the leg . . . I ran my hands downwards again. The leg was bolted to the floor through metal brackets.

I worked on the loop, pushing it upwards till I could get to my feet. Got there. Couldn't straighten because of the chain but at least I'd got myself off the floor. I stood hunched over, back bent, draught cutting my ankles now. What next?

I eased my head down to rest it on the bench and felt along the surface. There might be some tools around, something I could use. Nothing on the bench but a metal vice, too far away, impossible to get the chain links into it.

Pushing towards the back I worked as far up the wall as I could which was only a couple of feet; nothing. Resting my forearms on the bench I stretched my right foot out, feeling the floor with my toes; no luck.

My left foot found some damp sackcloth and I dragged it slowly within finger reach, shook it hard to clear it of insects and debris and pulled it across my shoulders. It was very damp and cold but I couldn't possibly be any colder than I already was so it was worth wearing for a few minutes to see if it improved things any. If it didn't I would be in real danger of hypothermia.

Hypothermia – *ha!* You have to stay *alive* long enough to catch it.

Where was I? Where was he? Why hadn't he finished me off like Gilmour and Donachy? Why the hood? If he was going to kill me what did he care if I saw his face?

The little straw-clutcher inside me started reaching out:

Maybe this was just a lesson, a reminder that I shouldn't have ignored his note. Maybe he'd just hold me a couple of days then let me go. Or keep me locked up till he'd finished the killing.

Shit, what about my rides at Chepstow tomorrow? What day was it? He'd got me on Friday evening; I was assuming this was somewhere in the early hours of Saturday morning but there was no way of telling. I didn't know how long I'd been unconscious and with this hood on I didn't know whether it was day or night. It could be Sunday or even Monday. Bloody hell, Barber would be going crazy. Jack Delaney would be having a field day.

This was ridiculous. What was I worried about? The way things were going I wouldn't be seeing Barber or anyone else again.

Even Lisa. She was supposed to call me on Saturday.

I should have told her what my plans were, rung her every night to tell her my movements next day. Told her that if I disappeared suddenly it wouldn't be through choice. Okay, maybe she couldn't have done much to get me found but at least she'd know I hadn't let her down. And she could have told Barber I hadn't let him down either.

I should have but didn't.

Uncontrollable shivering took me now, vibrating the headache against the walls of my skull.

Still hunched over, leaning my head on my arms, I tried to jog lightly from foot to foot in an attempt to get warm, speed the circulation. It was tedious and tiring but it began to work. I kept it up as long as I could till my calf muscles burned and made me forget my headache for a minute. Eventually I warmed up from freezing to plain bloody cold.

I don't know how long I kept it up. All sense of time went after maybe an hour. My head became separate from my body, laughed at it jogging stupidly on the spot. My mind wandered till I was convinced I was above my body, watching that fool Malloy jogging pathetically, half naked, wearing that silly hood and sackcloth. I mocked myself cruelly and enjoyed it. All my thoughts seemed pleasant. The pain went away. So did the cold. So did consciousness.

I thought I heard a key click in a door. Couldn't be sure it wasn't just in my mind. Awoke slumped on the floor against the bench leg. Or was I? Maybe I was dreaming or still hallucinating. Became aware of some daylight through the hood. Door opening. Closing. Four footsteps.

His hands on my back now, gripping my sides. Turning me onto my hands and knees. I submit easily. No fight. Must be a dream. Someone pulls the sackcloth off my back. A hand on my head. Gripping my hair through the hood. Pulling my head back and up. Chain tightening. Choking. Pain now. No dream. Don't think so.

Something pushed from behind between my legs. Long and thin. Between my balls and my thigh. Like a long pencil high in my crotch. Drawing it back now, out. A foot. Two feet. Three feet. Leather. Yes, leather. Moving slowly now. A tab catches me, cuts into my penis. A

tab . . . a flap. A leather flap. A riding whip. That's it, a
. . . ahhh . . . ahhh hitting me now. My back. Stinging.
No dream now. No dream.

The whip bit into my back, my shoulders, my thighs,
my backside; I cried out, he hit faster, harder, grunting
with the effort, no direct aim just any piece of skin. My
arms and legs gave way and I crumpled onto my stomach.
He kept hitting, grunting, the leather-covered whalebone
singing through the air then smacking tightly into my flesh.
I was yelping now, almost squealing. I tried to stuff loose
cloth from the hood into my mouth so I could bite it.
Didn't make it. Tried to turn. To fight. Couldn't. Kept
hitting. Could hear him. Breathing hard now. Trickles
from my back warm on my freezing skin. Blood. And
pain. And blood and pain and grunts and whacks and
pants and cuts and screams and . . .

A noise woke me. A voice. It was dark again. Was I
awake? The pain was there. What was the voice saying?
Same thing. Over and over. What was it?

Listen . . . 'Work out your own salvation with fear and
trembling' . . . 'Work out your own salvation with fear
and trembling' . . . 'Work out . . .'

It was on tape. On a loop. Same thing. Deep, forced
voice. Which part of the Bible was it from?

Who cares?

I lay on my front, joints and muscles stiff and sore but
scared to move. The pain in my back was worse. My neck
was raw from the chain. My head pounded. My gut ached
from hunger.

But I was alive. He hadn't killed me.

Outside, the wind had died down. The draught chilling
my right side was steady. Trying to relieve the stiffness I
moved a couple of inches to the left and almost screamed
as I felt a cut creak open, the wound edges tearing themselves slowly apart.

I lay still, panting, waiting for that eruption of pain to subside back to bubbling point along with the rest. I tried to think what to do. Something positive. I couldn't. Nothing came.

The tape loop kept turning: 'Work out your own salvation with fear and trembling.'

I'm trying. Honest to God, I'm trying.

Maybe if I could get to my feet again.

Huh? Big laugh. As much chance of that as flying.

Must try.

I sucked the hood, caught some cloth between my teeth and bit down. Forced my arms up under my face. Heard the dried blood cracking and parting on my shoulders letting the pain weep from the cuts. Felt the cold sticky oozing wound under my right buttock as I drew my leg up. Heard my body say in panic, *What are you doing! You're opening these cuts. They're bleeding again. Lie still!*

I got as far as my hands and knees, breathing hard now through my nose, blubbering through the snot, sweating in the hood, eyes crushed closed, trying not to faint with the pain, trying to control my movements, my thoughts, block out the taped voice taking over my mind . . .

I bit through the cloth and passed out.

Still darkness when I woke. Pain still there. Tape still playing. Same words. Interminably. Filling my mind. Where was it, the tape machine? On the floor somewhere. By my feet. Near the door. I stretched a leg slowly towards the sound. Felt the plastic casing with my toe, the handle. I kicked.

Pain-burst.

The machine fell over. The voice stopped. The tape was off. In its place some music. Then a terrible screeching interference. Must have knocked it onto radio. Local station, maybe. Find out where I am. Screeching interference. Worst I've heard. Wish I'd left the tape on.

Blacked out again.

Daylight when he came back. Didn't hear the door open or his footsteps. Only knew he was there when he switched the radio off and there was silence. Deafening silence.

Heard him breathe.

Maybe he'd speak.

No. No words. Just a sound. A quiet sound. Swish. Swish. Swish. The slow singing of the whip.

Terror grabbed my gut. A pathetic groan of fear and shame escaped my throat, making me rage at this man who'd reduced me to a petrified child. 'Who are you?' I asked. The words came out like a desperate plea, making me even angrier at myself, at my own fear. '*Who are you?*' I screamed it this time.

He didn't answer.

Guessing where he'd be I kicked out grunting with pain and effort in a weak attempt to fight him, to let him see he hadn't beaten me.

My body turned as I lashed out, the wounds on my back grinding splinters from the floor. Before I could turn onto my stomach again he lashed me twice on the chest and groin.

I stifled a scream, determined to go out with some dignity.

I cringed waiting for the next blow, heard him stretch as he raised the whip then jerked silently as it bit like a red-hot saw blade. I waited for the onslaught.

It didn't come.

Just the swishing noise close to my ear. The stretch as he raised it but didn't hit me. The swish again. Then three hard horrific smacks in quick succession.

I lay praying, begging God to make him stop but all the time

Swish . . .

Waiting . . .

Swish . . .

. . . for the next one.

He would hit me maybe once in three minutes then twice in ten seconds. The agony of not knowing when the next stroke would come was worse than the blow itself. Then, like last time, the grunting started. Hitting faster. Grunting to a sexual intensity.

Now the frenzy. Almost a relief. No more teasing. No more waiting. Pure pain. Quickly bringing . . . Blessed unconsciousness.

I woke up in Heaven. Or that's what I thought. No pain. Warm bed. No voices. No whips. Just quiet. A pleasant groggy peacefulness.

A nurse came. A beautiful nurse who smiled like my mother.

'You're awake,' she said.

'I think so.'

'Somebody did a right number on *you*!'

Scouse accent.

'Afraid so,' I said.

'What did you do to upset him?'

'Wish I knew.'

She hadn't stopped smiling. 'Try and get some more sleep. If the pain comes back I'll give you something for it.'

'Where am I?'

'Shrewsbury General Hospital.'

'How did I get here?'

'Ambulance brought you in early this morning. Somebody found you in the car park of the local supermarket . . . Without a car, and without much else either.'

'What day is it?'

'Monday.'

'What date?'

'Eighteenth of March.'

'Oh shit.'

'Forgot someone's birthday?'

You can always count on scousers for humour in a crisis.

'I need to make a phone call.'

'I'll bring you the phone trolley.'

When she tried Mac's number the operator said, 'Sorry, you can't make transfer charge calls to an answering machine.' Yeah, very good. I was about to ask her to try Lisa when I realised I didn't have the number.

I tried Barber. Whoever answered wouldn't accept the charge. Silly bitch.

The nurse lent me money for the call. Barber wasn't there. The nurse looked up Lisa's number for me. Lisa wasn't there. I rang McCarthy's number again and left a message. Around 4 p.m. he rang back.

'Lots of people looking for you, Eddie. Where've you been?'

I told him and he started firing questions. I said, 'Come and get me out of here and I'll tell you what happened.'

He agreed. And I asked him to bring a few things. Before he rang off I asked, 'Have you seen Barber?'

'Saw him at Chepstow on Saturday.'

'Was he mad?'

'About you going missing?'

'Yeah.'

'Well, he was before racing, but he seemed a bit happier afterwards. Both his runners won.'

'Oh no! Who rode them?'

'Jimmy Crane. Two bloody good performances. Don't want to depress you, Eddie, but I think you may be out of a job.'

Chapter Seventeen

A lot of the pain was back. I'd refused more morphine, settling for some painkilling tablets, so my head would be clear enough to let me ride at Nottingham next day.

I'd finally got through to Barber. When I told him I was ringing from a hospital payphone he said he'd best ring me back because we needed to have a 'long talk'.

I didn't give him the full story, just enough to get his sympathy. If I'd told him how badly injured I was there's no way he would have asked me to ride so soon. I said I'd give him all the details when we met at Nottingham. He said Delaney was stirring things up again and that if anything else happened to stop me riding then he was sorry but the job offer would be withdrawn.

After speaking to him I told the ward sister I planned to discharge myself as soon as McCarthy arrived with some clothes and money for me. She wasn't pleased. Five minutes later a doctor appeared with some advice.

His name-tag said, Doctor Thomson. He was square-faced and bearded with light brown hair and matching eyes and he spoke in that rhythmical, unintentionally patronising tone common to his profession. It must be an NHS time-saving device for doctors: speak to everyone as though he or she is an imbecile. This will save you working out how intelligent they are.

He said, 'I really don't think it would be wise of you to voluntarily remove yourself from hospital care.'

'I wouldn't argue with you, Doctor; I'm sure it's pretty unwise myself but needs must when the devil drives and all that.'

'You do realise that the hospital cannot accept responsibility for any deterioration in your condition should you leave here without our approval?'

'I do.'

Wedding vows. Oath-taking. I waited for the next one.

'May I ask why you're so anxious to discharge yourself?'

'I need to be back at work tomorrow.'

'No job is that important, Mister Malloy.'

'This one is.'

'What do you do for a living?'

'I ride horses.'

'What sort of horses?'

'Mostly slow ones, unfortunately.'

He stared at me. 'You're not a *jockey*?'

'I know a few people who'd agree with you there.'

'Are you telling me that, in your condition, you plan to ride racehorses tomorrow?'

'Over jumps.'

He sagged down and sat on the end of the bed. 'You're in the wrong hospital, Mister Malloy, you want certifying.'

I nodded. 'I know a few people who'd agree with you there, too.'

'Seriously,' he said, 'do you know how many stitches we put in your back this morning?'

'The nurse said forty-two.'

He nodded in confirmation, gravely waiting for it to strike home.

I said, 'I hope they're flexible ones.'

He wasn't amused. 'Mister Malloy, if you take a fall tomorrow you are looking at permanent severe scarring . . . At best. At worst you could get blood poisoning so bad it could kill you.'

'I'll be careful.'

He looked at me for a while then said, 'Your flippancy doesn't impress me, you know. I don't see your attitude as brave, just foolish.'

'I told you, Doc, I agree with you. I'm not trying to impress anybody . . . Look, it's a long story. It's the story of my bloody life and if I had time to tell you it . . . shit, this sounds like a bad scene in a movie . . . What I'm saying is if you knew what was behind it all you'd probably understand why I've got to ride tomorrow.'

He shook his head slowly. 'I doubt it. Whatever it is it will be downright bloody stupid and irresponsible of you to ride in a horse-race tomorrow.'

'I'm sorry, Doctor, that's the way it is. It's my life.'

'Oh it's your life all right but when you're back lying in hospital again tomorrow night as you undoubtedly will be, it's my colleagues and I who have to patch you up again, which can be just a *little bit* galling. And it's the man in the street, the taxpayer, a man who has a humdrum job and an average wage who will be paying for you to lie in that bed. A bed, incidentally, which you will probably be depriving someone else of. Someone who may have been suffering on an NH waiting list for some considerable time. Someone who did not *choose* to go and injure himself!' He got up. 'Think on that, Mister Malloy!' And he set off down the ward, stopping after ten paces then hurrying back, brows like storm-clouds. 'Have the police been to interview you yet?'

I shook my head.

'I'll ring them again and remind them. Maybe they can talk some bloody sense into you!'

He went away leaving me feeling very small indeed.

At 9 p.m., along with McCarthy, came the police, Starsky and Hutch themselves: Kavanagh and Miller. Kavanagh, unbuttoning his raincoat, smiled and said, 'Long time no see, Eddie.'

I looked at him. 'Yeah, I missed you.'

'Me too,' he said.

I glared at McCarthy who read it correctly as, Why the hell did you bring these two? He said, 'I thought it best to call Inspector Sanders since you're the first, uh, survivor.'

'And witness,' Kavanagh added.

I said to Kavanagh, 'Isn't this out of your patch?'

'Special arrangement with the Shrewsbury lads.'

Miller, more satanic looking than usual in black coat and matching polo-neck, spoke from the bottom of the bed, 'We told them you were a difficult guy to deal with.'

I nodded. It hurt. 'The doctor will confirm that,' I said.

'So, what's the story?' Kavanagh asked.

'Look, can't it wait till tomorrow? I'm tired and sore and it's a long way home.'

Kavanagh said, 'You're not going home tonight?'

'I've just been through all this with the doctor. He's left me in no doubt that I'm a silly selfish bastard. He's right. You're right. Everybody who disagrees with me is right. I'm not arguing. But I'm going home tonight and I'm riding two horses at Nottingham tomorrow for Hubert Barber. It might kill me but I'm going to do it. I hope I've made myself absolutely clear 'cause I'm not talking about it any more.'

'Oh,' Kavanagh said, 'we are a bit tired and emotional.'

I ignored it and turned to Mac. 'Did you bring some gear?'

He nodded. 'But no way will it fit you.'

'Don't worry about it, it's just to get me home.'

He put a leather holdall on the end of the bed, took out a pair of brown corduroys, held them up and said, 'You could probably get into one leg of them.'

Kavanagh chortled, 'Failing that, you can always blow them up and hire them out as a bouncy castle.'

Miller laughed. First time I'd heard him. A strange girlish giggle. McCarthy wasn't amused. He said, 'They're far too big for *me* now too since I started my diet!'

'For God's sake,' I said, 'we'll be here all night. Just leave me the bag and draw the screens so I can get changed.'

Kavanagh's face hardened. 'We need to talk to you, Malloy.'

I struggled to push myself upright. Half grunting, I said, 'I know you need to talk to me, Kavanagh. I'm going home. You can either follow us back or come and see me after racing at Nottingham tomorrow . . . Even better, why don't you travel with me in Mac's car and you can do all your questioning on the way over . . . Help take my mind off the bumpy roads.'

He looked at McCarthy. 'That all right with you?'

Mac shrugged. 'Makes no difference.'

Kavanagh turned to Miller. 'You don't mind following us over?'

'All the same to me,' Miller said.

That was good news. Miller's company I could definitely do without.

'Fine,' Kavanagh said, smiling again, 'that's what we'll do.'

They left me to get changed, an exercise which made me think again about leaving hospital. Though my shoulders, back and thighs were heavily strapped and dressed I could feel the wounds pulling and straining at the stitches like patches in an old wind-battered sail. Sweating and swearing, starting and stopping I eventually got myself into Mac's old cords, a T shirt and a jumper.

There was no mirror but I felt like I'd lived quite comfortably in these clothes then someone forgot to feed me for three years. Too sore to draw back the curtains, I slipped through a gap and shuffled up the ward in a pair of old training shoes. Eyes swivelled from pillow height on either side as the other patients watched me weave along the floor, stooped like some demented hunchback, trying to hold the trousers tight at the waist without rubbing them against my back.

I signed the discharge papers and, flanked by my three visitors, hobbled away down the long corridor. We moved slowly, me hoping the pain would ease by tomorrow, them hoping silently, no doubt, that they wouldn't meet anyone they knew and have to explain what they were doing with this ragged shambling lunatic.

Mac drove. Kavanagh got in the back with me, so close I could smell his sweet aftershave. Thankfully, Mac had remembered to pack the thick blanket I'd asked for to help pad my back on the journey. The pain itself was like a big throbbing pad and each time we hit a bad piece of road I had to stifle a moan of agony. Mac would say sorry and I'd say don't worry.

The pain was making me sweat again and each time we passed under a street-lamp the orange light showed Kavanagh my twisted glistening face. 'You okay?'

I nodded, not trusting my voice any more not to start crying once it heard how pathetic it sounded. Kavanagh said, 'I'll wait till we're out of town, till we hit the motorway, before I ask you any questions.'

Jaw muscles clenched, I thanked him with my eyes, wondering if I'd stay conscious long enough to reach the motorway. I did and the smooth surface made things, if not painless, a good deal easier. Kavanagh looked at me. 'Can we talk now?' he asked.

I nodded. He said, 'Mister McCarthy said the guy caught you at home, that right?'

'Yes.'

'Friday night?'

'Yes.'

'How did he get in?'

'I don't know. I'd just got home. There were no lights. I thought a fuse had blown but when I went to check I saw someone had switched the power off at the mains. Then, like, all at once I smelt the ether and felt a gunbarrel in my neck and a pad being clamped over my mouth. He was strong.'

'Big?'

'I think so.'

'He say anything?'

'No. All the time he had me he never spoke a word.'

'And you didn't get a look at him?'

'He put a hood on me, tied it to a chain collar.' Involuntarily I swallowed and felt a mild, memory-induced panic.

Kavanagh said, 'How long were you unconscious?'

'I don't know. I woke up freezing cold, bollock naked . . . something made me think it was the early hours of Saturday morning but I couldn't be sure.'

'Tied up?'

'Chained by the neck to the leg of a big bench or something. Somewhere outside, an outhouse, a shed or an old garage, maybe.'

'You hear any sounds? Traffic? Trains? Aircraft?'

'Nothing like that though I was out of it a lot of the time so there might have been . . . Just small animal noises, mice, birds . . . and the smell of rotting vegetation. I remember that, you know that sort of sweet sickly smell?'

Kavanagh nodded, though I could see he didn't know what I meant but I didn't care. 'Somewhere in the country, I'd guess,' I said.

'Why'd he dump you in a car park in the centre of Shrewsbury, then? He could easily have been spotted. Why not a country lane? A field? An old barn?'

'Dunno . . . Maybe he didn't want to shit too close to his nest.'

'The countryside's a big place, Eddie.'

'Look, I don't know why he didn't *dump* me, as you put it, somewhere else, I just don't know!'

'Okay, okay, no big problem . . . When'd he start on you with the whip?'

The instinctive burst of fear I felt when he mentioned it took me by surprise. I swallowed hard. My mouth dried up. I had to forcibly detach myself from the memory of it before I could tell him about the whippings. And about the tape loop.

'What did it say?' McCarthy asked from the front.

'It said, "Work out your own salvation with fear and trembling."'

Mac said, 'Is that from the Bible?'

'It's worth checking,' Kavanagh said, then, 'We've got a real weird bastard here . . . What was the voice on the tape like? Would you recognise it again?'

I nodded. 'But it wouldn't count for anything, it was one of those put-on voices, like an impersonation of the devil, deep and sort of growly at the back of your throat. Something you'd do to scare the kids.'

Kavanagh said, 'And the guy himself never spoke once?'

'Not a word. Just grunts. He grunted hard and fast when he was really going at me, just before I passed out each time . . . I couldn't make up my mind whether it was exertion – that was making him grunt, I mean – or, well, it sounded like almost sexual.'

'A deviant,' Kavanagh said.

'I don't know. I'm just telling you the impression it left on me which might not be all that dependable on account of me thinking I was being beaten to death. You could hardly say I was of sound mind at that particular point.'

Kavanagh nodded slowly and was quiet for a while. Then he said, 'Know something? I don't think this is our man.'

McCarthy said, 'Of course he is! He's got to be! Exact same modus operandi as Gilmour and Donachy. The note, the ether, the biblical stuff . . . no one else could have known about that. None of it's been released to the Press, has it?'

Kavanagh said it hadn't. McCarthy asked me, 'Have you mentioned it to anyone, Eddie?'

'Not a soul.'

'Well,' McCarthy said, 'the only person I've told is my boss who has probably told the Senior Steward. So unless it was one of those two who was beating the shit out of you over the weekend then it's got to have been our man.'

Kavanagh said, 'Only one difference in the guy's m.o. from Gilmour and Donachy . . . He didn't break one of Malloy's legs and put a bullet through the middle of his forehead.'

'There must be a reason for that,' McCarthy said.

'Yeah,' said Kavanagh, 'the reason is it's not our man.'

McCarthy said, 'No. I just can't agree with you. What do you think, Eddie?'

'I don't know what to think. I'll tell you one thing, when that ether pad went over my mouth and I remembered Gilmour and Donachy I thought it was him all right! I thought I'd breathed my last.'

Kavanagh asked, 'You still think it's him?'

I thought for a few seconds then said, 'I don't know. Did I tell you about the threat I received before the Gold Cup?' They looked mystified. 'The note . . .' I prompted. Nothing. Obviously I hadn't mentioned it. I filled in the details.

Kavanagh was angry that I hadn't called them as soon as I'd got it. I was too sore and weary to argue but we discussed the note and none of us could make up our minds whether it was connected with the murders, my abduction or anything else. Things were becoming more confusing.

Mac still tended towards the theory that it *had* been the killer who'd kidnapped me.

Kavanagh shook his head. 'Nah, sorry, but it just

doesn't fit.' He looked at Mac, catching his eyes in the rear-view mirror. 'Do me a favour, Mister McCarthy, and just check with your boss, and the Senior Steward if you can, if they've mentioned the notes or the ether to anyone else.'

Mac said, 'I'm sure they won't have.'

'I'd be grateful if you'd check, all the same.'

I couldn't see Mac's lips in the mirror but his eyes told me they'd be pursed.

Kavanagh said he didn't think he could learn any more right now and asked Mac to stop at a service station. Miller followed us in and Kavanagh transferred to his car, promising he'd send the forensic boys to the lodge in the morning to pick up the Cheltenham note (if my kitbag was still there) and check the place over. He warned us to disturb as little as possible when we got back.

It was dark again when we drew up at the lodge. McCarthy didn't carry a torch. We got out of the car and virtually groped our way towards the door. I cursed as I remembered that I didn't have a key but Mac clicked the thumblatch and the door, undisturbed since Friday night, creaked open.

My stomach turned over and I had to steel myself to follow Mac in. I told him roughly where the mains box was and he fumbled his way forward leaving me holding on to the door-jamb feeling totally alone in the blackness.

A heavy click then the lights came on, blinding me. I narrowed my eyes and looked around. Nothing disturbed. Bag on the floor where I'd dropped it. No signs of a struggle. Then again I hadn't put up much of one. Same in the living room.

It was very cold. Mac built a fire and offered to make tea. I settled for a glass of water and some painkillers. I'd already asked Mac to stay the night if he didn't mind sleeping on the sofa. It was too far to drive back to Lambourn, I told him, but maybe the real reason was that the memory of Friday made me scared. I needed someone with me.

Mac searched all the rooms and found a broken window at the back where the intruder had forced his way in.

He helped me upstairs to bed and he helped me undress. I was grateful for that and for his company. Even more grateful when, at 2.30 a.m., he heard the screams from my room and came running.

Chapter Eighteen

By the time Mac reached me I was awake, sweating and shaking, the nightmare as fresh as the new pains in my back. Mac switched the light on as he barged through the door, his face pale and panicky then relaxing as he realised no one was there.

He offered to stay, to sleep in the chair by the bed but he'd only have nagged me about wanting to ride next day so I sent him back downstairs, took a sleeping pill and slept restlessly till 8 a.m.

Along with my riding gear I packed the bottle of strong painkillers, determined not to take any until just before my first ride. After half an hour's driving I was so sore that I couldn't lean back against the soft velour.

I stopped, adjusted the seat and drove on perched on the edge of it, grimacing and sweating like a chronic constipation case. One half of my mind was insisting that I had to ride today and the other half was laughing uproariously at the absurdity of the idea.

Nottingham racecourse lies within cantering distance of the city centre. A flat, fair course with no tricky fences to catch you out, I reckoned I had a good chance of getting Barber's two horses home safely from start to finish . . . maybe not in front but in one piece.

If I did have a fall I had to hope it would be a soft one. A fall I'd get up and walk away from, one which wouldn't make the course doctor want to examine me too closely.

If he saw the state of my back he'd ground me till it healed
and once I was grounded I was out of a job.

Standing by the weighing room I sipped black tea from
a styrofoam cup and watched my hot breath mist the cold
air. From the top of my spine to the lowest wound on my
right calf the aching soreness was pulsing now and I was
trying to think of something to take my mind off it.

All I could come up with were questions: who had done
this? Why? Was it the killer or was Kavanagh right, was
it someone else? If so, who and again, why? If it was
someone else he'd undoubtedly wanted me to think he
was the killer; and the ether and the Bible quote told me
that. It also narrowed the field. The only people who
should have known about those things were insiders,
people in The Jockey Club or in the police. Maybe
McCarthy's people were leaking information.

Things around the weighing room were getting busier;
most of the jockeys and valets had arrived and I set about
planning the best way to hide my injuries from them.

Tipping the last half inch of tea onto the grass I turned
to go inside when I heard something I didn't want to hear,
not yet anyway: Barber's voice.

'Eddie!'

Slowly I did an about-face and saw him hobbling
towards me across the tarmac, his over-long white hair
billowing like hovercraft skirts beneath his cap. He looked
anxious. I cranked up what I hoped was a disarming
smile.

He stopped in front of me, red-faced, puffing,
unbuttoning his long army coat to let the cooling wind in.
'You okay?' I asked.

'Put in a bad weekend, Eddie, a bad weekend.'

I waited.

He went on. 'I feel as if I've been fighting battles for
you for years rather than bloody weeks and you're never
there to back me up. Delaney's been mouthing off again,

he's ringing round my other owners . . . Now *they* know what he's like, which is lucky for you, but some of them are beginning to question my judgement in defending you all the time.'

Up till now I'd been prepared to bluster my way through, give Barber enough bullshit to try to get his commitment again but what I was now seeing in his face was genuine hurt and puzzlement that I should keep letting him down. Sure, it was hardly my fault but Barber wasn't to know that.

It came home to me that he had a life too, a career which no doubt meant as much to him as mine did to me . . . the way things were going I was helping wash his down the tubes along with my own.

A combination of guilt and the now brutal pains in my back pushed me into a full confession. We went and sat by the empty parade ring and I told Barber exactly what had happened over the weekend along with most of the other stuff, though with Kavanagh's warning in mind I didn't mention the notes or the ether.

As I talked I watched the trainer's expression change down through aggravation, wonderment, relief to sympathy.

He said, 'Jesus, Eddie, I knew there had to be good reasons. I knew you wouldn't just have let me down.'

I nodded. 'Look,' I said, 'you'd better sort out someone else to ride these two for you today.'

'You're feeling that bad?'

I nodded slowly, knowing I was admitting defeat. 'I could just about stay on them, I think, but there's no way I could give them a proper ride. I've messed you about long enough, Mister Barber, you've got yourself and your owners to think about.'

The relief I saw in his eyes, the acknowledgement that he didn't have to argue me out of it, told me I'd done the right thing.

Reaching forward he gently squeezed my arm. 'Take some time to recover, Eddie, I'll keep the job open. How long do you think before your back heals up?'

'A week maybe, I don't know.'

'No problem. A week, two weeks, whatever . . . don't worry.'

'Thanks, Hubert.'

I knew he meant it but if you think a week's a long time in politics it can be a bloody eternity in racing. Barber's stable was in good form and in the course of a week he might have twenty runners. If whoever took my place rode a few winners Barber would be under strong pressure from his owners to keep the new guy on.

He was still holding my arm, looking sympathetic. I smiled, 'Go and book someone for those two horses, Mister Barber, or you'll be too late.'

'Right. Fine.' He stood up, glad to be escaping. 'Let me know if there's anything I can do, Eddie . . . Keep in touch.'

I nodded and he turned and limped off, his step unmistakably lightened by the burden he'd left behind.

I sat still, the pain fading to the back of my mind as the realisation of what I'd just done sunk home. Unless Barber's stable suddenly hit a bad patch while I was grounded I'd probably just written my resignation as stable jockey.

Back to square one . . . and what a cold and bloody lonely square it would be.

I felt marginally better having come clean with Barber but even that satisfaction was tainted with the knowledge that by race time I knew I wouldn't have been able to get into the saddle anyway. As the day had worn on the pains had worsened, bringing cold sweats at visions of someone slapping me playfully on the back to wish me luck before I went out.

Slowly I got to my feet. What the hell, I was still alive,

still breathing. Square one wasn't exactly unfamiliar terri-
tory. I'd survive. I'd be back.

Wearily, achingly, I set off for the weighing room to
pick up my kit, swallow some painkillers and try to gee
myself up for the drive back home. My skin creaked and
stung as I walked and I promised it two days of me
lying motionless on my front if only it would ease off. It
didn't.

I told my valet I wasn't feeling too good and was going
home. He helped me get my stuff together and I thanked
him by dodging his sympathetic hand aimed at my shoulder as though I'd just discovered he was a leper. Mumbling
something about a jarred collarbone I apologised and
headed for the door. As I reached slowly to open it someone came through from the other side. It was the course
doctor and he looked to be in a hurry.

'Sorry!' he said as he barged through then, stopping
quickly, 'Eddie! You're the man I'm looking for.'

I knew Doctor Donnelly quite well, well enough to
know that the look in his eyes meant he thought I was
hiding something. I had a brief stab at a defence, 'Sorry,
Doc, but I'm off home; can it wait?'

He half-smiled. 'Just a few minutes of your time,
Edward.'

I followed him to the ambulance room; tall man, thin,
long wax coat, green wellies, nice round bald spot on his
crown shining through brown hair. He had hollow cheeks
and a big light brown moustache stained dark in the centre
by nicotine. He spoke to me over his shoulder as he
walked, 'Going home? Not feeling well?'

'Felt better.' I was going to plead flu but I knew it was
pretty hopeless.

'Where are you living now?' he asked.

'Leicester. Henry Kravitz's old place.'

'God, I haven't seen Henry for ages, how is he?'

'Haven't seen him myself for a while.'

We went into the warm ambulance room, all drab greens and browns rather than hospital whites but the smells were there. Doctor Donnelly closed the door. We were alone.

'Sit down,' he said.

Trying to keep the pain from showing I lowered myself into a hard plastic chair and perched on the edge. He looked down at me. 'Sit back, Eddie, relax.'

I stared at him. 'All right, Doc, who told you?'

'That's not important.'

'It is to me.'

'It was for your own good, Eddie.'

'*I* know what's for my own good, that's why I'm taking a couple of days off.'

'From what I've heard you might need longer.'

He was sitting back against the table, legs crossed, arms folded, big honest brown eyes waiting for my next weak offering.

'I'll be okay in a day or two,' I said.

'You sure?'

'Positive.'

'You won't mind if I take a look then?'

'Doc, listen . . .'

'Eddie,' his voice softening, 'it's my job. Your job is riding horses, mine is trying to make sure you don't kill yourself in the process; now I *have* to take a look at your back.'

I hung my head, rubbed my eyes, stared at the floor. 'I don't think I can get my shirt off,' I said quietly.

He came towards me. 'I'll help you.'

I'd put on two shirts in case some bloodstains spread from the bandages. They had, in big patches on both shirts and through to my sweater. After calling me a crazy, crazy bastard several times the doctor, with the help of two painkilling jabs, managed to change my dressings.

Then he took my medical book and stood me down for

fourteen days, no argument. 'Get a lot of rest, make sure the dressings are changed every forty-eight hours and come back and see me in two weeks.'

The Grand National was in two weeks. Not that I was likely to be offered a ride . . . not now.

'Doc, do me one favour, tell me who reported me.'

He shook his head. 'Someone who obviously had your best interests at heart.'

'I doubt it.'

'Some day you'll thank him.'

'I hope I get the chance.'

He offered to fix me a lift home. I told him I'd make it myself if I could get there before the jabs wore off.

The painkillers just about saw me home in the bright cold afternoon. I parked and the wind across the flat land ripped the car door open as I sprung the catch then cut icily through my sweater as I made for the door.

The identity of Doctor Donnelly's informer had bugged me throughout the drive and it still gnawed away as, shivering, I clumsily built a fire, stocking it high in case I couldn't move too well later.

The first suspect had to be the doctor at Shrewsbury Hospital, the one who'd been angry with me. I washed up, made coffee and rang him. He remembered me, said he was extremely glad I'd been stood down but flatly denied contacting the racecourse doctor: 'I've better things to do with my time than continue to look after patients who have foolishly discharged themselves.'

The other man who'd crossed my mind was Barber. Although I'd asked him to keep it quiet maybe he'd let something slip, though it would have to have been in a hell of a short space of time.

If he didn't do it that only left McCarthy and the two cops, they were the only other ones who knew but I couldn't see how any of them would have a reason.

I rang McCarthy's office. He was in Newmarket on

stable visits. I raised him on a crackly mobile phone line but he hadn't spoken to the doctor or anyone else.

I got Kavanagh next, his lazy voice and manner laid back as ever. He'd mentioned my injuries to no one and nor had Miller to the best of his knowledge though he'd check.

When I told him I'd only one more guy to eliminate he perked up a bit.

I said, 'Barber's the only other person I've told. If he didn't report me there's only one more guy who knew the state my back was in . . .'

'. . . the guy that did it.'

Barber's secretary gave me his mobile phone number but it was switched off. I kept trying and got him about half four on the way home from Nottingham.

'How'd your horses do?' I asked, not sure if I wanted to know the answer.

'Stuffed, both of them.'

'Sorry to hear it for your sake, Mister Barber, though I can't say I am for mine.'

'At least you're honest.'

'Mister Barber, did you speak to anybody today about . . . about my injuries?'

'Not a soul, Eddie. You asked me not to.'

'Of course, I know but, well I had a run in with the course doctor . . . he stood me down for fourteen days.'

Silence for a while then, 'Now, *I'm* sorry to hear that, Eddie, for both our sakes.'

'Me too but there could be a clue in there somewhere that might be useful to the police. I just wanted to double check that you hadn't let anything slip, even by accident.'

'Definitely not, Eddie. Absolutely not.'

Slightly offended.

'Mister Barber, I had to check, no offence intended.'

'None taken, Eddie.'

'Good, thanks again, I'll keep you in touch.'

'Do that.'

I rang Kavanagh back and told him.

'Did you ask this doctor who tipped him the wink?' he said.

'Several times. He's not saying.'

'Well he'll be saying when I ask him. Do you know where he'll be tomorrow?'

'Southwell maybe, possibly Worcester. If you ring the track in the morning they'll tell you.'

'Where will you be?'

'I'll be here by the phone. Probably lying flat on my belly trying not to move, but I'll be waiting for your call.'

As the night wore on and the wind howled around the lodge the pain came again, slowly like small biting animals hatching all over my back. I passed on the painkillers settling for half a bottle of whisky which dulled the soreness in my body in exchange for a spreading melancholy of self-pity.

Fractured thoughts floating around, ruined career, screwed-up comeback, broken relationships, nobody to turn to . . . I wallowed a while then something that had been nagging at me all day finally surfaced – I hadn't spoken to Lisa. She'd probably be thinking I was trying to avoid her.

I found her number. It rang eight or nine times before she answered. 'Eddie. How are you?'

'Okay.'

'Listen, can I ring you back?'

'Tonight?'

'Five minutes, give me five minutes.'

'Fine.'

I hung up, feeling better already. She sounded all right, not mad or anything. I thought about pouring another drink, considered what two weeks of inactivity would do to my weight then said what the hell and half-filled the glass.

The phone rang. I reached for it. 'God, that was quick! Thought you said five minutes?'

Silence.

'Lisa?'

Nothing.

'Hallo . . . ?'

'Eddie . . . ?'

That sweet soft Irish voice, sounding hurt, unsure.

'Jackie! Where are you?'

'Who's Lisa?'

'She's just a friend; tell me where you are.'

'No. I just wanted to make sure you were okay but obviously Lisa is seeing to that.'

'Jackie, come on!'

'Barely two bloody weeks . . . *you bastard!*'

'Jackie, listen, for God's sake!'

She hung up.

Shit! What a day this was turning out to be. I gave a little laugh of frustration and relief. At least Jackie was okay. It had been a good clear line, maybe she hadn't gone back to Ireland after all.

The phone rang again. Jackie or Lisa. I answered carefully, 'Hallo?'

'Eddie.'

McCarthy, sounding tense.

'What is it, Mac?'

'David Campbell Cooper's disappeared.'

'Since when?'

'Yesterday. He didn't show up to ride at Fontwell today . . .'

'He's done that before.'

'He was due at his mother's house in London last night for her birthday party. Didn't turn up.'

'Maybe he doesn't like parties.'

'Don't be facetious, Eddie, I've spoken to the police, they're treating it seriously.'

'Meaning they think they'll find him dead.'

'They didn't exactly say that but they are concerned.'

'The kid's probably just got sick of his old man's bullying and buggered off somewhere.'

'You know the boy's father?'

'Unfortunately, yes.'

Mac said, 'He's just been ranting at me for the last ten minutes. He wants to put up a twenty grand reward for the boy's safe return. Both the police and I have advised against it in case he gets into a ransom situation with this guy.'

'And . . . ?'

'He's going to do it anyway.'

'Good for him. Gives me something to occupy myself with for the next two weeks. *And*, there's nobody I'd rather take twenty grand off than Jack Cooper.'

Mac was baffled. I explained I'd been stood down by the doctor. Mac said, 'If you're unfit to ride, what makes you think you can charge around the country looking for David Cooper? What if the killer *has* got him?'

'Mac, my career is sliding swiftly down the pan. The prospect of no job and no money makes twenty thousand pounds worth taking a lot of risks for.'

'So now you *do* think the killer's got young Cooper?'

'Dunno. I hope not, for his sake.'

'Yours too. The reward is for the boy's safe return only. No payout on corpses.'

We talked a while longer and Mac wasn't pleased when I said I thought there was a leak in his department. Somebody had reported me to the doctor at Nottingham. Somebody knew about the notes and the ether. As if the prospect of being on the killer's list wasn't bad enough somebody else was out to end my career.

Mac said, 'That's wild speculation, Eddie. You'll have to name suspects.'

'Okay . . . I'll give you two.'

Chapter Nineteen

I told Mac it had to be either Con Layton or Claude Beckman. Both had major grudges against me; Layton for obvious reasons, Beckman's motive I'd yet to discover. Mac disagreed. Accepting my theory meant admitting there was a problem somewhere in his department. He wasn't ready to do that yet. We didn't say goodnight on the best of terms.

Next morning I sat down to plan the practicalities of searching for David Campbell Cooper.

Money: things had improved substantially owing to my winning percentages and cash presents from happy owners in the last couple of weeks. I'd paid the most pressing bills and diluted the red ink contents on others to a pale pink. I was still owed my five per cent of second prize money in the Gold Cup, around fifteen hundred quid. Things could have been worse.

Transport: wouldn't win any Formula Ones but was fast enough to get me out of most troublespots.

Health: not good. Back still very sore, driving long distances looked out. Have to do what I could on the phone for the first couple of days and hope for improvement.

Thoughts of the telephone made me realise Lisa hadn't rung me back last night. Maybe she'd tried a few times. Mac had kept me tied up for a long time. I rang her number. No answer.

Straight-backed and suffering I shuffled to the kitchen for coffee and toast then sat down to list people who could tell me things about David Cooper.

May as well start at the top. I found his father's office number in *Directory of the Turf* and rang him. He remembered me well and his first instinct was to hang up. I persuaded him it was in both our interests to forget the blow-up we'd had at Southwell and let me concentrate on trying to find David.

He answered my questions with more irritation than enthusiasm.

I made notes while he told me about his son's background. This was limited to education, friends (that he knew of), places they'd lived . . . I asked about girl-friends. Cooper couldn't name any ('He's not fucking queer, if that's what you mean!'). The Coopers had divorced when David was twelve. Was he still close to his mother? Cooper said the kid never talked about her.

I'd expected at least a couple of nostalgic reminiscences about the boy's childhood but Cooper kept it practical. It seemed to me in the end that he hardly knew his son. Memories of my own father came briefly back . . . our relationship hadn't been much better. Makes you wonder why people have kids.

Cooper quickly grew impatient with questions on domestics and told me to get cracking on the basis that the boy had been abducted by Gilmour and Donachy's killer.

David had last been seen by his father's trainer, Bobby Watt. He'd gone to his yard on Monday to school a couple of horses. Watt's place was near Uttoxeter in Staffordshire.

The trainer couldn't help me much. 'The kid seemed okay, quiet as usual. He arrived about eight, schooled three for me, had breakfast and buggered off.'

'Did he say where he was going?'

'Nope. He wasn't racing that day, I know that.'

'And he seemed all right?'

'I told you, the boy's so quiet you wouldn't notice any difference. He could be suicidal and you prob'ly couldn't tell.'

'He finish his breakfast?'

'As far as I know. I don't wet-nurse him.'

'Didn't mention his mother's birthday party?'

'Not to me he didn't.'

'Is he close to anyone in the yard, any of the lads?'

'I think Pauline's got the hots for him but I doubt it's mutual.'

'Can I talk to her?'

'She's out with the second lot just now.'

'Ask her to ring me, will you?'

'Sure.' He took my number.

To satisfy my own curiosity, I asked him who would ride Cooper's horses while the kid was missing.

'Nobody. Jack told me to withdraw two today and two tomorrow and not to make any more entries till the kid's found.'

'So you'll be suspending his training bills out of sympathy?'

'Fat fucking chance.'

Pauline rang within an hour. She had a grating Lancashire accent. After a five-minute conversation I was convinced she knew more than she was telling and decided, though I didn't warn her, I would pay her a visit.

The nerves in my back seemed suddenly jumpy at the prospect of driving north. Still, Uttoxeter wasn't that far, a couple of painkillers should see me through.

Hauling two pillows from upstairs I propped them behind me in the driver's seat and set off.

The journey was reasonably smooth, the pain never unbearable. I found Watt and he took me to meet Pauline who was cleaning tack.

Eighteen or nineteen, she was plump and plain looking with dirty-fair hair. She wore a yellow polo-neck with strands of straw sticking to the hem, tight jodhpurs which needed washing and blue rubber splash-boots. Watt introduced me, told her it was okay to answer my questions then left us alone in the tack-room which was dark and depressing.

The girl was nervous, avoiding my eyes. I suggested we take a walk, up to the gallops maybe. Outside it was mild but windy. Pauline seemed less unhappy walking by my side but still unenthusiastic about answering questions. I changed course and talked about her and her horses for a while and she brightened considerably but clammed up again when I came back to David Campbell Cooper.

'Pauline, why won't you talk about him?'

'I don't know nothin'.'

'You were pretty close to him, weren't you?'

She shrugged slightly but took it as a compliment. 'We talked sometimes.'

'Do you think he was happy? I mean, was anything bothering him?'

'Dunno.'

'He would have told you if there was . . . ?'

Another shrug. 'S'pose so.'

'What did David think of his father?'

Slight hesitation this time, then, 'Dunno.'

'Was he afraid of him?'

She didn't answer. I stopped walking. She did too, reluctantly, and gazed at the grass. I said, 'Are *you* afraid of him – Mister Cooper?'

She dropped her head even further now, staring at her bootlaces.

'Pauline, I give you my word I won't mention anything you say to David's father or anyone else.'

Still avoiding my eyes she said, 'He'll tell Mister Watt to sack me and I won't get a reference.'

'Who will?'

'Mister Cooper.'

'No, he won't. I promise you. He won't even know we've been talking.'

'Mister Watt'll tell 'im.'

'Pauline, listen, all Mister Cooper is interested in is getting David back. If you can give me a clue as to where he might be there's no way his father will sack you . . . he'll probably give you a reward.'

She scuffed at the wet grass with her heel, scoring a long dark bruise. 'David won't want to come back to his dad,' she said. 'I don't think he likes him all that much.'

'Who doesn't like who?'

'David don't like his dad . . . and he don't think his dad likes him, he's always mitherin' him about gettin' better, bein' perfect, like.'

'Would it have bothered him enough to have run away?'

She shrugged again, still scraping earth. 'Dunno.'

'Pauline, look at me.'

She stood still and slowly looked up.

'David *has* run away, hasn't he?'

'I dunno.'

I stared at her accusingly. She got a little angry. '*I don't know!*'

I believed her. 'Okay, I'm sorry, I had to be sure.'

She cooled quickly back to docility and we started walking again. I persevered another ten minutes and had a minor breakthrough when Pauline said David had talked vaguely about moving to France with his mother sometime soon, but she knew no details. He *had* mentioned his mother's birthday party and intended going on the evening he'd disappeared. He hadn't said what he'd planned for the rest of the day and no, Pauline hadn't walked him to his car so couldn't say if he had a suitcase with him.

I reassured Pauline her job would be safe, gave her my

phone number, said goodbye to Watt and settled carefully
back into the car.

Heading south again I thought the next best lead would
be David's mother. If he was close enough to her to talk
about accompanying her to France then he wouldn't have
run away without telling her. If he'd absconded to escape
his father there was every chance she'd know where he was.

How much she'd tell me was another matter and keen
as I was to avoid a trip to London I didn't rate my chances
of getting much info from her on the phone. I rang her.
She sounded convincingly anguished about David's dis-
appearance and said she'd be happy to see me and help
in any way she could. I drove home to pack an overnight
bag.

Lisa had left a message on the answerphone saying she
had tried to get back to me last night. I called her.

'Not working today?' I asked.

'On vacation for two weeks.'

'That's right, you told me. How's Susan?'

'Not at all well, I'm afraid. They took her into hospital
last night.'

'Jeez . . . that bad?'

'On the edge of a complete breakdown . . .'

She sounded strained. I said, 'Are *you* okay?'

'Fine . . . I just feel desperately sorry for her.'

I sympathised and we talked for a while. She asked how
I was doing and I told her what had happened over the
past few days. She listened with alternating reactions of
anger and incredulity. When I reached the part where the
doctor stood me down she told me she'd been at Nottingham that day and overheard a discussion between the racecourse doctor and Claude Beckman, the Stewards'
Secretary.

'Beckman was saying something like, when he does
come back I'll have him in front of the Stewards. I didn't
know who they were talking about.'

'Can you remember what time it was?'

'It was after racing. I was on my way home. Why?'

'I was just wondering if Beckman could have been the guy who tipped the doctor off, but there's no way Beckman could have known.'

'That man does not care for you *at all*,' Lisa said.

'It's getting to be mutual. What do you know about him?'

'Not much. Was a bit of a mummy's boy. Lived with her till she died. Now lives on his own somewhere in the Welsh Borders, I think. Never married.'

'Gay?'

'Dunno.'

'Does he bet?'

'He's not supposed to.'

'Doesn't mean he doesn't. Maybe Beckman lost a lot of money on one of my horses, maybe that's why he can't stand me.'

'I don't think he does bet. I'd have heard it on the grapevine.'

'He's beginning to bug me.'

She said, 'Let me nose around and see what I can find out about him.'

'You'd better be careful, you've got a job to protect.'

'Least of my worries.'

I told her I was going to London to see David's mother and that I'd keep her in touch.

She said, 'What about your back? Can you drive okay?'

'A bit like Quasimodo in a milk-cart but I get there.'

'Why don't I drive you?'

'To London?'

'Wherever . . . I'm doing nothing for the next ten days.'

I could think of many less pleasant travelling companions but she really would be risking her job. I told her it wasn't worth it. She convinced me the job meant little to her and with a mixture of trepidation and pleasant anticipation I agreed to pick her up in an hour or so.

'You might want to pack an overnight bag,' I told her. Unsure if I was reading too much into the ensuing pause, I added, 'Just as a precaution, it's not a come-on.'

'Of course not.'

Again I couldn't read her tone and wished I could see her face. She said, 'See you when you get here.'

She must have been watching from the window of her flat. As I pulled up she came striding towards me in that easy athletic gait I'd noticed at Haydock. Her fawn knee-length coat swung open revealing tight black ski pants and a jade velour top. Her black high-heeled ankle boots clicked on the flagstones. Trying not to grimace I eased myself out of the car and straightened slowly as she reached me.

We both smiled. The sun was behind her in a clear sky. Her short thick hair shone, the whites of her brown eyes were luminously clear beneath a dark fringe. I couldn't see a trace of make-up on her soft almost perfect skin and when she parted her pink lips her teeth gleamed. I remembered her perfume from the Gilmours' place. Standing close to me on that bright cold afternoon I thought she was the healthiest, most vibrant human being I'd ever seen.

'You look . . . very well,' I said awkwardly.

She smiled wider and said, 'Thanks. I wish I could say the same for you. Your back must be hurting like hell.'

'Is it that obvious?'

'You're an awful colour.'

I smiled. 'I can see this is going to be a really uplifting partnership.'

She touched my arm. 'Sorry, I should keep my mouth shut.'

'Forget it.'

I moved my makeshift backrests to the passenger seat, Lisa adjusted the driving position and mirrors and we headed for the M4.

On the way we talked about Beckman and the killings, young Cooper and his father, Susan and the children (staying now with their grandparents in Devon) and chatted about things in general. Nothing too personal but by the time we stopped for coffee just outside London we seemed reasonably familiar and comfortable with each other.

As I brought the cups to the table Lisa reached to the floor for the small black clutch bag she'd brought. Her heavy hair fell over her face then swung back as she straightened and opened the bag. 'Mind if I smoke?' she asked.

'Feel free.'

She lit a long white-tipped cigarette then held it up, blowing smoke. 'Menthol. Trying to give it up altogether.'

'Why does everybody who smokes have to apologise all the time?'

''Cause we're persecuted by all you pious non-smokers, that's why. Murderers are treated better than we are.'

'Pack it in then.'

'I'm *trying*!'

I smiled at the spark of anger. She smiled but not in response, at something that had crossed her mind.

'What is it?' I asked.

'You read much?'

'Only formbooks.'

'There's an American writer called Garrison Keillor, he –'

'Who?'

'Garrison Keillor.'

'I think you've got him mixed up with a cavalry fort in the Utah desert.'

'Very funny. He wrote a story about the last four smokers in America. They're holed up in a canyon somewhere and there's this mother trying to get a message out to her son scribbled on an old cigarette packet.

Something like, "This is it, son. They've been closing in for days. The helicopter gunships are overhead, getting closer . . ."'

It was good to watch her, the enthusiasm, the animated face.

'You should go into acting,' I said.

'You really think so?' She posed with the cigarette, a puckered smile fronting the fake Hollywood accent. I laughed lightly. She would be very easy to get to like.

As Lisa manoeuvred us skilfully through the city traffic I called Kavanagh's office and spoke to Miller. His buddy was on his way to Southwell to speak to Doctor Donnelly.

I said, 'Can you ask him to ring me on this number when he reports in?'

Miller grunted something and I gave him the number with the impression that he was reading his newspaper rather than taking it down.

We found Mrs Cooper's place and before I went in I rang Kavanagh again. 'Did you see the doctor?' I asked.

'Yep.'

'Did he say who reported me?'

'Yes and no.'

I waited.

'His informant was anonymous. Left a note.'

'Saying what?'

'Saying, Take a look at Malloy's back, he's badly injured and shouldn't be riding.'

'Don't suppose it was hand-written?'

'You suppose correctly; type-written.'

'Any clues there?'

'We're working on it.'

'Couldn't be the same typewriter that produced the Cheltenham threat?'

'You are very perceptive this evening, Mister Malloy.'

'It's the same?'

'Might be. The jury, as they say, are still out.'

'And if it is?'

'Another clue, isn't it? Another piece in the jigsaw, another pattern in the great tapestry of justice.'

'You been at the cooking sherry again?'

'How can you tell?'

'Sharp perception, like you said. Will you let me know as soon as something's definite?'

'You'll be the first on my list.'

He prattled on, still flippant, telling me they couldn't get too serious about young Cooper just yet, even under the circumstances. 'If we had to go looking for every nineteen-year-old who didn't go home for a couple of days . . .'

Before hanging up he promised to ring me in the morning.

David's mother lived in a nice big house in Kensington with three Birman cats which were the snobbiest creatures I'd ever seen. She was dark, slim, pale, quite elegant. David took his looks from her. Contrary to what her ex-husband had told me she claimed a close relationship with her son and said he phoned regularly, wrote the occasional letter and would see her 'certainly' six times a year.

When I suggested he might not have been happy under his father's influence she agreed but tempered it by saying that David had always been sensitive and careful not to play them off against each other.

'If he planned to leave home would he have let you know in advance?'

'I'd certainly [one of her favourite words] like to think so.'

She said she knew nothing of any planned move to France and could offer no suggestions as to David's whereabouts. Repeating Cooper's fears of the boy's abduction she suggested I looked on it in that light. But if she really believed her son had been taken she wasn't convincing in her concern. Though determined to keep an open mind I left her house with a definite twinge of suspicion that she, at best, knew a bit more than she was saying.

I rejoined Lisa in the car, she said, 'There was a call on your mobile.'

'Who from?'

'Peter McCarthy.'

I looked at her. 'Hope he didn't recognise your voice.'

'Well he sounded a bit surprised, especially when I told him Mister Malloy was in a meeting.'

I smiled. 'What did he say to that?'

'Just asked that you call him as soon as possible.'

I dialled his number. He said, 'Who was that who answered your phone when I rang?'

'Oh, that was my new secretary, Lucretia.'

'Come on, Eddie . . .'

'It was just a friend, Mac, just a friend. What can I do for you?'

'It's what I can do for you. Young David Cooper was seen with your favourite Stewards' Secretary early on Monday afternoon.'

'Claude Beckman?'

'Uh-huh.'

'Where?'

'At a service station on the M1.'

'Doing what?'

'Drinking coffee and chatting amiably, according to what I hear.'

'So Beckman could have been the last person to talk to the kid?'

'Very likely.'

'Any objection to me paying him a visit?'

'None at all.'

'Where is he tomorrow, do you know?'

Mac said, 'He starts ten days' leave. Want his phone number?'

'And his address if you've got it.'

He gave me both.

I hung up. We sat in the darkness, Lisa watching me as I sighed and leaned back against the pillows drained of energy. She said, 'You're not fit for this trip back, are you?'

'A couple of painkillers and I'll be okay.'

'You won't. You look absolutely exhausted.'

Pivoting my head against the seat I looked across at her and managed a weak defeated smile. 'I'll find us a hotel,' she said.

It was a small place, softly lit. Lisa wouldn't let me carry her bag. I asked at reception for two single rooms. The man behind the desk said, 'Sorry, only one twin room left.'

I said, 'Thanks, we'll find somewhere else.'

Lisa, standing beside me, said, 'No, we won't, we'll take it.'

The man smiled.

Chapter Twenty

She wore cream silk pyjamas with teddy bears on. I wore bloodstained bandages. We sat on our separate beds sipping hot chocolate. She said, 'Didn't you bring fresh dressings?'

I shook my head. 'Couldn't have changed them myself.'

'You knew I'd be with you.'

A tiny shrug was all I could manage. 'Didn't want to appear presumptuous.'

She shook her head slowly but I thought I saw a spark of gratitude in her eyes. She got dressed again, went downstairs and came back with a big first-aid kit.

An hour later she was asleep in the bed nearest the window.

I lay on my side listening to her soft breathing. Pale light from a street-lamp filtered through the curtains. Every few minutes a vehicle passed on the road below. Tired but too sore to sleep I realised how grateful I was that Lisa was with me. Not for romantic or sexual reasons (I somehow felt inadequate, afraid of any expectations on that front) but just as you'd feel about an old friend. Whether she'd thank me for that sentiment was another matter.

Next morning we set off for Beckman's place, an old cottage at the foot of the Black Mountains. McCarthy had given me directions as best he could after saying it was 'in the middle of nowhere'.

Explicit directions from the landlord of a small hotel saw us to the bottom of the steep track leading to Beckman's place at eleven-twenty. If Beckman *was* around he was the last person we wanted to spot Lisa so I asked her to return to the roadside hotel and come back for me in half an hour.

'What if something goes wrong, Eddie?'

'Like what?'

'Like you not being here when I come back.'

'I don't see there being any problems but if I'm not here maybe you could wait half an hour then go back to the hotel. Wait there another hour then phone Mac. Don't tell him who you are, just say you dropped me off at Beckman's and I haven't come back.'

She got serious. 'You know Beckman dislikes you intensely . . . probably hates you?'

'That's one of the reasons I'm interested in him, I want to find out why.' I got out.

'Eddie, be careful.'

'Don't worry. See you in half an hour.'

Although the sun was now out in a watery sky it had been raining heavily for two days and turbulent streams of varying widths splashed down the steep heavily rutted track. My shoes and trouser bottoms were quickly soaked as I climbed and the ache in my wounds seemed to worsen.

The white-walled red-roofed cottage lay at the end of a path bordered by young trees. A silver Audi was parked outside almost touching the heavily creosoted picket fence. I went through the gate and along the pebbled path but stopped suddenly as a familiar smell reached me. I stood sniffing lightly, trying to place it.

A faint breeze carried the smell along the narrow tunnel formed by the side of the cottage and a high board-fence. It came to me: that sweet scent of dying vegetation, all the more pungent now as the sun warmed the rain-sodden ground. I'd last smelt it lying helpless and naked and covered in whip wounds.

That made me reconsider. It could be a complete coincidence; that smell must be rising from a million overgrown gardens, fields and woodlands all over the country. Or it could be that this was the place I'd been held. It wasn't such a long way from Shrewsbury where I'd been dumped.

If Beckman was the man who'd abducted me, if he was home just now and I walked blithely in not only unarmed but seriously unfit to put up a fight . . . he was a big man, probably quite strong. I looked around for a concealable weapon, a rock, a bottle maybe, a short heavy stick, but it was possible Beckman was watching me from the house. If he saw me pick anything up he'd know I knew and that would probably make him a hell of a lot more dangerous. If I stood around much longer he'd get suspicious too.

Just for show I patted my pockets and looked forgetful as though I'd left something in the car, then I moved on towards the door.

It was open. Just slightly ajar, maybe an inch. I pressed the big enamel weather-stained bell button and the ringing hammered out like a fire engine, startling me. You could have heard it on the main road.

I waited fully a minute; nothing. I reached forward again, more tentatively now, and gave the button a short stab. Another minute . . . silence.

Putting my ear to the gap in the door I listened hard . . . all I could make out was the faint ticking of a clock. I put my finger on the door and pushed it gently. It swung noiselessly open. I went in.

Slowly and quietly along the hall on the worn wrinkled carpet . . . All the doors were wide open: kitchen and toilet on my left, two bedrooms on my right, the living room at the bottom where I could see the side of the big ticking grandfather clock as I approached.

Stopping outside the living-room door I peered through

the narrow gap at the hinge side to make sure no one stood behind it. I saw only a thin slice of the room: yellowed wallpaper on the ceiling, dark curtains, old brown sofa, mother-of-pearl tiled fireplace surrounding an unlit gas fire, dark carpet, maybe brown . . . no occupant . . . silent . . . not a breath.

Leaning forward, I put my head around the door.

Empty.

An old TV on splaying legs in the corner; a wooden magazine rack stuffed untidily full. Two watercolour landscapes on the wall, no mirrors. On the mantelpiece a six by four brass frame held a black and white photograph of Beckman's mother aged around forty. The resemblance was quite noticeable. I also felt, for some reason, that I knew her.

Her son was nowhere to be seen. Still moving quietly, I searched the house. In the kitchen a shrink-wrapped chicken lay in a glass dish, defrosting instructions uppermost. Beside it a bottle of red wine had been opened, it was still full.

Wherever Beckman had gone it looked like he'd intended to be back long before now.

From the kitchen window I could see a long back garden, badly overgrown. At the bottom stood a big shed. The keys were in the kitchen door. I went out.

That smell was strong now.

The shed rested on railway sleepers. Sackcloth tacked inside covered the windows. The door was padlocked. I went back for the bunch of keys which hung in the kitchen door. The smallest one on the ring opened the padlock.

A loose bottom hinge left the door jammed against the base of the frame. I lifted it slightly and it creaked open letting in daylight. Against the back wall was the heavy bench. On top of it lay the hood with the chain sewn in and on the floor I found my bloodstains.

So it was Beckman. I felt a sudden powerful urge for

revenge; no curiosity, no 'why me?', just a violent impulse to get my own back. If I could rescue David Cooper at the same time then fine, but my main aim at that moment was to find Beckman, get him back to this cold wooden torture chamber and give him exactly the same as he'd given me, stroke for stroke.

Returning to the house I searched as neatly and methodically as I could through drawers, in cupboards, even in the hollow body of the grandfather clock. I found nothing to link Beckman to either of the murders. Two scrapbooks filled with Press cuttings gave me hope for a while. I was convinced when I opened them I'd find something relating to the murder of Gilmour or Donachy but there was nothing, just general racing pictures and race reports.

One odd item in the scrapbook: a defaced black and white picture of the finish of a race (looked like Sandown) where the second horse and jockey had been slashed beyond recognition. Why put a ruined picture in an album? On the telephone table I found a scrap of yellow paper with the words, 'check Ruger' and what looked like a telephone number. I pocketed it.

Suddenly remembering Lisa I glanced at my watch; I'd been here almost half an hour. I hurried out past the Audi then stopped and went back to it. The door was open. I quickly searched inside; nothing. Just a few odds and ends in the glove compartment. I sprang the interior boot-catch, got out, raised the lid and saw inside, an old type-writer without a cover.

Smiling, I reached down to lift it. Behind me someone shouted, 'Leave it!'

I turned. At the top of the back garden about a hundred yards away Claude Beckman was climbing the fence. He had a gun. I grabbed the typewriter and ran.

Just through the gate I heard a blast then the hedge to my left being peppered by shot. I raced down the track

scared to look round in case I overbalanced and praying
to God the car would be there.

It was. Lisa saw the panic on my face and started the
engine. I jumped in and Lisa pulled away with my door
still swinging open. I looked up the track expecting to see
Beckman taking aim but there was no sign of him.

Stabbing McCarthy's number into the phone I told
Lisa what had happened. Couldn't get a signal out to
McCarthy, bad reception among all these hills. I told Lisa
to stop at the hotel again and we'd call Mac from there.

We stopped in the car park. I leaned back slowly in the
passenger seat, sweat prickling my scalp. Lisa lit a cigarette. Her brown almost-oriental eyes looked at me as her
cheeks hollowed sucking in smoke. 'Think he'd have killed
you?' she asked.

'Put it this way, I wouldn't like to go back and give him
another shot.'

'What if he's following us in his car?'

'My guess is he'll be packing his bags and heading in
the opposite direction.'

'I hope you're right.'

The landlord was in the hall trundling an old manual
carpet sweeper back and forth. He was small and round
and his fat shiny face showed no surprise at seeing me for
the second time and Lisa for the third.

He stopped and leant on the handle of the sweeper
and said in his strong Welsh accent, 'Not lost again, are
we?'

'Just wanted to use the phone,' I said.

'Up the stairs through the door,' he said. 'Only takes
fifties.'

'I'll reverse the charges,' I said as we started climbing.

McCarthy listened in silence, broke off to call the cops
then rang me back. He said, 'So it looks like we might
have a little PR problem on top of everything else.'

'What are you talking about?'

'The Jockey Club, I mean, with Beckman being, well, an employee.'

'Big deal. He'll need more than a PR man once the police have paid him a visit.'

Lisa, sitting on the chair, smiled up at me. Mac said, 'What do you plan to do now?'

'I plan to ask you to find out as much as you can about Beckman, especially his past and to get me names of his friends and acquaintances, any clubs he's a member of, what he does in his spare time, all that sort of stuff. I want to know why he bears a big enough grudge against me to half beat me to death then have a second go with a shotgun.'

'I'll see what I can do.'

We went downstairs and had a ploughman's lunch and a short talk with the landlord about Beckman. Short because he knew little about him other than that he was involved with racing. Beckman had been in the cottage about six years and had never, to his knowledge, even been in the hotel for a drink.

We started the long drive across country, planning to stop at Lisa's place so she could pack a few more things and move in with me for a couple of days. Around midafternoon I nailed something that had been niggling me for hours, the scrap of paper I'd found on Beckman's telephone table.

I dug it out and reached for the mobile then realised the number was only six digits and that I'd need a dialling code.

'Shit,' I said, 'it could be anywhere in the country.'

Lisa said, 'Try Directory Inquiries for the code local to Beckman's area. If it was outside that he'd probably have written the code as well.'

I tried the operator. Lisa was right. The number rang out, then an answerphone clicked on and in a cidery accent someone thanked me for ringing 'Sparky's' (at least I think that was what he called it), apologised for his absence and said that opening hours till April were six till ten weekdays and ten till ten weekends.

Sparky's . . . what kind of business were they running? What did Beckman have to do with it and who was Ruger?

It was after seven when we got back to the lodge, the night lit by a full moon. The place was cold but seemed much more welcoming to two than one. Mac had left a message on my answerphone: when the police reached Beckman's place he'd gone. The shed I'd been held captive in was a smouldering heap of ashes. They had alerted other forces to be on the look-out for Beckman. Nothing else we could do at the moment.

Delving into my dwindling stock of low calorie packet meals we ate dinner and shared a bottle of wine then settled down by the fire to plan the next day's moves. Lisa rang the hospital. Susan was still under sedation.

I remembered Sparky's and got the number out again.

No West Country burr this time, the voice at the other end was young and vigorous. 'Sparky's.'

I chanced my arm. 'Can I speak to Mister Ruger, please?'

A few seconds' silence then, 'You winding me up?'

'Not intentionally.'

'*Mister* Ruger?'

'That's who I was told to ask for.'

'Somebody's winding *you* up then.'

'How come?'

'Ruger is a make of gun.'

Just to make sure he hadn't misheard me I said, 'Different from a Luger?'

'Completely different.'

'Oh, well, I guess Claude Beckman was pulling my leg.'

'That'd be a first.'

I hesitated, wondering how far to push my luck. 'Oh, he finds his sense of humour sometimes.'

'I'll take your word for it . . . Listen, are you going to be seeing Mister Beckman soon?'

'I hope so.'

'Tell him the gun's arrived, will you, and we've paid for it up front.'

'That'll be the Ruger?'

'The Ruger Blackhawk.'

'Will do, thanks.'

I hung up. Although the puzzle pieces seemed to be coming together the picture wasn't getting any clearer. I rang McCarthy and told him about the gun club. He said he'd let Kavanagh know then told me he himself had dug up some stuff on Beckman.

'Two different sources have told me the same thing but can't support it with any evidence. I'm still trying to get verification,' he said.

'What is it?'

'It looks like Mister Beckman, in the past, has been a very bad boy.'

Chapter Twenty-one

Mac said, 'Beckman studied law at Oxford for three years then dropped out to take a job as a management consultant in London. After a year in the UK he moved into international management consultancy which turned out, according to my sources, to be a cover for what do you think?'

'I dunno, Mac . . . drug-running?'

'Try gun-running. He was an arms dealer.'

'Hardly looks the type, does he? Anyway, that's not illegal, is it?'

'Depends. If you obtain proper end-user certificates and export/import licences from the governments concerned then you're okay. It seems Beckman stuck to the shady side, forging the certificates, bribing officials; he's supposed to have made a few quid and got out. Bought his mother a couple of racehorses, got himself a boat, took a respectable job with The Jockey Club.'

'Didn't your people check him out?'

'Of course. Rock solid. Impeccable references.'

'Probably wrote them himself. How long was he gun-running, then?'

'Maybe as long as seven years.'

'Was he involved in Ireland?'

Mac hesitated. 'Do you think he had something to do with the deaths of Gilmour and Donachy?'

I sighed. 'I don't know what to think. If Beckman's the

killer why didn't he kill me when he had me locked up? To beat me the way he did he must have hated my guts but still not badly enough to kill me . . . How could he have killed the others?'

We kicked it around a while longer and Mac said he'd see what else he could find out.

A lamp glowed in the corner of the big room and the fire was going well, sounding like a small furnace as the air in the chimney sucked up the flames. Lisa sat on the rug, I lay on my front at the far edge of it, the heat warming away the ache on my right side. Lisa held a wine glass. I sipped whisky and balanced my chin on the rim of the glass.

Lisa said, 'That glass'll break and you'll have more scars.'

'Mmmm.'

We were silent again for a while, staring at the flames. Lisa said, 'When I was a kid I always dreamed of living in a place like this, big and old in the middle of nowhere, a roaring fire in a dark room, making toast with a long golden fork and drinking hot chocolate . . . listening to the wind and rain battering the outside, making me feel cosy.'

Chin still on glass I mumbled, 'Bit short on golden forks, I'm afraid.'

'You're not too well stocked with hot chocolate or bread either.' I smiled. She said, 'What did you want to be when you were a kid?'

'A jockey.'

'Always?'

'Well, after hearing the shattering news, when I was about three, that I couldn't be the king.' I raised my elbows now to prop up my chin and looked at Lisa. 'You know,' I said, 'I'll always remember that, the first time anyone had ever asked me what I wanted to be when I grew up. Well it struck me that kings and queens had a pretty fine life of it and that's what I'd set my heart on. My mother laughed and said it was impossible 'cause you had to be born into the proper family. It was the first time I can recall feeling a sense of injustice.'

'At three?'

'Around then . . . well, I dunno, maybe five or six.'

'You don't get much more precocious than that.'

'Nah, first signs of an incurable romantic, that was all.' She drank and the flames danced through the clear liquid.

'What about family?' she asked and waited in open-faced anticipation for the start of my life history. I thought about changing the subject but ploughed on reluctantly.

'My parents are still alive and I've got a sister some-where and a nephew but I don't see any of them.'

I wasn't looking at her. She hesitated then said, 'Family feud?'

'Sort of.'

She saw I was uneasy. 'You'd rather not talk about it.'

'Not tonight.'

'Fine. What are the plans for tomorrow?'

Next morning at seven I was wakened by the telephone. It rang about twenty times before I got downstairs to answer it. It was Jack Cooper looking for news of his son. I mentioned he'd been seen with Beckman though I decided, for two reasons, not to tell him Beckman had also disappeared.

One, I didn't think Beckman had the boy or he'd have been locked up in the house or the outhouse as I'd been. And two, I didn't want Cooper senior flying off the handle at the inference of a homosexual relationship.

'So you haven't really made any headway?' he said.

'I suppose not.'

His language made me glad he wasn't employing me direct.

'David had his own place, didn't he?' I asked him.

'I bought him a nice flat in Sutton Coldfield.'

'I'd like to see it.'

'Fine. Pick the keys up at my office.'

'*You* carry a set?'

'Why not? It was my money that bought it!'

'Only asking. You been there since he disappeared?'

'I was there yesterday.'

'Was all his gear still there, clothes, shoes, passport, stuff like that?'

'How would I know?'

'I thought you might have looked. Why did you go there?'

'To see if he'd left a note or something.'

'And did he?'

'Don't be so bloody silly! Look, I haven't got time for this. Come and pick up the keys, they'll be with my secretary. Let me know what's happening.'

He hung up.

Lisa was impressed with David's flat. It had a big floor area, all wood with a few rugs, no fitted carpets. Six steps led you three feet above the sitting-room floor onto a broad interior verandah with a curving handrail. Opposite this a room divider made the place look much smaller and concealed lighting added to the cosy effect.

The furniture was floral, cottagey except for a wooden rocking chair by the fire. There was a narrow floor-to-ceiling bookcase with few spaces and watercolours hung above big pot plants.

Lisa said, 'Well there's your answer about the girlfriend, he's got one.'

'You think so?'

'Definitely. This is a woman's house.'

'So all men have bad taste in decor?'

'Maybe not bad but not as good as this. Look at the lighting arrangement, the plants.'

'Maybe he used an interior designer.'

'Maybe . . . a female.'

I shook my head. 'Grab a seat, I'm going to have a look around.' The bedroom had three tall narrow windows all on one wall. White paint, carpet and bed fabrics. Glass-topped tables either side of the bed held black anglepoise lamps, a phone and a book. A portable TV sat on the table below the window and binoculars lay on the bed. The white wardrobes were built in and held a lot of clothes.

Young Cooper had always dressed well and if he'd gone of his own accord he'd left plenty of stuff behind; half a dozen suits, two blazers, maybe ten shirts, four pairs of shoes, a rack of ties . . . I skimmed through the big shallow drawers: underwear, more shirts, odds and ends of cufflinks, a couple of pens, aftershave, tissues.

In the bottom drawer were two padded envelopes, three feet by two, unsealed. I slipped them out and eased framed watercolours from the open flaps. Both were country scenes, very well done. And very similar in style to the ones on Beckman's walls.

Why weren't *these* on David's walls? I looked closer. David Campbell Cooper's signature was on both. I called Lisa through.

'They're beautiful,' she said.

Going back to the living area we checked the pictures on the walls: all David's.

We persevered for a while longer but found nothing important, no passport, no wallet, no toiletries even, though that meant little. If he'd left on Monday with the intention of travelling to his mother's house that night he would have taken an overnight bag.

'We'd better get going,' I said.

Lisa said, 'Just let me finish the plants.'

She hurried through to the sitting room and picked up a half-full plastic jug. 'You never know how long he'll be gone, don't want them to die of thirst.'

David's flat was in a block of four. Hoping for a clue we tried all the neighbours: nobody home.

We had lunch at a country pub and sat down to take stock of progress. This was Friday afternoon. The boy had been missing since Monday. Whatever way you looked at it we were about as far forward as a snail on a treadmill.

I told Lisa how similar the paintings in David's flat were to those in Beckman's house. She said, 'So their relationship could have been as simple as buyer and seller?'

'Exactly.'

We decided that Beckman might have made some friends among the other members of his gun club, someone who, at least, might have been able to confirm where he'd got the watercolours. Failing that I'd ask the police if we could go back to Beckman's place for another look around.

On the way to the gun club, Lisa rang the hospital: Susan was stable but wouldn't be seeing visitors for the next few days. Lisa was upset. She talked about Susan for miles, about their schooldays, happier times.

The gun club, about twenty miles from Beckman's place, was a long building, its strip of floodlights on the roof visible above a high wall. As we approached the glass doors two men came through them. I knew both: Kavanagh and Miller.

At his syrupy best Kavanagh said, 'Mister Malloy, how nice to see you!'

I tried to remember if he'd met Lisa before and hoped he hadn't. I introduced her as a friend. Even Miller smiled.

''Fraid we beat you to it tonight, Mister Malloy,' Kavanagh said.

'Looks like it,' I said. 'Find out anything useful?'

Kavanagh kept smiling, darting show-off glances at Lisa as he teased me. 'Plenty.'

'But nothing you can talk about.'

'Not to the, uh, general public.'

'Fine. I'll bear that in mind next time I have some information.'

'Don't be childish,' Kavanagh said, 'it doesn't suit you.'

'What about Beckman's place?' I asked. 'You been there?'

'Hours ago.'

'Did you notice two watercolours hanging in the living room?'

'Can't say I did. Why, thinking of setting up as an art critic?' He flashed a little aren't-I-clever smile at Lisa.

'Forget it,' I said, and turned away.

They sniggered as we headed for the club and Kavanagh said, 'Goodnight, ma'am, nice meeting you.'

Suddenly remembering Beckman's typewriter, which was still in my car, I called Kavanagh back and gave it to him.

'Try not to lose it,' I said, 'you'll probably find that my Cheltenham threat and the anonymous tip-off to Doctor Donnelly were typed on it.'

Kavanagh sneered. 'How very clever of you.'

I ignored it. Lisa and I went inside.

We wasted half an hour talking to several people. Nobody there had ever known Beckman socially. He was a regular on the range but very much a loner. No one could remember his even having a drink in the club bar.

I said to Lisa, 'We'll get a break soon. We're due one. You'll see.' I wasn't sure if she believed me.

Back late at the lodge, fed and watered, wounds tended, sitting together again by the fire, I rang McCarthy and told him about meeting Kavanagh and Miller at the gun club. 'Heard anything from them?' I asked.

'Their boss rang me. Beckman was a long-term member there. He had a case full of guns.'

'All kept at the club?'

'Yep. Strictly legal.'

'I'm sure.'

'Among his collection was a Model Ninety-two F Beretta, the same type that was used to kill Gilmour and Donachy.'

'How significant is that? Statistics wise, I mean.'

Mac sighed. 'That's the point, around forty per cent of their members have that gun and the club owner thinks that would be a fair reflection countrywide. But we'll soon know. The police have Beckman's gun and it's being sent for tests.'

'Does Inspector Sanders think he killed Gilmour and Donachy?' I asked.

'He won't commit but I think Beckman's quickly becoming chief suspect.'

'I think he'll find himself on the wrong trail.'

I told Mac about the watercolours then asked if he minded me doing my own thing over the next couple of days, talking to Beckman's colleagues and maybe a few of the Stewards, sniffing around discreetly in high places.

'What's the point? You said you don't think Beckman's the killer?'

'That's right but I'm still anxious to know why he bears me such a big grudge. *And*, in the absence of anything else, he's still the only link I've got to young Cooper.'

'Okay, just try to upset as few people as possible.'

Lisa and I talked till late making plans for the weekend. Any discretion would be as much for her benefit as The Jockey Club's. I was still very much aware of her job security even if she wasn't. She changed my dressings, we drank one whisky each then went to our separate rooms.

Saturday and Sunday were spent making appointments by phone and driving fast to keep them. We spoke to a number of Beckman's acquaintances, none of whom could tell us anything useful. We even traced a couple of David

Cooper's old schoolfriends, though we'd nothing to show for it.

Sunday evening found me pretty dispirited and my mood began seeping into Lisa. The combination of a lack of success and confusion – in my mind at least – about how we really felt about each other made me think we needed a break.

I suggested she might want to go home that night and take Monday off, then maybe we could both come back with a fresh approach. She seemed relieved, packed her things, kissed me lightly on the cheek and said to ring right away if anything sudden came up.

I watched her drive off with mixed feelings but when I closed the door I knew I was glad to be on my own again with my thoughts. I've been a loner most of my life, acutely so in the last six years. Didn't know now if I'd ever adjust to the idea of a regular partner. And on this Sunday night I didn't much care.

Seven-thirty next morning the phone rang. I hurried downstairs cursing Jack Cooper and making a mental note to leave it off the hook at night.

It was McCarthy. I could feel the tension in his voice when he said my name.

'What is it, Mac?'

'Another corpse.'

'David Cooper?'

'Garfield Rowlands.'

I couldn't place him.

'Used to be a trainer,' Mac said, 'retired two years ago.'

'He wasn't Irish?'

'English through and through.'

'Shot?'

'Centre of the forehead, shoulder broken this time rather than his leg.'

'Bloody hell . . . Any note?'

'One was pinned through the flesh of his throat with a sharpened nail . . . usual chapter and verse numbers.'

'Which translate to?'

'"And I looked, and behold a pale horse: and the name that sat on him was death."'

'Was the same gun used?'

'We don't know yet.'

We were both silent for a few moments. I said, 'This is getting serious, Mac.'

He said, 'I'm heading for Yorkshire now. Want to meet me up there?'

I pondered. 'Mac, I don't know what to do. I'm supposed to be trying to find David Cooper and it now looks like the killer doesn't have him. Which, if I want this twenty grand reward, kinda sends me off in another direction.'

He got agitated at the thought of me pulling out. 'But the boy could be anywhere! It could take you years to find him!'

That was an argument too. I was becoming increasingly convinced that the kid had simply run away. 'Look,' I said, 'let me ring his father. I'll call you back.'

I think Jack Cooper was quietly impressed at me ringing him so early in the day. I told him about Rowlands and he didn't hide his relief that it hadn't been David. I also explained about Mac and how my loyalties were divided.

He said, 'Listen, Malloy, go after this crazy bastard. If you're right and he hasn't got David then at least I'll know the boy's probably safe.'

'And what if David turns up while I'm helping trying to track the killer down? I've suddenly done twenty grand, haven't I?'

'Tough titty. What are The Jockey Club paying you to help out?'

'McCarthy can authorise a fee depending on results. It

might feed me for a month or two but I won't retire on it.'

He was quiet for a moment then said, 'Look, I'm feeling generous. If David turns up safe *and* you help catch this maniac, you get paid.'

'What if I help catch him and David doesn't turn up?'

'Too bad. You get nowt. It all revolves around my son coming back home in one piece. Fair enough?'

'Fair enough.'

I called McCarthy back. 'Where do you want to meet?'

Chapter Twenty-two

I called Lisa. She was at the lodge just after nine. Fifteen minutes later we were heading for Yorkshire.

Rowlands' place was in Middleham, a sort of Newmarket of the north. McCarthy said he'd meet me there so we could go and speak to Jeff, the dead man's son. Rowlands' wife had died two years ago and Jeff, their only child, was reputed to be difficult to deal with. Mac was certain he wouldn't talk to me on my own.

I warned Lisa that she'd have to bail out before we met Mac and that I'd pick her up later.

She said, 'Why don't you take this investigating up full-time, Eddie? Then I could leave my crap job and come and work for you. We wouldn't have to go all around the houses then, making sure no one sees me.'

I looked across at her as we buzzed up the A1 in bright sunshine. 'I'm not sure I could afford you.'

She smiled. 'I work cheap.'

'How cheap?'

'What can you afford?'

'*That* cheap?' She laughed. 'Anyway,' I said, 'it's all right driving a nice comfortable car around, anybody can do that but when it comes down to the important stuff, the detailed investigation . . .'

'Detailed investigation! What *detailed investigation* have you been doing recently?'

'Well, there's lots of sort of subliminal stuff; I'm always quietly assessing things, storing data.'

She smiled, knowing I was winding her up.

The rest of the journey (much of it spent weaving through the orange acne of road cones) passed in good humour considering the prospect that was ahead and the three corpses that lay behind. At least there was a chance of a fresh lead instead of bouncing from pillar to post on the Beckman/Cooper trail.

We stopped in Northallerton, about twenty miles from Middleham, and Lisa got out in front of a big hotel. She said she'd window-shop to pass the time and that afterwards she'd wait in the reception area of the hotel. I got behind the wheel and even allowing for my still sore back it felt strange to be driving again.

Mac and I had arranged to meet in a pub. He was there when I arrived. Big place, packed with Sunday lunchers. Mac was by the window trying not to look guilty and I guessed temptation had got the better of his diet again. I sat down. Mac said, 'Are you hungry? I've just eaten . . . been here a while.'

'What'd you have?'

'Just a raw salad.'

'Uh-huh, and when did they start serving seafood sauce with raw salad?'

'What?'

I nodded towards the pink blob on the bottom of the dark blue tie overhanging his belly. He flushed slightly. 'It was just a small one.'

'As the actress said to the bishop.'

'Gimme a break, Eddie, you're worse than Jean.'

'So what did you have after the prawn cocktail?'

'A steak,' he said quietly. 'It was grilled. Very little fat.'

'And a couple of glasses of wine?'

'Just one. There aren't many calories in wine.'

'Compared to steak and chips.'

I ribbed him gently a while longer and he made me promise not to tell his wife. I ordered a sandwich and a beer and McCarthy, from habit rather than hunger, looked longingly at both.

He jogged my memory about Garfield Rowlands whom I now recollected vaguely from my riding days, though I'd never actually ridden for him. He'd trained for around fifteen years before giving up two years ago to concentrate on farming since when he'd built up a successful business. He kept a couple of horses and had hunted regularly. Rowlands was sixty-two when he died.

His son, Jeff, was well known to the Security Department as a big punter on the racecourse. He'd been in financial trouble more than once and only just escaped being warned off for gambling debts. Mac suspected him of some shady dealings with jockeys but had never been able to prove anything.

He had agreed readily to see us when Mac had phoned this morning though he looked less than agreeable by the time we got there. Shushing three barking dogs he ushered us into a large kitchen, apologising for his temper.

'Fucking Press!' he explained. 'Been driving me crazy all morning. The phone hasn't stopped. I had to take it off the hook. Six of the bastards are roaming around outside like jackals . . . try to be civil with them then it's (mimicking in a strained high voice) When did you find him? Where was he? How bad were the wounds? Anything missing from the house? Did he have any enemies? . . . Stupid bastards!'

We stood, nodding, trying to be sympathetic. Rowlands Junior was around forty; good thatch of fair wavy hair, strong jaw and nose, only his bulging blue eyes stopped him short of handsome. Slim and fit-looking in a casual mustard shirt, brown checked trousers and a light grey pullover, he slid two chairs back from the big dark table and sat us down.

He made coffee, moving around the kitchen in sharp
start-stop moves, like a robot. We offered condolences.
He sat opposite us and a black labrador sidled up for a
comforting pat. Rowlands looked down at the dog and,
rubbing its broad head, said, 'He's gone, old fella . . .
gone.' The big black eyes stared up at him waiting for a
better explanation.

Still comforting the dog Rowlands said, 'Even the animals are fucking shattered.'

Then resting his elbows on the table he massaged his
face with both hands and sighed, which seemed to settle
him a bit. 'I'm sorry,' he said. 'What can I tell you? How
can I help?'

From then on in he was as charming as you could expect
a recently bereaved son to be. We explained about the
other murders and how we thought they were linked and
he said the police had mentioned that.

Was there anything in his father's past that could possibly have set him up for this? Anything that could have
riled some lunatic sufficiently? No, nothing.

The only time his father had ever done anything to upset
anyone was when his head lad had been caught embezzling
money from the farm. The guy, the aptly named Nick
Canning, had helped himself to over twenty grand in a
two-year period and when caught got three years in jail.
Garfield Rowlands, despite promises by Canning to pay
him back and pleas from Canning's wife not to leave their
child fatherless, had testified at the trial.

Jeff Rowlands did point out that at no point had Canning threatened his father and also that Canning, although
involved in fraud before, had no history of violence.

He didn't know where we could find Canning, who'd
been out of prison almost a year, and suggested we
ask around as the man had been in racing most of his
life.

Thinking of Gilmour and Donachy, I asked, 'Do you

know if Canning might have had a grudge against anyone else?'

He shook his head. 'Not to my knowledge. I think you're on the wrong track there anyway. I heard he'd got converted in prison; born-again Christian and all that.'

Mac and I hesitated waiting for him to realise the implication in what he'd just said. It didn't seem to sink home. I said, 'Who told you about this conversion, can you remember?'

Rubbing his forehead he said, 'Christ, no . . . it was ages ago.' Then it reached him and he stopped the tired rubbing and looked at us. 'Did the others have these Bible quotes attached to their bodies?'

Mac, in a particularly bold move for him, admitted, 'Yes, they did . . .'

Rowlands stared.

'. . . but I know the police are especially keen to keep that quiet.'

Rowlands' curls bobbed as he nodded, stunned. 'So Canning *may* have had something to do with it.'

Mac said, 'Put it this way, we'd certainly like to speak to him. I'm sure the police would too.' Mac left him two cards, one with my number, and he promised to get in touch if he found anything out about Canning.

Before we left I asked Rowlands if the quote found on his father meant anything to him: 'And I looked, and behold a pale horse: and the name that sat on him was death . . .' He frowned for a while, staring at the floor, then shook his head. 'Not a thing,' he said.

Outside the main gate stood two journalists and a photographer. They waved us to a halt as we drove through. Mac opened his window. A young eager looking guy in leather bomber and jeans looked in. 'You guys cops? D'you know anything?'

Mac said, 'We know you're making the man in that house very angry.'

'Where is he? Is he coming out? What's he doing just now?'

I leaned across and nodded secretively. The boy bent low and close, looking expectant. I said, 'He's been too busy this morning to feed his rottweilers. At the moment he's baiting them with a rolled-up tabloid newspaper. Then he's going to let them out for a nice run round the farm. That's why we're leaving. Goodbye.'

'And good luck,' Mac said, smiling.

We headed back for the pub to pick up my car. Mac said, 'What do you think of young Mister Rowlands?'

'I don't know, to be honest. If all that Canning stuff was an act, planting the suspicion, pleading on the guy's behalf then just carelessly dropping in the born-again stuff, well, he's an awful ham. It was so bad it makes me think he might well be genuine.'

'I don't know so much. I checked around with a few bookies this morning; Rowlands owes almost eighteen grand, he is in severe trouble.'

'And he's an only child and sole heir to the farm?'

'Correct.'

'Do the police know about his gambling debts yet?'

'I haven't told them.'

'But you will?'

He nodded.

'Kavanagh and Miller on this one too?'

'Yep.'

Smiling, I shook my head. 'No wonder so many villains are running around loose.'

Mac rang Kavanagh on his mobile and asked him to check out Canning. Kavanagh said he'd come back on it.

It was after two-thirty when I reached Northallerton. Lisa sat in a big soft chair, hair falling forward as she concentrated on the magazine in her lap. On the table in front of her was an empty coffee cup. She hadn't noticed me come in.

'Bored?' I asked.

She looked up, clearing the mask of dark hair with a toss of her head. 'Thoroughly,' she said.

'Sorry I've been so long. Mac insisted on me hearing all his theories.'

'Which are?'

'Come on, I'll tell you on the way home. My back's killing me.'

She got up, dragging a plastic bag full of groceries from under the table. 'Been shopping?' I asked.

'For some decent food. I'm sick of that shitty packet stuff you've got piled up in every cupboard.'

I smiled.

On the journey I told her what had happened and that Mac thought Jeff Rowlands might have something to do with his father's death.

'Which would mean,' she said, 'he had killed the others as well.'

'Most likely, but where was the motive for the other two? Okay, so he stands to inherit a million quid's worth of estate from his father, but why would he have killed the other two?'

She thought a while then said, 'Maybe he planned it that way to make it look like some mad serial killer was on the loose. To have killed Tommy and the other chap with absolutely no motive would give him a near perfect alibi or at least a very effective smokescreen for his father.'

I made a face, 'Well . . . I don't know, he just doesn't seem the type. I could just about believe that in total desperation he might have killed his father, but not with such violence. He'd have set up an apparent suicide or something with an overdose or left him sleeping in the car with the engine running. I can't see him breaking his father's shoulder, blasting him between the eyes then nailing something through his throat. God, you'd need to be

completely heartless and deranged to do that to a total
stranger never mind your father.'

'So you think Beckman's still favourite?'

'The police think he is, according to McCarthy, but I'm
still not so sure. I just don't think he has the bottle for it.
The profile's wrong too. The people we spoke to over the
weekend mentioned nothing about Beckman showing any
signs of fanaticism. Now I'd bet Jack Cooper's twenty
grand reward that this guy is an out and out fanatic, some
sort of religious psychopath.'

'Maybe that's what he wants you to think.'

'Maybe, but I doubt it. I mean I'm sure Beckman
abducted me but that was for his own ends. He typed
those notes too, the one at Cheltenham and the one passed
to the doctor at Nottingham. Whatever it is it's personal.
I don't think he's ever killed anyone.'

She braked hard as a Merc pulled out in front of her.
Her eyes blazed. I said, 'Temper, temper.'

Cooling again quickly she said, 'But if Beckman has
some grudge against you, why not the others? I mean,
you don't know why he hates you, maybe he felt the same
about Tommy and . . .'

'Donachy.'

'. . . Yes.'

'And Garfield Rowlands?' I said.

'Sure, why not?'

'So why didn't he hassle them beforehand the way he's
been doing with me? Why weren't their notes typed, like
mine? Why did my note at Cheltenham have the actual
quote written in full while the others had only chapter and
verse references? . . . Why did he kill the others and not
me?'

She pondered a minute then said, 'You're right, that's
a pretty convincing lot of whys.'

'Thank you.'

'So who the hell's doing it?' she asked.

'The sixty-four thousand dollar question.'

'And what's the motive?'

'If we knew that,' I said, 'we'd be halfway there.'

We were quiet again a while, both thinking. I said, 'Do you know the most puzzling part for me . . . ?'

She waited.

'. . . this limb-breaking thing. With Tommy and Donachy he did it less than an hour before killing them. I'd bet the autopsy on Rowlands will prove the same thing. What's the point? If he wants to cause people real suffering before killing them why not beat them senseless? Why not break *two* legs and leave them in agony for hours? I'm sure it's a ritual of some sort, the same as the Bible notes are a ritual, but where the hell do they tie together?'

Lisa said, 'And it was Rowlands' *shoulder* he broke?'

I nodded. Her brow furrowed. She said, 'Why? Why not his leg like the others?'

I shrugged. 'Wish I knew.'

She thought a while then said, 'Was it the same leg with Donachy and Tommy?'

'I don't know.'

'That could be relevant.'

'How?'

'If it's some kind of ritual . . .'

'I'll ask McCarthy.'

Trying to work out the motive we fired intermittent could-bes and what-ifs at each other over the next twenty miles but the possibilities ran out before either of us could come up with a credible theory. We moved on to Beckman again, speculating on his reasons for abducting me, wondering how he'd got to know the details he needed to try this copy-cat thing to scare me but we came up empty once more.

Back home, Lisa, shivering, fixed the fire. There was a message on the answerphone. It was from Jack Cooper's secretary telling me that her boss was in hospital, intensive care. He'd collapsed with a heart attack just after speaking to me this morning and his secretary wondered if maybe I'd given him some bad news on the phone.

I called her and told her what Jack and I had discussed. She said he was still critically ill. I offered my sympathies saying I sincerely hoped he'd pull through. I had no great love for the man but the practical side was that if he died there'd be no reward money.

Lisa said, 'Did he have a heart problem?'

'The way he behaved the man was a walking heart problem. Always rushing around on full steam abusing everybody, he . . .'

The phone rang. I answered.

'Eddie . . . ?'

Rough voice I didn't recognise.

'Ah've been tryin' tae reach ye all day . . . Johnny Angell, we spoke a wee while ago.'

The Scottish newspaperman. 'Of course, how're you doing?'

'Ah'm doin' fine. This murder caper's bubblin' up nicely now, eh?'

'I suppose you could put it that way.'

He paused and I sensed him drawing on a cigarette. 'Whit'd'ye know?' he asked.

'Not a lot.'

'Come on! You were intae this from the beginnin', tryin' tae find out stuff about Tommy Gilmour.'

'Well that was for personal reasons, nothing sinister.'

'It's all sinister in your business, Eddie.'

'That's the way the media like to paint it.'

He paused again for more nicotine then said, 'Know anythin' about a guy called Beckman?'

'I know of him.'

'What's he like?'

'Personally?'

'Aye.'

'Wouldn't know. We're just about on nodding terms, nothing else.'

'D'ye know he's been missin' for a coupla days?'

'I'd heard.'

'We're goin' ahead with a story tomorrow that he is suspect *numero uno* for these murders.'

'You must have some good evidence or some good libel lawyers.'

'We've got both.'

Angell persevered for a while trying to get something quotable but it wasn't too difficult to keep dodging around and in the end he rang off no wiser, leaving the impression that his 'evidence' was based mostly on racecourse gossip.

I phoned McCarthy and told him about Angell and Jack Cooper. He said he'd just heard from Kavanagh about the ex-Rowlands groom, Nick Canning.

Mac confirmed that he had become a born-again Christian in prison. I said, 'I wouldn't read too much into that. I think a lot of these guys do it to help their parole chances.'

He said, 'Maybe, but listen, Jeff Rowlands was mistaken. Canning has a number of convictions for violence, two of them GBH and, listen to this . . . he once broke a guy's forearm with a hammer . . .'

I waited.

'. . . they've found out where he's living and they're going in at dawn tomorrow.'

Chapter Twenty-three

Canning lived with his girlfriend in a grubby rented flat in Lambourn village. We sat a few streets away in Mac's car shivering in the pre-dawn gloom. The police had wanted to go in at 6 a.m. but Mac persuaded them that as half of Lambourn would be up by that time, it would have to be earlier.

It was four-thirty. Cold and windless . . . silent. Pools of knee-high mist visible under the street-lights. Six tense armed cops behind the steamed-up windows of a white van. Eight more in two back-up vehicles. Now and then a cigarette tip glowed.

At four-thirty-three they all got out, softly closing doors behind them, moving quietly through an alley towards Canning's place. We'd been told to stay in the car. Kavanagh glanced back to make sure we were obeying.

Neither of us spoke. I rolled the window down and listened. Three long minutes of complete silence then the echoing crash of what I took to be a door being smashed in. Then a shout and two shots in quick succession.

Ten minutes later most of them came back and got in their vehicles. No sign of Canning or anyone else. Kavanagh and Miller appeared as lights started going on in the houses around us. I got out. Mac followed.

They saw us crossing towards them but didn't stop. We reached them just before they got into their car.

Kavanagh, unusually, looked strained. Miller was his surly self.

Mac said, 'You didn't get him.'

Kavanagh said, 'He wasn't there.'

I said, 'Who got shot?'

Kavanagh said, 'There was a dog in the bedroom, under the bed . . . It ran out suddenly.'

Miller got in the car and slammed the door. I said, 'Any clues where Canning's gone . . . ? Anything on Rowlands' murder?'

Kavanagh shook his head. 'We're still looking,' he said and opened the passenger door to get in.

I said, 'Mind if we have a look around the flat?'

Miller, his face distorted by the wet screen, shouted, 'Yes we do fucking mind! We mind a lot! Now piss off home and give us some fucking peace!' He revved the car and pulled away almost driving over our toes. I said, 'I guess he's not at his best in the mornings.'

Mac said as we walked back to the car, 'It was probably him that shot the dog.'

A bright but heatless sun was up when I got back to the lodge. I'd driven myself to Lambourn, leaving Lisa to sleep. I was tired and sore now.

I lay on the sheet we used for changing the dressings. Lisa said, 'I don't think it's getting much better, Eddie. Maybe you should go back to the doctor.'

I breathed into the pillow. 'There won't be anything else he can do, he'll just tell me to rest . . . It isn't infected anywhere, is it?'

She fingered the unbroken areas very lightly. 'Well, no, I don't think so . . . There's a lot of bruising, discoloration, but there don't look to be any *bad* bits, if you know what I mean. How sore is it?'

'I'll live.'

Some of the later editions of the newspapers carried the story that the police were now anxious to trace Beckman so that they could eliminate him from their inquiries. No mention of Canning.

I laid the newspaper down on the deep sill of the window. Sunlight speckled it through the dirty glass. Lisa moved around in the kitchen making lunchtime sandwiches. The phone rang. It was Mac. He said, 'Major embarrassment for your friends Kavanagh and Miller.'

'I'm listening.'

'I just spoke to Inspector Sanders to get the official line on the raid on Canning's house this morning . . .'

'Uh-huh.'

'The reason Canning wasn't there is that he's been in jail for three months. Assaulted a barman in Newbury. Got a year for it.'

I couldn't suppress a smile.

Mac said, '*And*, they shot his girlfriend's dog, a pedigree poodle she used for breeding. She's suing.'

I suppose I shouldn't have but I laughed. 'That pair wouldn't even get into the Keystone Kops. What's their excuse?'

'They say an informant let them down.'

'Badly,' I said.

'Anyway,' Mac said, 'Canning's out of the running, we're back with Beckman.'

'You might be and the papers might be but he's not for me. The killer's a psycho, a "man with a mission" type. I'm sure of it.'

Mac said, 'So what's the mission?'

'If we find that out we've got him . . . There's *something* in his mind that links the victims so far, some definite tie-up.'

We dissected things again for the umpteenth time and I suggested we'd been looking too closely at the personal lives of the dead men, searching for a connection in their nationalities, their family problems. The only solid link all three had was racing.

'Why don't we have a really close look at the formbook?' I said.

'What for?'

'I don't know, but at the moment we've got nothing else. We might turn up some connection.'

Mac said, 'You're talking about a mountain of work. Where the hell do you start?'

'Weatherbys. They'll probably have everything on computer.'

'Mmmm.'

(Weatherbys are administrators for The Jockey Club.) I said, 'What do you think?'

'Let me make a call.'

Dressed in my dark suit with white shirt and navy and wine floral tie I looked maybe half as good as Lisa in her tight black ski-pants and black polo. We sat in the reception area of Weatherbys in Northampton waiting for our contact, Colin Tindall.

He came smiling towards us, offering his hand three strides away. Mid-thirties, short and thin, maybe nine stone, thick brown eyebrows, grey eyes, he wore a tan shirt and brown trousers.

Lisa had assured me that no one here would know her. I introduced her as Linda just to be safe. I explained to Colin we were there simply to do some research into certain trainers and jockeys.

'How far back do you want to go?'

I thought of Rowlands. 'Could be twelve, fifteen years.'

He made that teeth-sucking noise which pleases people who know something you don't.

I said, 'You're going to tell me it's not on computer.'

'Most of it probably is . . .' He smiled. 'But the system's down at the moment, I'm afraid.'

Lisa asked, 'When is it likely to be up again?'

'This afternoon, hopefully.'

We sat at a long table in a room brightly lit by neon strips, one of which buzzed so annoyingly that I stood on a chair and removed it.

'Let there not be light,' Lisa said.

I said, 'Let there be peace.'

Blue-covered formbooks stood piled around us sand-bagging us in with their weight of information. Each contained a full season's worth of results. Every runner in every race listed right down to last place, every faller and every horse which started but didn't complete. Everything we needed was hidden in those tissue-thin pages but we didn't know where to begin.

What we needed was a huge database where we could key in: list full information on all horses ridden by T. Gilmour, i.e. owner, trainer, breeder, finishing position, betting fluctuations, etc. The same then for Donachy and Rowlands and we could even have tried David Cooper in there in the hope that some link would be thrown up.

That was what we *wanted*.

What we *had* were thousands of galloped miles and forests of jumped fences filtered clean of the bruises and sweat, the shouts and the whip-cracks, the joy and the sadness . . . just dry records, names and places, dates and prices.

Lisa said, 'Maybe we should start with *Horses in Training*, find Mr Rowlands' horses then start checking them one by one in the formbooks.'

I sighed, 'Okay.'

'At least it's a start, Eddie, cheer up.'

'I'm cheered, I'm cheered,' I said, reaching for a copy of *Horses in Training*. 'I'll take last year's if you do the year before.'

'All right. Do you know how long he trained for?'

'Around fifteen years, Mac said.'

Opening her book she raised her eyes to heaven and

said, 'They'll find our skeletons in here covered in cobwebs.'

After an hour I put my pen down, shoved a space among the pile of books and laid my head wearily on the desk, encircling it with my arms. 'God,' I said, 'talk about needles in haystacks.'

Lisa said, 'Eddie, you know the saying, an ounce of persistence is worth a pound of talent.'

'Maybe, but there's got to be an easier way.'

Lisa said, 'Let's list everything we know again.'

'We've done that a hundred times!' I said.

'Maybe we overlooked something.' She was admirably, annoyingly calm.

Pushing myself wearily upright I reached for my note-pad and flipped to a fresh sheet. We went through it all again: victims, names, cause of death, which limb was broken, what the Bible quotes said, traced back the last runner each had had, mixed and matched, stood things on their heads . . . nothing.

Back to the formbooks.

Three fruitless finger-licking cross-eyed hours later McCarthy rang. 'Find anything?' he asked.

'The computers are down and we're not far behind them.'

'We?'

'Me and my fingers,' I improvised. 'It's looking like a very long job, Mac, I think I'll chuck it till the computer's working again. It's like ploughing a field with a fucking fork.' I glanced at Lisa but there was no rebuke for the inadvertent curse, she didn't even glance up.

'When will it be fixed?' Mac asked.

'God knows. This morning they said this afternoon. It's now almost three o'clock . . . I'll give it another hour.'

'Listen,' he said, 'I've been checking the sort of people who use ether regularly . . .'

He did his usual tail-off, waiting for the prompt. 'And?' I said.

'. . . the most common users these days are Animal Research labs . . .'

He left it hanging in the air for my instinct to sniff at. I wondered if he had more to offer. 'Anything else?' I asked.

'That's all.'

'They use it as an anaesthetic?'

'On small animals. They also use it as a sort of cleaning agent.'

'Mmmm . . .' My mind sieved the facts, automatically trying to shake out the relevant pieces . . . fragments tumbled around, *dead jockeys, broken limbs, animal research, crazy quotes* . . . Scraps of Rowlands' Bible verse came back to me: *A pale horse . . . the name on him was death . . . horse . . . death . . .*

'Mac,' I said, 'I think you've cracked it.'

Chapter Twenty-four

Lisa had put her pen down and was watching me. Mac said, 'You think this guy *works* at one of these labs?'

'The opposite,' I said, 'I think he raids them. Probably burns them down.'

Mac said quietly, 'Animal Rights . . .'

I sat smiling, cradling the phone and doodling. Lisa's questioning frown asked if she could be let into the secret. Teasing her a while longer I said to Mac, 'Makes sense, doesn't it?'

'Maybe.'

'No maybes. I'll bet each of the victims has been involved with a horse being killed on the racecourse.'

'That's not saying much,' Mac argued. 'If he was killing people on that basis we'd be piling the corpses into horseboxes.'

'Maybe he's just started, Mac.'

I could almost hear him shiver down the line. 'Don't say that, Eddie.'

I said, 'Look at the evidence. Just assume for a minute what I'm saying is right and look at it. What happens when a horse breaks a leg?'

'It gets destroyed, shot.'

'Where?'

'Between the eyes.'

'Right. Now suppose this madman has decided someone is directly responsible for each horse death. What would

be his idea of perfect revenge . . . ? Letting them suffer
the exact same fate! Break one of their limbs, leave them
writhing in agony for about as long as it would take to get
a vet there, then put them out of their misery with a bullet
in the forehead.'

Knowing it was the best theory so far we kicked it
around a while longer, aware that we had to narrow the
field. Mac had a point, anything up to a thousand horses
had probably died on racecourses in the past decade.
Somehow this guy had to be fining it down. We had to
uncover his method of selection.

Watching Lisa as we talked I saw she'd picked up the
thread and halfway through our conversation she knew
exactly what we were on to. She started working back
through the formbooks.

Mac asked me to ring Hubert Barber and find out if
any of *his* recent fatalities had been ridden by Tommy
Gilmour. He said he'd contact Jeff Rowlands and Donachy's main retainer with the same question.

He hung up. I held the receiver ready to dial Barber's
number. I smiled at Lisa. 'Guess you caught the gist of
that.'

'Uh-huh,' she said, not looking up from her book.

I said, 'What are you doing?'

She looked at me from beneath her dark eyebrows.
'Sleuthing.' She said, 'Is that what you call it?'

I nodded, smiling, and dialled Barber's number. He was
out racing. I tried his mobile. No answer. I put the receiver
down waiting for Mac to call back. Lisa was still engrossed
in the formbook.

Amused at her commitment, especially now that we'd
cracked it, I watched her; hair hanging heavy and luxuriantly forward like drawn curtains on her fine features,
shaped paint-free nails on elegant fingers slipping softly
between pages then slowly up through the shield of hair
to be moistened by her tongue . . .

'*Sleuthed* anything yet?' I asked.

'Just about,' she lilted, like an incantation. I smiled again, relaxed in her company, happy in the glow of success. Lisa glanced up. 'You look like the cat that's got the cream,' she said.

I nodded. 'Double helpings.'

She flicked over one more page tracing a finger down it and said, 'Shouldn't start licking my chops just yet.'

'Why not?'

She closed the book, threw back her hair, tidying it with her fingers, then rested her chin in cupped hands. She said, 'You want to know how this guy's targeting people?'

'Mac should be calling back in about two minutes with that info,' I said.

'I'll tell you now, if you want . . . who he's going for and in what order.'

'I'm listening.'

She tossed her hair again. 'Well, it's sort of good news and bad news . . .'

I waited.

'. . . his target is people involved with horses killed in the Grand National. He's taking them in chronological order, in reverse. Tommy last year, Donachy's horse was destroyed the previous year and one trained by Rowlands, a grey incidentally, hence the "pale horse" quote, the year before that.'

I was staring at her now. 'Brilliant,' I said and moved quickly down beside her. She showed me the pages, carefully marked. I read through. She was right.

'How did you twig it?' I asked.

'The Grand National's only two weeks away, it was in my mind. There's always some sort of protest there anyway so I thought it was a good bet for the first shot. I hit lucky.' She smiled, pleased but not triumphant. I'd have been doing handsprings. I felt like kissing her but thought she might consider it patronising.

I settled for squeezing her shoulder and saying brilliant again and well done.

I tried to get back to a businesslike tone. 'So we also know who's lined up next?'

She nodded. 'That's the bad news . . .'

I could tell by her eyes. 'Me?' I asked.

She nodded.

'Can't be,' I said, lifting the books again. 'I didn't ride the year before Rowlands or the year before that.'

'No fatalities in either of those Nationals,' Lisa said. 'In the previous one there were three . . . you rode one of them.'

My mind went back six years . . . Mylah, big black horse, took a horrible fall at Becher's, broke his neck . . .

Lisa, arms folded, watched me. 'Who were the other two jocks?' I asked.

She glanced at her notes. 'A. Crawford and M. Pelham.'

I remembered. 'Alan's retired,' I said, 'Mark is still riding.'

'Well we'd better get in touch with them pretty damn fast.'

I dialled McCarthy's number – engaged. I rang Kavanagh while Lisa scanned the paper to see where Pelham was riding today. Kavanagh, as usual, was about as receptive as a rubber lightning rod. I said, 'Look, it's the best theory we've got *by far*.' I told him Pelham was riding at Sandown and that he'd better make sure he got some protection.

Finding Alan Crawford was going to be more difficult. Many ex-jockeys stay in racing in some capacity but from what I could remember Crawford had disappeared altogether. I told Kavanagh what I knew of him which wasn't much and said I'd try and get more info from McCarthy.

I rang him – still engaged.

Lisa had the formbooks open again. I said, 'Take a break. You've done enough.'

She didn't look up. 'Might as well keep tracing back through the Nationals, see how long a list we might be looking at.'

'I'll give you a hand,' I said and hauled another ten years of formbooks off the shelf.

Opening the first one near the back, I sprayed page-edges off my thumb at a hundred a second till I reached early April and the three-day Grand National meeting.

Almost whispering, Lisa asked, 'Think they'd mind if I smoked?'

'Probably, but what the hell.'

Head down I heard her fumble in her bag, open the packet and click the lighter . . . I waited for the mild smell of menthol tobacco to reach me.

The next half-hour of searching was interspersed with companionable mumbling and throwaway comments that sought no response stronger than a grunt or an 'Mmmm'. When another name was added to the list I'd picture the face. Very few were unfamiliar to me. Lisa knew her fair share too.

I tried McCarthy again. Still nothing. We ploughed on, silent for a long spell. Lisa stopped once and said, 'You know Rowlands? I wonder why he killed the trainer rather than the jockey?'

It was a good point. I didn't know the answer. We ploughed on.

Making notes, Lisa said, 'The further back you go the more fallers there seem to be.'

'Mmm, they say the fences have got easier in the past few years.'

'Have they?'

'I haven't ridden in it for a long time but I doubt if they're that much different. The people who say it's not as tough are mostly fat journalists who've never sat on anything wilder than a bar stool. Put them on half a ton of snorting steeplechaser and aim them at Becher's at thirty miles an hour, then ask how easy the fences are.'

'So how come there are fewer fallers lately?'

I shrugged. 'Maybe the jocks are getting more sensible.'

'Doubt it. I think the fences *are* easier.'

I glanced up. A glint of devilment was in her eyes. 'You're just trying to wind me up.'

'Makes a change from the other way around,' she said. 'You know something, I –'

The door opened. McCarthy came in, smiling as he saw me. He closed the door and saw Lisa and the smile disappeared. She looked at me. I looked at him. He said, 'Tell me it's not true.'

My brain, weary from scanning small print, refused to come up with a plausible excuse or one of any kind for that matter. I simply nodded. Mac took his trilby off and dropped it on the table with an air of resignation and defeat. Drawing a chair out he sat down slowly. Lisa and I were at opposite ends, she on his right, I on his left.

Unbuttoning his brown tweed jacket he looked at me and his whole face said, I knew you were stupid, Eddie, but I didn't think you were this stupid.

I said, 'Mac, I needed help.'

He kept staring.

'I needed a driver and I needed somebody smart and somebody who could keep their mouth shut.'

He shook his head slowly.

'Lisa didn't want to do it, I talked her into it.'

Lisa said, 'Didn't take much persuading, Eddie.' She was smiling. Mac looked at her and said, 'Don't tell me any more. I *do not* want to know any more.'

I said, 'Lisa's found the key – the Grand National. We'd have been struggling for a long time without her.'

Mac said, 'Why are you trying to justify it? You can spend all day saying this and that but in the end you know you shouldn't even be talking to each other, never mind working together.'

I said, 'What's the problem, Mac? Lisa's not even in your department, you've got no responsibility for her, just forget you came here.'

His jaw muscles bulged as he ground his teeth. 'Eddie, I've got a *responsibility* to enforce the bloody rules of racing! That's what my job is!'

'Come on, it's hardly a rule of racing; a personnel department rule, maybe but . . .'

'Same bloody thing to me, isn't it?'

'Calm down, Mac, we'll work something out.'

He raised a hand, pointing at me. 'I'm warning you now, Eddie, don't try and tie me in to any of your schemes.'

I did my 'honest' gesture, open hands, wounded look. 'No schemes, promise . . . let's get through the important stuff and work this out later. Lisa found the link, it . . .'

He was still angry. 'Eddie! Don't –'

'Mister McCarthy . . .' Lisa spoke quietly but firmly. Mac turned to look at her and she held him calmly and confidently with her gaze for a few seconds then said, '. . . I wouldn't compromise your position in any way, I'd resign first.'

McCarthy's face tried weakly for a chivalrous look but it was relief that appeared. He blustered, 'Well, there's, uh, there's no need to talk about that . . . not at this stage.'

Smiling, she said, 'I just wanted to reassure you.'

He nodded, stuck for words. I got up, dragged my chair and books alongside him and motioned to Lisa. 'Want to move along and show Mac what you found?'

And she did, with enthusiasm and warmth and that pulsing vitality that made me think she was capable of anything. The commitment and dedication in her eyes, that singular intensity when she sat close and spoke to you had Mac looking mesmerised and miserable after ten minutes because he was so taken with her by then he knew he'd never be able to hand her over to the sheriff.

When Lisa finished talking I tried to draw McCarthy into a three-way debate, an analysis of what we had so far. He stopped me short.

'Can I have a word outside?'

I nodded. He got up, smiling apologetically at Lisa. She looked at me and pulled a big-eyed face that said, You're in trouble now!

In the corridor Mac said in a tight-throated, aggravated whisper, 'Eddie, don't try and get me in any deeper! How can you expect me to sit and discuss confidential business with . . . with a Jockey Club stenographer? For Christ's sake! You're putting my bloody job on the line as it is!'

'You seemed pretty receptive in there when she was talking.'

'Well I came to my senses when she stopped . . .'

He was speaking more naturally now, though anger still simmered in his eyes. He said, 'Look, I'm willing to forget I came here today but you drop her right now. You're doing her no favours and you're not helping yourself.'

'What's that supposed to mean?'

'It means if anyone finds out what she's been doing she'll lose her job; it's not worth it!'

'Listen, nobody's –'

His face told me an especially nasty thought had occurred to him and he interrupted, 'Tell me you haven't been visiting yards with her or talking to anyone . . .'

'I'm not that stupid, Mac; look, you're over-reacting . . .'

'That's your answer to everything, Eddie, fend off all criticism as over-reaction. You never stop to think of other people, of the position you're putting them in. No, no . . . as long as it suits Eddie Malloy then everyone else can go to hell in a handcart.'

His chubby face reddened with anger and from the exertion of moving his hands around so much while he talked.

It was pointless arguing with him in this mood. He took my silence as acquiescence. That turned his thermostat down and he started cooling off.

Pacing a few strides back and forth he composed himself and said quietly, gravely, 'We've got a lot of work to do, a lot of planning. Now please tell Miss Ffrench her services are no longer needed and ask her to go home. You can reassure her that I won't mention our meeting to anyone but if it happens again I will be forced to . . . Okay?'

Trying to look deflated, repentant, I nodded. Mac stood straight, looking proud of himself for having been so forceful.

'Gimme a couple of minutes,' I said quietly. He nodded imperiously, granting the request. I smiled as I turned away.

I told Lisa the choice was hers, she could quit now or stay on. I told her what Mac had said so she knew the risks.

'It's only a job, Eddie,' she said, 'there are others. I'm not quitting now, it's just getting interesting. I'll pack my job in.'

'When?'

'Now.' She smiled and reached for the phone.

I suddenly felt very serious and responsible. I grasped her elbow gently. 'Lisa, listen . . . what are you going to live on? It's not as if I can pay you . . . Well not much anyway.'

She was dialling, still smiling. 'I've got that worked out.'

'But when this is finished, I mean I'll just be a jockey again. It's not as if I can set up as a detective agency or something, what will – ?'

She hushed me with a finger to her lips as the call connected. She spoke to her boss and told him she was leaving. He tried to talk her out of it, then tried to hold her to her notice period. He dropped that quickly when she said she was getting involved in something that would

probably compromise The Jockey Club. He asked her to
fax her resignation immediately.

Putting the phone down she crossed her arms and leant
back against the table still smiling and enjoying my
bemusement.

'You don't hang about, do you?' I said.

She shrugged. 'Procrastination's the thief of time and
all that.'

'Sometimes impulsiveness isn't much better. What are
you going to live on?'

'How about half of the reward money for finding David
Cooper?'

'And how long do you think that's going to take?'

She smiled wide and picked up a formbook. 'Not long
at all because, courtesy of this little book, I know where
he is.'

Chapter Twenty-five

I leant, straight-armed, on the table and looked at her. She said, 'Well, I don't know his exact location but he's with the killer.'

I waited.

She said, 'He abducted David by mistake.'

It was obvious she was confident in what she was saying. 'Who'd he mean to get?'

'Rowlands' horse wasn't the only one to die in the race three years ago. A Mister D. Cooper's horse fell at Valentine's and broke a shoulder. Cooper was an amateur in his early forties. I remember reading an article about him. He retired at the end of that season.'

I stared at her. 'He's got the wrong man.'

'That's why his corpse hasn't turned up.'

'Yet . . .'

Lisa said, 'Think he knows about the reward money?'

'Bound to.'

'Twenty grand buys a hell of a lot of ammunition.'

We had a big meeting that evening at my place. Kavanagh and Miller came. McCarthy brought one of his men along: Tim, short, thin, fair, scrawny-necked. He carried his own herbal tea bags and pretended to gaze intently at whoever was speaking while stealing quick little glances at Lisa who sat cross-legged in a deep chair.

It went quite smoothly apart from the occasional

belches of sourness from the two cops, pissed off as expected that we'd beaten them to it. They weren't delirious about Lisa being there either but we ignored most of the jibes and they gradually settled down to constructive planning.

Protection had already been arranged for Mark Pelham. Alan Crawford was tracked down working in a stud in Dubai. The Sheikh who owned the place promised him two bodyguards. Lisa had come up with seven more names from the last ten Grand Nationals and between Mac's department and the police they were trying to trace them.

The debate was whether to give *all* of them police protection. If the killer stuck rigidly to chronological order everyone else was safe till Pelham, Crawford and I were dead.

Kavanagh said with some satisfaction, 'You'll need a babysitter too, Malloy.'

Resisting a sarcastic reply I nodded, 'Fine.' Kavanagh rang Sanders, his boss, and told him we wanted to keep the Animal Rights connection from the media for the moment. Sanders gave us forty-eight hours. He was being pressed for results and was anxious to publish news of any progress.

We decided not to tell Jack Cooper about his son in case he hired a posse of strong-arm men to round up every known AR activist in the country.

Beckman's name was mentioned. He still hadn't turned up but both McCarthy and his sidekick were confident he'd never shown any leanings towards Animal Rights.

Miller told us about a special department at Scotland Yard which had a file called ARNI, Animal Rights National Index. ARNI held details of all AR people known to the police. Miller and Kavanagh planned to go there tomorrow for a full briefing.

'Can we have another meeting after you've been there?' I asked.

Kavanagh said, 'We'll see,' but his cold look meant, no, we can't. I suggested asking Mark Pelham to help us trap the killer by pulling his bodyguard away and having a team follow him unobtrusively.

'Why don't you be the stool-pigeon, Malloy?' Miller asked scornfully. 'You're pretty good at volunteering others for dangerous jobs.'

Lisa looked at me. Everyone looked at me. I said, 'I'd be happy to but if the killer's working in strict chronological order *backwards* then he'll try for Pelham before me. He was last to fall.'

Mac said, 'You really think he'll be that thorough?'

I shrugged. 'He's been pretty precise so far. Breaking the exact bone each horse had broken, leaving them to suffer for about as long as it would take to get a vet there . . . he even chose a quote for Rowlands that fitted the colour of the dead horse. I think we're dealing with a very picky man.'

'A psycho,' Tim said looking as surprised as the rest of us at the first sound of his voice.

Overruling my protests that they might at least consult Pelham on the idea, they threw it out, though they did agree to my sticking around Pelham for the next few days.

McCarthy thought that was a bad idea. 'You're offering the killer two birds with one stone.'

'There'll be a bodyguard there too, Mac,' I reminded him; 'it won't be easy to take three of us.'

'But you obviously think he'll try or you wouldn't be tagging along.'

I shrugged. 'It'll pass a day or two till we've got some solid information together on the Animal Rights people.'

He didn't like it any better but said no more. He was tired and hungry and wanted to get home. By eleven they'd all gone, leaving Lisa and me alone.

She knelt by the fire with a drink and I made scrambled egg, toast and tea. She washed up afterwards then switched the lamps off and we sat opposite each other sipping neat whisky and listening to the crackling logs.

Comfortable in silence we stared at the flames each with our own thoughts. I watched her. She didn't notice. Propping the glass carelessly against her chin she gazed at the fire. It winked back, a gold glint in her whisky, silver in her dark eyes.

I'd been interested in women since I was thirteen. Fifteen years later I was sitting across from the most remarkable one I'd met. Cool, intelligent, good-looking, athletic, intense and impulsive when she wanted to be, no girlish coyness, not an intentional flirt, undemanding, independent – oh, a hundred per cent independent and *completely* confident . . . naturally, genuinely, no effort at all.

So what was she doing looking contented in the company of a twenty-eight-year-old neurotic obsessed with the juvenile ambition of being better than some other crazy bastards at riding dumb animals over big fences. Surely she could do better than me.

Maybe I amused her.

I wanted her. I knew that. But I didn't want to run the risk. Either way I'd lose. If she rejected me it would make it impossible to carry on the way we were going. If she took me on she'd probably expect me to live up to her standards. Big strain meeting people's expectations. I tried it for a long time then gave up. Not worth it.

Lisa glanced up, knew I'd been watching her for a while. It didn't faze her. She smiled and said, 'Scared?'

I nodded. 'A little.'

'Me too.' She drank and gazed at the fire again. 'I feel we'll get him soon,' she said.

'One way or another.'

We were quiet again, then she said, 'Mister McCarthy still wasn't comfortable with me being there tonight, did you notice?'

'Probably thought you were stenographing everything.'

She smiled. 'The kid that was with him was pretty weird.'

'I don't know, he had good taste in women.'

She raised her glass, toasting me, and sipped. She said, 'Do you intend to stay with Mark Pelham . . . sort of, twenty-four hours?'

'Would that cause you problems?'

'Not in the least. I've got something in mind to help pass the time.'

She was getting as bad as Mac. I waited. She said, 'I'll spend the morning with Susan and in the afternoon I'll ferret out, if that's the right word, my local Animal Rights Group and see if they want a new member.'

I drove up to Haydock next day reaching the course just as Mark Pelham went out for his third ride.

I watched him throughout the race crouched nervously behind his mount's head in a much lower style than usual. Vehicles using the M6 were easily visible from the far side of the track and the thought of what a particularly loud backfire might do to Pelham's nerves brought a brief smile.

He finished third and I moved down from the stand to walk in alongside him. Seeing me he nodded briefly. His tightly strapped riding helmet gave him premature forehead wrinkles and squeezed a few dark curls out just behind his ears. His brown eyes flicked nervously across the faces in the crowd. A couple of times he turned to look back. Veins stood out in his neck and I could see the clear beat of a pulse there. His white breeches bore mud and grass-stains which told me he must have had a fall earlier.

Standing by the entrance to the winner's enclosure Kavanagh watched him come in on the dark steaming horse. Then he saw me and looked perplexed, though he didn't speak. Pelham guided his horse into third spot and vaulted down. His trainer and the horse's owner asked him how it had gone and must have been surprised to find him clutching their arms and gathering them around him in a human shield.

I hoped for Pelham's sake that whatever was going to happen would happen soon because his nerves weren't going to stand many more days of this. I drifted over and stood beside Kavanagh. He spoke from the corner of his mouth without looking at me.

'What do you want, Malloy?'

'Just wondered if all was quiet on the Western Front. Pelham looks a bit nervous.'

'And you're so cool.'

'That wasn't what I meant.'

He was still staring straight ahead. He said, 'Look, you shouldn't be talking to me. For all you know the killer could be watching.'

'So?'

'He might twig that I'm a cop.'

'Think that would make any difference?'

'Just piss off, Malloy.'

'What about *my* protection?'

'Just stick around Pelham till we get a chance to talk. His bodyguard's the guy across there in the dark coat and glasses.'

'With the silvery tie?'

'Uh-huh.'

'Fine. I'll stay by the weighing room and wait for Mark.'

I stood it for about another two hours then realised why Pelham's nerves were shredded. Kavanagh and the bodyguard behaved as though they expected the gunman to walk round the next corner, step from a doorway, spring from behind a tree, drop from the roof, pop up through a drain. The tension stretched between them like a fraying hawser. Sooner or later it had to snap.

If this was what protection did to you, I told Kavanagh, I didn't want it. He made me sign a disclaimer putting him in the clear if I got shot and I left at five and headed back to the lodge.

Lisa had gone. I rang her flat. No answer. I moped around for a while wondering, now that I was alone, about the wisdom of refusing a bodyguard. With Pelham being watched closely the killer might take the easy option and come for me.

He had a gun. At least one. What did I have? A metal baseball bat. It could crack your skull, cave your ribs in but I wouldn't swing it quite so fast with a bullet in my head. Or my lungs full of ether.

The sweet pungency came back to me.

Where was Beckman?

Why did the killer use ether? You stick a gun in someone's face they tend to be reasonably obedient. Why knock them unconscious?

Maybe he had to set them up in the right position for limb-breaking. What did he use, a hammer? He'd have to put his gun down then, I suppose, to hit them in the right place. Maybe that was why he used the anaesthetic.

I unhooked the bat from the coat stand. Twirled the handle in my palm, squeezing the rubber grip. Opening the door I took it outside. It was bright, cloudless. Strong wind. I walked to the rear of the building twirling the bat as I went, watching the sun glint off its swollen stainless-steel end.

Only twitches of pain now from the ten-day-old wounds on my back. I widened the arc of the swing, gripping one-handed then double, turning and crouching, imagining a bone-rending connection with the killer . . . or Beckman. I definitely wanted to get Beckman whatever else happened.

By the shed at the back lay a heap of bulging black refuse sacks. I brought the bat down hard on the top one and it burst like a ripe plum, spraying out long-dead leaves.

The wind helped suck them through the gaping hole then blew them swirling in all directions. I spun and whirled, turned and dived, swinging the bat at the flying leaves like a maniac trying to swat a swarm of locusts, keeping it up till all the leaves had gone.

Then I stood panting, laughing, half-moaning as my back ached and the wind riffled my hair then patted it down as though saying, Try again some other time, little boy.

Much of the earlier tension gone I wandered back along the side of the lodge, the bat now my comfortable companion. Though if someone had offered me a gun . . .

Evening. Alone in the lodge. Waiting. Couldn't settle. Strange without Lisa. Where was she? How was Susan? How was Pelham?

Dead yet?

This was hopeless. I couldn't stand it, the waiting around, the tension. I rang McCarthy and told him I was back home.

'Who's with you?' he asked.

'Nobody.'

I told him about dumping the bodyguard and signing Kavanagh's disclaimer.

'You're crazy,' he said.

'I know, but I've decided to take my own precautions.'

'If they're illegal I don't want to know.'

'They're not. I'm just going to make myself hard to find. I'll move out of here for a few days, stay off the racecourse. If this guy wants me he's going to have to come looking.'

As we discussed the best place for me to go I realised it wasn't where I was that was screwing me up it was the fact that I was doing nothing.

'Heard from Miller today?' I asked Mac.

'Not yet.'

'So you don't know if he saw these ARNI people at Scotland Yard?'

'I'm assuming he did.'

'They're just taking the piss, Mac, you realise that? Him and Kavanagh *and* your man, Inspector Sanders. We give them leads, they promise to keep us informed, then we get nothing.'

It didn't take long to persuade Mac I was right. He knew some people at Scotland Yard and I talked him into arranging a meeting for me with one of the ARNI people.

'Give me half an hour, I'll ring you back,' he said.

The ARNI man's name was Kevin Sollis. I was to meet him at ten next morning. Just to stay on the safe side, to avoid any midnight visitors, I set off for London that evening.

Sollis, one of two guys on the ARNI unit, was friendly looking, thirtyish; big square face, light brown hair, thick moustache, skin pitted ruggedly but evenly like orange rind. He wore a checked lumberjack shirt loose over khaki army-type fatigues with loads of pockets, the bottoms tucked into high Timberland boots – a regular backwoodsman who'd been born in the wrong country. He was very helpful, didn't seem at all miffed about me being a 'layman' and had the general demeanour of quiet patience and inner calm that you see in Jehovah's Witnesses.

He'd spent some time with Miller the previous day and said he didn't mind giving me the same info and advice he'd dished out to him.

First he gave me a potted history of the Animal Rights Movement in Britain. Set up in the mid-seventies, they operated in individual cells with no overall structure. Engaging in raids on Animal Research establishments, farms, pet shops, butcher shops, burger bars, department stores, fox-hunting yards.

They carried out rescues or arson attacks, their main

tactic being economic sabotage of any business they per-
ceived as being involved in animal abuse.

Of late they'd started branching into 'consumer terrorism', threatening to contaminate food and drink manufac-
tured by companies whose policies they didn't approve of.
The police reckoned around two thousand activists were
currently operational in the UK.

To combat them ARNI had been set up in 1984 and
officers from the unit had made a number of arrests over
the years, securing convictions and jail sentences in some
cases.

Only a handful of activists had been convicted of individual acts of personal violence and Sollis had concentrated on those in drawing up a list of possible suspects
for Miller.

He had pinpointed the four most likely and graded them
on an educated guess basis as to which we should aim for
first.

I said, 'Only four? I thought there'd be a *few*.'

He smiled, teeth hidden under the big moustache. 'It's
a funny game, you know. Most of the people involved
realise they've got, if not the support of the general public,
then a grudging sort of sympathy. As long as they stick
to raiding research labs, burning down furriers and dis-
rupting foxhunts then they know they'll be looked on as
crusading outlaws. Once they get involved in violence, it's
a different story.'

I argued that the movement, by its very nature, must
attract fanatics but Sollis said they're quickly weeded out.

'Then where do they go, the weeds?'

He shrugged. 'Who knows? A few are just violent for
the sake of it and find somewhere else to practise it, gangs,
football terraces, pub fights . . .'

'But the true Animal Rights fanatic, maybe one who's
tired of what he sees as peaceful protest, might well blow
a gasket and go on a spree like this.'

'Every chance.'

I thought for a while. 'So, if the movement itself is eager to keep a non-violent image, there's a possibility someone there would blow the whistle on this guy if they knew who he was?'

Sollis said, 'Your real problem would be getting them to admit any association with this guy.'

'But if I could convince them he was definitely on an Animal Rights kick?'

He smiled his slow smile. 'It's well worth trying.'

I asked him what Miller's thoughts had been on this list. Sollis said he'd just taken the names, along with a note of their last known whereabouts, and headed back north saying he'd be in touch.

'A dedicated detective,' I said sarcastically.

Sollis shrugged, refusing to rise to it. 'Some like to use different methods.'

I left it at that.

The Animal Rights Movement had no recognised leader but Sollis told me my best bet for information was a guy all the other AR people looked up to.

He'd just been released after serving five years for arson and was living in a London flat provided by a sympathiser. He was known simply as Buck, a name he'd adopted in memory of the ill-used fictional dog hero in the *The Call of the Wild*.

The flat was in North London halfway down a shabby backstreet. I pressed the bell. A minute later the door was opened by a thin pallid man wearing a white T shirt and blue jeans. He was barefoot, his toes long and pale, fair hair cropped short, a day's beard on his narrow jaw and wearing glasses so thick that each blue eye seemed to fill the lens. He blinked, almost startling me. I said, 'I'm looking for Buck.'

'Who are you?'

'My name's Eddie Malloy.'

'What do you want with Buck?'

I was trying to place the accent but couldn't.

I said, 'I need his help.'

Buck stared at me a while longer, blinked again then led me inside.

He sat on the edge of a square table, sharing the space with a big blue typewriter and piles of letters, half of them unopened. Smoking roll-ups and drinking strong black coffee from a panda-badged mug he talked about Animal Rights with the controlled passion of a fanatic tutored by a PR man, a mixture of persuasive reasoning and colourful sound-bites: 'Vivisection labs and factory farms are the concentration camps of the Human Reich.'

When I steered him round to what I wanted to discuss he said, 'Everyone involved in horseracing is a fucking moron.'

I said, 'Well all these morons are building themselves a nice fund of sympathy in the public eye because this bloke is going around knocking them off. He must be setting your cause back years.'

He stopped halfway through a slug of coffee and said, 'Don't try and con me with that shit, man.'

I shrugged, 'Nothing to do with conning you, it's a simple fact. Racing folk are involved in sport, they're not vivisectionists or factory farmers, they're innocent people trying to make a living and this guy is murdering them.'

He loosed off then about whipping and making horses jump fences and I listened without interrupting too many times but I kept driving him back to the point because he knew I was right. I mentioned the names Sollis had given me and Buck smoked a while and thought.

He said, 'I'd have to make a phone call. You want to come back later?'

'If it's privacy you want I'll wait outside.'

'Okay, gimme five minutes.'

Chapter Twenty-six

I put my ear to the door but could hear nothing. I wondered where his phone was.

After three or four minutes he opened the door and I went back in. He said, 'Reid moved to the Shetlands a few months back, he's either studying seals or working on the oil rigs, depending what story you believe. Craven's hanging around with some of the so-called New Age Travellers, last heard of in Dorset about three weeks ago.'

'Where in Dorset?'

'Dunno.'

'What about the other two?'

His magnified eyes stared at me blankly, saying he thought he'd done enough. 'No information,' he said.

'You haven't got it or won't give it?'

'Haven't got it.'

We exchanged mistrusting glances for a few seconds then I handed him a card. 'I'd appreciate a call if you do find out anything about them.'

He took the card without comment, a hint of sourness creeping in, regret, maybe, that he'd helped me. I left. He didn't say goodbye.

I rang McCarthy and asked him to speak to the Dorset police and find out the movements of whatever convoy this bloke Craven was with.

He said, 'Maybe we should get Kavanagh to do it.'

'Maybe we shouldn't. Listen, Mac, Kavanagh doesn't

give a toss; the guy is a *bad* policeman. So is Miller. He took the same list as I've got and buggered off back home without giving it any more thought.

'If Kavanagh finds out about Craven he'll either ignore it completely or go barging in among these travellers like Geronimo attacking a waggon train. They're sure to point him towards Craven then, aren't they?'

He gave in without further argument. 'Okay, Eddie, I'll ring you back as soon as I've spoken to the Dorset people.'

He sounded under pressure. Maybe the case was getting to him. The papers were still full of it and his boss was probably giving him hell. Tough life.

I left London under a grey overcast sky for the green pastures of Dorset and all the way a fine rain fell with that irritating inconsistency that makes intermittent wipe too much and no wipe not enough. I cursed the clouds, then chided myself for letting such tiny things annoy me.

Mac rang. 'Spoke to a sergeant at Shaftesbury who reckons they're in Wiltshire. There was supposed to be a rave party on Friday night near Castle Combe but the local police stopped it from turning into anything of decent size. Anyway the Shaftesbury bloke thinks they may well still be around Castle Combe.'

'Are there many of them?'

'A couple of hundred, he reckons.'

'Mmm.'

'Also, I didn't tell him exactly what we were about but I got the distinct impression you won't get a result there.'

'How come?'

'Too tight-knit . . . they live in a world of their own, treat outsiders as if they come from Mars.'

'I think you'll find money talks, same as it does anywhere else.'

'You can only try, I suppose.'

His mood hadn't improved, still down. 'You sound pretty low, Mac, you okay?'

'I'll be fine,' he said quietly, 'it's been a long . . . life. Keep in touch.'

As I parked in a layby way above the travellers' encampment a moist dusk settled over everything, no discernible rainfall just very wet air. It didn't dampen the campfires which bubbled like yellow geysers below.

The big field held maybe fifty ramshackle vehicles, trucks, caravans, an old ambulance, an ancient mobile library with a sixties registration plate, a dilapidated horsebox . . . these people might be weirdos but there must have been some bloody good mechanics among them.

Peering through my binoculars as the light faded I saw people wandering around, long hair, dreadlocks, old clothes, dogs yapping at their heels, children playing in the mud, lights of varying size and intensity; lamps flickering behind the small windows of vans, campfires flaring like furnaces as they filled the lens, pinpoints of yellow glowing on the ends of sucked cigarettes . . . and happy relaxed faces, some laughing, many smiling . . . maybe not such a bad way of life after all.

One thing for sure, Mac was right, there was no way I was going to march in there and get answers – bribes or no bribes. I didn't doubt they'd take money but God knows what kind of shit they'd feed me in exchange.

The ARNI man, Kevin Sollis, had given me a picture of Craven which I pretty much had in my mind but I took it out for another look. Very dark, blue-black hair long and thick, heavy eyebrows over deep-set dark eyes, leathery complexion and, in this picture anyway, a moody scowl. I checked the notes I'd made:

Thirty-three, divorced, convictions for violence going back sixteen years, twelve of which he'd spent in jail for murdering a man who'd kicked his dog (the judge had allowed for a certain degree of provocation).

Most of Craven's convictions could be blamed, it

seemed, on his terrible temper. He could take offence at the mildest comment and lash out immediately with whatever was to hand, which, given his taste for drink, was often a beer glass.

He had a soft spot for animals, going back to his childhood in Cornwall where he was raised on a farm, often forgoing pocket money or payment for work in exchange for the life of a lamb or a pig, despite his father's mockery.

At seventeen he'd joined a hunt saboteurs group but was banished by them after frenziedly attacking a huntsman who'd become detached from the main group when his horse went lame. It had taken five of Craven's fellow saboteurs to drag him off the unconscious huntsman.

When told by his 'colleagues' he was no longer welcome he'd set about them as well, putting two in hospital.

Jailed for murder just as Animal Rights Groups were setting up their economic sabotage operations, Craven had supported them from his jail cell in the form of a stream of letters to newspapers, few of which were printed.

He looked a reasonable bet from a violence point of view but there seemed to be no Bible connection and the only link with horses was that first incident at the hunt. Why would he have latched on to racing?

Raising the binoculars again and resting my elbows on the roof of the car, I scanned slowly, faces only, back and forth till my eyes hurt and my shoulders ached and, finally, the darkness hid them all.

Driving back into the village I found a charity shop and noted its opening time of nine next morning. A flashing 'Vacancies' sign, which looked garishly out of place in such a pretty, demure village, drew me into a fifteen-quid-a-night guest-house where the landlady promised, as she led me to the third floor, that climbing the stairs would keep me fit.

Small room, single bed against a radiator, tiny sink, narrow wardrobe, a stool and an old TV which offered the same channel no matter which button you pressed.

I flopped on the bed, belly down out of habit. I was hungry and tired and must have dozed. Brief dreams of Craven's dark face, then Lisa's white body.

The two old ladies serving in the charity shop were in general agreement that the worst thing ever to happen to Castle Combe was being voted England's prettiest village. They recalled the days of horse-drawn carts and bountiful harvests when everyone worked on the land rather than in craft shops and tea rooms, the days when tourists hadn't been invented.

I chose a pair of old jeans a size too big, two tatty jumpers and a shapeless coffee-coloured T shirt, thick socks with clumps of darning, well-worn leather boots and an ancient canvas rucksack: twelve pounds fifty the lot.

In an antiques/second-hand shop I collected some pots and pans, an enamel plate and mug, some mottled cutlery and a Swiss army knife. From a small grocer's I bought beans, soup and a tin of hot-dog sausages, a loaf, firelighters and matches and a bottle of cheap fortified wine.

I changed in a public lavatory, put my normal clothes and things in the car and checked my face in a wing mirror. I have a natural heavy beard growth and already it looked dirty, though my hair was a little too neat. I mussed it up a bit then locked the car and, pots and tins rattling in my rucksack, set off towards the travellers' camp.

Tramping through the village I couldn't pass a shop window without staring at my scarecrow reflection – all I lacked was a battered old top hat.

A couple of miles on, feet already aching from the ill-fitting boots, I cut into the woods covering the hill above the encampment and worked my way to the deepest parts, not bothering to duck soggy branches or to avoid nettle stings.

In the unnatural morning twilight below the heaviest canopy I gathered twigs and broken branches – damp but kept combustible by the shelter above – and lit a fire. The greasy white firelighters roared in the stillness sending flames curling around the moist greenery till it dried and ignited releasing spicy smoke which I stood over while it wandered through my clothes.

I stayed there for the rest of the day, keeping the fire going, seeking out the smoke till my hair, my skin and everything I wore were impregnated with the smell. Digging my fingers into the debris of the forest floor I forced dirt under every fingernail, wiped my hands on my clothes then my face and hair.

As the light died I walked to the edge of the wood and stood watching the camp, waiting for dusk. When it came I clumped noisily down the hill and into the field, pans and tins clinking as I approached the nearest campfire, hoping dearly that none of the holes in the old rucksack was big enough to let my mobile phone slip through.

It turned out to be much easier than I'd thought. I was welcomed by most of the travellers with no question more searching than 'How long you been on the road, man?' A young couple let me doss down (wrapped in a makeshift sleeping-bag sewn together from ancient army blankets) in the back of their van and shared their breakfast of smooth porridge and toast with me.

By Saturday afternoon I judged it safe enough to start dropping Craven's name into casual conversations. Within an hour I learned where he was.

He'd been travelling with the convoy in an old estate car since the previous autumn but hadn't wintered too well in the open air. After spending the coldest months with a worsening hacking cough and spitting gobs of phlegm 'the size of fried eggs' Craven had been admitted,

six weeks ago, to a Bristol hospital, suffering from tuber-
culosis.

My informant, a bearded pony-tailed fattie, owned the
converted ambulance on whose steps we sat while he told
me this. He'd been drinking beer all afternoon and got
up to 'take a leak' leaving me without a lead any more,
back at square one, rubbing my grimy eyes and face
wearily with dirty hands and wondering what the hell to
do next.

As the afternoon light faded I sat there thinking how
agreeable these people's lives were compared to my own.
No pressure, no ambitions, no social jousting, just a free-
and-easy existence – talking and music, drink and soft
drugs, sex and companionship. Their friends meant much
more to them than things material and that in itself created
an atmosphere of warmth and closeness.

I looked at my own life: career going nowhere, no real
friends, estranged family, my thirtieth birthday not all that
far away and the months accelerating like inflation, only
worth twenty days each now compared to when I was a
kid . . .

I can't say I wasn't tempted to stay with the travellers.

I got up and gathered my things together, thanked my
hosts and trudged away across the field, legs heavy not just
from the caked mud on my boots but from the weariness of
having no direction.

Dumping the old boots in a waste bin in the car park I
pulled on my shoes and drove to Bristol where three
pounds fifty bought me half an hour in the sauna suite of
the local swimming baths. A pound coin dropped in a big
glass-fronted machine activated an arm which pushed a
bottle of green shower gel off a rack and down the exit
chute.

I used the whole bottle, lathering myself under a luke-
warm shower, the water cool enough to soothe my scarred
back. Changing into my normal clothes I stuffed the old

gear in a plastic carrier and left it by the bin in the shower room.

Shampooed, clean-shaven and smelling nice, with the cold night air making me feel even fresher and with some optimism returning, I drove to the hospital to see Craven. I wasn't sure what I was going to say to him and I knew the visit seemed pointless but he had been the only link left and I went to see him because I just didn't know what else to do.

I was Craven's only visitor. He sat propped up on pillows, wheezing gently, looking much less threatening than in his photograph. The thick dark hair was stringy and grey-streaked, the cheeks sunken, the eyes dull. His thin lips were clogged at the corners with white sticky matter. A shallow enamel bowl curved to fit the chin lay on his bedside table, its bottom coated with red-speckled phlegm. Beside the bowl stood two get-well cards.

I sat down and introduced myself as a journalist but I could see from the start he didn't buy it. I told him I was working on the jockey murders and had got on to the Animal Rights angle and that there'd be a few quid in it for him if he could give me one or two inside stories.

He said nothing. I might as well have been talking to his pillows. He lay staring at me as though he pitied me, shaking his head slowly a couple of times at what I said. When for the third time I asked if he thought any Animal Rights supporter could be capable of murder he spoke for the first and only time: 'Fuck off, you prick,' he said weakly, his eyes finally showing an edge of hardness.

I got up and lifted the cards from his table. He frowned and wheezed as I opened them. The first one was from Mary and urged him to get better for the summer. The second one said, 'Get fit and come out fighting!' It was from Buck.

I sat in the car in the hospital car park knowing the bold

Buck had put me away and wondering how significant it was. In telling me Craven was with the travellers in the West Country he'd given me sufficient information, if I was smart enough, to track Craven down to his hospital bed.

Why hadn't he simply told me he didn't know where he was? Why hadn't he told me Craven was in the Shetlands along with the other guy – what was his name? – Reid . . . Was he just trying to keep me off Reid's tail, was Reid our man?

I reached in the glove compartment and dug the ARNI cop's card out: Kevin Sollis. I rang and persuaded him to join me for a drink around ten o'clock. It was eightish now, I had time enough to get back to London for ten. He said to meet him at The Yard and I pulled out and headed for the M4.

Sollis, big as a beer truck and still wearing his backwoods gear, stood outside on the pavement idly throwing soft kicks at a lamp-post and whistling quietly. The same lazy smile was there under his moustache as he reached to shake my hand. 'You like real ale?' he asked.

'Don't think I've ever tried it.'

'Want to?'

'Sure.'

He turned me with a hand on my shoulder. 'There's a good place about five minutes' walk away.'

'Fine.'

We ambled companionably along the wet street, Sollis telling me lovingly about the qualities of real ale, stopping every now and then to expand on a point, never once asking why I'd invited him out. By the time we reached the pub he'd made me feel I'd been his friend for years, his close friend.

I guessed he had a gift for doing that with everyone, but it didn't make me like him any less. A few more of his kind in the police force in exchange for the Kavanaghs and Millers might not make the law any less of an ass but it would certainly improve its image.

Comfortably settled in a smoky corner of the busy bar, Sollis watched me take my first sip of real ale. It was hellish sweet but I didn't say so; nodding and licking my lips I assured him it was the best I'd ever tasted. That made him happy and he sat back to listen.

When I'd told him about the last couple of days I said, 'Now there's got to be a chance that this Buck character is involved somewhere, or at least knows more than he's saying.'

Sollis nodded slowly, looking at his knees. We were side by side and I sat turned towards him trying to draw the line between being heard above the general buzz and not being overheard. From time to time Sollis would incline his ear closer to my mouth. He did it as I said, 'What would be the chances of a phone tap?'

He turned, raising an eyebrow, 'On Buck?'

I nodded.

'Got one,' he said and sipped beer.

'Now?'

'Uh-huh.'

'Who monitors it?'

'We tape everything and play it back each morning.'

I felt the sudden tension of expectation. 'So who did he call to get the info he gave me on Craven?'

'Nobody. He was just bluffing you.'

'But there must be something. He must make some calls?'

'Oh, he makes calls and he gets calls but it's all domestic stuff. He knows we're listening in.'

Deflated again I asked, 'So what's the point of tapping the line?'

Sollis shrugged. Reaching for his glass he said, 'Procedure, I suppose.'

'Sounds a bit daft to me.'

He shrugged again, happy to accept my judgement. I said, 'He must make calls from elsewhere, I mean he must have some contact with these other Animal Rights people.'

Sollis said, 'I'm sure he does. He'll get a call asking him to ring back and he goes out and rings from a call-box.'

'So why don't you bug the call-box?'

'He always uses a different one. Anyway, we'd have trouble getting clearance for that; Buck's been squeaky clean since he came out.'

A woman sat down at the piano in the corner and tried to start a singalong. Sollis looked across at her and smiled. I said to him, 'Why didn't you tell me on Wednesday about the phone tap?'

'You were enthusiastic. I didn't think Buck would give you anything, but I couldn't be sure. You deserved the chance to try.'

I looked at him. 'I was thinking of going back tomorrow,' I said, 'confronting him with the fact that he'd known all along Craven was in hospital.'

Sollis drank and shook his head. 'Pointless. He'd just laugh at you.'

'So what do I do next?'

He shrugged. 'We can try and locate the other three on your list.'

'How long is that likely to take?'

'No way of saying but we can start in the morning.'

I sighed and nodded slowly, downcast. Sollis punched my shoulder gently and smiled. 'Cheer up. It's not the end of the world.' He started singing along with the pianist as tuneless as he was jolly.

Sollis invited me to stay in the spare room of his neat little terraced house in Chiswick. We got there at midnight and Mrs Sollis, a pretty, chubby Filipino in her mid-twenties, fussed around making me welcome, heating delicious home-made pizza and pouring red wine.

Around 2 a.m., alone in my neat little room, I thought of Lisa. It had been four days since we'd spoken. We'd agreed if there was anything important and we couldn't get in touch we'd leave messages on my answerphone which could be played back remotely.

Depressed and missing her I rang my number as much in the hope of just hearing her voice as anything else. I connected and pictured the phone ringing out in an empty house. The answerphone clicked on and I punched in the playback code.

Lisa's voice was there right enough telling me she was just checking in. No real news, though she *had* joined an Animal Rights Group which she said, so far, was 'the bore of the year'. I smiled.

After Lisa another female voice played back, a stranger. Identifying herself as a Mrs Pritchard she carefully gave her address and phone number, saying she would like to give me some urgent information on Claude Beckman.

Chapter Twenty-seven

Next morning, Sunday, I returned Mrs Pritchard's call. She was nowhere near as keen to see me as she'd seemed on the answerphone, saying that she wasn't sure it mattered much any more. Eventually she agreed to see me at her house near Finsbury Park around ten-thirty.

I skipped breakfast, thanked Sollis for his hospitality and promised I'd be in touch. On my way to North London a newspaper banner caught my eye. I stopped and bought three papers. Inspector Sanders had released the Animal Rights 'line of inquiry' saying he felt confident the public would respond positively with any information.

With the Grand National less than a week away the Press, predictably, made a major story of it with most of the tabloids carrying it as their big front-page spread. I wondered how the killer felt as he read it over his breakfast.

Mrs Pritchard watched from behind a curtain as I climbed half a dozen steps towards her door and I waited without knocking. She was six feet tall in flat shoes, maybe forty-five, pear-shaped under a knee-length herringbone coat, pale-skinned, long-faced, sad-eyed, she didn't invite me in and suggested we have our chat in the open spaces of Finsbury Park.

It was cold, grey and drizzly. She carried a big black brolly. I turned my coat collar up.

Between long splay-footed strides on the wet pavement she spoke little, though the noise as buses and cars splashed past would have drowned conversation anyway. We turned through the gates and took the diagonal path across the park, the traffic-hum decreasing as we went. In a grove of trees by the railed-off duckpond she said, 'I am Claude Beckman's sister.'

I waited for more.

She said, 'I was . . . concerned when some of the papers were alleging Claude might have been involved in those jockey killings.'

She'd obviously become a lot less concerned when she'd seen this morning's headlines, hence her sudden reluctance to see me. I said nothing. She continued. 'Claude couldn't kill anyone, it's not something he'd be capable of . . . much as he may sometimes like to think he would.'

We walked on past a kid throwing bread to the ducks. Without looking at me Mrs Pritchard said, 'Claude had a very big chip on his shoulder about you but he had nothing against the men who were killed and the newspapers shouldn't have implied he was involved. He hated you because you took a race away from mother just before she died, the Whitbread Gold Cup.'

I thought back. I'd finished second in the Whitbread, one of the biggest races of the season, about six years ago. But I'd got the race after objecting to the winner for bumping me on the run-in . . . God, I couldn't even remember the name of the horse who'd originally 'won'.

Mrs Pritchard said, 'Mother had always wanted to win the Whitbread. She'd been ill for some time but had gone to Sandown that day with Claude. When her horse passed the post first she told Claude that she could now die happy. Then you objected and they took the race away from her. She died two weeks later . . . Claude doted on her.'

Unfortunately for me.

My mind went back to Mrs Beckman's picture on

Claude's mantelpiece. Now I knew why she'd seemed familiar. I also remembered the defaced photo in his racing album and realised the slashed, scarred jockey was me.

'Do you know where Claude is now?' I asked.

'I haven't seen him for more than three years. We were never particularly close but I felt I owed it to the family name to try and clear it in his absence.'

'So how do you know he hated me so much?'

'Because for ages after the Whitbread he talked about nothing else but getting revenge on you, then within a year you'd lost your licence and your livelihood and Claude was ecstatic. Then, last summer when I read that you'd got your licence back I knew Claude would be raging. I thought of warning you but I knew he was working for The Jockey Club and I didn't want to jeopardise his position.'

'But you didn't mind jeopardising mine.'

Offended, she stopped and looked down at me. 'If I'd thought you were in any real danger I would have warned you.'

'A bit late for that,' I said.

A jogger passed us, panting, squelching across the grass.

She said, 'What do you mean?'

'Just over a week ago he drugged me, hauled me back to his garden shed, stripped me and laid into my back with a horse-whip till he was too tired to lift his arm. Then he dumped me naked in a car park.'

She stared, frowning, thinking, then said, 'But he didn't kill you.'

'So that justifies it?'

'Of course not. I'm sorry he did that but what I meant was he's not a killer.'

She turned and slowly started walking again. Producing a cotton hankie from her pocket she tried, as elegantly as her long nose allowed, to clear her sinuses.

I said, 'So why doesn't your brother come out and defend himself against these allegations in the papers? Where is he?'

'I don't know.'

We walked a few strides in silence then she said, 'Do the police know he assaulted you? Are they looking for him?'

'They know what he did and they're sort of looking for him in a half-hearted manner.'

'So *they* don't really believe he killed those men?'

'They can't make their minds up. At the moment they're pursuing, as they would say, several lines of inquiry.'

'So,' she said indignantly, 'why are the papers allowed to publish these allegations? How can they get away with it?'

I shrugged. 'If you look closely you'll see they're not really alleging anything, not outright anyway, it's the way it's written – for those who read between the lines, if you like. They use terms like "confirmed bachelor" which is libel-free doublespeak for homosexual.'

She said, 'They used that expression for Claude.'

'And is he?'

She looked down at me like I smelled bad. 'He *is* a confirmed bachelor. He is *not*, as far as I know, a homosexual.'

'As far as you know.'

'We were never that close. I didn't keep tabs on his private life. What has Claude's sexuality got to do with it anyway? It would hardly give him reason to murder people.'

We wandered on for twenty minutes through the cold drizzle, walking the same oval path past the duckpond. Mrs Pritchard continued an ever-weakening defence of her brother. Her heart wasn't in it and she left the impression that she had never really cared that much for him and was speaking up only because she thought it was what her mother would have wanted from her.

I asked why she hadn't contacted the papers direct; she said she didn't want them camping on her doorstep. She'd rather hoped that I would put them straight after talking to her. I told her I didn't want the buggers on my doorstep either. She accepted with a shrug and we left the park.

On the walk back I learned she was divorced and ventured out seldom, preferring a quiet life with her cats. Two of them were in the window as though waiting for her and it was the only time I saw her smile. She went up the steps without a goodbye and, duty done, conscience clear, stepped through the door back into her own private little world.

I called McCarthy from the car, updated him on Beckman and told him my trip to Wiltshire had led me back to square one. He said he'd told Kavanagh about 'this Buck character' and that Kavanagh and Miller intended taking him in for questioning. I told Mac he'd probably run rings round them.

'So what's your next move?' he asked.

I sighed. 'I'm going to stay away from the lodge for a few more days. Sollis has been helpful. Says he'll get to work today on tracking down the other three names on my list but I honestly feel we're running out of time. This guy must have something big planned for Saturday, some major fireworks.'

'I know. I've got a meeting with the Aintree executive tomorrow morning to discuss security.'

'Better tell them to get the army in.'

'Cheer up, Eddie, we've still got a week to get this guy.'

'And he's got a week to kill a few more people. Me included.'

'Stop being pig-headed then, take the offer of police protection.'

'Mmmm. Wouldn't mind Sollis as a minder. He's built like the proverbial brick shithouse and laid back with it.'

Mac said, 'If he's had firearms training I could probably arrange that.'

'Okay, see what you can do.'

Next I rang Lisa. She sounded glad to hear from me. I told her what I'd been doing and asked how Susan Gilmour was.

'Improving. Very slowly, but she is better.'

Lisa had joined an Animal Rights Group in Cheltenham and quickly befriended one of the most dedicated members, a young girl called Lucy.

Lisa said, 'She's only eighteen. You'd be amazed at the number of kids in these groups. Some of them are only about fourteen!'

'The idealism of youth,' I said.

Lisa had only been to one big meeting but had spent a lot of time with Lucy. She said, 'They've got quite an effective recruitment campaign. Once somebody shows a spark of interest they bombard them with statistics on factory farming, research labs and stuff. They hand out horrendous pictures and show videos of foxhunts and horses taking some terrible falls in races. I'm trying to find out if they've got any footage specific to the Grand National. Maybe somebody in the movement specialises in it.'

'Lisa,' I said, 'you've just given me an idea.'

We sat in Sollis's office. He'd just brought in a box of videotapes and was pushing one into the VCR. He said, 'Aintree last year, that was where you wanted to start, wasn't it?'

'Might as well.'

Pressing the play button he settled back. 'Got loads of these, you know,' he said, 'foxhunts to fashion shows. See a lot of the same people in each one. Mostly peaceful. A few skirmishes but no violence on the scale you're talking about.'

The tape opened on about a dozen protesters on the road outside Aintree racecourse. Their banners had pictures of fallen horses under big slogans like YOU BET: THEY'LL DIE and they could be seen appealing to race-goers, though there was no soundtrack.

Most people ignored them, a few openly taunted them. When the camera closed in on faces Sollis leant towards the screen and pointing with his pen ran through a few names and gave brief biographies of each.

'You'd make a good racecourse commentator,' I told him.

He smiled and continued till a teenager appeared on the screen. Reaching quickly for the remote control he froze the picture. I looked at him. He'd gone serious. He said, 'I'd forgotten about this.' Nodding towards the shimmering freeze-frame he said, 'A few hours after this was taken that kid was dead. Crushed under the wheels of a horsebox.'

I tried to see the boy's face. It wasn't clear. 'What happened?' I asked.

'This protest was on the Friday, the day before the National. Early next morning they appeared further up the road to try and prevent horseboxes driving into the stables. They had a sit-down protest and our lads had to drag them away to let the boxes through.

'This kid wriggles free and runs after one of the boxes, tries to jump up on the driver's footplate, misses and goes under the wheels.'

I cringed. 'You got film of it?'

He nodded. 'But you don't want to see it.' He stopped the tape, ejecting it. 'How about the previous year's?' he asked.

I shook my head slowly, still thinking about the dead boy. 'How old was the kid?'

'Sixteen, I think.'

'Was there an inquest?'

'Death by misadventure.'

'Were you there?'

'At the inquest – no. My mate was, had to show this tape and give evidence.'

'Can I talk to him?'

Sollis looked at me. 'Think you're on to something here?'

'Dunno, but I suspect somebody somewhere threatened revenge. What about the boy's family?'

'I'm not sure. You'd be better talking to Polly, he was dealing with it.'

'Polly?'

'Jim Perkins. We call him Polly.'

Sollis got him on the phone and we had a long chat. The boy's name was Christopher Roe. Roe's mates had tried to attack the box-driver straight after the incident and the driver had subsequently received death threats by post and telephone, though all that calmed down after a couple of weeks.

The only family the boy had was his father who he'd lived with on a farm near Hereford. His mother had been killed three years previously in a tractor accident.

Was his father at the inquest?

Perkins said, 'Yes. I remember watching him as the box-driver gave evidence. Now from what I'd heard, if anyone was cut out for taking revenge it was Victor Roe. Ex-SAS man, tough as nails, supposed to have killed half a dozen terrorists in his time.

'But he was as calm as you like. You'd almost've thought he was in church. Peaceful looking? I'd have called it serene. Not a hint of animosity on his face. Just sat there clutching his Bible.'

Chapter Twenty-eight

Perkins was confident that after the inquest Roe had gone back to live on his farm and get on with his life as best he could. I was more of a mind that he'd found justification in his Bible to avenge his son's death.

It was mid-afternoon. Sollis was still waiting for official approval to take over as my bodyguard. I rang McCarthy again to tell him about Victor Roe and to ask him to press hard for Sollis's clearance.

While we were waiting I found out the name of the box-driver involved in the kid's death and rang his stable. I was put on to Tony Greenway, the head lad, who I knew quite well. We exchanged pleasantries and I told him as much as he had to know before asking him if I could speak to Sampson, the box-driver.

'He left last year, Eddie, around the beginning of July.'

'D'you know where I can find him?'

'We've already tried a few times.'

He told me Sampson had phoned him one night out of the blue saying he wouldn't be back, that he couldn't forget the kid's death. Sampson had worked there for five years. A recovered alcoholic and ex-vagrant he'd made a lot of friends at the stable. Tony reckoned he was drunk the night he rang and might have ended up back on the streets.

He said, 'Every month or so one of the lads goes to London and spends a night trawling the streets to see if we can find him.' He sighed, 'No luck so far.'

'You sure he was drunk the night he called?'

'He was pretty emotional, crying. That wasn't like him. It was a bloody shame. I remember him saying to tell Liz, that's our cook, that he loved her and he was sorry he'd never got round to telling her that himself. Terrible . . .'

'And not a word from him since? Not a sighting?'

'Nothing.'

I thanked Tony and told him I hoped Sampson would turn up. Personally I had grave doubts.

I tried ringing the Northern police to give them the info on Roe. Kavanagh and Miller were both in London. Inspector Sanders wouldn't speak to me. The desk sergeant gave me Kavanagh's mobile number.

Kavanagh answered sounding smug and said it wasn't really convenient to listen to my 'latest theory'. He said, 'We have a gentleman with us now who is going to be very helpful and co-operative . . . aren't you, Buck?'

I said, 'I think you might find Buck giving you plenty of information. How much of it will be reliable is another matter.'

'Leave us to worry about that, Malloy. You just keep your head below the parapet.'

'Mark Pelham still okay?' I asked.

'Last time I saw him.'

'Good. When you've finished chasing your tails ring me. With a bit of luck I'll be getting some help from a *good* cop by then.'

I hung up. Sollis smiled. Over a quick lunch in his favourite pub we worked on the best and safest way to approach Victor Roe. Sollis wondered how much his ex-bosses in the SAS would be willing to tell us.

Nothing, was the answer. We rang a captain at the Hereford barracks who denied ever having heard of Roe. Sollis pressed him without saying outright that Roe was suspected of involvement in the killings.

The captain still maintained that he personally knew

nothing of Roe and that if we wanted more information we would have to request an interview by letter with his superior and also provide details of when Roe was supposed to have served at Hereford.

Sollis got back on to Perkins who said he understood Roe had left the SAS four years ago just after his wife had been killed. He didn't know what rank Roe had held nor could he confirm the 'terrorist killing' stories. He admitted he'd got the information on Roe from a man at the inquest claiming to be Roe's neighbour. He didn't know the man's name.

'Brilliant,' I said. 'How the hell do we corroborate it?'

Sollis smiled. 'Don't worry. Let's just get an interview fixed up. They'll know something at the barracks. Standard procedure in the SAS to disclaim all knowledge of individuals.'

We sent the letter by fax to the SAS HQ then spent the afternoon waiting around for a reply and for approval for Sollis on the bodyguard front. That came through just before six. We waited another half-hour for a reply from the SAS. None came.

I said, 'Let's just go up there. This is a waste of time.'

Sollis agreed and asked a WPC to ring us if a fax arrived from Hereford. After completing paperwork in triplicate in three different offices Sollis checked out a Smith & Wesson pistol and fifty rounds of ammunition. We got in my car and headed for the M40.

The big man beside me was relaxed enough to start dozing off after fifteen minutes on the motorway. I felt better than I had done since this thing started. For once I wasn't on my own. Sollis was more than co-operative. He was friendly, trustworthy . . . and he was armed.

It's amazing how much confidence you have when you've got a gun on your side.

It was dark by seven. We were forty miles from Hereford when confirmation came through that someone at the barracks *would* see us. Sollis took over the driving while I dialled Lisa to update her. She wasn't home. I rang my own answerphone to leave a message for her and to play back anything else that had come in since last night.

Lisa had left a long message: 'Eddie, tried to get you earlier. No luck. Listen, remember we were wondering why Rowlands was killed rather than the jockey? I spoke to a few people who said Rowlands had run the horse after it had taken a bad fall in the Gold Cup a couple of weeks before. There had been several protests in the Press before the National about Rowlands running the horse. People were saying it should have been retired for the season.

'Rowlands obviously ignored everyone and the killer seems to have taken the view that *he* was to blame for the horse's death. Anyway, the point is it got me thinking about the others, your race for instance. What if the guy was hunting around for someone other than the jockey to blame?

'Don't know if you've ever heard of a vet called Digby Craddock but I found out today that he was responsible for giving the horse that Mark Pelham rode a clean bill of health when it was sold just before the National. The horse died of a heart attack and the gossip is that Craddock must have known about it. Some think he did it for a backhander from the vendor.

'I've tried to talk to Craddock on the phone to warn him but he thinks I'm a crank so I'm driving up there to see him. Not far, Bromyard in Worcestershire. I'll try you on your mobile once I've spoken to him or I'll leave another message here. Take care.'

Suddenly I had an empty feeling in the pit of my stomach.

I grabbed the phone and punched in McCarthy's number.

'Mac!' He read the rising panic in my tone.

'Eddie, what's wrong?' he asked.

'Do you know a vet called Digby Craddock?'

He thought for a few seconds. 'Heard of him, don't know him. Why?'

'Lisa thinks he might be involved in all this, she says he had something to do with a dead horse in the National.' My voice was tight, tense.

Mac murmured, 'Craddock, Craddock, Craddock . . . no, can't think.'

'Look, do me a favour, he lives somewhere in Bromyard. Find out exactly where and get the police there as fast as you can.'

'Eddie . . .'

'Listen, Mac, Lisa's gone up there to see Craddock and I *know* something's gone wrong! Now get somebody there. We'll start heading in that direction now. Ring me as soon as you have the full address.'

'Eddie!'

'Do it, Mac!'

About fifty minutes later I reckoned we were no more than a couple of miles from Craddock's place when McCarthy rang again.

'Eddie . . .'

I could tell by his voice. 'Lisa?' I asked and held my breath.

'Craddock . . . he's dead.'

'And Lisa?'

'She's not there.'

'Thank God!'

'Eddie, they found her handbag . . . I think he's taken her.'

There was still some heat in Craddock's fat body which lay on the cold tiles of the kitchen floor. The cops were waiting for their medical man to arrive but a grey-haired world-weary sergeant reckoned the vet had been dead less than an hour. The corpse showed no obvious signs of violence. The note in the pocket of his pale blue shirt read: Jeremiah 17:9. No one had tried to find a Bible.

Lisa's handbag had been discovered under the kitchen table. The worktop bore signs of a struggle: a pool of coffee spilled from a broken mug, a small bunker of sand which had burst from a shattered egg-timer, jagged slivers of a broken whisky glass in the stainless steel sink.

I told the sergeant Lisa was my girlfriend. He said, 'Tough break.' He wouldn't let us nose around. 'Nobody touches anything till SOC get here.'

'Scene of Crime Officer,' Sollis told me.

Kavanagh and Miller were also on their way. The sergeant said I'd best wait till they got there. I didn't think so.

I rang Mac from the car and updated him, then asked, 'Have you got a Bible?'

'Somewhere, hold on . . .'

I heard drawers being opened, stuff being shuffled around then he came back. I gave him the details and he mumbled quietly as he leafed through the pages, then said, 'Got it. "The heart is deceitful above all things, and desperately wicked."'

I said, 'Mean anything to you?'

He pondered. 'Something's clicking in the back of my mind with Craddock . . . can't pin it down. Let me ring Frank and come back to you.'

'Frank who?'

'Robinson, my collator . . . Give me a couple of minutes.'

McCarthy's department employed someone solely to collate information for cross-reference. The collator welcomed everything, from the nastiest gossip to documented evidence. His job was noting and sorting it all, someone else would decide how valuable it was.

I told Mac to save his breath. 'The key word in the quote is heart. Lisa found out Craddock knew the horse had a dicky heart but still passed it A1 to run in the National. You can tell the pathologist to start the autopsy by looking at Craddock's heart.'

Sitting there in the silent darkness I thought about Lisa and felt angry at her foolhardiness, then guilt at allowing her too much rope.

Worry followed, twisting maliciously in my gut, sending nasty little questions as to why he'd taken her, feeding images of brutal rape to my mind's bulging eye, then murder . . . I couldn't switch it off, the more I tried the more vivid the show became.

Sollis tried to reassure me. 'Maybe she got away.'

I shook my head. 'Her car's still there. He's got her all right.'

We sat in silence.

Sollis said, 'What's she like? Will she handle it?'

I sighed. 'As long as she stays alive, she will.'

'If it is Roe he might be heading back to Hereford right now. Want to try and keep this appointment?'

I looked at him. 'Be ten o'clock before we get there. Think this captain guy will still see us?'

'I'll drive. You ring him.'

The captain said he'd be there. Sollis pushed the car up to eighty and tried to make me feel better by giving me the pistol to load.

Mac rang with confirmation of Lisa's story on the dead vet. Or at least confirmation of the rumour.

'No proof then?' I asked.

'None, or he would have been struck off.'

'How widespread *was* the rumour, Mac?'

'Frank seems to think not that many people had heard it; it was no big deal really compared to some of the other stuff that goes on.'

'Doesn't it make you wonder how our man got hold of

it, then? He'd have to be pretty heavily involved in racing to have heard it first-hand, wouldn't he?'

'S'ppose so . . .'

'Unless he has a ready source of inside information.'

Mac paused then said, 'You think somebody's setting people up?'

'A ready source, Mac . . . David Campbell Cooper. Under duress of course, but that must be why he's holding him.'

'You think he's maybe torturing the boy to get it?'

'Big possibility.'

The next thought in my head, and Mac's too, I think, was Lisa . . . it went unspoken.

I said, 'Who was the vendor who knew that horse had a dicky heart?'

'I don't know.'

'Well you'd better find out 'cause he might be next.'

Mac said, 'With Mark Pelham off the hook you maybe better face the fact that *you* might be next.'

'Mac, the way I'm feeling the sooner this bastard comes for me the better. I'm ready.'

'Just stick close to Sollis,' he said, then, 'By the way, if it helps with your Victor Roe theory the gun used to kill Gilmour and Donachy is among those on standard issue to the SAS.'

We sped on, headlights cutting through the dark, my anger and frustration bubbling as I tortured myself with the thought that we were probably driving in the tracks of the killer, following him, never knowing what turn-off would lead us in a different direction.

At the SAS camp two armed soldiers took away Sollis's pistol and ammunition and escorted us to a sparsely furnished office in the basement of a darkened building. They left Sollis and me alone there for about twenty minutes.

Quickly sussing between us that we were either being

watched, listened to or both we stuck to talking about Roe and the killings.

The door opened and a soldier came in introducing himself as Captain Gavin: early thirties, slim, looked and acted mildly effeminate. Not what I'd expected. Maybe just a ruse.

He listened carefully and almost silently to our story as we listed piece by piece why we suspected Roe was involved. When he'd heard us out I asked, 'Can you confirm that Victor Roe was part of the regiment here at one time?'

'Yes, I can.'

'And that he left when his wife was killed around four years ago?'

'About six months prior to that actually.'

'Do you know why he left?'

'Religious grounds.'

'Can you be more specific?'

'He became one of these *born-again* people, renounced violence.' The captain seemed contemptuous.

I said, 'Did you know his son also died in an accident this time last year?'

'Oh I know that,' he said, 'but what you gentlemen obviously don't know is that Victor Roe killed himself three months later.'

Chapter Twenty-nine

The captain told us Roe had been found dead in his living room, a shotgun on the floor nearby and half his head blown off. He'd left a note saying he couldn't go on after the death of his son.

Having built up my expectations of raiding Roe's place tonight and freeing Lisa I felt angry and frustrated to the point of tears. After all the disappointments and wrong turnings over the past three weeks I was raging against fate. I couldn't accept that we were back at the start – with nothing.

I'd have bet Jack Cooper's twenty grand reward money that Roe was the killer.

We found a pub offering accommodation, booked in for the night and ordered drinks. Sollis drank beer. I sipped whisky. I'd been ranting for a while and I was aware of Sollis watching me, waiting to see what I'd come out with next.

I said, 'It could be an SAS cover-up, you know . . . to protect an ex-member. Maybe he didn't commit suicide. Maybe he *is* still running around.'·

Sollis nodded, but I could see he just didn't want to get into an argument. He was happy to listen to me sounding off till all the steam had gone. He said, 'We'll go and see the local police in the morning. Get full details. See if anything funny shows up.'

I drank, and smiled ironically. 'Thanks for humouring me, Kevin. I appreciate it.'

He looked mildly hurt. 'I'm not! It's worth a shot. We're here anyway. Won't do any harm.'

We finished our drinks and went to bed. I lay awake for ages and as soon as my subconscious knew I was asleep it locked the good dreams in their rooms and let all the devilish ones come tumbling out to play.

Next morning we visited the local police station, more because we just didn't know where to turn next than in any real expectation of finding something. Sollis charmed the desk sergeant into letting us see the file on Roe's suicide. Sitting in the small interview room we worked our way through it.

On 7th July last year Roe had placed a shotgun under his chin and blown the front of his head off. The body hadn't been discovered till almost a month after his death when a social worker visiting Roe to help him get over his son's death had found his badly decomposed corpse in the living room. Reading the report of the officer in attendance the first thing Sollis noted was that no swabs had been taken of Roe's hands.

He explained: 'In any shooting there'll be some blow-back, some chemical discharge from the gun onto the hand holding it. It's a simple way of proving a suicide. No trace of discharge, then somebody else pulled the trigger.'

'Would it be standard procedure to take a swab?' I asked.

He shrugged. 'Not exactly standard, I suppose. Depends on the officer in charge.'

'Would the swab still show something after a month?'

'Oh yes. Would be faint but it would be there.'

Flipping the report over he picked up the next piece of paper, read it and passed it to me. 'Suicide note,' he said. 'Probably the reason they didn't take a swab.'

I looked at Roe's sloping handwriting: '1472 days since

Isobel's death. 63 since Christopher's. Along with my God they both await me in Heaven.'

I looked at the figures, their neat uniform height. Sollis flicked a picture across of Roe's wasted, insect-ridden, unrecognisable body. I gazed at it for a while then at the figures again and I smiled.

Sollis frowned at me. I said, 'He faked it.'

'What?'

'He's still alive.'

Fifteen minutes later the Northern police faxed us a copy of the other notes Roe had left on his victims along with the one he'd sent me. We sat comparing the figures on the chapter and verse numbers with those on Roe's 'suicide' note. To my eye they matched exactly.

Sollis, although not as convinced, agreed there was a very strong chance my theory was right.

To help build my case I got the number of Roe's social worker and rang her. She confirmed what I'd suspected, that Roe had known the exact date she was next due to visit. In the first three weeks after his son's death she'd gone there once a week, then Roe had said that a monthly visit would be fine.

'So what was his thinking there?' Sollis asked.

'To make doubly certain the body was unidentifiable . . . by sight anyway. First he makes sure the shotgun blows the face away, then to cover any discrepancies in build he gives the corpse maximum time to rot knowing it's unlikely that anybody except the social worker will call at the farm for a month.'

Sollis nodded slowly, then said, 'So who's the dead man?'

I leaned back, comfortable with my thoughts, happy that I'd put everything together in my head. I said, 'Who do you think? Who'd be most likely?'

Hands in pockets, Sollis shrugged. 'A jockey? Trainer?'

'How about Sampson, the box-driver?'

He frowned, puzzling. I said, 'Roe's a religious man. He has to find justification for killing. Who would he have felt justified in killing within ten weeks of his son's death under the wheels of a horsebox?'

The big man's frown dissolved; he smiled.

I said, 'The guy's supposed to have conveniently disappeared just a few days before Roe kills himself, slipped back into the anonymous life of a vagrant. He rings the stable in a very emotional state to say he won't be back, which means, theoretically, nobody will be looking for him.'

Sollis nodded slowly.

I said, 'How'd you like to bet Roe had a pistol at the poor bloke's head as he spoke?'

The more we went over the whole thing the more convinced I was I was right. Sollis was on my side. Mac too, when I rang him. He decided to drive straight up and join us.

By the time he arrived, mid-afternoon, we'd read the contents of Roe's will. He'd asked that the animals be given free to good homes and that the farm be sold and all proceeds donated to the RSPCA. He'd added an interesting rider: 'As a memorial to my wife and son the farm should stand empty for a period of one year before being sold.'

I looked at my companions. 'Guess where Mister Roe is based,' I said.

The farm lay five miles north of the town. Sollis had persuaded me that we had to wait till nightfall before going in. We were on our own. Kavanagh and Miller, acting on information from Buck, were scouring the flatlands of East Anglia trying to find their new 'chief suspect'.

Inspector Sanders had gone to Bali on holiday and his stand-in was of the opinion that we didn't have a shred of solid evidence to justify a raid on 'a dead man's house'.

British summertime had begun the previous night and

I had to suffer the additional frustration of waiting an extra hour for darkness. If anything happened to Lisa between now and the time we went in it would take a lot of living with.

As dusk fell Sollis and I lay crouched on the crest of a small hill about five hundred yards from Roe's farm. McCarthy had volunteered to stay back down the road with the car 'in case we needed to make a quick getaway'.

No lights showed in the farmhouse though we faced only the outer walls of the rectangular building. There could have been some sign of life within the quadrant it formed.

Sollis checked his gun for the tenth and final time and darkness wasn't quite on us when we started creeping down the hill, Sollis whispering, 'This is the most fun I've had since the superintendent fell in the fire.'

I wasn't sure if he was joking.

Reaching the corner of the building I peeped out across the yard. One light was on in the house. There was complete silence.

I turned to Sollis. 'I'm going to work my way along that wall to the window. If he's inside the house he won't see me. If he's outside he can only be in the big barn to your left or by the gable end at the top. Can you try and cover those two areas?'

He nodded and said, 'Be careful.'

'I'm only going to take a look through the window, no heroics.'

'Good luck.'

I slunk out crouching and scuttled towards the corner. Working my way along the rough sandstone wall, scrutinising the doorways and deep windows of the barn opposite, I felt my senses so keenly tuned I could have seen an atom or heard a feather land on snow.

I reached the lit window and peered in: an empty kitchen, bare ceiling bulb casting harsh light on the sink

unit, table and chairs, dirty dishes, a toppled cereal box
and various packets and tins. Glancing back towards Sollis
I saw his silhouette against the last of the light in the
evening sky. I moved on towards the door.

In the shadow of the doorway, just as I reached for the
handle, the door was opened from the inside. Sollis saw
it too and shouted, 'Down, Eddie!'

But I stayed upright and saved the life of David Campbell Cooper.

The boy told us Roe had left two hours previously, then
he led us to where Lisa lay in a bedroom. Hearing us
come in she got to her feet looking defiant, obviously
thinking it was Roe. When she saw me she tried to smile
but her face crumpled and her body slumped and I caught
her just before she fell and just after she started to cry.

He'd kept her tied up, using blue and yellow mountain-
eering ropes threaded through heavy metal rings fixed to
wall-beams. Her wrists and ankles were raw from
rope-burns.

She clung to me, head on my shoulder, weeping quietly
and I was perversely happy that her cool efficiency, her
hundred per cent competence had finally broken down.

Sollis said, 'Eddie, he might come back any time.'

Lisa jerked upright, her wet wide eyes staring at me.
'You haven't caught him!'

Half puzzled I shook my head. 'No, he left two hours
ago, according to David.'

Lisa looked horrified. She said, 'He's gone to kill Vanessa Compton!'

Vanessa Compton was an owner who lived in Richmond, Yorkshire. Roe had told Lisa that although Compton had been warned of her horse's failing eyesight she'd
forced her trainer to run it in the National where it had
fallen, breaking its back.

When talking about it Roe had kept quoting to Lisa,

'If the blind lead the blind then both shall fall into the ditch.'

Sollis rang the Richmond police telling them they'd probably have time enough to set a trap for Roe and asked them to contact us at Hereford police station as soon as they knew anything. He and McCarthy took over control of operations organising a welcome party of armed police at the farmhouse in case Roe aborted the Richmond attack.

Before leaving to take Lisa back to the lodge I reminded young Cooper to call his mother and father. He nodded, looking a bit perplexed by everything. He told me he'd found Roe waiting in the back seat of his car the day he set off for London and his mother's party.

Roe soon realised he had the wrong D. Cooper but couldn't let him go and had kept him locked in the basement below a heavy trap-door. The night we turned up was the first night the kid had tried to open the trap-door from the inside, and succeeded only to narrowly avoid having his head blown off by Sollis.

Roe never appeared in Yorkshire nor did he return to his farm. That worried Lisa enough to talk me into moving out of the lodge again. Roe had told her how frustrated he was that he couldn't trace me and keep up his strict chronological killing order.

He'd known too that I'd been trying to track *him* down, though Lisa couldn't say how he'd got that information or how he'd known about the rumours surrounding Digby Craddock and Vanessa Compton.

Mac had checked out the Compton 'blindness' thing and, as with the vet, confirmed that it had been a fairly tightly kept piece of gossip.

I asked David Cooper if Roe had been pumping *him* for information, but he denied it.

Officially Sollis was still my bodyguard and he shadowed

us discreetly over the next three days. We spent them in Southport, close to Aintree, and moved each night to a different hotel. That seemed to ease Lisa's mind about Roe.

She was sure he was still after me and by Wednesday evening she almost had me convinced too. But he'd have his work cut out.

His face was all over the newspapers and the TV bulletins. There had been numerous reported sightings in the last forty-eight hours, all of them checked out by the police, none leading to anything other than increased Press hysteria.

We heard that young David Cooper had paid a brief visit to his father who was now off the danger list but barred from attending the National in which David was to ride his horse, Gospel Oak. Jack Cooper sent me a message via McCarthy congratulating me on finding the boy (but no mention of thanks) and promising a cheque soon.

I told Lisa we'd have a fortnight in Antigua when the money arrived but she'd have been happier just to come to terms with what she'd gone through. I hadn't been sure how she would react to the ordeal, though I'd thought she'd be depressed and weepy for a while. But there just seemed to be an air about her of suspended belief.

During the twenty-four hours she'd been held Roe had spent a lot of time with her, spouting propaganda, talking passionately about animal rights then sliding into weepy reminiscences, repeated over and over, of his wife and son.

Lisa had tried arguing the case for the sanctity of human life over animal life but he'd said, 'Not *evil* people, you can't defend evil people.'

Though she wouldn't admit it I think there was something in her that felt sorry for Roe. Trouble was it was battling with the part that hated him for what he'd done.

We spent our nights in the same bed but all it did was make me regret that we hadn't made love before all this happened. I wanted to know what it would have been like 'untraumatised'.

Silly maybe, but lying holding her I couldn't rid myself of the impression she was clinging to me for fear and for comfort and the promise that life, some day, would return to normal.

She was especially tender with the still fresh scars on my back, treating them almost like old friends, like something unchanged, reassuringly familiar.

On Wednesday night I lay awake cradling her as she slept, sad now for her and maybe for me too that her shell had broken and the confidence, the independence, the pure zest for life had started leaking out.

The Aintree management declared they were taking unprecedented security arrangements for the whole meeting and intended to search every single racegoer by means of a scanning machine. They also said that armed police would be on duty strategically placed around the course 'to deal with *any* situation'.

Neither of us was really in the mood for Thursday's meeting and we spent the day wandering on the coast. On Thursday evening Mac called to tell me Jack Cooper's trainer, Bobby Watt, was trying to contact me. I rang him.

'Eddie, just had a call from Jack Cooper's secretary saying I should offer you the ride on Dunstable in the first at Aintree on Saturday, interested?'

'I'll be interested if the doctor gives me the all-clear on my back.'

'What's wrong, been lying on it too much?'

'Yeah, very funny. I'll see the doc tomorrow, I should be okay. Will you be there tomorrow?'

'I've no runners, but I'll be there.'

'Can I tell you then?'

'Okay.'

'How's your National horse going?'

'Great guns, if the kid's bottle ain't been screwed up with this bloody kidnapping caper he'll have a fine chance.'

'Jack Cooper had a big bet?'

'I don't think so, got to keep his excitement to a minimum.'

'*You'll* be glad he's on the mend, anyway.'

'Damn right. He's a bloody nuisance at times but I know which side my bread's buttered.'

'See you tomorrow.'

On Friday morning Lisa did one final clean-up on my back and we packed our bags and headed for Liverpool.

More than the usual number of fallers on the Friday meant that the course doctor was kept exceptionally busy and when I persuaded him to spend a minute examining my back he hiked my shirt up, passed his hands over the healing scars and said, 'You'll do.'

He made the appropriate marks in my medical book and gave it back to me. I hadn't expected it to be that easy and was now faced with the prospect of my first ride in a fortnight.

I sat on the scales: ten six. I'd put on three pounds. No matter, Dunstable was set to carry eleven seven. No wasting in the sauna would be necessary for next day.

Lisa and I spent the rest of Friday in a private box as guests of Frances Crosbie, a race sponsor and an owner I rode for occasionally. We drank too much champagne – though it seemed to make Lisa forget things for a while – and had to get a taxi back to our hotel.

Alone with me again Lisa became moody and depressed as the alcohol effects wore off. The hotel was full of people we knew and I persuaded Lisa it was best if we sought out as many of them as possible and spent the rest of the evening with them.

If any of them brought up the abduction, fine; at least she'd have a chance to talk about it, get it out of her system. It would be better that sitting moping in the room.

In the company of a dozen or so we had a great night spiced with the delicious anticipation of every Grand National eve. Four of the lads had rides in the race and three others had runners.

Comparisons were made, bets were struck, information sought, plans revealed . . . it was everything I'd remembered it as and the only bitterness came from the fact that I had no ride in the race.

But even that resentment wasn't nearly as strong as I'd expected it to be. Maybe, after the events of the last few weeks, my values were finally changing.

We went upstairs around one and Lisa flopped down on the bed looking sad again. I felt a sudden desperate responsibility for her, a deep tenderness that caught me unawares. Taking my jacket off I sat beside her, pulling her towards me. She linked her arms weakly around my waist and rested her head on my shoulder. I stroked her hair, the side of her face, then felt the warm tears through my shirt.

She cried herself quietly to sleep and I laid her down, gently eased her dark velvet dress off and drew the covers over her. Quietly undressing, I switched off the light and got in beside her. I lay for a while watching her pretty face, thankful for the peace sleep had given her.

If the demon of Victor Roe was going to be exorcised we wouldn't have much longer to wait. In his mind the killer had little to lose. With his picture in every paper they'd catch him sooner or later.

It was my guess he'd try to go out with a major bang and tomorrow had to be it. Grand National day – the first anniversary of the death of his son.

Chapter Thirty

I'd been looking forward to the Saturday and my first ride since coming back but Lisa's emotional and mental condition was making me wonder if it was safe to leave her on her own. Sollis stuck close now and accompanied us to Frances Crosbie's box.

Frances promised to keep a close eye on Lisa and with Sollis at my shoulder, gripping the loaded Smith & Wesson in his coat pocket, I went to get changed for the first.

Fighting our way through the crowds, reading newspaper headlines like Murderer's National Threat, hearing people discussing Roe almost as much as the horses, seeing armed police at every doorway, perched on roofs, riding big heavy horses, listening to the tense communications on security staff radios, watching the glint of danger in the eyes of ordinary people who, having been electronically searched for weapons, sensed that for once they could be as much a part of the drama as the jockeys and horses, the real impact of what Roe had engineered came home to both of us. We looked at each other earnestly and Sollis said, 'I wonder where the hell he is?'

There had been no reference in the Press to my part in freeing Lisa and David Cooper yet Lisa said Roe had known I was after him. Also, I was still next on his list.

It got home to me as I changed for the first race that Roe couldn't hope to stay free much longer *whatever* happened today. And he was already down for three murders so another one would make no difference to him.

If there was going to be a fourth the target had to be me. The day had to be today. The ideal race, for maximum publicity, would be the National itself. But I wasn't riding in it so if he wanted to shoot me he had about ten minutes.

We trotted out of the parade ring, the stable lad on my right, Sollis, wary of the slavering mouth and prancing metal-shod hooves, on my left. The jogging motion threw my already churning stomach into greater turmoil.

My eyes flitted from face to face then across the rooftops where, realistically, he'd have to be for the chance of a decent shot – with a rifle anyway. I counted the armed police up there: twenty at least looking down from the rear. The same number, I hoped, would be at the front.

What if he was down there in the crowd, Beretta in pocket? A couple of quick shots then he disappears in the panic . . . I pictured Sollis bending over my bleeding corpse.

I tried to force it from my mind as we cantered to the start.

The race passed without incident. I finished third, panting hard. Sollis met me as I came back in, no smile, eyes everywhere, tension tightening his face.

When I reached the safety of the changing room my adrenalin, which had been pumping like a burst hydrant, slowed to a steady stream. I promised myself a stiff drink as soon as I got back to Lisa.

The wattage was steadily increasing in the weighing room atmosphere among those with a ride in the big one and I would have liked to have stayed and shared it even though I had no more mounts. But thinking of Lisa again and that drink I showered and changed and went back to the box.

Lisa was much calmer. She'd been so tied up in thoughts of her own ordeal over the last few days that she seemed to have forgotten about any threat to me. I didn't remind her.

We watched the second race together and she backed the winner; fizzing with excitement she turned to me, waving her ticket, '*Sixteen to one!*'

'Brilliant!' I said and kissed her. She hugged me, eased her grip then hugged me again. She was smiling, the old vitality and intensity back in her eyes. I said, 'You seem better.'

She nodded. 'I think I'm going to be all right now . . . I'm sorry about last night.'

'Forget it.'

Her hand on my shoulder she guided me towards the door. 'You go back to the weighing room, I'll be fine here.'

'It's okay, it's not as if I've got a ride . . .'

She looked at me. 'I know you want to be there . . . go on.' She gave me a push. I turned. 'You sure?'

'Sure I'm sure, I'll be fine, see you after the race.'

Sollis put down his half-finished beer and we hurried back across towards the changing room. Sollis stood guard outside. I went in to soak up the atmosphere. With forty-five minutes left before the off the place was buzzing. There are two changing rooms at Aintree and both look as ancient as the race itself with their high ceilings, wooden walls and old metal saddle racks.

I sat in room two watching the nerves working on jockeys and valets. They each had their own way of handling it: some joked incessantly or played pranks, others went abnormally quiet, a few became surly and uncharacteristically abrupt, one or two developed high-pitched laughs, almost everyone mocked any colleague who appeared on the TV above them doing one of the endless live interviews with the BBC.

Looking at the screen someone said, 'Oh-oh, here comes the boy wonder.'

Most of us glanced up. The presenter was introducing

David Cooper, already wearing his father's luminous yellow colours with crimson sleeves.

The presenter turned to David and said, 'David, nineteen years old, first ride in the National, the weight of family expectations on your young shoulders and as if that wasn't enough to be going on with, earlier this week you were literally snatched away from the clutches of a madman . . . Tell us about it.'

Young Cooper, not at all awkward, stared his questioner in the eye and said, 'It was no big deal really, I learned a lot from it.'

'Like what?'

'Well, like what really matters in life, what it means to have proper values, how important it is to have the courage of your convictions.'

This wasn't the youngster's normally tongue-tied performance and the changing room gradually quietened as people paid attention.

The presenter smiled and said, 'I think everyone would agree with that but how do you feel about the man who, allegedly, murdered your colleagues, who kept you locked up in fear of your *own* life?'

'I admire him.'

The smooth presenter suddenly looked flummoxed, he said, 'You *admire* him?'

'That's what I said. Victor Roe is a man with total commitment to his convictions. The Grand National cost him the life of his only son. He considers the race barbaric and murderous and has had the courage to do something about it.'

Sensing a real news story the presenter perked up again. 'David, forgive me, but you sound as though you almost agree with the views of this Victor Roe.'

The changing room was now completely silent. This interview was going out live to millions of people all over the world.

Cooper said, 'I agree wholeheartedly with them.' He turned to face the camera which went in close on his face. He said, 'All of you out there are contributing to barbarism, to the practice of forcing dumb animals over huge fences. You are all condoning cruelty of the most horrific kind . . .'

At this point I heard the Clerk of the Course who was watching from the doorway say, 'Jesus Christ Almighty!' in a voice that suggested the world had come to an end.

'. . . a cruelty I will no longer be party to . . .' At this he ripped his silks off, the cameraman zooming out quickly to catch him throwing them to the ground. I thought of Jack Cooper watching this and his nurses trying to get his heart-rate down.

The boy went on, '. . . Every one of you should be ashamed of yourselves. If Victor Roe had had his way this race would never have gone ahead today. There is still a chance that it might not and I, for one, sincerely hope that will be the case.'

Without any acknowledgement to the now speechless presenter the kid turned and walked away, dumping his whip in a rubbish bin as he passed.

Lisa was convinced Roe had an accomplice – there he goes, I thought.

The director cut to another betting show. In the changing room we all looked at each other; Bomber smiled, shaking his head and said, 'Never thought the kid had it in him.'

For the next couple of minutes everyone forgot their National nerves as they discussed the interview. Suddenly I heard my name called by a weighing-room official. I went to the door. The man said, 'You're wanted.'

Looking over his shoulder I saw a frantic Bobby Watt beckoning me. I went over and he handed me the silks the kid had discarded. 'Get changed! We're trying to get special permission from the Stewards for a late change of jockey.'

I just nodded, dumbfounded; I'd been so wrapped up in young Cooper's performance it hadn't occurred to me that the horse would need a new rider. I hurried back into the changing room and found myself a valet who quickly replaced the buttons ripped from the silks by young Cooper.

Drawing my boots on I felt the smoothness of the leather ankle-patches and wondered just how many people, other than jockeys, appreciated their ankles. Clamped tight to the side of a blundering thoroughbred they could save your life.

A pair of boots stopped in front of me and Layton's furtive voice said, 'You're a jammy bastard, Malloy. Wouldn't be surprised if you put the kid up to that just to get his ride.'

I didn't reply, didn't even look up and Layton, no doubt smiling his snide smile, started to move off. I poked my toe out catching his heel and he tumbled forward, crashed against a bench and landed prone at the brown-brogued feet of Sir Marcus Talland, the Senior Steward.

Looking down, Sir Marcus said, 'No need to grovel, Layton, this is not a Stewards' Inquiry.' Everybody laughed, except Layton.

Sir Marcus gave us the usual pre-race pep-talk warning us of the need for fair play and to go steadily approaching the first fence. We nodded gravely, though all of us, Sir Marcus included, knew the advice would be ignored.

The bell rang telling us it was time to leave the warmth and safety of the changing room and, drawing final deep breaths, we all got up and filed through the door like paratroopers committed to jump though unsure whether our chutes would open.

Sollis stepped in beside me and we walked, shoulder to shoulder, towards the parade ring. I glanced around at

the police marksmen on the roof. If Roe was somewhere
up there with a rifle, had he heard the jockey change being
announced? Did he know I was now riding Jack Cooper's
horse? If he did he'd have no trouble picking me out in
these dazzling yellow silks.

Watt legged me up onto Gospel Oak, a big iron-grey
gelding. Detailed riding orders were pointless in the
National and Watt restricted himself to, 'He stays all day.
Don't be afraid to use his stamina, even if it means doing
the donkey work over the last two miles.' I nodded and
the stable girl led me round the ring abreast of another
horse. Sollis walked alongside though out of kicking and
biting range. Forty horses and around a hundred and fifty
people made things cramped in there.

The majority of my rivals had known of their intended
rides for months beforehand which left me at a disadvan-
tage. Knowledge of the strengths and frailties of others
can give you quite an edge in the National and I'd had no
time to make any detailed assessments.

Still, I was beginning to get a feel of Gospel Oak's
power from the way he used himself, his long swinging
walk, springy muscular jog.

Suddenly there was a sharp crack. Women screamed
and the crowd scattered as a horse went down three in
front of us, his jockey rolling, from habit, into the foetal
position on the grass. Sollis drew his pistol and aimed in
the direction the sound had come from.

People were ducking, staring wildly around. Two
policemen came rushing in from the far side. All TV
cameras swivelled towards the spot. Some jocks had leapt
from their saddles. I watched wide-eyed, trying to understand what had happened. The fallen horse was scram-
bling, trying to get up, but its lad sat on its neck gripping
the reins, immobilising it.

The rifle-crack noise had come from the horse lashing
out with a back leg and catching one of the stanchions

with a shoe, shattering its pastern. When calm was restored they wheeled the screens in to cover the stricken horse and its weeping connections and waved us out onto the course.

Sollis was white-faced and wide-eyed.

The jocks who'd dismounted, ducking for cover, were looking rather sheepish as we circled at the start. All the horses too were well on their toes. Equine and human nerves seemed intertwined, taut as twisted stirrup leathers.

The stands behind us and the enclosures on either side were packed solid. I wasn't the only jockey anxiously scanning the faces behind the rails, looking for some sign of madness, looking for the face of Victor Roe which stared out from the front page of every newspaper.

As much to break the tension as out of habit a bunch of us broke off and cantered towards the first fence. Gospel Oak immediately took hold of his bit and set off, gliding over the turf. Crossing the cinder-covered Melling Road he half jumped from instinct without breaking his stride and when we halted by the first jump he had the cheek to plunge his head into the belly of the fence, coming away with a mouthful of spruce.

In the last few minutes he'd told me all I had to know about him . . . I had no complaints.

As the starter called us in I emptied my mind of everything except tactics. I'd decided to go down the inside where the steepest drops lay. This would let me keep my eye on the leaders while hopefully avoiding the crowding and trouble which was inevitable at the first three fences.

We lined up and when we were all still and facing the right way a sudden momentary hush fell over the racecourse, then a huge roar as the starter raised the tapes.

Above the noise I imagined I could hear Sollis's sigh of relief.

We were off, the crowd noise already being left behind in the mad rush for a good take-off position at the first, most going too fast in the desperate quest for what seemed the same ten yards of fence.

I heard the crashing noises before seeing the signals of trouble in front of me. The leader of the trio just ahead must have come down because the tails of the two just behind him were erect and waving like flags as they tripped over the rolling faller.

Three horses thrashing around on the other side, but where exactly? There was no way of knowing and I pulled violently on my right rein to force Gospel Oak over at an acute angle. At full stretch the horse grunted in mid-air and landed inches from Bob Jenner who'd fallen towards the middle of the fence.

The horrified look on Bob's upturned face told me he'd lost his bottle, the worst thing that can happen to a jumps jockey. Once your nerve goes *you've* gone and as he caught my eye we both realised, he with embarrass-ment, me with sadness, that he'd soon quietly retire thankful that his bones were still the right side of his skin.

We raced on, my horse and I both sharper for the close call. Taking a good hold of his head I guided him over the next four without getting near another horse. Becher's Brook next and that cold little blob of extra tension tight-ened in my gut.

Seeing a good stride from a long way out we met the take-off bar just right and soared over . . . the thrill just as strong as it was the last time I'd jumped it, six years ago. That additional second you're airborne over Becher's seems like a moment frozen in time.

We were nearer last than first approaching the right-angled Canal Turn and I decided to take my chance to reduce the deficit. Pulling ten yards off the inner I then asked Gospel Oak to veer sharply left attacking the fence as acutely as we had the first though this time through choice in order to straighten the angle.

His common grey head missed the upright end of the fence by centimetres and we passed at least fifteen others who'd been forced to jump straight before being yanked around the right-angled bend to face Valentine's Brook.

Having improved our position so dramatically with little effort, we settled into a rhythm designed to conserve energy for the same spot next time round.

The spruce tops seemed to slip easily underneath us and when Gospel Oak flew over the huge Chair fence real hopes of running a very good race crowded my mind. With a circuit to go fate couldn't be tempted by thoughts of actually winning.

As we came to the first again, the seventeenth this time, I was glad to see Bob Jenner on his feet by the rails, a broken bridle hanging from his hands, horseless maybe, but in one piece. He looked up as we jumped past knowing he'd never be with us again and shouted, 'Good luck, lads! Good luck!'

Evidence on the second circuit offers both congratulations on having survived so long and admonishments to be careful: holes torn in fences, equine casualties hobbling back towards the stables, loose horses careering across the centre of the course, jockeys still on the ground being attended by medics, broken stirrup irons, deeply gouged furrows – drawing a breath I glanced around, about twenty left, some beginning to labour.

Approaching the Canal Turn again we lay fourth on the inside. I looked behind, maybe fifteen or sixteen left, most of them beginning to show signs of weakening. None of the others looked to be going better than we were. It would soon be time to kick on and try to break them.

Taking the fence less acutely than last time I glanced back again at those still jumping it. Among the cavalcade of vehicles following on the road inside the rails something struck me as not being right. The horse sensed my concentration drifting and his stride faltered slightly bringing me back to the job in hand.

We faced Valentine's, the first of four fences in the long straight before the turn for home. Still unsettled a hundred yards before the fence I looked over my left shoulder again: the usual vehicles tracked us, camera cars, ambulance, stewards, vets . . . then I realised what was strange, the ambulance was weaving in and out as though trying to overtake the others.

I turned my attention back to Valentine's, saw a good stride and we sailed over. I glanced back, one was coming after us, black colours, could be Layton.

Three more in the straight. From the corner of my left eye I saw the ambulance drawing alongside me on the road. He should be at the back waiting for casualties not up with the leaders. I turned to look directly at him.

The driver's window was down, he looked grey as wood ash. Upright behind him, leaning against the passenger door, stood a man with what looked like a rifle. He was aiming it at me.

Instinctively I crouched low, the horse's stride changed as he guessed at what I wanted, the next fence was yards away, I stayed low, no help to the grey, and he rose a full stride too early and only the gap punched in the fence on the first circuit saved us.

We raced towards the next. I looked again at the gunman, the ambulance seemed to sway, the rifle swung in a ten-inch arc and he fired. I heard the bullet pass my head. The horse didn't falter . . . Jesus, what do I do? Slow down? Speed up? Stop? Couldn't stop, that would be like shooting fish in a barrel.

He drew slightly ahead of me now looking for a broader target, aiming at me face-on. I moved over towards the inside trying to narrow the angle. He slowed and broadened it again. I ducked right down below the horse's neck,

God knows what the commentators were saying about my performance . . . Another bullet went singing past as I heard the riflecrack.

How long before he gets his range?

Over the next . . . flew it again, the horse seemed totally unaware that someone was trying to kill me. Where the fuck were the police? They must have twigged something was wrong by now.

One left to jump before the home straight. The ambulance level again. The incongruous sight of a man in a St John uniform trying to shoot me, the poor driver crying with terror now and trying to keep the vehicle straight. After this fence he would run out of road. Either he turned away or came crashing through the rails to follow me.

Hoofbeats behind me, getting much closer. I glance round, it's Layton, driving his horse on, grimacing, shouting something at me, seems unaware of the ambulance. At my heels now, trying to force his way past, up the inside and I'm so tempted to let him come through and give me cover . . .

He screams, 'Give way, you bastard, Malloy!' and barges his way through knocking me off balance as we rise at the fence. Mine hits the top with his front legs and starts to topple. I let go the reins and instinctively pull my feet from the stirrups . . . going down, almost slow motion, a gunshot, Layton screams ahead of me, the earth pounds the air from my horse in a cavernous grunt and I'm over his head, rolling clear, spinning forward, Layton's horse slumps in front of me, see-saws once then comes to rest lying on my legs . . .

. . . I can see the clouds, hear Layton moaning, turn my head but I can't move. The screech of brakes, boots running fast on a tarmac road, horses landing either side of me, their jockeys trying with wild disbelief to take in the scene; then Victor Roe's face above me, blocking out the sky, a terrible murderous madness in his wet eyes as he levels the rifle at my head. 'You made me kill the horse, Malloy!' Then screaming it, 'You made me kill the fucking horse!' I stare up at him, blank-faced, like a baby at the mercy of a giant. He rests the rifle barrel between my eyes and squeezes the trigger and I hear the sound but feel no pain.

Epilogue

I opened my eyes and the rays of the afternoon sun made me think I was in Heaven rather than a bed in Walton Hospital. McCarthy was there, so was Lisa and she smiled at me. I could see she'd been crying and she started again when I smiled back.

McCarthy said, 'You okay?'

'Am I alive?'

He nodded. 'And in one piece.'

'Good. What time is it?'

'Quarter to one, Sunday afternoon . . . What do you remember?'

'I remember Roe pulling the trigger and I remember hearing the shot.'

'As he was squeezing the trigger, half a ton of sweating steeplechaser landed right on top of him . . . one of the amateur-ridden stragglers determined, luckily for you, to finish the course.'

'Roe dead?'

'Badly injured but he'll live.'

'Layton?'

'Roe shot him in the knee, his career's over. The bullet went straight through and killed his horse.'

'That's what Roe was screaming at me,' I mumbled.

Mac said, 'What?'

'Nothing . . . who won?'

'Santa Lucia, the favourite.'

'Punters would've been pleased.'

Mac nodded. Lisa was squeezing my hand. I smiled. 'Must've been fun at the Stewards' Inquiry.'

Between them Mac and Lisa filled in the rest of the details. David Cooper was helping police with their inquiries on the basis that he'd conspired with Roe in giving him personal details about two people: Digby Craddock and Vanessa Compton.

It seemed Roe had treated the boy kindly from the start, explained his beliefs to him, even sought comfort from the kid over the death of his own son.

David, stuck with Jack Cooper as a parent, had taken to Roe as a worthwhile father-figure, someone to whom money meant nothing but the lives of defenceless creatures meant everything. This had blinded the kid to Roe's obvious madness. They reckoned a good lawyer would keep David out of jail and maybe even Roe would escape it for a mental institution.

And Roe's big plan for the Grand National? He had intended to release David Cooper on the Wednesday and have the boy claim he'd escaped. Cooper was then to help smuggle Roe into the weighing room on Saturday where he would hold all the jockeys at gunpoint and give his big anti-National speech direct to camera at the off time so that the broadcast went all over the world. With Roe's face in every newspaper and TV broadcast they'd had to settle for Cooper's mini-version.

Beckman has yet to be sighted.

I was on my feet in a couple of days and almost a hundred per cent within a week. The season was nearly over, I was tired and so was Lisa. Jack Cooper's cheque had come, along with the message that he was giving up his racing interests to spend more time with his son. Lisa and I decided to go away for a month and come back fresh for the new season.

We did some spring-cleaning before we left for Antigua

and I found the Bible which had been kept handy these last few weeks. Browsing through I found what looked like a suitable quote for Victor Roe. I scribbled out the chapter and verse numbers on a scrap of paper – St John 19:30 – and dropped it in an envelope addressed to the prison hospital.

We mailed it from the airport.

St John 19:30: 'It is finished.'